COLLECTED STORIES

COLLECTED STORIES

E. M. SCHORB

HILL HOUSE NEW YORK

ISBN: 978-0-578-50478-0

Cover sculpture of author: "The Writer," by Natale di LaPadura
Cover photo: Bill Giduz; Cover design: Selah Bunzey

ACKNOWLEDGEMENTS

Grateful acknowledgement is given to the following publications in which one or more of these stories first appeared:

5 A.M., The American Scholar, The Arts Journal, As it Ought to Be, The Bangalore Review (India), Best American Fantasy, Best New Writing 2015, Camera Obscura, The Carolina Quarterly, The Chattahoochee Review, The Coe Review, Cutbank, Cutthroat: A Journal of the Arts, Eclectica Magazine, ELM: Eureka Literary Magazine, Folio Literary Journal, Gargoyle, Ginosko Literary Journal, The Great American Poetry Show, Vol. 3, Gulf Coast, Haight Ashbury Literary Journal, The Interpreter's House (England), Mike Shayne Mystery Magazine, The Milo Review, The Mississippi Review, Modern Day Fairy Tales, Mudfish, Offcourse: A Literary Journal (NYU Albany), Oxford Poetry (Magdalen College, England), The Roanoke Review, Short Stories Bi-Monthly, The Timber Creek Review, University of Windsor Review (Canada), Wascana Review (Canada), Willow Review, The World of English (China, "A Fable" English and Chinese translation), Writers' Forum, The Writing Disorder, and The Yale Review.

"Candy Butcher," "The Sandal Shop," "An Actor Prepares," and "Gravity Flow," with small edits, are excerpted from the Eric Hoffer prize-winning novel, *A Portable Chaos.*

Special thanks to Shea Thompson, director of the premier performance of "Marijuana at Monticello" at the *M.T. Pockets Theatre* in Morgantown, West Virginia.

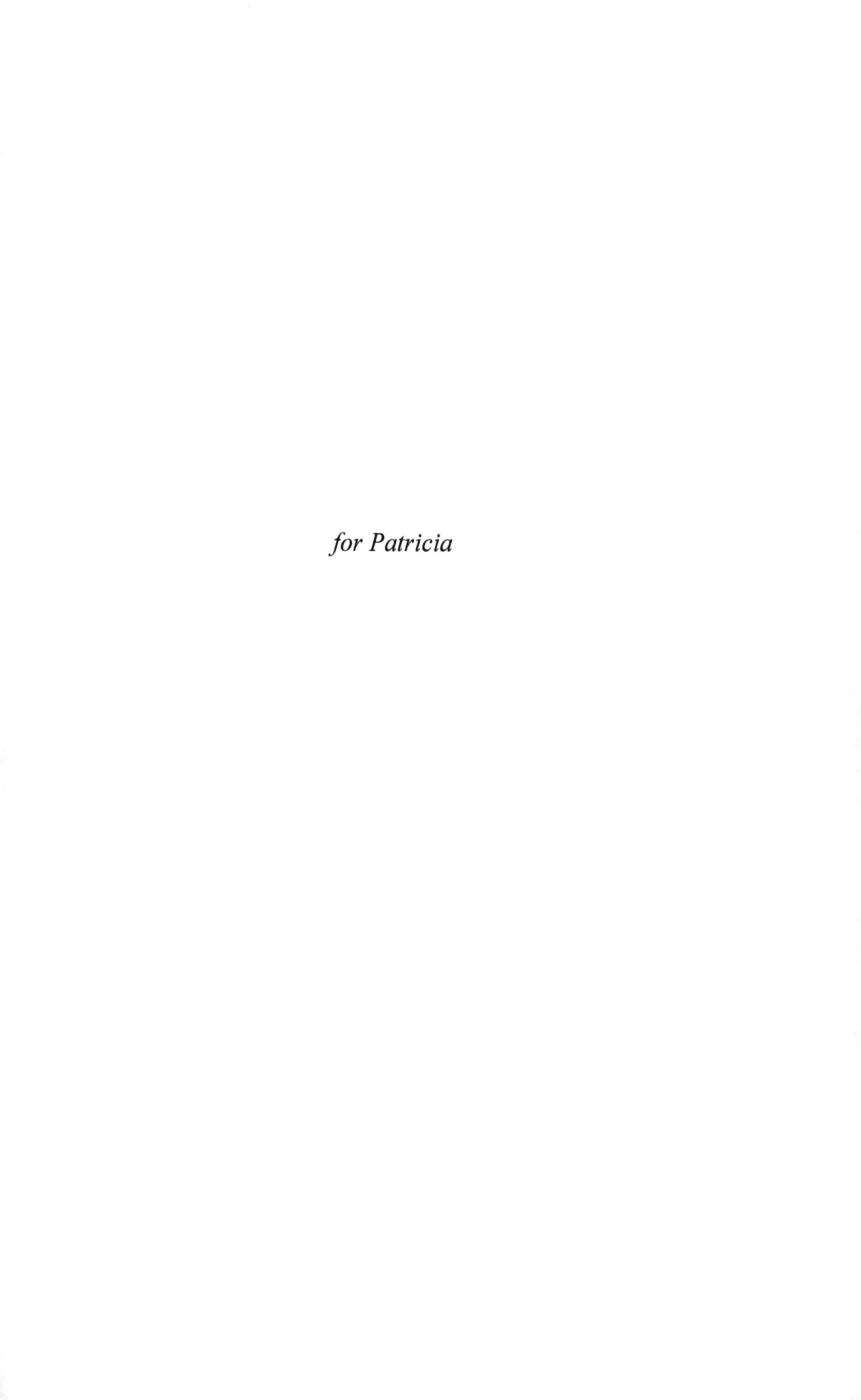

for Patricia

CONTENTS

I.

II.

III.

IV.

V.

INTRODUCTION: AN AMAZING VARIETY

Whether you follow the page order or skip back and forth, smart and dear reader, this book will amaze you by the variety of what it offers. The title calls them all stories, but this is somewhat misleading. Stories they are, of course, but they vary in length from flash fiction to novellas; you will find a one-act comedy mixed in, featuring Thomas Jefferson and his marihuana plantation ("Marihuana at Monticello"), and a specter of genres from fairy tales for children ("The Golden Squirrel") to the most cynical noir. In between, there are action-packed thrillers like "Haydn's Head," with double-crossing spies, copious guns, and devastating uppercuts. As for locale, these narrations will take you from North Carolina Outer Banks to Polynesia and points in between, with sorrowful or merry stays in New York Greenwich Village. A character, Jimmy Whistler, appears in several stories set in the Village, and this recurrence of actor and locale is a skillful esthetic counterpoise to this amazing variety of riches.

From Schorb's bio in his web page we learn that he attended NYU, probably in the early sixties, when I, too, was studying for a PhD at the Courant Institute of Mathematical Sciences. On Sundays, from my window at the NYU graduate dorm (Judson Hall), I could watch and listen to the wonderful jazz improvisational playing on Washington Square, while, who knows, Schorb might have been there too, together with his actor friends. Did he go to the Five Spot Café on St. Marks Place, near W. H. Auden's apartment, and listened to Thelonius Monk?

In one of his Jimmy Whistler stories, "The Sandal Shop," we are taken back to the East Village in those glorious times. There, Jimmy meets his first beatnik, a character oddly named Marsayas—perhaps intended as a combination of several musician names: the unfortunate Marsyas, who challenged Apollo to a contest, either with a double flute or with a lyre, and ended up being skinned alive by the god as a reward, and of the renowned musical family Marsalis, virtuosos of many instruments. Whatever the case may be, Marsayas complained that he could not live with his family. "Impossible!", he said, his whole family were "convention-racked lunatics," or "business fiends" or "materialist maniacs." Marsayas, instead: "I'm a Zoroastrian. I believe in the power of light to conquer the forces of darkness. I believe in universal love." That's the first beatnik I know of who did not claim to be a Buddhist of some sort. A Zoroastrian! Those were truly the new, hip Sixties: something unexpected and far out at every turn.

Schorb has an ear for the manifold accents of American speech, and that adds significantly to the amazing variety of this book. From the slangy speech of the car salesman in "The Hat Trick" to the refined, elliptic staccato of "Snowbound," the artist who went in search of a vision and is dying of cold: "He feared nothing but the thought of no vision, not the loss of his wife to another, nor the loss of his life, nor the meaning of loneliness, but for the vision forsaking all." And let's not forget the hippie slang of "The Code of the Blue Commune," where one of the young male members of the free sex, peace and love commune, Mooncalf, addresses the detective, Marshal McCool, "Look, fuzz, I had nothing to do with this thing," and the whole thing promptly becomes as vicious and violent as anything by the Coen brothers.

To understand one of the masterpieces in this book, "Murphy's Star," it is useful to recall that Schorb, again according to his bio in the web, has been an actor and has long been involved with the film industry. It is the description of a despicable personality, Murphy the actor, a super-charged Narcissus, transfixed by his own star. It makes you think of other narcissistic, selfish, or Don Juan types in the market, from Don Juan himself to Henry Crawford of Jane Austen's *Mansfield Park.* And you realize that no Narcissus of previous times could possibly measure up to Schorb's Murphy, for there was no Hollywood back then and no TV, which have increased the audience size, hence the capacity for narcissism, more than a thousand fold. One must say, though, that independently of his acting past and his film experience, Schorb has a special touch, almost Dickensian, for depicting egoism in enduring ways and unforgettably despicable characters.

Aunt Gertrude in "Movie Money" is one of them. She is Jimmy's aunt, the owner of the rooming house where the boy Jimmy and his mother are staying. But is this boy Jimmy Whistler, or some namesake? We are not told; the rooming house, however, is not in the Village but in Newark. Aunt Gertrude is a miser with mafia connections, who keeps Jimmy and his mother in thrall by the promise, not always kept, of giving them money for the movies on Fridays. Newark, however, is, for Jimmy, a sort of vile annex of the Village, as we surmise when we read "Candy Butcher," another Jimmy story, where people go to see "burlesque" — "to see at the Adams Theatre in Newark what Mayor La Guardia had banned from New York." What can I say? La Guardia didn't deserve an airport.

When I was fifteen, I saw my my first and last burlesque at the Teatro Babilonia in Buenos Aires Retiro Park. The audience were mostly old gizzards, plus me and three of my high-school buddies: today, none of us has forgotten the vedette, Sombra Duval (a name suggesting shade of the valley, or shaded valley), who, having done her bump-and-grind, twirled the tassels on her pasties, and snapped her G-string (as Schorb describes), having furthermore sung her salacious song, imbecile but indelible, proceeded to strut off in her spike-heels, proudly showing us, while the old gizzards roared in heat, her naked shady valley. It was for us an important detail of what Flaubert sarcastically called the sentimental education.

Back to Schorb's depictions of egoism. Aunt Gertrude with her dog Wiggles ("a very old bitch with tumorous, pendulous breasts"), memorable as they are, do not achieve the artistry of what is perhaps my favorite story in this book, "A Practical Nurse." Lorna Chandler, a young woman who plays the practical nurse, and Cora Freemantle, a rich, older woman, are the two characters. The older woman is in bed, unable to walk; her dog Suzy Wong is the only living thing she cares for: this fact, and the others pertaining to the older woman's repulsive personality, are revealed in the dialogue, through expressive phrases and tones of voice. Thus the means of achieving the desired effect are as spare as they are effective.

The initial story, "Charlie . . . for the Lord," shows Schorb painting a very different character, an orphan from the South, good hearted and naïve to the point that his co-workers, the other young salesmen, consider him a "jerk and a dumb turkey." Fairmore, eighteen years old, has a soul too fair for this world, and so he cannot last. Yet his death has a wakening effect on his boss, the Manager, a cigar-chomping veteran of WWII who believes himself to be a no-nonsense, hardened businessman. The Manager's unlikely redemption is a rare instance of a Schorb story ending on an uplifting mode.

By contrast, look at the final story, "The Devil's Tavern," a future dystopia worthy of Jonathan Swift or H. G. Wells, in which an all-powerful Ministry of Wellness controls the lives of the people to the smallest detail. I'm not complaining. There are too many final-redemption stories in the market today, which is a cause for a demoralizing depression. That's something you, sharp reader, will not experience in reading this amazing collection.

Ricardo L. Nirenberg
Editor, *Offcourse Literary Journal*

I.

CHARLIE . . . FOR THE LORD

1

Through sad morning eyes the Manager surveyed his dirty dozen, sighed, and stuck a fat green cigar between his sooty teeth. He was under orders from his doctor not to smoke, having suffered a minor heart attack earlier in the year, but cigars had come to be his greatest pleasure, though they, and coffee, sometimes made him bilious. He was overweight, and had high blood pressure, but he had worked very hard all his life and told himself that he needed food for energy—coffee too, caffeine and nicotine, to get himself going, and to keep himself going. Thus he had at first tolerated, then made use of, what had become an institution at the Harlem branch of the American Home Supply Company—the pre-work coffee-klatch. It gave him the chance to look his boys over, to see how they were doing.

Some of these boys would be going to Viet Nam soon. The Manager was a veteran of what he called "War Two." He had a Silver Star and a Purple Heart.

"But that was a long time ago," he told Fairmore, the newest of his boys. "You weren't even born yet."

"I want to serve my country," said Fairmore. His Adam's apple bobbed over the big Windsor knot in his stained pink tie, pink as his cheeks, as he swallowed coffee.

"But," said the Manager, "we were fighting for something good. I don't know about this war."

"But I want to serve my country," Fairmore repeated doggedly.

"Well," said the Manager, "you're probably on the right track. Where are you from? You don't sound like a New Yorker."

Fairmore told the Manager that he was an orphan, had no home. He had started from a foster home in New Orleans and had wandered to California.

"That's the Golden Land," Fairmore told the Manager.

When the eighteen-year-old Fairmore mentioned California the middle-aged Manager felt his golden dream being touched, a dream of the past. The Manager had spent the best time of his life in San Diego, before being shipped out to the Pacific Theater. He had met and married his wife there, and she had become pregnant with their son there.

The Manager said: "How do you come to be here, in New York?"

"Oh, I worked for this moving outfit in L.A. Just one truck, the boss, me, and another guy. It wasn't even licensed. The boss got a haul to Chicago. In Chicago, he got a haul here. He was supposed to pay me here, but he disappeared. I only had fifty dollars left from California—then I saw your ad. I was sure lucky to see that ad, I can tell you. I was getting a little scared."

The Manager realized how innocent Fairmore was, despite his knockabout life. He talked about all the places he had been and all the things he had done in a way that showed that he hadn't understood many of his own experiences. The manager decided to keep an eye on him.

His own son would have been a bit older than Fairmore now, had he lived. The Manager might have counseled him not to go into the present war. He might have told his own son to go up to Canada and stay there. But maybe not. What would his wife have thought, had she lived? Why had he survived the accident, to go on alone like this? What had been the point of these ten years? Work! And later, his lady friend, Mavis. When he had had his heart attack, she had acted as if she hadn't known him for the past five years. And he had bought her so many nice things! A good time girl, that was Mavis. What was it? A fair weather friend! What was the point?

That week the Harlem branch of the American Home Supply Company was pushing 18" x 23" imitation-gilt-framed portraits of Christ. The portraits were of a life-sized, Hollywood-handsome Christ, hair combed, and not too long, a wavy chestnut-brown; neatly trimmed goatee; shoulders covered with an azure mantle. But the great selling feature was the eyes. They were ingeniously made to follow you wherever you went. Step this way, step that, they were on you.

Fairmore had no car, of course, so every morning he strapped eight or ten of the pictures of Christ together and carted them off toward 125th Street, where he was told to go—"then pick a tenement, and start climbing stairs." It was a big hopeful load and it was a summer hot not only with racial friction, but with extreme August heat and humidity, so Fairmore did a lot of sweating as he lugged the pictures. And by mid-week, it came to the Manager's attention that Fairmore had been placing a record number of items in a record number of places, coming back to the store two or three times a day to get another and yet another stack of eight or ten pictures and going out again, an inspired look on his face.

The Manager prided himself on being a tough man; but there was something about Fairmore—his innocence, his eagerness—that touched him through his city armor, and it had occurred to him, as he chomped his green cigar, that Fairmore might not understand that his smile was only meant to be a mask. Vaguely, he grew concerned that Fairmore might be placing more pictures than could be covered by his commissions—even that he might be seeding his record number of placements with his own money. The Manager did not care, usually, who paid, so long as his salesmen did not place any items with junkies or drunks, where you couldn't count on getting them back. But he was worried about Fairmore. On Thursday morning, while the crew was having coffee, he spoke to him.

"Remember, Fairmore," he said, "you're a salesman. Your job is to collect that dollar down. You're getting it, aren't you?" He stuck his cigar back between his teeth. He felt dyspeptic. Mavis wanted him to take her on a trip somewhere. He thought of California. San Diego. His wife and son. "Aren't you?" he prodded.

Fairmore looked sheepish. "But I'll get it back in commissions, won't I? I mean, it's only a dollar, but I still get four. I get five dollars on each one, isn't that right?"

The Manager held his stomach with one hand and took his cigar from his mouth with the other. "Only when it's collected, Fairmore—only when it's collected. You get the first five that's collected. But the dollar down you keep now. You want to have some money at the end of the week, don't you?"

"Yes, sir."

"Don't put in your own money. A good sale, a good placement, is a solid placement. Make them put up their money—to show good faith."

"Lots of them don't have any money. But I can see that they want the Lord. That's why I know they'll pay."

"No, they won't, and we'll have to repossess the damned things. Make them pay up." He became aware that he was being paged, but he continued to study Fairmore's face. "Haven't you been peddling anything but those pictures?" he asked. "Just those Christ pictures? Let me see your order book." He was paged again, this time with greater urgency. A pain gripped his side. He said, "Never mind. Later."

2

On Friday evening Fairmore stepped into a tenement building, the last picture of the day, and of the week, under his arm. He was tired and hungry, but he wanted to place the picture before he quit.

The building had seven floors and an elevator, but the elevator stood open with an *OUT OF ORDER* sign on it; and, in it, curled in a profusion of dirty newspapers and greasy rags, which had apparently been used in a recent attempt to repair the broken machine, slept a black man with bristling gray hair and a puckered, sullen face, one large hand clenching the neck of a half full half-gallon of cheap, red wine.

Fairmore climbed the marble stairs, delighting in how they had been worn away by countless footsteps, and feeling, as his feet pressed through the thin soles of his shoes into the concave surfaces, a sense of community with the people whose feet had worn them away.

At the seventh floor he began to knock on doors.

He could hear voices behind the first door: a man and a woman talking, her voice high, even, his deep, and rumbling. They paid no attention to his knock.

He stepped to the next door. Here a large young black man, naked to the waist, poked his head and one shoulder out of the door.

"Good evening, sir," Fairmore said. "I represent the American Home Supply Company. I am going to various homes in the neighborhood . . ."

"No, man; can't use it! don't need it! don't want it," said the man, and pulled the door shut.

Undaunted, Fairmore stepped to the next door and knocked.

A young girl of about his own age answered, and he said, "Good evening, miss. I represent the American Home Supply Company . . ." and so on. But the girl seemed uncomprehending. Fairmore might have wondered at the tracks on her arms, but he could not see them in the poor light. It's doubtful, however, that he would have realized that she was high on heroin. The range of his experience did not include hard drugs.

She stared at the picture that Fairmore was holding up and did not seem to see him behind it. He paused, then repeated, "I am going to homes in the neighborhood to show people this beautiful portrait of our Lord which my company is putting out for only a dollar down and a dollar a week for one year. It's a hundred dollar value for only half the price; but, really, due to its religious nature, it's beyond price—"

"Is that the Lord, Charlie?" the girl said finally.

"Yes, miss," Fairmore said, and then in the half dark and shadows he saw that she had her blouse unbuttoned, just hanging open, with her young, swaying brown breasts just covered at the nipples. Her eyes were fixed and strange and wide, and he could see that her body was still covered with a layer of baby fat, and that her breasts were swaying as she swayed, pushing her blouse aside first this way and then that.

"Why he stare at me?"

"His eyes move, miss."

"He watching us." Her concentration, more even than her state of undress, held Fairmore wordless and waiting. Then she said: "How much, Charlie?"

"Just fifty-two dollars, miss," Fairmore said, trying not to look at her breasts. "One dollar down and one dollar a week."

"I want the Lord," she said flatly.

"One dollar—"

"Charlie." She looked at him for what seemed the first time. "Mister Charlie . . ." She tilted her head for him to come in. "For the Lord, Charlie . . ."

She took his hand and drew him into the apartment.

3

It worried the Manager that Fairmore did not return to the store on Friday night. He asked several members of the crew if they had seen him, and when they said that they hadn't, the Manager toughened himself, shrugged, and said, "He'll probably turn up tomorrow. He'll want what he's got coming, if he *has* anything coming."

"He's a jerk," said one of the boys.

"A dumb turkey," said another.

"Why?" demanded the Manager. "Because he's decent?" He stuck his cigar between his teeth and puffed angrily. He was counting out commissions. Fairmore *was* a dumb turkey, he told himself. *Go west, young man!* Now what made him think of that?

The Manager was more worried on Saturday. He thought of calling the police. But, in New York, that was a ridiculous idea. He sighed and went on with his work. Several of the crew were quitting and he was going to put another ad in the Sunday papers, actually to notify them to run last week's ad again. But he had forgotten and now it was too late. He blamed the missing Fairmore for distracting him.

After the crew were off and had left, he worked with a few of the regulars on inventory. What to order? More of those damned pictures of Christ. Fairmore had sold them out.

4

Through the plateglass windows of the Harlem branch of the American Home Supply Company the Manager saw a police car pull in to the curb outside. A couple of local cops, familiar to him, got out and came up to the locked front door. The Manager signaled, made his way through the plastic-covered furniture and lamps and opened the door for them.

"A boy named Fairmore work for you?" asked a cop.

The Manager realized now that he had known that something had happened to Fairmore. He had known it all day.

"Dead. Got his head bashed in."

5

The Manager tried to tell Mavis about it later that night. They had had several drinks before he brought it up. He didn't know quite how to explain how he felt about it.

"Sounds like just another dumb kid," she said.

The Manager was a little drunk. He searched for words. It would have something to do with his wife and son, those ghosts, and with the wars, the one in which he had served, as a Sergeant, so proudly, and this one, in which he would have advised Fairmore, and his own son, were they alive, not to serve.

"Don't serve, I would have told them."

"Why not?" asked Mavis.

"Because what we were doing was honorable. I don't feel that anything we do nowadays is honorable."

And it had something to do with Mavis, and this trip she wanted them to take, of which, he became aware, she was now speaking.

He broke in on her. "Let's go to California, Mavis. Let's dump everything and go out to San Diego and get a little apartment and start fresh."

"San Diego! Are you crazy? What's out there? Besides, I like things fine right here in the Big Apple. All I want's a vacation."

The Manager thought of how Mavis had acted when he had been ill, with his heart attack. He thought of her indifference, of her selfishness, of her callous attitude about Fairmore's death.

"Maybe I'll go without you," he said.

6

The Manager didn't go into the Harlem branch of the American Home Supply Company on Monday morning. Somebody else would have to open up. In fact, he was fairly certain that he would never open up again.

The formula of his life must change. Yet he needed some final thing, an emotional stamp. So instead of opening the Harlem branch of the American Home Supply Company that morning, he made his pilgrimage to see the black girl, the last puzzle-piece in the week-old saga of Fairmore. She was in the Women's House of Detention in Greenwich Village.

His police friends had told him the facts of the case, so when he asked her about them it was not in the manner or for the purpose of finding them out, but to hear her tell it, to feel her before him as in his knowledge she had stood before Fairmore, and to try to understand what it had meant.

She spoke in the blurred voice of a junky of how her father had come in and hit Fairmore over the back of the head with a wine bottle. He was drunk, she said, and didn't want her whoring, especially with no Mister Charlies. She said that he was always a little crazy when he first woke up, and he had been sleeping somewhere in the building, else he would have seen nothing was happening—"that little white boy scared shitless," she concluded.

Yes, the police had told the Manager that the old man had told them much the same thing. The girl had fallen silent. To keep her talking, the Manager said:

"But if your father didn't want you to do it—"

"I got a big habit, but I wouldn't of gone 'gainst my daddy if I wasn't so high and that that boy had sumptin I really wanted."

A pain twisted in the Manager's side.

"What?"

"The Lord," the girl said, with final banality or profundity.

The Manager summed it up this way: he had been the Manager of the Harlem branch of the American Home Supply Company, and Fairmore had worked for him, and this girl was one of their customers, and Fairmore would have gone broke giving his own money away, come out at the end of the week with nothing; and he, the Manager of the American Home Supply Company, would have taken this girl's money, had Fairmore got it, and Fairmore's money, and spent it on a vacation for Mavis, and the American Home Supply Company would have lost nothing. The American Home Supply Company never lost anything.

He studied the girl's pretty, dark face, at once alien and familiar, and realized, saw with simple, startling clarity, that Fairmore had had his head bashed in and half his blood spilled over the bed of a girl even younger and more lost than himself, one of the dollar-down, faceless ones, for him no longer faceless, no longer alien.

MURPHY'S STAR

1

You won't find Murphy's star on the Hollywood Walk of Fame. It should be there, according to Murphy, but who listens to him, anymore, aside from me? He's a nonentity, an old crank who's been on social security for years and supplements his income with what little extra work he can find in Hollywood. Marie and I have spotted him in crowd scenes—here a dottering old Arab, there one of the geezers in the background in a nursing home. He never gets a line, but I've caught him throwing in a silent grunt or two, gratis.

He has a bad leg from his days as a stuntman, which, with old age, has become a problem to him; and I occasionally run into him on Hollywood Boulevard, limping along on a cane, long ratty hair down to his shoulders, looking a little like Howard Hughes, and wearing a dirty old toga, or some other incongruous costume, perhaps on his way to or from a mob scene, or perhaps merely wearing what he has to wear, a scarecrow Father Time among the seamy-side hip-hop rappers, junkies, and baby prostitutes of modern Hollywood, a ghost from the golden days.

In fact, the last time I ran into Murphy, it occurred to me that I might be able to make something out of his story of a Hollywood rise and a Hollywood fall.

I'm mulling this over.

What got me inspired about the project, the *potential* project, was not so much that the scenario, the outline of events, was unique for Hollywood in those wonder years, but that what caused Murphy to fail was built in to his character, not a character he played on the screen, invariably heroic, but his own personal character, what there was of it. For the first time, my mind crossed the matrixes, and I connected Murphy with Greek tragedy—no, I must go easy, that's really a bit much—let's say, with the tragic flaw, the Achilles heel, that brings down the Greek heroes. I guess I couldn't see him like that before because I didn't much like him, but there has been a several decades march of time since his glory days, and now all I see is a pathetic old man, no better than he ever was, I suppose, but harmless and on his way out.

2

The Glory Days?

In the late Thirties, Murphy and Marie were a couple of ambitious kids from Brooklyn who eloped more from the alphabet poverty of the New Deal Depression than they did into the natural hopes and dreams of a picket-fence-and-babies marriage, and went West, not to pick grapes like the Oakies, but to become movie stars. A good-looking young pair of wildcatters, I guess they thought they had nothing to lose and everything to gain. "Pure arrogance," Marie says. "Ignorance on my part, and pure arrogance on Murphy's."

They worked odd jobs at odd hours, anything they could get—Murphy actually did pick grapes for a time—and put all their money into their tuitions at the Hollywood Dramatic Institute, where Murphy quickly gained the notice of the directors.

He had the kind of looks that startled. He was six-feet-four, broad shouldered, and, for all the observable power of his physique, had a waist like a girdled girl's. What the directors saw in him was not a brilliant actor—Murphy was not brilliant at anything, though he was adroit at everything—but a potentially valuable property, and they did everything in their power to improve his natural assets, including his speech and voice, which were uncultivated—to this day Murphy can convince you that he was to the manor born, if he so desires. He can also be as rough as the street kid who came out here, and perhaps even more vulgar, for time has desensitized him.

He was cast in showcases where he began to be noticed, and it soon became evident to Marie that there was only one career between them that was worth pursuing.

In those days, Marie admired everything about Murphy, and some things with good reason. He had physical, if not intellectual, intelligence, and the boy from Brooklyn could ride, rope, and shoot from the saddle in no time, which is how he got into stuntwork. I'd say that Murphy had a quick but shallow mind, which in those days Marie took for something more—emotional depth, seriousness. But Murphy was not a serious actor, he was an actor who wanted to be a star. His end in view was a life of money and fame, which is fine, but Marie mistook him for a serious artist, and set to work in earnest, as a waitress, supporting herself and Murphy, while he continued his career.

His physical daring led to work as a stuntman, and that in turn to bit parts, which was where his career stood at the onset of the Second World War. The knee injury, acquired when Murphy fell from a horse, made him 4-F, and the scarcity of attractive young men began to make life easier for him. Soon he was playing second leads, then, occasionally, leads, in dozens of shoot 'em-up, grade B films on Poverty Row, where, if you worked hard and often enough, you could make a living.

Poverty Row was a factory. Films were made in three weeks, in two weeks, in one week. Nobody waited for a finished script. Sometimes hacks like myself would stand by the director and feed words to the actors. The idea was to keep things moving, turn things out. Sometimes the stories didn't make sense, but if you kept the action going nobody seemed to notice. That was how I got to know Murphy, and at first we hit it off. He was the kind of guy who even appealed to men, the hero type, the kind all of us want to be when we're kids; but I soon began to see what a flawed character he was.

I guess it was the incident of the ingénue that tipped me off. I'm hardly a prude—there must be one somewhere in this business, but I've never run into that rare bird—but I don't like to be made to lie, and Murphy asked me to do just that. Somebody stole, lost, or misplaced several reels of film—the loss of film can be a disaster—and shooting had to stop. Murphy took advantage of the lull to go off with the ingénue. But first he asked me to stop by his home and tell his wife that he had to go on location for a couple of days, out to a false-fronted western town in the Mojave Desert.

"Why don't you call her?" I asked him.

"No, I don't want to talk to her. She can hear it in my voice."

"Why don't I call her?"

"Because it's more convincing if she sees your face."

I thought it was lame at the time, but I went along with it because I was curious to see what kind of paragon would put up with Murphy. What hadn't occurred to me at the time was that Murphy was throwing me at her. It has since, and I've told Marie about it, of course, and she agrees. But she says, "Murphy will never know how grateful I am." I think they were already through, even if they didn't know it yet.

Marie and I hit it right off. She invited me in for coffee, and an afternoon-long conversation ensued. Naturally, we talked about Murphy. He had what it took to be a big star, she thought, but she was no longer under the illusion that he had what it took to be a big man. She was quite frank about it. "When I see him on the screen, it makes me wonder if Gable is really Gable, or if Errol Flynn is really as much fun as he seems."

"Gable is really Gable," I told her, "and Flynn is really fun. Stars can get into all sorts of trouble, but there has to be some real character there, or they won't glitter on the screen. They call Hollywood the Dream Factory, but the camera is a truth machine."

"Do you think Murphy's got it?"

"I don't know," I said.

"Because, if what you say about Gable being Gable is true, then maybe Murphy won't be a star, after all."

I saw that she was no longer in love with Murphy, if she ever had been. I also saw that she was losing faith in his ultimate success. I could tell, too, that she had heard that "on location" story before. I guessed that she had grown up during their marriage, and suspected that her investment in Murphy's career might not be rewarded.

She had an optimistic eager nature which showed when she laughed or spoke of her early dreams for Murphy and herself; but, in general, she seemed sad and disillusioned. She was not quite defeated, but I could see she was thinking about throwing in the towel. That afternoon I fell in love with the eager girl who emerged occasionally from the saddened young woman. But I kept my feelings to myself.

3

Murphy no longer needed Marie. The trailer he had bought to be their home became little more for him than a dressing room, and she its attendant. And now that he no longer needed her, he no longer took pains to keep the knowledge of his amorous adventures from her. He even seemed to feel satisfied at the distress he caused her.

It also satisfied him to drop his heart's current queen suddenly and finally and without explanation, so that the woman would wonder what had caused the break. The women who befriended him, he punished with confusion and doubt.

I asked him about his behaviour with regard to women, once, when we were having a drink together, and he seemed inclined to talk, and he told me that it was a payback to his mother, whom he both worshipped and hated.

It was a rare glimpse of his inner workings, and not a pleasant one. I took it that his mother had dominated his early life and then died, leaving him feeling deserted. He told me that in running off with Marie, he had deserted another girl, who was pregnant. The girl had killed herself. A sixteen year old. He had never told Marie about it.

"What difference does it make?" he said. "She was a loser, or she wouldn't have done it." That was the period when I most disliked Murphy, when he was still on the rise and becoming more arrogant with every success. He seemed to me then to be a cruel and stupid man.

Then he met Sarah Orbisson. She was a former actress, sister of a legendary studio tycoon, independently wealthy, and currently married to Harry Orbisson, who had been producer on several films in which Murphy had had parts. Sarah was a large woman, tall and voluptuous, combining the Magna Mater and the siren. She had been a great beauty, but had let herself go, provoking her husband to call her "the cow." Murphy disliked Harry Orbisson, and I had to agree with Murphy that Harry wasn't a very pleasant person. But who was Murphy to talk?

The trouble between them started during the filming on one of the pictures they made together. Murphy had had an affair with a young actress who was Orbisson's protégé, and Orbisson had had him fired. A couple of years had passed, the protégé had disappeared, and Orbisson had forgotten the incident; but Murphy had not. Murphy had a long and vindictive memory, and maybe that earlier incident played a role in what happened later. Knowing Murphy, it probably did.

4

By now, the Murphys had two children, both boys; and so, needing room, they bought a bungalow out in the hills. I arrived one evening to give Murphy some new lines. The kids were asleep and the place was quiet. We sat down together at the kitchen table, the script spread out before us. After a few minutes, I thought I heard Marie crying. The sound was so muffled, I wasn't sure at first, but when she came in the room later to make coffee for us, her eyes gave me no doubt.

Murphy and I finished up.

Murphy went to the radio and turned it on full blast. Marie asked him to turn it down. "The children are sleeping," she said. Murphy turned the radio down and apologized for his thoughtlessness, but the act had triggered something in Marie.

"They're you're children, too, you know." she shouted. "Don't you care about them? Don't you care about anyone but yourself? You're like a spoiled child."

Murphy's face went stony and red and there was heat in his eyes. Was he acting, I wondered, was this the opportunity he had been waiting for?

"How do I know they're mine?" he shouted back. "Because you say so? Ha! The oldest one may be mine, but the other one could be his," and he pointed an accusing finger at me. "He could have had this script delivered; but no, he's got to bring it out here himself. Any damned excuse to see you! I know he comes out when I'm not here," he said conclusively.

I was nonplussed. It was such an incredible accusation that I thought for a minute he was joking. But there was also insight in it, because, as I had realized from our first meeting, I was in love with Marie.

"How can you say a thing like that?" Marie cried. "You're *never* here. And Felix is like a second father to the boys. You mustn't love me at all to say a thing like that—you mustn't ever have loved me!"

"That's right," Murphy yelled, "I don't—never did, come to think of it—and why can't you be quiet about it? You're lucky as things are!"

"Now, hold on, Murphy," I said, standing up, and Murphy whirled about and knocked me cold.

I woke up sprawled on the couch, with Marie sitting beside me, holding ice to my chin.

"He's gone off," she said. She looked at me for a long moment, then leaned over and kissed me. A few days later, Murphy moved out, and I moved in. The new situation pleased everyone. Marie filed for divorce, Murphy apologized to both of us and fully cooperated, and, eventually, Marie and I married. "No hard feelings," Murphy said, shaking my hand, and I was certain that there weren't any, at least on his part, because I was also certain that he had got just what he wanted.

5

At war's end, Murphy was an established professional, but he was not making the progress he had expected to make. He had expected to be a star by now; but he was merely a working actor in a booming industry, one day a Stetsoned cowboy, and the next a trenchcoated detective in a series of forgettable films, some of which I wrote.

His biggest hit to date was a film that was shot in three weeks: *Fast Draw McGraw.* The kids loved it. Murphy went out on a theater tour, appearing on Saturday mornings at theaters where they were showing *Fast Draw McGraw.* When the film was over and the kids were still shouting, he ran down the aisle in his buckskins, waving his hat and shooting blanks into the air. Any little boy of sixty can probably still remember him.

But Murphy believed himself to be a talented actor, and he wanted to use himself well. I had to admit that his self-assessment was correct. Murphy had the stuff of a star, at least the superficial stuff, the looks, the body, the manner, and the camera loved him. But nothing happened, or, rather, typecasting happened, and it looked like he was destined to be Fast Draw McGraw forever. That is, until Sarah came along.

Sarah showed a proper appreciation of Murphy's talent, as well as of his face and physique, just as Marie once had. But Sarah had power, and, finally, through her influence, Murphy got a couple of relatively good roles under a new name and persona. They were secondary roles but in grade A films made at a major studio. The studio signed him for a long-term contract based on the notice he got in the parts, and it looked like he was finally on his way to stardom.

At last, he was out of Poverty Row! He felt himself rising again, buoyed by this maternal Ishtar. All his defenses fell. He admired Sarah's brilliance, respected her judgments on the industry; and Sarah had beauty, if a little too much of it, education, which Murphy scorned but secretly admired (he was thrilled to discover that I had graduated from Princeton), and influence. He still felt himself to be commonplace, never having mastered off camera any of the polish that he was occasionally able to portray on it. And so he plunged on, with rising passion and recklessness, in pursuit of this tarnished bronze goddess; for now he was free to be with his wondrous Sarah, his Sheba, the matriarchal bosomy queen of his nights. But it was a hot, tropical love that Murphy had with Sarah Orbisson and the rainy season was setting in.

Of late, "the cow" had acquired another bullock. This should not have surprised Murphy, for Sarah had a dubious reputation to maintain, but it did. In my opinion, it has left him dazed until this very day, which proves to me that Murphy was in love—or was in something—with Sarah; and it was probably the first time in his life that he had been in anything with anyone, beside himself.

Rumors of her infidelities to Murphy were by now being constantly delivered to his ears, but he did not, would not, could not, believe them. Why, he asked me, and others, would she want anyone else when she had him? It was ridiculous.

6

It was difficult for Harry Orbisson to believe that anyone took Sarah seriously; for, as I say, she was notorious in Hollywood for vulgarity and nymphomania, and Orbisson's only reason for staying with her was that her brother was Martin King, one of the most powerful men in the industry, a king-maker and -breaker, who had made Harry a little king, once upon a time, when Sarah had still cared for Harry. For his own part, Harry by now considered Sarah's antics to be amusing and her sex-menagerie ludicrous.

Therefore, few things could have been more surprising to Harry Orbisson than Murphy's attack upon him. It was an attack in the name of chivalry, gallantry, or whatever, for Harry had referred to his Sarah as "the cow" once too often to suit Murphy.

He committed this egregious act on the set of Murphy's latest picture, *The Tall Stranger,* an adult western of Academy Award quality, if I say so myself, for I wrote the screenplay. I was also producing, though Orbisson would get the credit. This was the picture that was going to make Murphy a big star.

There stood Murphy, tall, rawboned, and angular. He was wearing a trail-driver's costume and his by now signature beaten-up Stetson, and he looked the hero he was acting and probably believed himself to be. He grabbed Orbisson by the collar and shook him, all the while warning him not to ever use that word again with reference to Sarah, who was too good for him.

The set went silent. Everyone froze. I knew what a fool Murphy could be—I knew what he was capable of, as well. Harry Orbisson was not a big man physically but he was a studio giant, even not considering his connections. At this moment, it was still possible to gloss things over, and I called Murphy's name in a warning voice:

"Murphy!"

But he was too deeply involved in his part, too much the tall stranger, and topped things off by laying Orbisson out with a powerful punch to the jaw, just as he had done me, once, and no doubt numerous others.

7

When Murphy was informed that Sarah considered him as already part of her past, and that she thought he should be punished for his assault on her husband, Murphy collapsed into bewilderment.

When weeks went by and she wouldn't answer his calls he grew paranoid and depressive and made the wrong kind of headlines by turning out a famous Hollywood hotspot, doing several thousand dollars worth of damage. He was arrested, tried, and spent a few months in the Los Angeles County Jail.

Upon his release, he vanished into the desert with the bimbo who had been waiting for him at the jail, and didn't turn up again for several months. "You've got to get ahold of yourself," I said, when I finally ran into him, looking drunk and disheveled, on the street. "Go back east for a while . . . do some stage work."

"I'm no stage actor," he said. "I'm a movie star."

But that was a delusion.

Murphy's attack on Harry Orbisson cost him his career, for Martin King lifted a telephone at his brother-in-law's behest, and Murphy was forever washed up in Hollywood.

But for once his career seemed to hold small interest for Murphy, perhaps because he didn't realize the enormity and finality of his act, or perhaps because his ultimate interest was elsewhere. Only once since his Ma's death had Murphy loved a woman, really loved her, and he had lost, lost in a horrible, annihilating defeat.

I met Murphy many times during the years when he was blacklisted, and during those years his version of his great misadventure changed. It wasn't long before he was saying that he had known all about Sarah. "Just like all the rest of them," he said to me one day. "Liars! They don't know how to love a man. My mother was the only woman who ever loved me. Her love was pure gold."

8

Sitting at home, sometimes, looking at pictures of all of us, Murphy and Marie and I together, Murphy as Fast Draw McGraw, Marie's changing but always beautiful face, Murphy's boys, *my* boys, who have families and careers of their own now—Marie and I have often pondered Murphy's enigmatic misadventure.

"I think he really loved Sarah," I've said.

But had he really loved her? Or had he considered her a means to an end? If I am ever going to make a screenplay of Murphy's story, I have to decide on that.

"I think he was just using her," Marie often says. "He used everyone, including you and me."

"But Sarah used *him*, and threw him away."

"I know what he'd say," Marie says, "he'd say that he never loved her."

And I guess I have to admit that Marie is right about that; because, judging by a recent conversation I had with the old goat, it has apparently become more comfortable for Murphy to think that he never loved Sarah, that he was using her, "milking the cow dry," as he put it, and that it was only a damned fool impulsive mistake that prevented him from becoming a star.

MOVIE MONEY

Aunt Gertrude had had no education—had been, due to the poverty and ignorance of her family, virtually a waif—but possessed noticeable innate intelligence. She kept several sets of account books, some of dubious public record and some honest, illegal, and secret. The house of her dominion may have been a rooming house in a Newark slum, but it was papered green with numbers racket hundred dollar bills that had to be accounted for.

She had been a buxom girl who had swollen into an enormous woman and subsequently shrunk back to a two-hundred and fifty pound mere shadow of her former self, leaving her sallow, inelastic skin loose and hanging. Jimmy's earliest memory of her—he was about four or five—was of that enormous middle-aged woman of sixty.

She sat across from him and his mother in a restaurant booth and he counted her seven ballooning chins. Tactlessly, he asked about them, though he was just as fascinated by the even larger balloons that rested side by side on the table top, that were deep-trenched and powdered and seemed to roll about of their own volition.

Of the chins, Aunt Gertrude told him that each represented a daughter and that, collectively, they indicated that she was the seventh daughter of a seventh daughter and was therefore possessed of magical powers, such as the gift of the evil eye.

Later, his mother told him that Aunt Gertrude had been stolen by Gypsies as a little girl—actually, farmed-out as a helper—and had lived in a Gypsy camp somewhere in the Watchung mountains of New Jersey for over a year, when finally her father had—reluctantly, for she had been a demonic child even before being "kidnapped," and some said that she had been given away—gone to retrieve her. Into her early sixties, she had developed ghostly cataracts that added impact when she gave you the evil eye, which she often did, and either had or feigned to have a heart ailment. By now, this doubtful heart condition had been present for as long as anyone could remember with no more dire consequence than that if anyone crossed her she would go spinning off across the room like a top on her little horny feet, her great, low bulk knocking a swath in the furnishings, and dive into a possum faint. This was called "swooning," and Jimmy's mother said that Aunt Gertrude had "swooned" or was about to "swoon." In truth, it was difficult to tell if her heart or her temper was the true culprit. She took—suitably—nitroglycerin for this condition, and smelling salts were always advisable. The smelling salts were carried in the pocket of another enormous, though much younger, woman, named Charity. Charity was Aunt Gertrude's flunky. She had culled Charity and Charity's husband, Donald, from the mildly-challenged ward at the mental institution at Vineland, New Jersey. Charity and Donald lived, as it were, by Aunt Gertrude's leave. Charity was a low, wide three-hundred pounds; Donald a high, narrow one-twenty-five. This couple existed upstairs and would plummet down a back stairwell at Aunt Gertrude's ear-splitting behest. Charity did all of Aunt Gertrude's domestic chores, more or less ran the roominghouse, including keeping in supplies—slow or not, she was a sharp bargainer—and Donald did the toting and fixing. They were well content, and even protective of Aunt Gertrude, who needed protection no more than did her favorite wrestler, Gorgeous George. Far from the least important member of this odd ménage was a canine. Wiggles was a very old bitch with tumorous, pendulous breasts. Aunt Gertrude, who had been at various times in an otherwise amoral career immoral on a professional basis, had been unable to have children, and had always felt the lack of a daughter. Wiggles served her as such. Jimmy took it that there had been other doggy-daughters before the obscene Wiggles, but for as long as he could remember Wiggles had been about, door-scratching and spitting horrid barks at any intruder, himself included, being dragged back and shushed, and traipsing off down the hall ahead of the menagerie, like an old woman who has just given a salesman an earful, nails clicking, upright stubby tail stiff, broad hindquarters naked, unappetizing. Jimmy was a fastidious little boy and Wiggles deeply disturbed him. She sat at table, wrapped in a bib, and ate from a dinner plate. Because she was an old dog and couldn't chew, all were subjected to the spectacle of Aunt Gertrude, or sometimes Charity, masticating morsels before placing them in Wiggles' worn-down chops. And often, not being content with her own portion, Wiggles would heave her clattering bulk to the floor and beg Jimmy's, which he must forfeit or incur Aunt Gertrude's wrath.

"Isn't she a sugarball? Give her some of your meat. Don't forget to chew it for her!"

Friday was the big day of the week. Fridays, Aunt Gertrude prepared to go to Long Branch, New Jersey, where she would be met by her paramour and dominant partner, Tony "Ice Pick" Scarpia, a nearly four-foot tall man with a twisted spine, her "little giant," who ostensibly sold live bait, hence, "Ice Pick," to the fishermen on the pier there, but who was actually a mob-sponsored bookie and runner with the need of getting large sums of money out of his possession and back to Newark, to the roominghouse he owned and which existed under the absolute dominion of Aunt Gertrude.

* * *

When Jimmy's nervous mother rang the doorbell on Fridays, sending Wiggles into a conniption fit, Aunt Gertrude would usually be applying a sulphur-based solution, which she used instead of a razor, to her jowls and chins and pulpy, varicosed legs, of which, no pun intended, she was very vain, and every recess of the house would reek of sulphur, like a brimstone pit. Jimmy's mother would adjust herself to the powerful, rotten-egg fumes while Wiggles was being calmed and sent on her haughty way. On recovering from the spinning heart-seizure his mother's entry had caused, Aunt Gertrude would tell her to get herself some breakfast (coffee would suffice for Jimmy's mother in such an atmosphere); then Aunt Gertrude would carry on with her toilet like Susannah herself, if sans Susannah's everything including the intrigued elders. If Jimmy's mother could manage to be pleasantly helpful during the course of the day on Friday, and Jimmy could join her after school, and do the same, Aunt Gertrude might give them the money to go to a movie and buy some popcorn.

What was required was that they take her to the station and wait with her until train time. Jimmy would carry her bags and his mother would make chitchat, larding her comments with compliments.

"What a lovely dress, Aunt Gertrude!"

"I don't care for it that much!"

"Don't you?"

"No!

"Well, maybe it is a bit . . ."

"A bit what? Don't you like it? You just said you did!"

"I *do*!"

"Well—" Huff-puff!

Jimmy invariably arrived at a crucial moment, for with Aunt Gertrude there were no non-crucial moments. By now her beard and leg-hair would have been peeled heart-attackingly off with the sulphurous pancake crusts that had mummified various parts of her anatomy, her top-hair would have been freshly dyed—this was Jimmy's mother's specialty—either jet-black or fire-engine red, as Aunt Gertrude's mood would have it, her too-small shoes force-fed by horn her horny feet, and, corseted, frocked, and fully decorated, she would look like a Woolworth's Christmas tree. But Wiggles would have to be left in the care of Charity and Donald, whom Aunt Gertrude did not trust to do right by her doggy daughter while she was away (albeit so in awe of her magic were the poor serfs of her household, that she had little to fear), and therefore had to be bathed and prepared for the weekend before Aunt Gertrude could take her leave in confidence. The galvanized tub would be on the kitchen table and Charity would be turning Wiggles fatly and stiff-leggedly about in it, soaping and scrubbing her under Aunt Gertrude's close scrutiny. Jimmy's mother would answer the door, lead little Jimmy back into the kitchen, and stand aside, eager to please, afraid to offend, baffled and thwarted, it being understood that she was not competent to be involved in this splashy task.

"Is there anything to eat?" Jimmy asked.

"Not now," his mother said, meaning of course not that there wasn't anything to eat but that Jimmy should keep quiet. Aunt Gertrude shrieked, grabbed her fat-buried heart, and fell back, knocking pots and pans from the stove. Charity had lost her soapy grip on Wiggles and the ungainly animal had slopped about in the bubbles.

"I thought she'd drown," cried Aunt Gertrude. "For God's sake, Charity, be careful with her!"

Jimmy sniggered.

"And just what do you think is so funny?"

One ghostly evil eye was on him, the other tightly shut.

His mother pinched him.

"Nothing, Aunt Gertrude."

"I should hope not!"

Charity got Wiggles rinsed, spread a bathtowel out on the table, patted her dry, turned her over, powdered her tumorous breasts, and put a nice clean jockstrap on her. These jockstraps served as double-D doggie brassieres, holding Wiggles' pendulous powdered breasts in place. There were several other elongated jockstraps hanging about the kitchen on towel racks, drying. Wiggles stood upright now, a small whale on four toothpicks, jockstrap at sway. Charity sweatered, harnessed and leashed her.

This was where Jimmy came in. He could not fathom what gave Aunt Gertrude the idea, but she was firm in her conviction that it was good for Wiggles to be walked after her bath, and it was his delightful duty to walk her, and not just in front of the house, where he would frowningly skulk, if he were not urged on, but all the way up to Broad Street and under the Lackawanna overpass, where the bus stop was, and many people were, and back. If not conscious, was it subconscious sadism that compelled Aunt Gertrude to force Jimmy to do this? On more than one occasion people had laughed out loud at the sight of the red-faced, embarrassed little boy in short pants and the enormously overweight, pendulously jock-strapped dog that seemed in charge of their direction. It happened again on this particular Friday, and one woman even pointed at them from a passing bus. Jimmy's face burned red as a tomato, and tears of shame and temper rolled down his cheeks. But Jimmy consoled himself with the prospect of the movie that lay ahead—maybe.

They couldn't be sure. Aunt Gertrude was capable of not coming through on her part of the unspoken bargain, just to show them. There had been sad times when they left the station with empty pockets and had had to be satisfied with just looking at the bright marquees, to imagine how good it might have been to see the pictures and to talk about how much they would have enjoyed them. Then they would go home cursing Aunt Gertrude a little but mostly laughing about the mishaps of Wiggles and Aunt Gertrude's swoons. Later, they would listen to the evening radio programs and look forward to next week, the eternal optimists—for, after all, being dirt poor, they had no choice.

Aunt Gertrude loved gin rummy and Jimmy was the only soldier in her small army who knew how to play it. But she had a method. She would set up the card table next to the television set, then a relatively new device with a huge, rabbit-eared antenna, and turn on wrestling, which she loved—Jimmy noted her adoration of Gorgeous George—and then, when in trouble with her cards, would shout for him to look at what was happening in the ring, and, while his attention was diverted, would cheat by changing cards or stealing extras. One time he caught her at it, though he had suspected her of cheating before this. Boldly, he accused her, and she accused him of being a thankless ingrate like his no-good drunken father. Jimmy sat fuming, about eight years old, then charged across the room like a little bull, goring her with his cowlick horns. She was terrifically strong, even then, and he could believe the family tales told of her by nieces and nephews whom she had lifted into the air in her lustier youth and thrown clean across rooms. This time she easily finessed him into a half-nelson, boxed his ears red, whirled, and, having subdued him, promptly fainted. Charity brought out the smelling salts while Wiggles and Jimmy's mother had hysterical fits of their own. No one was concerned with the crushed, defeated little heap under her—Jimmy. That Friday they did not get their movie money.

So Jimmy's eyes sucked back his tears and he held himself in and brought Wiggles back to the house.

"What did Wiggles do?"

"Sniffed at things."

"Was she cute?"

"Yes, Aunt Gertrude."

"Did she pee or poop?"

"No."

Thank God! That would have required removing the jockstrap in public and replacing it afterwards (he was always required to take extras along). It had happened before and was perhaps worst of all.

"Well, we are all ready to go then. Charity, get my pocket book! Donald, get my bags!"

When they took a taxi, the trip to the station wasn't so bad. Then it was just a question of stuffing Aunt Gertrude, her bags, and themselves into the back seat and setting forth. But sometimes she couldn't get a cab to come to the house at the right time; or else, for other reasons, preferred to take a bus. Jimmy thought she preferred to take the bus sometimes so that the passengers could get a load of her, all dolled up and, as she no doubt believed, dazzling. But this bus ride with Aunt Gertrude was nearly as much of an embarrassment to him as were the afterbath walks with Wiggles. Indeed, Wiggles and Aunt Gertrude had much in common. Aunt Gertrude's legs, however, were of stouter stuff than those of her doggy daughter. Jimmy watched her now, as they climbed the great wide ramp that led to the trains; and, though he could scarcely drag the suitcases that were attached to his weakening hands and weight-sloped shoulders, he giggled to see the bowed, varicosed, mouth-down megaphones of her legs triumph over the upgrade. Side to side she heaved, as if the whole station, and the whole world, were tilting.

As usual, she had bought them chicken salad sandwiches and coffee in the lunchroom down the ramp behind them, where everyone had seen them before, for many Fridays. As usual, she had complained about the expense. As usual, she had been rude to everyone, and as usual Jimmy felt a little sick. But it was a good sign. It showed that she was in a giving mood. Perhaps she was in a good mood because she was looking forward to making love to her little "Hot Pepper." He loved her, they all knew that, if not why. Perhaps because she seemed oblivious to his deformity. Perhaps because she only heard his deep voice or saw his handsome head. But then, there was the gambling money she would be bringing back from Long Branch to Newark on Monday, and perhaps she feigned her obliviousness to his deformity, and her orgasms, which were occasionally overheard and commented upon by the horror-struck tenants of the roominghouse, as she feigned her heart attacks. Who knew?

They boarded the train with her, as was their practice, and sat with her, waiting for the train to show signs of life. Jimmy wondered if she would give them their movie money, which he felt they had earned, and if it would be enough, and if they would be able to get off the train in time, and not be swept off with her, away from the many glittering marquees of Newark, while she strung it out, cat and mouse. She bullied. His mother strained to be dutiful. He perspired. Aunt Gertrude's perfume was dizzying. The train jerked with coupling. Steam hissed.

"We'd better get off, Aunt Gertrude," his mother said.

"You have plenty of time. You're awfully anxious to get away. Where are you going?"

"Nowhere," said his mother, cowed.

"Well, then, sit still! Oh, by the way, here are a couple of dollars. Why don't you go to a movie? 'Gone With the

Wind' is playing at the Adams on Branford Place." But she did not hand over the bills.

"All off!" cried the conductor.

Aunt Gertrude sighed, and handed the bills to Jimmy's mother.

They kissed her and got off the train. Now they must stand and dutifully wave until the heavily laden train puffed out of sight. If they did not stand long enough, she would call them on it next Friday, and they would not get their movie money then. Finally, the train completely disappeared, and they could leave the station and walk back to the center of Newark and study the other worlds of the magical marquees. In those days you really had a choice.

Or so it seemed.

THE LIAR

She came in to the cafeteria three or four times that week, would sit with her older friend, a kind of watchdog, but pleasant, in his section, and would smile at him when he came near. He was a busboy. No, he wasn't. He was an acting student. No, he wasn't. He had run out of money. But he was going to have more money some day, and then he would go to New York University and take dramatic arts.

He was about her age; but, somehow, in the circumstances, and quite un-intentionally, she made him feel younger. She looked like she had money, and he did not, look like he had money, that is. Of course he did not have any, or why would he be a busboy in a cafeteria? She must have been in her late teens, early twenties, but she had a mature way about her, serious, intelligent. He lived in Greenwich Village, but not quite. He lived on the great wall of Greenwich Village, 14th Street, in a shoebox of a room with a sagging single bed which he shared with a friend as poor as himself, a Puerto Rican boy of intellectual bent who had been in the Marines with him. They were not out very long, a matter of months. They had a G.I. Bill coming, but had to get tuition money together first, and be reimbursed. They seldom had car fare. They had few clothes, which they shared, on a first come first serve basis, so that neither of them could be sure what he was going to wear at any particular time. Who knew what would be left? First one up and out was best dressed. They were too poor to feed their roaches. Now he wore a white jacket supplied by the restaurant, an apron stained with food, old baggy fatigues, split in the crotch from squatting to pick up under the tables, and down-at-heels muddy shoes of military issue. They had white soap stains at toe and heel. He owned no others. It embarrassed him that this beautiful young woman, who looked like a movie star, kept smiling at him. The smile was sweet, intelligent, and kind. The smile was warm and friendly and respectful. But it hurt his pride, because she was so beautiful, and poised, and well-dressed, and obviously well-off, and established-looking. He would have thought that she was making fun of him or teasing him or something, but somehow he could see that she wasn't. She and her friend sat and smoked cigarettes after eating and he had no choice but to go to their table and collect their dishes. and he hated it, because of the way she looked and smiled; but he had no choice but to do it. The older woman said, in a pleasant voice, we've been watching you. My friend thinks you're very attractive. This horrified him, horrified him. What was he to say? He nearly spilled the stack of dishes. Careful, said the older woman, and laughed a little in a friendly way.

You take your break soon, said the younger one, you take your break about now, I noticed. Won't you bring us all some coffee and sit with us?

I can't sit with the customers, he lied. Nobody would care. It was a cafeteria.

Of course you can, said the older woman in a pretty full-throated voice. She was a bit overweight.

Please bring us some coffee and sit with us, said the beauty.

Can't you see she's smitten, said the other, and the beauty looked actually embarrassed herself. She wants to meet you. She thinks you're very handsome. What do you do? I mean, beside this.

I'm an actor, he said. Was he lying?

So am I, said the beauty. My friend, too. Are you studying?

Yes, he lied.

We thought you might be, said the older woman. Get the coffee and come and sit down. We want to talk to you.

So he sat with them that time and again the next time they came in. The beauty seemed nicer and more cultivated the more he saw her. She was so young, it had not occurred to him that she might be working, but it turned out that she was already pretty well-known. She was in a play on Broadway. So was the other one. They made him feel like a roach. It wasn't their fault, of course. They were as sweet as could be. He knew it was himself, his pride, but he couldn't help it. They made him feel like a poor ignorant slob, bussing dirty dishes, his old stained shoes stinking under the table. And yet the beauty made him melt, just melt. She was nice and nicer and it frightened him. It embarrassed him. She wanted him to ask her for a date, but where could he take such a girl, a girl rich and famous and successful? He didn't have any clothes to wear, let alone an extra dime to spend on her. Why did she have to pick on him? Where could he take her? Oh, where could he take her? And as if she knew what was in his mind, she asked him if they couldn't take a walk together sometime. Just go for a walk, she said. You don't have to take me any place special. I'd just like to be with you. We could go for a walk in the park. To the zoo.

I have no clothes that I can wear to walk beside you, he thought. I am only a busboy, not even a real actor. But he *was* an actor, for he said, No. It will do you no good to know me.

Why not?

Because, he said, looking down at his stained apron and muddy shoes, because, you see, like so many actors these days, I don't like women, I mean not in that way.

You mean, she said, you're gay?

Yes, he lied, and watched her gather up her things and leave, her friend consoling her; watched the most beautiful, wonderful girl he had ever known walk out of his ridiculous lying failure of a life forever. He gathered up their plates with deep sad relief, swearing to himself that he would get himself some new clothes, so that the next time this happened, he would be ready.

RED STATE BLUES

Enola Gay opened the doors of the Battle Flag at nine, but now, near noon, I'm still perched on a cushioned stool in an empty roadhouse in a nowhere crossroads named Downy, outside Atlanta, waiting for a fat wallet to walk in. Enola's left my Coors and me to dream while she counts cash or something down the other end of nowhere, and I dream of everything I had that mattered, make wishes on Battle Flag matches to get it all back, and blow them out.

I can see you, Maw-Maw, in a movie in my mind, waving two little stick flags on a Fourth of July, the Reb battle flag and the Stars-and-Stripes-Forever, your mouth stuffed with barbeque and slaw, beer suds on your nose, your round face flushed and happy, your white hair wavy as the snow on the ski-slope at Sky Valley where David took me and little Lee the winter before to teach us how to ski. Sometimes with my time-warp Star Trek X-ray vision I can see you when I wasn't there at all, taking a piss, sitting in that hot port-a-potty at the carnival that set up in that field of Queen-Anne's Lace and sneeze-making ragweed outside Downy last summer, white as blackboard chalk, but scarce able to sweat even in that boxed-in heat and with one evil fly buzzed down and landed on your pink putty nose which kids used to point at when you were younger and it was that port-a-potty like the Orgone Box cure-all I saw a picture of in my psych textbook when I still had educational ambitions, see you as if the door stood open, but the waiting crowd could only see it shut too long. Hodgkin's or loss of life force finally killed your body, if not your unkillable spirit of troublesome fun. That lives on in my heart. You were boozing with Bubba, Uncle Bubba, and he was blamed, unfairly, for once, and driven from the pack, eventually, sick of hearing how he took you out and killed you in the most embarrassing public way possible.

But somebody would have surrendered to your wish. It was your life's blood, the spirit of it, the laughing in the juke joints and calling young studs "sonny boy," the Nascar video games, the mechanical bulls, the pool tables, the pickled eggs, pale in their jars of anemic beet blood—two of them and a beer made my birthday breakfast this morning—the honky-tonk jukeboxes banging out country music, and all the rest of that laughing life before death.

Hey, Uncle Bubba, how many banks have you robbed? Maw-maw told me once that you'd wasted most of your life behind bars, but the family always stuck by you, leastways until you took your sweet sister out that night to die. Shit, I might as well be with you, wherever you are, as here in the same town with them sin-spitting Bible-thumpers who started driving me out at fifteen, when I had little Lee by someone I couldn't name for shame, just the way they Bible-thumped Mama out when she popped me, and she's as gone as you are, Uncle Bubba, leaving me for Maw-Maw to defend, me some kind of bastard halfbreed bitch Mama got from one of her Cherokee boyfriends she liked to run with up in the Smokies, a bastard and breed bitch left for Maw-Maw, who done her duty, then Mama's too.

"It's a bitch!" I tell Enola Gay, when she comes my way, about today, tomorrow, and yesterday—about anytime since God's marble blew up.

"Girl, you got Red State Blues," says Enola Gay. But what I got now is a coziness around me, like an Indian blanket, not the heat, just that sweet beer safety. Fact is, it's getting kind of hot in here, with the sun climbing. Enola plugs in the juke box and it lights up like Christmas. That's cool! I go over and slug it and come back to listen. It's Patsy Cline—"I Fall to Pieces." I look in the mirror and see a cowgirl sip at a Coors behind a cancer-stick cloud. That's me. That is *I.* See? The little whore knows better. She's not just trailer trash. She's been to community college. Thought I'd become a teacher or maybe a nurse, do some good in this good-for-nothing world. If it weren't for Lee, having to feed Lee after Maw-Maw got her Hodgkin's and anyway got too old to care for the sweet little brat, maybe I'd be saving lives instead of infecting them.

After I did David he came back like a persistent beau, and even brought me candy and flowers, Whitman's and roses, and I began to forget that he was a trick and we began to talk because he was a teacher and I still had some of my ambition for learning, and he had this nice patient nature, too, not like the slope-headed, hairy-assed truckers and rednecks and servicemen who come in here looking for sex and trouble. You could ask Enola Gay if David wasn't a gentleman and a kind of poet with his song lyrics he wrote himself and some of them were about me, too—eventually.

I'm gonna have another cold Coors.

It's summer out there, and none too cool in here, but shady dark toward the back, where I am, sunny toward the door, with a big splash of sun wavering on the floor like gold water on the yellow wood. The Battle Flag's got a good dance floor, big enough for shagging, or even line dancing. I just told Enola if she don't turn up the air-conditioning, I'm taking my beer back into the fridge.

Thinking back, I suppose the best thing was that David liked Lee, showed him magic tricks with cards and chemistry—he taught chemistry—and I stopped turning my own tricks, and signed up for courses, and we began to make a family. David always had money, an "ample sufficiency," he'd say, but that was what worried me, because he wasn't teaching; he'd just go off and never say where, what he was doing, and come back and be good as gold to us, and I would tell Enola Gay, who had troubles of her own. I could tell Enola Gay that I was in love, but, black-eyed, she'd only laugh, or, maybe worse, try to wink that black eye.

Then one day David and Lee took off and never came back. David's meth lab, that he kept secret from me, blew up. I had to go to the Sheriff to find out, nobody came to me. David's dead and Lee's dead, too, gone with him to pieces. Every blessed thing I care about is gone, like with the wind. All this shit happened before I was twenty-one, which is to say, that is the yesterday I've got to celebrate today. Today! Today's my birthday, but I got nobody to spend it with. Well, maybe not! Here comes a wallet walking on water.

CANDY BUTCHER

By the time La Guardia was re-elected, the word "burlesque" had been banned and, soon after, the Minsky name itself, since the two were synonymous.
—Wikipedia

1

This was a new kind of burlesque, Harold Minsky's burlesque of 1952, with big production numbers reminiscent of the great follies of an earlier era; and this was the Saturday night crowd, middle-class and wealthy people, husbands who had brought their wives, respectable theater-parties, even an occasional clergyman, come across the Hudson or in from the suburbs to see at the Adams Theatre in Newark what Mayor La Guardia had banned from New York. Now, for the sixth and last time of the day, the oily, tuxedoed singer leaped from the wings singing the theme song, a variation on "The Most Beautiful Girl in the World"—

Oh, they're handy—
Oh, they're dandy—
And Minsky girls

are the most beautiful girls in the W-O-R-L-D! The strippers did a bump-and-grind, twirled the tassels on their pasties, snapped their G-strings, and strutted off in their spike-heels. The chain of chorus girls disappeared into the wings with a sequined kick from its last link. The singer took several bows and stepped off into obscurity. The great purple curtains rushed from the wings, met center-stage, ballooned, and settled.

2

In his first week at Minsky's Jimmy had his hair cut into a ducktail and bought himself a white-on-white shirt, like the ones the older candy butchers wore. The second week he cut his penny-ante tonk rummy bets—the novelty of the ongoing game was keeping him up till all hours—and managed a pair of blue suede shoes. He had begun to smoke, holding his corktipped cigarettes between his teeth in imitation of Stoney, the hard-faced ex-Marine who was the chief candy butcher for Lou Schenk, the concessionaire. He even attempted to imitate the bitterness Stoney had acquired in an apparently brutal life that had been capped by the Korean War, without quite understanding it to be bitterness, taking it for worldliness, a kind of crude sophistication. But Stoney disliked innocence, and delighted in persecuting it. He practiced his persecution of Jimmy during the all-night card games in the little concession room in the basement of the theater with a form of verbal abuse that had its origins in Marine Corps boot camp and in the black street kids' game of "The Dozens"—piling up ingenious metaphorical insults about one another's mothers. Stoney was the great white hope of "The Dozens." "My balls itch. Whose Mama can get here first with a good ball-scratcher? You're young, Junior. Maybe your Mama's the fastest runner." Jimmy thought it prudent not to offer a rejoinder. Stoney was big and raw boned and quick to temper, as Jimmy had observed. No one said a word. Tex and Big Jim, both of whom had at least five years on Jimmy, just sat patiently on their deep, upended trays and played on.

3

Jimmy leaned on the plateglass of the candy stand, smoking, and saw sad-eyed Marge, the counter girl, staring up at Stoney's hard, handsome face. Jimmy saw her sad eyes and wanted to divert them to himself. He gripped his cigarette in his teeth and swaggered a little in his mind. Marge and Stoney were talking about someone named Sunny.

"Who's Sunny?" he asked.

"A tramp," Stoney said.

"She's not a tramp, Stonewall!"

"Sunny used to be my old lady when she was in the chorus in Bayonne," Stoney said.

"She never was!" cried Marge. "She was a lot too nice for you!"

Stoney ignored her. "She's an usherette," he said, "just hired."

"She's waiting for an opening in the chorus," Marge said, "like me."

Stoney snorted contemptuously. He took Jimmy's elbow and said, "C'mon, Junior. Let's find her."

They pushed through the heavy red padded doors of the lobby and into the auditorium. On stage, Flame O'Hair was strutting her stuff. Stoney led Jimmy toward a blonde in an usherette's uniform. "This is Sunny Day, Jimmy. She asked me to introduce you."

Sunny Day smiled, and said: "Hi! I've seen you around and thought we should get acquainted." She had small, pretty teeth and gray eyes. "I'll be off duty in a half hour. I'm going up to the box on the left side to watch the show. Would you like to join me?"

"I don't know," he stuttered. He realized that his knees were beating unrhythmically against the orchestra's drum gambade and that his heart was beating only between cymbal crashes and then in great, breathless gallops. He could feel his pointed ears burning and guessed they were red, perhaps enlarged.

When Jimmy joined Sunny in the dark, brass-railed box she was in street clothes and had undergone a transformation from the cute usherette into a woman of mystery. In the dim stagelight that rose up to them, he could make out the way her knitted dress clung to her voluptuous body. She said, "Hi, again!" as he sat down. Her wide-brimmed hat angled back to the stage. Feathery hopes, fears, and doubts fluttered Jimmy's heart. He was glad that he had stopped to comb his greased, ducktailed hair, and had put on Stoney's suit jacket. His scuffed leather jacket—which he had worn for several years as a Western Union boy, and which had grown much too small for him since he had taken up bodybuilding—would have been out of place, in what he now thought of as this formal setting. It would have completely hidden his white-on-white shirt as well. His knee-bulged dungarees were dark and dirty, but didn't show. He resented the lower darkness, though, for hiding his new, pointed, blue suede shoes.

On stage a long curving sweep of powerful powdered thigh rippled and flexed. From spiked heels two seams ran up mesh-covered flesh, were accented at the round hips and nearly met at the tiny, arching waist. Each gambade shifted the weight of the body from one jutting hip to the other, a pulsing, upside-down heart. Sunny put a hand on his knee and squeezed in rhythm with the music and the stripper's bumps and grinds. Jimmy sat, afraid to move, staring at the stage. Sunny unzipped his jeans, and in a few seconds there was a crescendo of music and motion. She pressed a piece of paper into his palm. "My address," and got up and left him alone in the dark box. He saw the comics come on but had no idea of what they were saying. He heard, "My address, my address, my address. . ." over and over, like the refrain of a song. He had never before had a woman touch him like that. Never before had such a thing been done, he thought, not in all history.

4

Jimmy waited for two weeks before going to see Sunny. He wasn't sure whether he had avoided the encounter for two full weeks because he didn't want to seem in too much of a hurry or because he was afraid. He was not afraid, he told himself, he just didn't want to seem too eager. Nuts! He was scared to death.

Sunny took Jimmy's leather jacket and woolen scarf and put them over the back of an armchair. She was just out of the shower and her hair was wrapped in a big yellow towel. She was wearing a quilted pink robe and pink pompommed slippers. Her feet seemed incredibly small to Jimmy, and the nail polish on her toes glittered like enamel roses. She made him breathless, yet he tried to breathe evenly. He wanted to be cool and smooth.

"Sit down," she said, indicating the couch. "That thing opens into a bed." She smiled at him. "Are you horny?"

"No, I ate. But I'm thirsty."

She laughed, shaking her head, said, "I'll get some beer," and went into the kitchenette.

Jimmy sat like a collapsed puppet on the couch and clumsily fingered a pack of cigarettes. Finally he tore the pack open and stuck a corked tip between his teeth. This was the tenth brand he had tried in as many weeks. So far, these were the best for biting. He took a drag. The smoke got into his eyes and he wiped them quickly with his sweatered sleeve. He heard Sunny getting the beer, the clinking of bottles. The kitchenette had an oilcloth across its doorway. The walls wore faded flowered wallpaper. There was a metal dining set with a plastic top and maple end-tables and a mahogany dresser with a mirror with cards and letters stuck in it. One of the items stuck in the mirror was a picture of Sunny in G-string, pasties, and spike-heels. His sixteen-year-old lust, which he had carried about in him like an overstuffed piñata, felt a near-bursting blow. Sunny came back with a tray, beer, and two stemmed glasses. She smelled of exotic perfume, passion flowers, his nose told him, not that he quite knew what they were.

"You've got a nice apartment here," he said.

"What, this dump? I rent it by the week."

"Isn't the furniture yours?"

"No, it's furnished. I just took it to tide me over when I came in from Bayonne." She saw his extended cigarette ash. "There's an ashtray."

She sat down beside him and her quilted robe flapped open, exposing a neat, pale knee.

"I never know how to open these things," she said, clinking a bottle-opener on a cap.

"Here," Jimmy said, opening the bottles with shaking hands.

"You're strong," she said. "I can see your biceps through your sweater."

"I lift weights," he said. "I've built myself up from a ninety-eight pound weakling, when I was thirteen, to my present size—almost six feet tall and a hundred and seventy-five pounds—in just over three years. I work out three times a week at the Y, and for the past few years I've done a lot of bicycle-riding. I was a Western Union boy. That really develops your thighs."

"Well, I understand that," she said, "being a dancer."

"I can see you have strong legs, too," he said.

"I have something else. I have something to celebrate tonight. I got a new job. I'll be shuffling off to Buffalo in a few days. A chorus job." She removed the towel from her head and shook out her damp, curly hair.

Jimmy could not connect with her words. He looked at her dark-rooted, orange hair, that looked to him like Rapunzel's golden locks, and wondered how old she was. Thirty? He couldn't tell about women. Then he realized that she was leaving town.

"I wish you weren't going away. I'll miss you."

He could never understand how women got their clothes to fit them as they did; how, for instance, they got their full hips through the narrow waistbands of their slacks. He had pondered these things.

"Why didn't you come up and see me sooner? I might not have taken the job in Buffalo."

"Well, I was kind of—"

"Scared? You've never been with a woman, have you? C'mon now, tell Sunny truth." She laughed, touched his cheek, and pushed back some of his fair hair. "I wish you'd change the way you wear your hair. It'd look nice without all that grease in it, loose and curly."

"I will—if you won't go away." He bounced his glass on the table and put his hand decisively on her knee.

She shuddered. "Oh, your hand's still cold!"

Jimmy held his ground for a moment, his eyes widening, then withdrew.

Sunny smiled, and affectionately added to the rumpled state of his hair. "That's all right," she said, putting his hand back. "Go ahead."

"Sure is hot in here."

"Why don't you take off your sweater?"

He stood up and pulled his sweater over his head, tousling his hair in a wild, electric disarray. "My," she said. "I think you've got something for me."

5

A few nights later, Jimmy groped through the littered outer cellar of his parents' basement home, which was the superintendent's apartment of a rooming house, guided only by the demonic red eyes and teeth of the roaring jack-o'-lantern furnace. He reached out before him in the dark, acutely aware of his new gloves. They would protect him should he touch something sharp or hot. Sunny had come to the theater to pick up her final check and had brought them with her. "For my curly-head," she had said. "Your hands looked red and raw when you visited me. But I shouldn't give them to you."

"Why not?"

"Because you told me a lie."

"What lie?"

"You pretended you had never been with a woman. But I know better, don't I?" She had kissed him quickly on the cheek and hurried off.

Now the tight smile of light from under the door of the basement apartment stirred mixed feelings. He wanted to tell somebody about himself and Sunny, but there was nobody to tell, nobody willing to listen. Once inside, he'd be doing the listening. He loitered in the dark, shadow-boxing without shadows to box. "Take *that!* Stoney—and *that!*" He wondered if Sunny had told Stoney about them. She had sworn to him that she had not told Stoney, but Stoney seemed to know and had been ragging him unmercifully. As he boxed there in the dark, it occurred to him that Sunny was probably in Buffalo. Would it ever happen again? His gloved hands dropped to his sides. It would never happen again—never, never! And he loved Sunny, *loved* her! Emotion shook through him. He wiped his eyes on his sleeves, the backs of his gloves.

Inside, his father sat at the table, wearing his mother's kimono. He greeted Jimmy with:

"Quoth the Raven, Nevermore!"

Immediately echoed by:

"Quoth the Raven, yourself!" Jimmy's mother rose from a bed in a corner. She was wearing his father's overcoat. "He's been like this for hours, Jimmy. *Quoth the Raven! Quoth the Raven!* I can't stand it anymore. He's been drunk for weeks. He's supposed to sell books. When was the last book you sold? Look at us, here in this hole in the ground! Look!" Jimmy looked at the dripping, crisscrossing pipes, the painted-over, black-speckled bricks of the walls, where the bedbugs lived, the faded linoleum roses. . . .

"The Wizard of Oz!"

Jimmy looked at his father. "Mom's right, Dad. Look at us! Look at this place! We can't live here. Nobody can!"

"That's what I've been telling him. That's what I've been saying. What I've been telling *you*! Nobody'll listen to me. It's mid-winter and we have no back wall, just a rug slung up to keep out the cold. If it weren't for the furnace outside the front door, we'd freeze. In fact, we ought to knock out that beaverboard partition so we can get more heat."

"Mom's right, Dad. This is the worst yet."

"Just one minute, young man," said his father, raising a finger. "Since when do you decide policy?"

"Since he sees his mother in this terrible condition."

"People can't live like this, Dad."

"People can and do. But let me propose the biblical solution to you both. If your home offends you, pluck yourselves from it!"

"He doesn't know what he's saying, Jimmy. Don't pay any attention to him."

"It is *you* who never knows what you're saying—or doing," said his father. He gave Jimmy a conspiratorial look. "Did you know that she found a woman's photograph in your suitcase?"

"Sunny's picture?" Jimmy looked at his mother. "Mom, you didn't have any right to go through my things. I have a right to *some* privacy."

"No, you don't! Not when you're only sixteen and might be getting into all kinds of trouble."

"Where is it?"

"I tore it up. What do you think? A picture of a half-naked tramp with 'I'll never forget you' on it! I only hope you didn't have anything to do with her. You might have a social disease."

6

It was Saturday night again, the big night, and the last show was over. Jimmy sat with his friend, Tex, in a bar that was catty-corner across the intersection from the theater. Through a soft, steady fall of snow he saw the Minsky marquee-lights dowse out. He had plugged the jukebox with a nickel to hear his favorite song, "Rags to Riches." The crooner understood how he felt.

"Look, Junior," said Tex, "the lady's got to live her life. She's got to take a job when she gets the chance. You can't go moping around like this—'taint good for you. Go on, now—drink your beer. The chorus line's full of girls who would be glad to sleep with you."

"Nobody else is like Sunny. She made me feel like somebody cared about me."

Stoney and his ne'er-do-well buddy, Big Jim, emerged from the backroom, where they'd been shooting pool.

"How's the virgin?" said Stoney. He was drunk and disgruntled, having lost a game and a fivespot to Big Jim. "Poor Jimmy Junior! Does he miss his ladylove? You dumb shit, Junior! Playing romance with these whores makes me sick. Haven't you figured out that I put her up to it?"

"What do you mean?"

"He don't mean nothin'," said Tex. "Don't pay no attention to him."

"I mean I told her to make a man out of you."

"He didn't, neither," said Tex. "He's just teasing you, Jimmy."

"Butt out, Tex!" said Big Jim.

"She liked me," said Jimmy. "She gave me these gloves."

"Let me see those," said Stoney. "Look!" He held the gloves out for Big Jim's inspection.

"These are *my* gloves, Junior. I lost them in Bayonne a year ago. Now you turn up with them. I must have left them at her place."

"They're brand-new," Jimmy protested.

"They were brand-new when I lost them."

"Put them on," said Tex. "If they fit, then we know."

"I told you to butt out, hillbilly," said Big Jim.

Stoney threw the gloves on the bar. "I don't have to prove anything to a punk like you, Junior. Keep the damned things." He gave Jimmy's shoulder a scornful pat. Then he smiled. "*C'mon!* She's just a whore. Hell, Junior, they're all *whores*."

Lou Schenk, their boss, got up from a booth and came over, tough and bulky. "Push off, Stoney," he said. "You're drunk. Go home and sleep it off."

Stoney looked at Jimmy and laughed ridicule, shrugged indifference, threw an arm over Big Jim's shoulder, and allowed himself to be walked to the door. Jimmy picked up the gloves and pulled them on, tenderly.

Suddenly he convulsed, his eyes making a small shower of tears. Standing, he gripped the bar-rim hard in his gloved hands and hung his head between his arms. He looked down at a brass rail and a tin spittoon filled with floating butts.

"She was a *pig*, Junior," Stoney called back from the door.

From deep in Jimmy's throat came a sound like the howl of a wolf, and he ran out into the black-and-white lacework street after Stoney. "You bastards!" he screamed after the snow-curtained figures who walked ahead. "You liar, Stoney! She *liked* me, you rotten son-of-a-bitch!"

Lou Schenk and Tex had followed Jimmy into the street, grabbing after him. In his hurry the heavy concessionaire slipped on the iced-over sidewalk. Jimmy was only vaguely aware of Lou's curses and Tex's nervous laughter.

Ahead, Stoney detached himself from Big Jim and turned back. "Apologize, Junior, or I'll come back there and teach you some Marine Corps manners. I warn you: *Apologize!*"

From somewhere Marge had appeared. "Stop it, Stoney!" she called. "Stop it!"

"Shut up, bitch!" Stoney yelled. He stalked forward, eyes glittering drunken anger, intent on Jimmy.

Jimmy hesitated. Then Tex said: "Go to, Junior! Git 'im!" Jimmy took a step forward.

"No, no!" cried Marge. "Stop them, somebody. You'll all end up in jail!" She held a cigarette and her gesticulations tracked up and down in the gloom.

Then Stoney slipped on the ice, and Jimmy pounced on him, pummeling him with his gloved hands, hitting his face, his shoulders, his flailing arms, sometimes just hitting packed ice. It was his life he pounded. Then he felt hot flashes on his face: Marge was burning him with her cigarette, sticking it in his cheek, his temple.

"You bitch!" he heard Tex say, and felt Marge being pulled from him. He heard her scream in short, shocking spurts. But he was in a dream, a nightmare. He pounded his life until he felt himself being pulled from Stoney's inert form by Lou Schenk, heard the concessionaire's deep soft calming voice commanding him gently to stop, to be still. Then he was being manhandled by a pair of burly blue policemen.

7

Jimmy's father said, "I have the shakes, snakes, and the dancing bears, but I'll be all right in a few days."

"I know you will, Dad."

"Now, what's this you want me to do?"

"I want you to sign me up so I can go in the Marines."

"You can't go in the Marines," said his mother. "You're not old enough."

"Always the nay-sayer," said his father.

"I'll be seventeen on my next birthday. That's old enough, if I have your permission."

His father looked at his mother. "He can do what he wants to do if he has the courage to do it." He smiled blearily at Jimmy. "I'll sign you up."

"And be rid of you," his mother said. "That's all he wants. He'd like to sign me up, too, but I keep the rooming-house going."

"I'd like to sign up your voice," said his father.

8

Stoney, Big Jim, Tex, and Lou Schenk were in the concession room getting ready for the matinee.

Jimmy felt a nervous embarrassed pride at seeing that Stoney had a black eye and a blue bruise on his jutting jaw. His stomach shook as he did a stationary swagger that said: Don't tread on me.

"Here he is," cried Big Jim. He looked at Stoney. "Aincha gonna do nothin'?"

Stoney shrugged, morose, subdued, sober.

"No," said Lou Schenk, "he ain't gonna do nothin', an' neither are you. I don't want no trouble among my butchers.

I got a business to run. If it wasn't for me all of you'd be in jail right now." He turned his attention to Jimmy. "I like you, Junior. You got a lot of guts, showing up here. I didn't think you'd have the nerve to come in today. But I got to let you go. Stoney's my number one butcher. I need him."

"That's O.K., Lou. I figured. I just came in to say goodbye, and no hard feelings to anybody. O.K. Stoney?"

Stoney nodded.

"So—well—that's it."

Tex walked Jimmy out of the theater. "What are you going to do?" he asked.

"I'm going to join the Marines, Tex. The Marines build men. Look at Stoney. If he'd been sober, why he'da beat the crap out of me. And right, too. I don't know what got into me."

"You really mean to join the Marines?"

"If they'll have me."

"Oh, they'll have you, Junior, don't worry about that." He thought for a minute, as if remembering. "Well, it ain't nothin' here," he said, indicating the darkened theater. "It's the big burlesque out there. Hell's bells, Junior, it's all a big burlesque. You do it all."

OPEN LETTER, CLOSED BOOK

Veilsville's quiet. Wind's playing low tunes through the whitened, skeletonized trees in the woods surrounding the house. I survive the nights with sleeping pills and bourbon, dull books and dying fires. But the days, George!

When I stepped out to collect the half-frozen milk this morning, a young woman poet was in the hammock on the porch. Late November! Bittercold! She lay snoring in a thin dress under a raincoat without a lining. Another of my crazy conquests. They come from all over, everywhere, anywhere! This was a good-looker. You'd be surprised at how many are good-looking. What do they want? I'm a serious man. I'm a heart-broken man. Don't they know? Where's all that much talked of poetic sensitivity? Can you imagine me, of all people, with stalking fans? It's too fantastic. Sometimes I think I've gone mad, that I'm hallucinating all this.

What was it? A year ago? A year ago! Here I was, a plain ordinary Professor of English in the English Department of a little backwater, jerkwater college with an enrollment of 600 students in the unheard of hamlet of Veilsville, Tennessee—and, George, I was happy! You, who weren't even satisfied to hold a chair in literature at one of the best—if not, etc.—Ivy League schools in the country; you, who must have power in New York as a critic; you, sophisticate, bon vivant, etc.; you, who have never been "happy"—you would not and probably still cannot believe it; but I was happy. I remember your constant jibes; your: "Why bury yourself with the hillbillies in the Appalachians?" Your Erewhon/Nowhere ribbing. But George, *you* were fully grown, a mature man. I've only recently been born. At forty!

I interrupted this letter for a few minutes to send my young stalker back to bed. Can you imagine? She's about twenty and "simply steaming" for me. Think of it! Charlie Fallon, a sex object! It's so ludicrous it must be true. Now don't cluck your tongue. Yes, I let her in—yes, I let her stay. Why not? She's of age, and I've never been so lonely in my life. Maybe she'll help. I don't know. Her poetry's execrable but her legs are great; and she must be healthy or she'd be sick from sleeping out last night. Not a clogged sinus do I detect. Don't worry about me; it doesn't matter anyway.

What I mean is, George, that the past—one might say my pre-birth years, the ones from that false start my mother gave me to that period of a year or so ago—seems to me now like some sweet dead happy dream. I'm in the real world now, bloody born at last. Now I'm like you—tough old George—in a way. Except—I have a dream of happiness and yes even of beauty to recall. I can draw on it, like a big bank account. The Pulitzer was nothing, George. I'm going to be a *great* poet now. I hurt enough to send me right up to and on past the Nobel and into history. What poor Kathleen always wanted!

I suppose you see them occasionally. The cocktail circuit, or The White Horse, or wherever the literary chic waste their breath these days. Pardon my ignorance. I was a literary anchorite. I never knew that life. Whistler is a good poet—hell, a fine poet, maybe a great one—but he's had no luck. Not really. How odd that I of all people should have had such luck! Strange, strange luck! Whistler offended too many important people. But five fine books! And I, with just my one absurd sad long account of forebemoaned moan, and suddenly—as one of the New York papers put it—I'm a Cinderella poet (my God!), a Big Prize Winner! I'm more popular—I shy from the word famous—even more academically respected (but there I've got Whistler who never stopped to pick up a degree) than poor Kathleen's hero roaring boy. Add to that, that, at the age of forty (now forty-one) my ridiculous career, unlike Whistler's, has been called "meteoric." The world is truly tilted. And that embarrassing letter I wrote to my subscribers a year ago, when I was in the middle of my worst agony and confusion. Did you ever see it? I don't suppose so. You never would subscribe to what you called "Charlie's Little Poetaster's Journal." I can hear you now: "Don't encourage him. If you do, he'll stay buried out there in the boondocks forever. Charlie's a dear soul. He's got talent, but he wants bringing out. He's pathologically retiring." No, George: perhaps I was simple but I wasn't sick. Now I'm sick—and I'll never be able to be simple again.

When I look over copies of "A Poet's Journal" now, I can't believe that I was its editor, that *I* chose the pathetic (sometimes bathetic) poetic stuff that mimeos its pages. Was that Charlie Fallon? Did I think such stuff of merit? It's a wonder you didn't kick me down the stairs, George, as it's said Schopenhauer's mother did him. But, you see, I must have been a happy man. Innocent beyond belief. But nothing, George, absolutely nothing, had ever gone wrong for me. Now I understand that I didn't understand poetry at all, though I taught it. Think! I spent my summers at The Writers' Camp, giving my seminar on "Poe and the Dark Side of the Mind!" Well, here's a copy of the letter I sent out to the subscribers of "Fallon's, A Poet's Journal." Don't skip reading it, George. As simple-minded as it is, it will become part of literary history—now that I'm such a famous fellow.

AN OPEN LETTER

Dear FALLON'S, A POET'S JOURNAL Reader:

I feel that you subscribers are members of my family, and because I find myself in such a despondent frame of mind, it is to you I turn.

Some time ago my wife, Kathleen, took our five-year-old son, Chuck, and left me. Her move to New York was completely unexpected. As far as I could tell our life here together in Veilsville was a happy one. However, I have since learned that another man was involved.

For weeks I have lived here alone, miserably, unable to tell if I were awake or still within some hideous nightmare. Although I have sought and obtained professional help, I have lost over twenty pounds and still find it practically impossible to carry out the smallest domestic task.

However, out of this period of despondency, one solid and good thing has come. I have been forced for the first time in my life to look deeply into my own soul. And out of that painful sight I have gleaned a sheath of poems. I have assembled this collection of poems into a small volume, called A Closed Book. *The heartbreak I have endured and still labor under was occasioned by my wife's leaving, and I am having the collection printed so that I might present her with a copy on what would have been our sixth anniversary. In order to have one copy printed, I have had to contract for 250 copies.*

I hope it will not seem crass to you, dear reader, that I now offer the remainder of these copies for sale. It is only because I think of you as members of my own family and because I feel that you might want to help me now that I do so. I ask, too, that if any of you have any thoughts which may be of use to me now—any ideas on how one so stricken might begin again and pick up the pieces of a shattered life—please send them to me. You will not be considered a "busy-body," let me assure you. I am asking for any assistance you feel you might offer me.

The holiday season is coming on and I wish each of you a happy time, though I know my own will be bleak.

Yours very sincerely,
Charles Fallon, Editor

I've read it so many times lately, George, I know it by heart. I just copied it out from memory. A few words here or there might be off, but that's the gist of it. I even put an order blank at the bottom!

You know part of what happened next, George. The wife of the top man at one of the big publishing houses was a subscriber. She was touched by my letter and sent for a copy of *A Closed Book*. Strange world, she was even more touched by the poems! Her husband's house published it—ten thousand copies first run! It was to be a gimmick. Another of those strange things called a popular poetry book, a trade book—no cultural endeavor—another *Stanton Street and Other Blues*—another *This Is My Love*.

None of us really knows what he or she is doing, do you think, George? But I suppose you think you do—that's your nature. But you can believe this, my friend: I do not even remember writing those poems, that book. Those first weeks after Kathleen went off with Jimmy Whistler—and took my darling little boy with her—those weeks—now—are a complete blank. It was so totally unexpected, George! There wasn't a hint.

Whistler had stayed with us, I remember, for about a week. He was drinking rather heavily—but who complains about a brilliant poet's drinking habits so long as he behaves himself? I'd only gotten a few issues of the magazine out at that point and I was all wrapped up in it, so perhaps didn't observe what was there to observe. I don't know—I don't *remember*.

Whistler and Kathleen and I all met at the same time, at The Writers' Camp. I was doing my Poe thing and Kathleen was a college junior up for the summer from Alabama to study creative writing. Whistler was putting the final touches on his second book—the one that would make him famous. I was 35, a full professor. Whistler an unknown 25 year old poet, with a few small press things to his credit. Kathleen paid no attention to him. In her eyes, it was I who was important. She developed one of those teacher-student crushes. At least I thought it a crush at first. Well, you know what happened. I don't know why I re-hash for you. No, it isn't for you. I'm trying to get it straight. But in short, Kathleen came up a few months later and we got married. She's a kid and I'm 35. But you know me, George—I'm a kid, too. Then my son is born. George, my whole heart is in Kathleen and that boy of mine. Suddenly I'm younger than I've ever been. I've got so much energy I can't contain myself. I'm happy-manic and forgetful. I'll publish a little magazine for poets. I'll teach at old Veilsville by day and edit and publish by evening and love Kathleen and the boy and even love my own silly poems, songs to them and to the sweetest and best of all possible worlds. I'm even dumber than you thought! I'm even happier than before. There's no end to my dumb happiness. But Kathleen's lonely out here in Erewhon/Nowhere. I should have heeded. She was young. But this was what I loved. Here I could write about my precious larks! I'm an innocent academic Henry David. Then Whistler hits it. Suddenly he's famous—famous as poets are famous. He writes me in response to a letter of mine congratulating him that he's dizzy with success, wants peace, quiet, etc. I invite him here. Well, you know.

He came here occasionally—even gave old Veilsville a free reading or two as a favor to me. Drank mostly. Kathleen went down south to see her folks. Only I gather that what she really did was to go into New York and make the rounds with famous brilliant Whistler. In those days it *was* The White Horse. But good old 40 year old Charlie Fallon, the perennial child, was too much of a dope to even dream it, what was "going down," as the jargon is. Then, just like that, it's over.

I can't work—I mean I can't teach. I get leave. I sit in here, a twisted, split-minded, broken-hearted creature, mooning over my vanished Kathleen and my taken boy. I drink and for the first time in my life, as it now seems clear, I write. What do I write? If I didn't have the book right here at my elbow I wouldn't know. Apparently I wrote these poems. They are terrible, sharable things to read. I was not myself. No, I became the self I am. I was born. But the tricks weren't done.

George, you know I don't know anything about literary politics. So I have never been able to explain satisfactorily to myself how a book of poems which was published to be a money-maker, a heart-throbber, could hit for The Pulitzer. But hit it did. Maybe it was the power of the publishing house. Obligations of the committee, etc. Maybe it was the tremendous popularity of the book—the first book of poems to hit the *Times* best seller list since . . . since I don't know what. Maybe it was the ballyhoo. Nothing to match it since *Love Story*. But there I am in New York, which I hate, and making the circuit, which I hate, and all I can think of is Kathleen and how she always wanted exactly this sort of thing to happen. I'll admit it was perverse satisfaction that occasionally tempered my misery. Indescribable misery, George—thinking how all of a sudden I have eclipsed Whistler. "Now," I would tell myself, "I bet she wishes she had stuck it out with me, with young-old Charlie. Now she's sorry, I bet!" But it wasn't any good. And hell, it's obvious even to me that if she hadn't left me I'd never have been what she wanted me to be.

Christ, George, can you make sense of it? Of course you can. You can make sense of anything.

Yeah, Georgie boy, I'll take your European Tour. I'll do a residence at Oxford, or even the University of Cracow. For your sake if for no other reason—so you'll get your clever fee, you old hustler. Christ, George, you're a crook! Any honest agent would take ten percent, not twenty-five. You didn't think I even knew that, did you? Well, George, you're a friend, so you can hustle me if you want to.

Damn, I feel old! I'd better go join my young literary stalker under the sheets while she's still steaming and I'm still able to ease her pressure. Would it be okay if I brought her along on the tour? She really has got great legs.

You know, George, for the first time in my life I realize what it is to be a poet, with all that it means in loneliness. See you in New York. Hey, let's sail over. What do you say?

HOW TO FLOAT

They found the coast of China colder than Kobe, the straits full of frayed fog, like a gray curtain, a fine, wet, disheveled lace, that seemed to rise from the gray ship's pregnant sides, and up into a threatening sky. About them distances opened like hall doors, and then they could see where they had been, or might be going, which was, a low, colorless land too distant to see clearly, too close and ominous for comfort. Oh why had they joined the Marines? Not for this murky ocean and that misty land. Their feckless rifles were aimed toward imagined Chinese hordes. Later, they read in the papers of how near to war they had been; the whole world was in fact near to war. But once more diplomacy resolved the terrible threat, at least for the time being, and, after two nerve-wracking, sleepless weeks of hazardous duty, of criss-cross cruising, the ship took a scudding turn in the Straits of Formosa, making a long, curving wake, followed by swooping, screaming gulls, famished for the jetsam and trying to land on the blurred, floating letters of farewell the Marines had written home. With hosannas of thanksgiving, their lucky ship set course for Hawaii, O happy day!

The 3rd Shore Party Battalion of the 4th Marines, Fleet Marine Force Pacific, Kaneohe Bay, Oahu, Territory of Hawaii, got a new education officer. Lt. Bland was assigned directly to Jimmy Whistler's outfit, Company B, and immediately held a white-glove inspection. Bland stopped at Jimmy's footlocker and dug into his books.

"You read Faulkner?"

"Yes, sir!"

"What's this?"

"Paradise Lost, sir. Milton."

"You're half through it?"

"Yes, sir."

"I read it at Stanford," said Bland, in cultivated tones. "I took engineering, but I read a lot of literature. I'm a Catholic—have you read Dante?"

"Not yet, sir. He's next—after Milton."

"I understand you box."

"My box?" Jimmy looked down at his footlocker—was something wrong?

"You're a boxer."

"Oh, yes, sir. I'm on the boxing team."

"And you're a weight lifter?"

"Yes, sir."

"How much can you bench press?"

"About three-twenty-five, sir."

"Not bad. I can do about three-fifty."

"That's very good, sir."

"You know I'm the new education officer for the battalion, don't you?"

"Yes, sir. I've been told that."

"I want you to report to my office after inspection."

"Yes, sir."

Jimmy duly reported and was told to sit down across the desk from Lt. Bland.

"Now here's the thing," said Bland. "I've looked over your records. I see you have a unit citation for hazardous duty in the Formosa business. I've never been in any kind of action. What was it like?"

"Boring—when we weren't scared, sir. We were put on three LSTs and sailed down from Japan and into the Formosa Straits. We sailed back and forth along the coast of China for about two weeks, then we got an order for our ship to peel off and come here to Hawaii."

"Go on."

"That's about it. We didn't know what it was all about until we got here and read it in the papers. Then we found out we were close to war. Ike—President Eisenhower—threatened the Communists with atomic weapons and they backed down. And we were given the medal."

"I bet you were glad to get here."

"Yes, sir. It was good to know I was back in the States."

"Do you think Hawaii will ever be a state?"

"Oh yes, sir! No doubt about it."

"Do you have any close buddies in this outfit?"

"You don't have friends in the service, sir, just military acquaintances."

"You're a bit of a loner, aren't you?"

"There's not many guys to share Milton with, sir."

Jimmy thought Bland was a very impressive fellow, friendly but sharp. He felt that here at last was a guy he could hit it off with—too bad he was an officer. He wondered what Bland was after. He suspected that there was a method in this apparently random questioning.

"What did you do before you joined up? I see you dropped out of school."

"Sir, I was a Western Union boy for a few years. Then I was a candy butcher at Minsky's Burlesque in Newark—hawked candy, orange drinks, popcorn, girly magazines, like that, sir."

Then Lt. Bland said, "How would you like to be a Naval Air Cadet? NavCad? You could become an officer and a pilot. I want to give you a series of academic and intelligence tests—are you willing to try?" Jimmy figured he had nothing to lose and said, "Yes, sir."

Jimmy wrote home and told his parents about this. His mother wrote back, saying that his father completely disapproved and she agreed with his father. Elliot Whistler had lost a son by a previous marriage, an RAF pilot, shot down in 1941. He would not have another son flying. So both were against him becoming a pilot, as his mother had been against him becoming a writer, a boxer, a weight lifter, a Marine, or just about anything. Even his father called her "The Negative Force." But his father joined her in being against flying, so it was two-to-one, or two-to-two, if he could count on Bland.

Night after night, Jimmy thought about his parents, often dreamed of them. They seemed always on the run from a bad check or an overdue rooming house bill, or in search of better sales territory or an even cheaper rent. Sometimes they moved twice in a week: twice a month was ordinary. Jimmy rarely attended school, and then it was usually only for a short time. Now they were superintending a rooming house in Newark. His mother had written because his father was on a three-month drunk. Someday Jimmy would come home, and go to work in a factory, and help support them, she suggested. Nothing must happen to him in the meantime. That was his future as they saw it. It seemed a very bleak future to Jimmy. He planned to go to school on the G.I. Bill. He intended to become a writer. Becoming a Naval Air Cadet would eliminate a good many steps in his progress. But soon a second letter came, this time from his father, who had sobered up: by no means should he follow this dangerous course. Look at what had happened to his half-brother! His father was a fairly good writer when he was sober. He had been a W.P.A. writer, and once wrote speeches for the mayor of Newark. Jimmy remembered his father walking him along the little wall that fronted the Newark City Hall, holding his hand. He must have been about five then, and so proud of his father. These days his father was a door-to-door salesman, and fancied himself an expert in making people agree with him. His father's letter put a damper on Jimmy's enthusiasm for cadet training. But the more tests Jimmy took, the closer he and Lt. Bland became, and Jimmy felt torn between the ideas of the two.

Despite the rules against fraternization, Jimmy and Bland began to meet at Waikiki. They would sit in their bathing suits in the shade of the Banyan Court at the Royal Hawaiian Hotel, drink Mai-Tais, and watch the waves and the surfers roll in. Bland loaned Jimmy a book on tank warfare, another on fighting the Huks in the Philippines.

"We must never get into a land war in Asia," he told Jimmy. "Read the book and see why." Bland was probably about twenty-five, but he seemed a fountain of wisdom, which was why Jimmy did not want to disappoint him.

"Think of it," said Bland, "you'll be flying the newest jet planes! Pretty exciting, eh?"

Jimmy thought of his mother and father, and Bland noticed his frown.

"Look what I've brought along," he said, digging into a duffle bag. "I'm going to teach you to play chess. I give us a week and you'll be beating me."

As a Shore Party Logistics man, Jimmy had made many beach landings, jumping out of the landing craft in helmet-high water while loaded down with a fifty-pound pack, rifle, cartridge belt, canteen, medical kit, bayonet, etc. Many times he had gone under, only getting his head back above water with the greatest effort, despite his strength. Even if he could swim, he couldn't swim in such a getup. And the truth was, that, in spite of all the time he had spent in Y.M.C.A. and other gyms, he had not learned to swim. He was taught again in the Marines, but it didn't take, and, though the Marines said he could swim, and had certified him, he did not believe it. He tried at the Armed Services Y in Honolulu, but could only keep from drowning by the most strenuous effort, which, despite his strength, he could not maintain. It was as if his forever negative mother was there to say, "You can't learn to swim at your age," as she had said, on his sixteenth birthday, when asked what he wanted to be and answered that he would like to be a writer, if he could.

"You can't be a writer. You have no education." She seemed to stand by the pool, scorning his efforts—and he sank, and sank again, and again.

Another beach landing was coming up. He wasn't a malingerer, but the redundancy of these landings was getting to him. He decided to goldbrick on this one, go to sickbay with a minor ear infection—why he had misheard Bland at the inspection—and spend a few days on his rack, reading and smoking Lucky Strikes. He had just started *The Revolt of Mamie Stover*, when a group of M.P.s appeared at the empty squadbay doors and called his name. He called back, and discovered that he had been assigned to a military police unit called the HASP, for the Hawaiian Armed Services Police. He stuffed *Mamie Stover* in his back pocket and found himself walking into her world of prostitution and violence. This is what he got for trying to get out of something. Served him right, he guessed.

HASP headquarters was on Ala Moana in Honolulu. The HASP itself was composed of a patrol section, a motorcycle section, an AWOL apprehension section, an investigative section, an aid station, and several lockups. All services were represented. Training was on the job. There was a barracks area on the second floor where Jimmy was assigned a bunk. This was something of a come-down from the beautiful surroundings at Kaneohe Bay, across the enchanted Pali mountains. Jimmy felt as if he had returned to

Kobe, Japan, or, worse, Newark. He was assigned to the patrol section, which meant that he had to walk about like a street cop with a forty-five pistol on his hip and a nightstick in his hand, and break up fights and arrest trouble-makers. Apparently, he had been chosen for this select outfit because he was big, strong, smart, and, most of all, available. If he had gone on the beach landing this would not have happened, he reasoned. But it was a lucky break in a way, too. Now he didn't have to decide between Bland's and his mother's and father's versions of his future. Not for the present, at least. That very night, he found himself patrolling Hotel Street, part of which was known as "Hell's Half Acre." This was where all the action was, bars, fights, killings, prostitution, etc. It was the job of the HASP to keep it under control.

He had been on the job for about two months, when one night he saw a transvestite followed into a men's room by two sailors. Suspecting the sailors of being up to no good, he followed them in in time to stop them from completing the beating of the transvestite that had already resulted in a long-lashed eye being popped out. One of the sailors had the transvestite's money, in an initialed clip. He arrested both sailors and took them to Ala Moana, where they were charged. An ambulance had taken the transvestite away from the bar. Next day, Jimmy received a letter from the Chief of Police, honoring his work. It turned out that the transvestite was a relative of the Chief's. Jimmy found himself to be something of a hero. Several other incidents added to his reputation. A bottle across his face also added a broken nose and several minor scars. But he was beginning to like being a cop—you could do some good, he thought. Jimmy was not what he called "a badge and a whistle man," self-important. He avoided seeing as much trouble as he could.

He wrote to Lt. Bland and told him he would not be going to NavCad. Bland wrote back, telling him he had passed his one year college equivalency test, and that his I.Q. score was very high indeed. He would be crazy, wrote Bland, to miss this opportunity. "It will change your whole life."

Up or down, which way would he go? Which way *should* he go? He wrote to his parents and told them he would not rise into flight, but continue to walk the soiled if solid ground of Hotel Street. It'll be Newark next, and Minsky's Burlesque house, back where I started from. Or a by-the-hour worker at the scissors factory on Halsey Street, or the chewing gum factory in Bayonne. That's what you really want from me, he thought. But still, he harbored dreams of his own. He thought he might go to a drama school, become an actor, and later a playwright. He filled his secret notebooks with poems and plots. He would think of lines he thought beautiful while patrolling among the low-life on Hotel Street, in the heart of "Hell's Half Acre." Above the street, with its tawdriness, was the sky, blue and cloud-scudding by day, and full of stars by night.

He would check into the Armed Services YMCA, when on liberty, and spend the weekend in his room, reading. He read the Pocket Bible straight through on one weekend. Occasionally, of a morning, he would try to swim the length of the Y's Olympic-sized pool, from the deep end to the shallow, just in case his strength began to fail. He could do it with the power of his arms and chest, but nothing would allow him to float. He had to use all his strength or he would sink and drown. It wasn't that he couldn't swim but that he couldn't float. Bland seemed to have given up on him. His parents seemed to have forgotten him again. No letters came. He had no girlfriend. There had been a whirl of military activity and travel that precluded getting to know any women, and he had no taste for prostitutes or even

B-girls, both of whom he worked among. He was lonely a good deal of the time, even in the middle of the noise and activity of Hotel Street.

And wherever you looked, people caused you trouble, or betrayed you. Jimmy had been sending money home, so that he might have a nest egg to start out on, and had recently written to his parents asking if his financial records matched theirs. They flat out denied ever receiving a cent. They had stolen his money—probably used it on booze—and didn't even have the good grace to be honest about it. If they had asked, Jimmy would have given them the money. It was the betrayal that hurt, the lying. They were all he knew of love and they sided together against him.

Suddenly he couldn't breathe. He was drowning in murky water, held down by an enormous weight, something on his back, a man or a woman, holding him under. His scream was a gurgle, and he waked, sitting up on his bunk, his whole body wet. What was he going to do?

Then, in the usual mysterious way of the military, Jimmy was transferred out of the HASP, and assigned back at the Kaneohe Brig to be a prison chaser, one who takes prisoners from one locale to another. The HASP had to keep their limited lockups cleared, so they would send mixed batches of Army, Navy, Marine, Air Force, whatever, to any brig or stockade that could house them, then sort them out, and the chasers would take them back to their own base lockups. Jimmy took the dog-faces to Schofield, the swab-jockeys to Pearl, and the flyboys to Hickam, shotgun at the ready.

One bright morning, Jimmy had to report to the Provost Marshal's Office over an incident in the mess hall. The prisoners had a schedule, and there was some pressure of time to get them fed and back to the brig. Jimmy had ordered about fifty prisoners to the head of the line. He had the authority to do this, but usually the prisoners had to wait their turn, along with the non-prisoners, all of whom ate in the same mess hall. There was a gung-ho corporal named Dunkel who was interested in getting ahead in the military police, another chaser, like Jimmy, but with more brig experience, though he lacked Jimmy's background in the HASP, and may have been jealous of it. Dunkel made a big stink about what Jimmy had done, demanded his sidearm and his armband right there in front of everyone, and made a virtual arrest. Now the question of who was right was going to be settled by the Provost. Jimmy didn't give a damn who won. If he won, things would go on as usual. If Dunkel won, Jimmy would probably be placed back in his Shore Party unit, which he missed. If he could get himself back under Lt. Bland's control, he might re-think the NavCad idea. After all, he had a right to his own life, especially after his parents had stolen his money, their latest betrayal. But the question was settled in Jimmy's favor. He had been thinking of the well-being of the prisoners and the safety of the situation. It was not a good idea to keep a large group of prisoners, anxious to eat, and to get on with their day, waiting for other units to go through ahead of them. He had used good judgment. On the contrary, Dunkel's actions had been considered over the top, extreme, generally not very sensible. Dunkel did not hide his hatred. Outside, he spit at Jimmy's feet, and Jimmy would have to work with him for God knew how long! Sometimes winning was worse than losing.

There was scuttlebutt about what was going to happen at the brig. For reasons beyond Jimmy's understanding, there was a dearth of rank on the base. The Turnkey was going stateside. He was a staff-sergeant. There were no more men of that level, only corporals, like Dunkel and himself, and privates first class and buck privates. The scuttlebutt was that one of the corporals was going to become Turnkey. Jimmy did not want the job. Let the gung-ho Dunkel have the job. Jimmy was content to ferry the prisoners about. But now he feared that the incident between himself and Dunkel might put him in the lead position to get the job. That was the last thing he wanted. He had a low opinion of power-seekers.

In an effort to get all his troubles off his mind, he took off by himself. He thought he would go down to Hotel Street, have a few drinks, and then go to a Chinese restaurant he favored and have a good meal. He was wearing slacks and an Hawaiian shirt. Blond, bronzed, and athletic, he passed the entrance to an upstairs dance hall. In his experience, these countless dance halls started young girls off as hostesses and quickly turned them into prostitutes. This was ordinarily none of his business. Bad things were always happening in Hell's Half Acre. But this time his attention was caught. A youthful female voice had cried out. An angry male voice had responded. Jimmy turned back and looked up the stairway. A man with the body of a Sumo wrestler had a pretty young Hawaiian girl pinned to the wall about half-way up a wide, twenty-foot stairway.

"What's going on up there?" Jimmy called.

"Help me," cried the girl. "I want to go home!" The girl was crying, and trying to twist loose from the big ape's grasp.

"Get lost," said Sumo, "this is none of your business." He was a bouncer type, part Polynesian, part Oriental, or some such mixture. But it was hard to tell. The light was dim in the upper reaches of the stairway. "You came here," he said to the girl, "now you stay."

"Let her go," said Jimmy.

"Mind your own business." The big man showed Jimmy his full face. Jimmy felt a cold chill run up his spine. The man's face wore a full tiger head tattoo. Jimmy got a grip on himself.

"I'm military police," he called up, and waved his wallet at the man. "Now let her go."

To locals, the Military Police was the same as the Civilian Police, since they worked together. The man let go of the girl. He seemed to be waiting for orders. Jimmy said, "Miss, you come down here." He pointed up at the man.

"You stay right where you are. Got it?"

The man gave Jimmy a surly, but assenting nod, and the girl broke free and stumbled, tears streaming, down the ten or so steps to join Jimmy.

"Stay put," Jimmy warned again, pointing at the man, and took the girl's arm and walked her briskly to the corner.

"There," he said. "You're free."

"Please, don't leave me," she begged. "I'm afraid they'll come after me, and I don't have any money." Now Jimmy saw that she was a beautiful child, perhaps sixteen, an exquisite Polynesian girl with eyes like black full moons. Sweet Leilani herself.

"What did you do, run away from home?"

"Yes. But it was a big mistake," she said, through tears. "I want to go home."

They walked a little way and Jimmy hailed a cab. "Tell the driver where you live." It was some place Jimmy had never heard of. He slid in beside her.

"Have you been—uh—molested?" he asked.

"No. But it would not be so, if you hadn't come along. I have only been here today. I have heard stories, but I didn't know how bad it was down here."

"Pretty bad," said Jimmy, looking out at Hotel Street.

"Oh, but it is beautiful. You mustn't think that it is all like Hotel Street. It *is* paradise."

"I guess I've just seen too many of the wrong places."

"You'll see, when we get to my village—you'll see how beautiful it is."

"Then why did you leave it?"

"I was full of curiosity about Honolulu. You're young. Aren't you full of curiosity?"

"I come from a tough town in New Jersey called Newark. I left there to go to a tough town in Japan called Kobe. I ended up here in a tough town called Honolulu. They all seem the same to me."

"You are a tough guy, aren't you?"

He looked at her. Was she kidding him?

"Not so tough, I suppose."

"No," she said, "not so tough, I suppose."

When the taxi pulled in to the bamboo village, it reminded Jimmy of the Jungle Jim movies he had seen as a boy. He half expected to see Johnny Weissmuller in his white hunter outfit emerge from one of the grass huts. What appeared to be the whole village of at least two hundred souls gathered around them, speaking a clicking, excited Polynesian tongue. It appeared that Jimmy's sweet Leilani was not just an ordinary girl, but a celebrity of some kind. She began to translate for Jimmy's benefit.

"They are relieved and happy to see me," she said. "Here come my father and mother." They came open-armed and seized their daughter in a loving embrace. Leilani told Jimmy that her father could be called "the Chief," so that was how Jimmy thought of him. He was the apparent head of the village, his wife the Queen Bee. Now Jimmy saw that his Leilani was a sort of Princess.

Jimmy had expected to let the girl out, and have the cabbie take him back to Honolulu, but the Chief pulled Jimmy from the cab and sent it off without him. For a moment, Jimmy thought he was going to be lynched, but then he realized that everyone was smiling. Then he thought of cannibals, but he had never heard of any on the islands. Finally, Leilani told him that her parents, indeed, the whole village, considered him a hero, who had saved her from a fate worse than death, and the big luau being prepared was now in his honor for that very evening. So he would eat, not be eaten. He was much relieved, and told Leilani so, who at first laughed at his apprehension, and now laughed at his flushed embarrassment.

"But I didn't do anything," he said. Leilani turned to her father and said a few words, then back to Jimmy: "Yes you did! I told them all about it, what the tiger-faced man was trying to do to me, and how you stopped him and brought me home."

Jimmy received the first of many affectionate pats on the back from Leilani's father.

Hours passed until morning light showed through the jungle fronds and fans, but the luau was still in full swing—deep drums and grass skirt dancing—and the Chief forced bowl after bowl of a powerful Polynesian drink on him. He shrugged and chugalugged and the party continued right into the full red dawn that came to that true paradise, blue Hawaii.

The secret machinery of the Marine Corps had decided. Jimmy received orders to report to the Provost Marshal's office to receive orientation. He was to be the new Turnkey at the Kaneohe Marine Corps Brig. Jimmy had just finished reading *From Here to Eternity*, and ugly visions of Fatso, the Turnkey at Scofield, who had brutalized Maggio in the novel, came to mind. How could he, Jimmy Whistler, have gotten himself into such a situation? He bet Lt. Bland was behind this unwanted advancement. Bland knew by now that Jimmy was not going to take him up on his offer to send him to NavCad training. This was either his way of advancing Jimmy, or perhaps his way of punishing him. As he had always proclaimed, people either betray you or get you in trouble, even when they don't mean to. Shun friendship, stick to military acquaintanceship. Keep people at a distance! Jimmy went to the base Chaplain.

"Isn't there some way you can get me out of this, sir?" he asked.

"Why should you want out?"

"I don't want to be a Turnkey, sir. I'm not right for it."

"The Marine Corps thinks you're right for it."

"They're wrong."

"I doubt it. Now, if you have any other problems . . . ?"

"Don't you see, sir, this is a mistaken attempt to help me along in my career. Lt. Bland is doing this because he thinks I ought to be in charge of something."

"I doubt if Lt. Bland has anything to do with this. This is probably the result of the incident that brought you to the attention of the Provost Marshal's Office in the first place." Jimmy returned two more times to state his case and received the same answer: "The Marine Corps thinks you're right for it. You can't outguess the Marine Corps, son. Now just go and do your duty."

There was nothing to be done. Jimmy was Turnkey of the Kaneohe Marine Corps Air Station Brig, and he would have to like it or lump it. He promised himself he would be the most humane Turnkey in history. He would not allow the chasers to pull any rough stuff, especially Dunkel, who was always eager to use force. Dunkel was the kind who, if given free rein, would end up as a war criminal. But Dunkel was not going to get his way in any brig run by Jimmy.

"I'm not going to let him push those guys around," he told Leilani on one of his many visits to her village. They held hands and took walks through the jungle to the nearby beach. Leilani was teaching him to swim.

"There is so much tension in your body. You must relax. It is because you are so tight inside that you can't float. Try to forget about Dunkel and your mother and father and even your friend Lt. Bland. Now breathe in slowly and ease back on my arms."

"You can't hold me up," he told her, but found himself floating on her brown arms, and looking up at her great dark eyes that reflected the sunset over the horizon. "You're so beautiful," he said. She took her hands from beneath his back and pushed him under.

"You'll learn someday," she said, when he had shaken the water out of his ears.

"Learn what?" he said, laughing.

"You are like a rock, but you will learn to float. You will learn to be a floating rock. That's a rare thing."

"Impossible," he said.

"No, the islands have lava that will float."

"I don't believe it."

"You don't believe anything. That's why you can't float. Look," and she leaned back into the water and swam into the sunset, so that his eyes couldn't find her, and then she rose up beside him, sleek, like a seal, lithe and laughing.

Months went by, and under Jimmy's supervision the Brig ran smoothly. But it *was* a responsibility of nightmarish proportions. Sometimes it got the better of him and he'd spend the night in an Hotel Street bar, drinking into forgetfulness. One night a couple of HASP patrolmen made a routine stop in a dive and, recognizing him, started a conversation.

"Hear you're the Turnkey at Kaneohe now," one said. "Look, do you need a ride back to base? We'll get you one." They seemed concerned about him. Perhaps Jimmy looked too drunk to maneuver. One of them said, "We better get him back to his brig."

"No, no," Jimmy protested, then everything went blank. Next thing he knew, he was brought to the brig barracks and dropped off. It was late, after lights-out, and he found himself deserted. He stumbled his way through the bay's faint, indirect light, moonlight and watchtower light, thinking sleep, and more sleep, but there was a surprise awaiting him. Dunkel was sitting on Jimmy's bunk, holding a glittering bayonet in each hand. Dunkel said, "I've been waiting to cut you up, you son of a bitch." Jimmy couldn't be sure, in his condition, but he thought Dunkel was drunk, too. Ah yes, beside Jimmy's bunk glittered a bottle of booze. Jimmy tried to summon whatever alertness remained to him. He sized the situation up this way. If he turned and ran, Dunkel would surely pig-stick him with one of those bayonets. But Jimmy was a boxer. He knew that if you can get in close to a long-armed opponent, that opponent's arm-length, otherwise an advantage, becomes a handicap. Dunkel would find it impossible to turn those bayonets around on him.

Jimmy dove at Dunkel, between his arms, and hugged the flailing chaser up and back into a metal wall locker. One of the bayonets went through a metal door and stuck, the other bounced from Dunkel's hand. They struggled there, and suddenly the wall lockers, the whole row of them, went over. Somebody turned on the lights, and Jimmy and Dunkel got a first clear look at each other. Both were bleeding. Jimmy swung, connecting with Dunkel's chin, and Dunkel sprawled on the floor, out for the count.

"He tried to kill you," someone said.

"He's drunk," Jimmy said. "A couple of you guys put him on his bunk. And don't mention this to anyone. Nobody says a word, hear me?"

Jimmy was going home, leaving blue Hawaii and bound for the Golden Gate. The emerald islands of paradise were disappearing from view. He stood on the bow of the troop transport, smoking a cigarette. There was a lot that he would never forget, but, alas, a lot that he would. He knew that. After all, he was a writer, wasn't he, and knew things beyond his years?

Leilani had finally taught him to float, but he doubted if he could do it without her. He hoped that he would come back and see her someday, in the not too distant future. He would come back and she would be married to some local boy and have a couple of cute little brats. He had never laid a lustful hand on her virginal beauty. He loved her; she would always be his sweet Leilani, his sweet dream forever, his sweet little sister.

He looked along the gangway and saw a queue of young men that seemed to vanish in perspective. The first in line stepped up to him. "We don't want to bother you, sir, but we want to thank you for the way you treated us when we were in the brig. You could have made it very tough on us, but you didn't. Thank you, sir." Brig orders had required that the Turnkey be called "Sir."

Jimmy said, "Don't call me, sir. I always hated it."

That one stepped away with a nod and a smile, and another stepped up, saying much the same thing. And they just kept coming. Jimmy was overwhelmed. "Thank you, thank you, thank you." They ignored the fact that his eyes had dampened. Then Dunkel stood before him.

"I owe you," he said. "You could have had me court-martialed and sent to Leavenworth. You knew I wanted to make a career in the Corps, and you gave me the chance to do it, even though we never got along. Semper fi, buddy."

"Semper fi, Dunkel." Jimmy looked out at the ship's wake and the long waves beyond it, the white tops floating with leis, and the island, green and paradisal. On an impulse, he reached out and seized Dunkel by the shoulder.

"Dunkel, you know, I learned something while we were here."

"What's that?"

"How to float."

THE THIN DISEASE

Note: In Africa, AIDS is often referred to as the thin disease.

Nearly seven feet tall, a skeleton made of giant bird bones, a bird-cage rib-cage, his heart a little pulsing robin, Kwame from Ghana on the old Gold Coast was my best friend. Kwame had to reach down to tap me on my red head.

"Dutch, we're going to cadge some drinks. You do the talking. Tell them I'm King Quazi of oilrich offshore Quaziland, and I can't speak English. Tell them my kingdom is ten miles long and a quarter mile wide, including beaches."

Kwame had purple-grey skin and was so thin he looked like the shadow of a pole, but his head was large and noble, with cheekbones carved in slate, and royally crested with a pompadour befitting the son of a son of a king from the ancient West African Empire, though he was always churchmouse poor.

We worked on the New York docks, off-loading ships, on-loading trucks. He wasn't very strong. He drank a lot and bled from the rectum when he worked. They had to cut the grapes away. Like a daddy longlegs and a flat red beetle, we wobbled to a bar near St. Vincent's, a knot of stitches still in his new tight ass. He could ignore the pain for the booze. He put his arm over my shoulder.

"Dutch, I'm going to die. I've got the thin disease. I'll never go back to Ghana."

"Sure you will. You'll go back."

There were good times yet. But he died. He died. He died. The white bed was empty but for a wave-crested, welted head, and limp hoses, some of which were black and leaked their fluids. Ghana was far away, a dream, but I was there, near, here, his friend, holding his hand, our funny different fingers entwined, though pulling apart.

ARGONAUTS

Verde que te quiero verde.
Verde viento. Verdes ramas.
—*Garcia Lorca*

We stripped down to whatever we intended to wear as swimming togs and sat down on the hot stone to enjoy some cold beer from sweating cans before taking the first plunge. There was a small concrete bridge down below the deeper pool and a pickup truck whizzed by over it, otherwise no sound but water and talk and laughter, shrill cries from the kids. Below the bridge the water dropped in a steep fall and then, after a rushing meander, into the lake. The lake was very large and dark and it was claimed that Good Peter, a phantom Oneida chief, beat an ominous tattoo upon a tom-tom out there at night. He lamented—*The voice of the white birds from every quarter cried out, You have lost your country, You have lost your country!* His whole tribe had been wiped out by the white man and he was out for justice (scientists said the night rumblings were made by natural gas, a less impressive explanation). After the beer we took a plunge in the water and then Ed had an idea. He had heard that somewhere upstream was a great waterfall, one that fell for perhaps a hundred feet—not a Niagara, but a fair cataract and it was supposedly located in a canyon of considerable beauty—and would I like to hike up the stream with him to find it. I said I would and we started off together up the shallows. Ed had been roughing it in a woodland way now for several years and moved along at a good pace over the slippery rocks, sometimes through the water, sometimes along the bank, but more often through the water, because the bank was quite steep most of the way and often it was non-existent, only a sheer wall of rock in its place. He looked a mythological figure of a man, tall and broad and beefy of shoulder, red and bushily bearded, sharp-eyed, visored cap pulled low for the slanting sun: he moved sure-footed as a goat—or not quite that, for he did slip occasionally, but even a mountain goat might have slipped on these watery stones. I kept apace about twenty yards behind and it took my whole attention focused upon where I was next to step to keep me from dropping farther behind. I was about thirty-five, Ed nearly forty, so we were no longer boys and this delicate goat-walking on watery stone was an effort, of the body but then more of the will. Where were we going? Where? And why? Why make the effort? Back at the lower pools near the bridge there was rest on the hot stone with beer, kept cold by the cold purling water and the shade of the rock over it; so why this little odyssey, this minor quest? Why be Argonauts? When I looked up Ed had disappeared ahead of me and I saw a long gently rising glassy piece of water, reflecting mountains, bushes, trees and below the crazily slanting mountains, bushes and trees all the little gems half buried in a slippery silt, as if the flow of the water had discovered a sunken treasure, brightly colored arrowheads, axes, peacepipe fixtures, as yet all unmanufactured—the raw material of a stone culture, the proud stuff of the phantom drummer of the lake and casting over it all, over the reflected, layered escarpments, over the faint tiny rock flowers, little bits of bright blue, scarlet, and gold, fool's gold, the reflected sky and the mysterious shadows of unseen birds, wind-caught leaves, swaying lazy branches and I wondered where was Ed: had I fallen so far behind in this amazing world, was all this sudden glare and shadow too much to be accepted, was I no longer any part of it, that could flow with it all at will, or without will, without the consultation with will, as I imagined the red shadows who were men and women that had flashed here once had been able to do? But then I saw Ed, as I came wading knee-deep in water around the long bend and he was standing on a rock his arms akimbo and breathing hard; I could see his back heave; he turned to me and motioned and pointed up through the trees and I followed his gaze and saw deeply hidden a small cabin grayed by weather. Ed grinned and pointed. "A poet!" he called and turned to his task of getting from one rock to another, the mountain goat. Again we came upon a small waterfall with a sharp declivity and we had to work our way around it up the steep embankment of black mud and moss. Our feet and fingers ripped and upheaved the fine smooth moss as we scurried, a bit fearful of taking a long uncontrollable slide backwards and on to the jutting rocks and then we were able to drop down again into the cool water at the top of the fall and the mud was washed from our feet and I dipped my hands in the water and rinsed the mud from my knees. The water here was only about four inches deep but stepping into it I was alarmed by its pressure and for an instant thought it might overtopple me and send me headlong down the fall to crumple my poor head on the rocks below, but I was learning already that to deal with nature one must relax: it is the only "safe" way. I had already learned not to fight the stone under my bruised feet but to put down a foot with all its muscles loose and to let it find its shape on the earth: otherwise it will not be accepted and rejection is the danger. Had I begun sliding down the muddy bank I should have forced myself to relax, to go limp and to accept my fate and I was already winning a faith that helped me believe that I should have merely slid over those jutty rocks like a piece of mossy mud and gone on sliding down and down and down the great fall under the bridge and meandered, making with my body some mystic hieroglyphs in the water, until I fell gently into the lake without hurt. I might have passed my wife and children and called to them to wait. I might have been ushered into that dark frothy water by low drums at twilight. Would life be so bad? But now we came upon an exceedingly long and narrow place which, except for the fact that it was all moss and stone and gurgling, rushing water and the fact that it was so terribly deep a trench in the high mountains, reminded me of one of those canals that city workmen dig in which to lay pipe for sewers and I felt like a workman on break now as Ed and I sat, panting, and smoked a cigarette and looked up the long alley at the fall there, perhaps a hundred yards ahead and Ed said "What do you think? Should we keep on going?" I don't know what it was that made me sense the larger fall beyond the smaller, perhaps it was some accurate unconscious reading of the lay of the land, or something vibratory in the rocks, but it seemed something else which I am forced to say was a kind of indescribable sensation: I sensed a great booming mystery that was also a sort of magical silence beyond and I said yes, let's go on. This was a treacherous place, for the water was deep and rushing with great, foaming force down its narrow confines and there was just moss-slippery rock edging steeply up into the thickest bramble and tangle of green life I could remember having seen: but somehow we found our way onto a wide open flat place and the water was gentle again, almost still but for a slight observable upper purling, a rippling and it was all open here, wide and open again and I felt as if I had been in a tunnel and now I was out again in the open. But there was still a sense of being low and it must have been due to the sense of height ahead, because we were already quite high up: we had come nearly two miles steadily upward and that was from a high place itself. Yes, the feeling of being low must have been because of the great height I sensed ahead. Or because of the mountains rising all around me: or because the azure and pink-streaked sky still seemed to be so high above. I had an image of men casting for trout with long, flexible poles, men with wading boots and colorful flies pinned all over their hats: pipes in their mouths. And when I looked up Ed was gone—gone again! And for all I had learned my feet were badly bruised, cut even and I would have been limping had I been walking on soft grass, so I had to take these ridiculous delicate little steps, like a baby's steps and I'd probably be left so far behind I'd be ashamed to be such a tenderfoot. And I wondered, with my Zen Master, what were the punishments of them that serve the Evil One, of those who cannot make their living except through violence to Being. And I saw Ed, ahead, standing in the center of a great open place and the water up to his ankles and he pointed up, crying over the natural sounds "Look! Look!" And I took one last look at my poor wretched feet to see that they were well placed on the slippery-as-ice rocks and looked up to where he pointed and saw an over-awing escarpment circling round us in deep beautiful folds of rock and placed us in a kind of canyon. And my feet slipped and up they went most idiotically into the air and down I went plunging and thrashing and laughing like a fool, but I kept my plaid slouch hat that Ed had given me above the water and a bit of my forehead and I came up making an absurd joke of how the beauty of the place had knocked me over and Ed at first afraid I had hurt myself began to laugh and I looked in my hat and best of all my smokes were still dry, and so I scampered on in the sun drying off and caught up with Ed and right around a bend in this enormous place—there was the waterfall. We pulled ourselves up on some rocks and Ed lit a joint and passed it to me. We looked around and I thought I must never let the details of this quest blur in memory. I must get right back to

Ed's ramshackle old farmhouse and scribe the magic of it all. Oh—The waterfall came down for fifty feet or more, then hit an odd rock and fell out like an opening fan across itself; so it was like two falls, one down, one crossing that, like translucent lovers entwined and undulating and above them, below a deep blue twilit heaven, a great cliff hung, weighted with trees. I knew a mystic place when I saw one; a tabernacle. So did Ed. And an Oneida Chief stood on the cliff in full regalia. He was smiling.

THE SANDAL SHOP

Or

How, while Being Pursued by the Divorce Demon,
Jimmy Whistler Discovered the Beats,
and was Saved by Marsayas, the King of the Beasts

1

The office of Magazine Subscriptions Unlimited was a bustling place, filled with telephones, none of which had time to ring for being dialed. Men and women of all races, creeds, ages, and costumes kept them leaping to their ears and slamming back for an instant's cradling before another leap and dialing. Jimmy Whistler estimated that at least fifty people crowded the place: workers, that is; aside from those, like himself, who waited to be interviewed for a job. Smoke hung heavy in the air, an ectoplasm.

There was a man seated across the table from Jimmy, a man with great broad shoulders, made to appear broader because of the heavy overcoat he was wearing. (It was February, and bitter weather: a fine time to come to New York from California; but nothing Vera and he did made any sense!) The man was big, but not fat. On the contrary, one could see—for he sat pushed back from the table in a sprawling, easy posture—that, where his coat fell open, his waist was neat and narrow. His legs were long and delicately shaped, seeming to be of a lighter bone structure than his upper body. Jimmy could see them plainly through the thin, blue, much-too-shiny summer slacks he wore. But what greatly interested Jimmy about him was that he wore a beard—a rarity in the clean-shaven Fifties and a pronouncement that the hirsute Sixties had arrived—every strand of which was thick as wire and glittery, coppery red. It was nearly a foot in length, and all of a piece, so that it moved with his jaw. It rayed from his chin like a Blakian sun. All this blinding hair began directly under a sensual, long lower lip, flexible and pink as the innertube of a bicycle tire. His kinky hair puffed over his ears and down to his frayed collar. On top he was nearly bald; though Jimmy was to learn that this, his first Beatnik, was only twenty-eight. The big fellow seemed ill-at-ease, perhaps because Jimmy had been studying him so intently—and rudely, too, for that matter—or perhaps because he was waiting, in a place he did not wish to be to do something he had no wish to do.

In any case, after completing his application form, he behaved restively, crossing and uncrossing his legs, smoking cigarette after cigarette, thumbing through magazines, and throwing them back in the pile with a look of irritation on his benignly satanic face. Finally, he started fishing with very long, delicate fingers in an empty cigarette pack. He crumpled the pack in his fist, and startled Jimmy out of his contemplation of him by leaning across the table and, with a show of white teeth and a whisk-broom movement of beard, nearly sweeping away several magazines, asking if he could have a cigarette from him. Jimmy said, “Sure,” and gave him one.

He told Jimmy he had just come back from Germany, where he had left his German wife and his two children, a boy and a girl. He had been a language teacher there, for Berlitz: had taught English to the Germans. He was in the process of breaking up with his wife, by his description a stuffily middle-class Hausfrau. He was staying with an aunt and uncle, a staid old couple, out on Long Island. They had ordered him to look for a job; and so, to appease them, he was making this half-hearted effort. But he had other things in mind, for the long run.

He told Jimmy that he had picked up a young woman on his first day in town, while wandering about in Greenwich Village, a big, strapping Fraulein, with an enormous bust and a Madonna-like face. Not the least of her virtues was that she had a sister and a brother-in-law who were "really hip, swinging." They ran a sandal shop in Brooklyn Heights, had a baby who never cried, never wore a diaper, and who was allowed free use of the floor for urinary and defecatory purposes. The brother-in-law plunked the bass fiddle, studied Zen, kept a Mulligan stew going for a month at a time, made sandals, and did odd jobs in his neighborhood. The sister was a mysterious beauty who smoked pot and sang lullabies. And in many other ways, apparently, this couple led an idyllic and primitive existence of which Rousseau would have voiced his approval. "Call me Marsayas," he said.

Marsayas told Jimmy that he was going to work his way in down there (which wouldn't prove difficult, as Rolly, the brother-in-law, had already accepted him as his guru), and stay with them for a while, at least until he could get Joan (his girlfriend) to get him a studio of his own. He was a painter, you see, and a poet, too. "Any old how," he said, "I've got to get out of my uncle's house. The old folks are driving me up the walls. Too much, too *much*! *When are you going to get a job? What are you going to do about your wife and those dear little kiddies of yours? Life is real, life is earnest. You must look to the future.* Would you believe it? They want me to be in the house by midnight!"

Jimmy agreed that that was a bit much to ask of a grown and married man, and especially one with two kids.

Marsayas said that his whole family was that way, "Impossible!" His whole family were "convention-racked lunatics," or "business fiends" or "materialist maniacs."

Not Marsayas. "I'm a Zoroastrian. I believe in the power of light to conquer the forces of darkness. I believe in universal love." Jimmy was impressed, even impressed with the holes in the heels of the argyles of this gleeful gargoyle as he walked to his interview as one walks to the gallows.

2

They were hired, and started the next evening at six.

Jimmy worked as fast as he could, thinking of Vera, of the latest peace pact, and worried that he might not be able to find a good, full-time job before the next rent fell due. But Marsayas, though Jimmy had heard him try a few times at first, had already given up the outlined pitch, and was engaging in long, relaxed conversations with, as the boss called them, "the Zombies."

Jimmy discovered that, though he had a certain talent for making people say yes, by the next evening, when the supervisor called them back to verify the sales, his customers had often changed their minds. They'd claim that they had not agreed to buy a subscription at all. They'd claim that they had only accepted his offer to send them a free dictionary.

Well, either he hadn't heard right, and had pressured the "Zombies" too hard in his financial desperation, and they had changed their minds as soon as his persuasive voice had clicked from their receivers; or his supervisor was a swindler, as some claimed, and was simply stealing his sales by canceling them in Jimmy's name and putting them in his own. This Jimmy suspected, but had no way of confirming, as the sales were checked by others and the order forms were out of his hands.

Rightly or wrongly, his sales were being canceled faster than he was making them. And this was the sort of thing that just could not be explained to Vera. He confided his plight to Marsayas, whose own sales hadn't added up to enough to get a cancellation from, and to his amazement Marsayas was surprised that Jimmy should be worried. "For Chrissakes, Jimmy, I thought you were just working here for beer money, like me. Why don't you get that Frau of yours off her ass and out into the labor market? She an invalid?"

After work they stopped in a midtown bar and had a few beers. It was one of those dives that have a food bar, and smell of corned beef and cabbage, stewed potatoes, cheap wine, draft beer, and sour people.

As they had agreed to do the previous evening, they had brought their poems to work with them, and now they sat and read each other's work. "GuraaaAH!" Marsayas sounded, and sipped his beer, leaving a broken ring of foam in the bristling red wires around his mouth.

He slammed Jimmy's little, stapled booklet on the table, chug-a-lugged his remaining beer, and vanished. Then he was back through the crowd like an ecstatic Bacchus with four huge mugs of slopping broth, two in each hand. He shouted: "You, you poor fool, are among the elect, the elite, the only *true* elite on earth. You are a *poet*!"

"Do you like them?"

"*Like* them? They're real *poems*, good as anybody going!"

Jimmy was thrilled. No one but Marsayas had ever encouraged him in his yearning to be a poet, everyone else thought he was foolish—especially Vera.

It would be quite a let-down, after such stimulation, to have to take himself home to Vera and her cranky, middle-class Bohemianism. Midnight was looming, Marsayas's curfew hour.

"Well, it won't always be like this," said Marsayas. "I'll be out of that bourgeois scene before the week-end. I'm moving into the sandal shop. Then we'll be able to drink and talk all night."

"I wish Vera would help me with tuition for school," Jimmy said, dreamily. "I'd like to be a writer, but I need more education."

"There's all kinds of writers, boyo—and all kinds of education. If you want to write, first read, read, read, then write, write, write! But if you want to go to college, well, that's a different story. I've got a masters, but I can't write poetry like your stuff." He drained a mug. "Chrissakes, Jimmy, who the hell is the boss in your house? Look at the lion. The king of the beasts! The lioness goes out and kills the quarry, then steps back and guards the old man while he eats."

"That's lions—not people."

"Well, people then. Do you know that the Indian brave never worked. He sent his old lady out to do it. *He* stayed at home and talked, talked *war* and *peace*," he shouted, and the whole bar, which seemed to be filled with middle-aged, unshaven men, turned to look at him, interest in their eyes, even hope. "That's what women are meant to do," he roared on, after a bow. "Let them make the nest pretty and wait like the votary bird to be impregnated. Then you take over until the egg is laid. *Only* until then. And then you go back and keep the nest warm with wine and good conversation while they go and forage for worms. Worms of milk for the baby and worms of wine for you. I tell you that is their biological role. *They* know it, so why don't you? Don't they all want to go to work nowadays? Don't they? Well, for God's sake, let them!

"This guy Rolly I've told you about, he makes sandals—because that's art, but Jean, his wife, chews the leather. That's right. She *chews* the leather—makes it soft so Rolly can work with it. Rolly only makes one pair of sandals a week, he tells me; but Jean, with those beautiful sharp little white teeth of hers, chews enough leather for him to make twenty! He keeps her at it all day—chewing, chewing—except when she's nursing the baby, or turning on. Now that's a *wife* for you! They're in the battle for survival together—it isn't all thrown on *his* back. That's *life*—and listen, that's *love*! I tell you, Jimmy, once I get to Brooklyn, I'll never work another day in my life. That's my oath. I intend to dedicate myself completely to the muses."

Jimmy wondered if Vera would chew leather for him. Marsayas was opening new vistas. He was an inspiration!

3

Jimmy got an idea. Friday night, pay night, he would have next-to-nothing coming, so over the weekend he would need all the moral support he could get. He thought that the hard edge of the weekend might be softened if Vera could hear Marsayas present his version of things before he presented his own. So they made a date for Marsayas to come to Jimmy's place on Saturday and help him out.

Marsayas didn't mind telling Jimmy that he thought he was quite a coward for being so afraid of a woman, and over such a little thing as not having any money. He had never heard of a wife who wasn't at least willing to help her husband, if asked. But Marsayas had no idea what Vera was like, or what she was capable of, if angered. And Jimmy had to admit that it was more than a modest proposal that had induced him to ask Marsayas over. He was also interested in finding out what would happen when these two forces of nature came into contact. Perhaps they would vanish in a clap of thunder, and leave only a little mushroom cloud behind.

Marsayas showed up at noon on Saturday, toting a case of beer and a gallon jug of purple wine. Jimmy saw him through the window, striding down Horatio Street. He had told Vera a little about Marsayas, and that he was coming, but he did not, could not, do him justice. He went over and stood by the expensive new coffee table (which Vera had bought the day before with the last of their savings, and upon which she had laid out all the tea-time and cocktail-hour delicacies a Happy Homemaker could conceive), and waited to enjoy the immediate impact his wild man find would have upon her.

The knock came, and Vera, who was near the door, opened it; then stood, as if transfixed, gripping the knob until her little fist turned white. Jimmy thought for an instant that she was going to slam the door in his friend's face, and start screaming. But she collected herself, asking:

"*Marsayas*?"

"Vera, I presume?"

"Ha—yes!" said Vera, looking up into the aimed ends of his red rays, and finally bethinking herself to step back. "Please come in—come in, please—*please!*"

Marsayas gargoyle-grinned, and slippity-slapped into the apartment on shower shoes. His naked feet were dirty, and red-and-raw-looking with the cold. Jimmy saw Vera eyeing them distastefully as the guru set his burdens down in the midst of the hors d'oeuvres.

Jimmy had hoped that it would take Vera longer to get her wind back. He had hoped that from first sight this imposing giant would keep her off balance. But, plain to see, she was coming around, resilient as ever.

He indicated a chair for Marsayas, and Marsayas seated himself, moving Vera's tidbits aside and putting his feet up on the table, between a bowl of cheese dip and a platter of cold cuts. Vera looked at him wide-eyed; at Jimmy, narrow-eyed; then pulled a tight meager smile back to her downy ears, and sat. Jimmy had received the first dirty look of the day. And he knew something about Vera. One dirty look meant more to follow, and maybe even along their trajectory one might find, in an hour or so, a vase, or a bottle, flying.

The thought flashed that he had better move quickly to prevent Marsayas from saying what he knew Marsayas intended to say. But then he was distracted. Marsayas said, from his recumbent position, "I hope you kids don't mind, but I took the liberty of inviting some friends of mine down—my girlfriend's sister and her husband. I thought it might do you good to meet them."

Vera stared at Marsayas, as one might stare at an oddity, trying to figure out what to make of him.

"Do us good?" she said.

"Yes. They do everyone good."

"How do you mean?"

"They're an example, an inspiration."

Marsayas removed his feet from the table long enough to fill two glasses with wine and stick them before Vera and Jimmy. He waved aside Jimmy's apology for not having done the honors, placed his horny heels back in the cold cuts, jug neatly draped on an elbow which he raised in salute, and yelled "PROSIT" loud enough to make Vera blink. They picked up their glasses and yelled "Prosit!" back at him. It seemed like the right thing to do.

Then Marsayas made his gleeful gargoyle face, which put on display for Vera his big, beautiful white teeth, and said, "Why didn't you tell me you had such a pretty wife?"

Vera perked up. "Why, thank you," she said.

"Yes—yes—I must paint you some time. But first you're going to have to become more natural. These are the new, hip Sixties, Vera. Hang loose! You're the very personification of the uptight Fifties. You seem . . . *constrained*—yes. Even your hair—is it dyed? A Lana Turner helmet. You'll have to get that stuff out of your hair and let it down—let it be natural—yes—" He moved the thumb of his free hand in a painterly gesture of measurement. "And you stop Jimmy from being a wage-slave and help to develop him as a poet. He's the real thing." The wine bottle remained cradled in his other arm, like a baby.

Fortunately, for Jimmy could see Vera revving up for a reply, a knock came at the door. It was the Reuters.

Rolly Reuter was a little fellow with big, lugubrious brown eyes, long black hair, and a long, silky black beard. Jean, his wife, was a striking young woman, with chatoyant greenish eyes, and beautiful long ebony hair that swam, like a dark, glittery stream, down neck and chest and out, over a more than ample, T-shirted bosom, to twin falls, stippled by nipples.

Marsayas picked up the thread of what he had been saying. But the atmosphere was irrevocably altered. Vera was discontent. She no longer listened to Marsayas, but interjected odd, pointless questions, as if only to attract attention; and the conversation became forced and jittery. Even so, Jimmy was able to attend to the Reuters enough to see what Marsayas had meant about them. It was simple. They were in love.

He looked at Vera, popping off about something or other, that hard, mean look about the mouth, those hurt, jealous eyes, and he knew what was going on in her mind; knew that she wanted this pleasant vision of love out of her sight. It was too much for her, too uncomplicated.

Jimmy envied Rolly his beautiful Jean—and he saw that Marsayas envied him, too—but tried not to show it. If Jimmy let on to the slightest admiration, Vera would make him pay—make them all pay, possibly.

The Reuters stayed for two hours and then went on their way. But Marsayas sat on, like a great blood-bubbling fixture. He finished off the last of the wine and started whittling down the case of beer he'd brought; then he dragged Vera up and danced her about to the phonograph.

Vera's mood brightened after Rolly took his beautiful Jean away. When Marsayas went to the bathroom, she kept on dancing by herself, whirling about the living room like the ballerina she had been trained to be. Once, she stopped, and tried to pull Jimmy to his feet to dance with her. But he refused. There was even something in her gaiety that made him nervous. He knew all too well how quickly it could change into angry hysteria. Yet she seemed happy, now; and if it hadn't been for all the misery she had caused him he'd have been glad to see her so. He'd have got up and danced with her, but for that.

4

Marsayas slept, head hanging forward, in an antiquated easy chair near the lumpy couch on which Jimmy woke. A young woman sat on the floor at his feet, propped up against his legs, asleep, with her head in his lap. She wore a quilted kimono, and one breast bulged into view where the kimono fell open. She was a bigger, heavier version of Jean.

Jimmy looked around, through puffed, uncertain eyes. There were sandals, belts, pocketbooks, all manner of leather goods, hanging in festoons from walls and ceiling. He must have moaned; because, then, from somewhere up near the ceiling, in a dark corner, in the rear of the shop, a soft, purring voice drifted down, asking,

"Got a headache?"

It was Jean. He could see her now, or see her eyes, like a cat's, high up, glimmering in shadows.

"Are you levitating?"

"I'm on a platform. This is where Rol and I sleep. How's your wife?"

Jimmy looked around, and there behind him, under a heap of coats, was Vera. She looked a mess. Her lipstick was smeared, there were Mascara-tear-stains down her cheeks, and her hair looked like a burning bush.

Well, was it paradise? Was this absurd little sandal shop a heaven on earth, a sanctuary? No, he guessed not; it was just that he had come from a small, unimportant hell. And why have anything to do with any hell if you can stay in a little, bright heaven? It was just too bad that there wasn't one more of these plump, lovely creatures around, another sister, for him.

He had been drinking beer with Marsayas for two hours before Vera grunted and woke up. She had a hang-over, was angry, had slept badly (so she claimed—been mashed by him), and wanted to get out of this (whispers, harsh, in his ear) "filthy place." She would not have Jimmy drinking again today. It was Sunday. "What *are* you, an alcoholic, like your so-called friend, Marsayas? He's a filthy beast and the sandal shop is a stinking zoo." She stomped outside "to get some clean, fresh air."

"She walked out on you last night—do you know that?" Marsayas seemed much amused by Jimmy's pickle. "You fell asleep in the car—I dumped you there, on the couch, and she got into a temper tantrum trying to wake you up. Feel your leg."

Jimmy felt around, looked at the place on his calf that hurt, and there was a large purple bruise. "It'll soon be time to go back to California," he said. "D.D. is catching up with us."

"Who's D.D.?"

"The Divorce Demon. He's been pursuing us since we got married."

"She gave you quite a pummeling before I could stop her." Marsayas laughed.

"You were inert—wouldn't, or couldn't, move for love nor money."

Jimmy was beginning not to like the way Marsayas looked, the beast. He seemed to think that Jimmy's problems were a joke. But then, who could blame him? It was the truth, after all. Vera and he were a joke. They had been making public fools of themselves for three years. Why shouldn't people laugh? The thought occurred to Jimmy that maybe he had finally come face to face with the Divorce Demon. Then Marsayas broke the news:

"Your phonograph and your TV were stolen last night. Some of your clothes, too."

Rolly came in from the back and sat down, looking lugubrious. Now he reminded Jimmy a little of Chico Marx. "That's the trouble with having possessions," he said; "it's not that they get stolen, but that it should hurt when they are. *Things*!" He sighed. "It's no good basing a life on *things*!"

He wore such a sad face. It struck Jimmy funny that he should seem to be suffering more over Jimmy's loss than Jimmy was.

"Oh, but it's true," Rolly said, as Jimmy laughed. Then he looked at Jimmy's feet. He had given him a pair of sandals to wear. Jimmy had them on over his socks. Quite a bumbling novitiate beatnik he was. "Do they fit?" he asked. Jimmy said that they did, quite comfortably.

Marsayas went on to tell Jimmy that, after he had pulled Vera off him, she had run out into the street and stopped a car by standing with outstretched arms, like a crucifee. The car had gone off with her. Marsayas said that he had been too drunk to follow, but that after taking a nap he had driven up to Manhattan to see if he could get her to come back. He said that he had found the front door wide open and Vera hysterical. She told him that the man who had driven her home had threatened her, and that she had given him everything he asked for and was afraid to call the police.

Trouble! *Trouble*! Four hundred, maybe five hundred, dollars worth of his hard labor stolen! His most prized possession—his typewriter. More disorder! More chaos! Well, Rolly was right. He was a fool to work for *things*.

He wasn't angry; he was just disgusted, with himself and with Vera. What a dreadful pain in the ass they must always seem to people! Ah! He thought to himself that he would go right ahead and get just as drunk as he damned well pleased; and he would start right now to demand, through an iron-clad indifference to anybody's harangue, his *rights*!

But just then Vera appeared at the door, eyes shooting hot tears like sunstruck diamonds.

"I want to speak to you," she said, choking in temper.

Marsayas bent down and buried Joan's neck in the red excelsior of his beard.

"Do you hear?" Vera shouted. "I said I want to speak to you!"

Her smeared lips were pursed, her grim, green eyes on Marsayas.

Rolly peeked in through the curtain, from the back, but withdrew his scared, comic-Christ face when he saw Vera.

"Step outside, please," said Vera, and Jimmy felt as if he were being called out by a barroom bully. Her breath was hot, and he thought he saw a flame leap from her mouth.

He got up and walked outside, onto Henry Street, a pretty, quiet, Sunday view, reminiscent of Utrillo. He could hear tugboats tooting in the harbor, beyond the esplanade.

Vera had her coat on. He was in shirtsleeves, a little chilly. He shivered. He thought that he must look like hell, unshaven, disheveled. So did Vera.

"I want you to come home with me," she said. "I've been waiting in that church over there for nearly an hour. I was not going to step one foot back in that filthy zoo of a sandal shop, with that smell of dead skin, but I did, for *you*. Now you come along with me, do you *hear*?"

"I'm staying here for a while," Jimmy said, affirming his rights. "You go ahead. I'll be along."

He was a bit tipsy—not much, but a bit; enough to think he was going to get away with facing her down—enough to think he was going to win, this time.

"No!" she said. "You come now!"

"No!" he said. "Later! I am a lion."

"You are not the king of the beasts. You're a pussycat. I suppose you'll want to grow a beard now."

"You just listen to me roar," he said.

"If you don't come now, I'll kill myself!" she shouted. The sentence rang down the hollow, empty Sunday street like a ricocheting bullet.

"No," he said; but he was weakening.

"You'll see," she yelled at him, turning, and running around the corner. "You'll see," she yelled again, farther down, out of sight.

He stood still for what seemed a long time, determined not to give in, determined to hold his ground. But then he heard her yell, "*You'll see*," from far down, toward the docks, and he thought of the harbor and the water.

It came to him. She means to throw herself in. But then it occurred to him that she had won medals for swimming. How could she drown herself? And what could he do if she did take it into her head to jump into the drink? He couldn't swim at all! But he had lost already. Even to think about it was to lose.

He started running down the block, around the corner, to the river. He slowed down, occasionally, wondering what he would do when he got there. He couldn't save her! Three years in the Marines hadn't taught him to swim. He wasn't going to learn in the next five minutes. And she couldn't drown, was an expert!

He stopped running once, and began to laugh. The absurdity of what was happening struck him. He had a stitch in his side. What kind of damned crazy show was this? And what part was he intended to play? The clown who gets fished out of the drink by his wife? But, then, in an instant, he was frightened again. What was she going to do? She was capable of anything.

He started running again, and he got to the dock just in time to see Vera take off her coat, and, looking back to make sure he was watching—he felt she would have waited for him to catch up had he taken longer—jump in.

He walked the next hundred or so feet. He wondered what sort of expression he wore. Whatever it was, that miraculous crowd that gathers out of nowhere at public events such as the one taking place under the esplanade in Brooklyn Heights did not like it at all. He did not move a wee bit faster, however. In fact, he sauntered. Meantime, until three or four burly firemen, who were stationed on a fireboat docked nearby, swam in three or four strokes to rescue her, Vera swam gracefully about, doing a lovely backstroke of the sort that had won her the medals. Then she allowed herself to be saved by the florid knights of the fireboat. Unfortunately, thought Jimmy, it wasn't even necessary to knock her out; they swam back to the boat in a beautiful formation, like well-trained frogmen, Vera on point, and the knights of the fireboat took her aboard.

As for Jimmy, he just stood where he was. He may have been laughing, or he may have been crying, but whatever he was doing, it roused no sympathy for him in the heart of the crowd. It was thumbs down for him.

Then one of the big, fire-colored knights stepped up to him.

"You that young lady's husband?" It sounded as much like an accusation as it did a question.

"Yes," Jimmy admitted, "I am."

"Well, whatsa matter widja? Why dinja jump in after huh?"

"I can't swim."

"Call that a 'scuse?" the fireman demanded.

Jimmy thought that he had best be careful now. He might be lynched.

"No," he said meekly.

"Well, now . . ." the fireman said, thinking. It must have been quite a search that went on in that big head, but he came out of it empty-handed. All he could say in his state of indignation was "Get aboard!"

There was a cop on the boat. "Are you prepared to take your wife home?" he asked, adding, "Otherwise I'll have to take you both to the station." Jimmy wanted to ask what he had done, but thought better of it. He said he was. He looked at Vera, who was sitting wrapped in blankets, three or four firemen asking her questions, consoling her, and no doubt condemning him. Vera saw him, then, and stood up, stretching her arms out to him through the blankets.

"Oh, Jimmy," she cried, "take me home."

Sure he would. What did it matter now? Something had happened, something had snapped. Vera thought she had won again, but she hadn't. This time he had won. And so had protean D.D., the Divorce Demon, in the form of Marsayas, poet, painter, prophet, and king of beasts.

II.

LEGACY

He that hath wife and children
hath given hostages to fortune . . .
—Francis Bacon, Essays

I.

Biology, loneliness, and love have always been busy on Fortune Island; even now, no doubt, in the year 2000, when the island is almost completely deserted, when all that is left at least of the human aspect of things is the administrative building housing the few officials who tend to its history, natural and human. To the best of my knowledge, the island was named for a plundered and derelict Spanish galleon, the *Buena Fortuna*, that, according to one history, "scuttled on the treacherous Outer Banks of North Carolina" in the Sixteenth Century. It's said that the gathering dunes eventually buried all but the prow of the ship, leaving only half of the name in plain sight, and so newcomers to the island looked upon the name of the ship as the name of the island and Fortune Island it became.

By the Eighteenth Century Fortune Island was a considerable port-of-call, with a fluxuating population of around eight hundred people. These included fishers, shrimpers, lobstermen, and tradesmen of all sorts involved with water traffic, and, of course, in many cases, their families. But then the great disasters occurred, one upon another. A hurricane in the mid-Nineteenth Century shut the main inlet while opening another miles up the Banks. People left in droves for the new port. The "fixed" population dropped to about a hundred, and continued to drop with the coming of Union troops during the Civil War. When the troops withdrew at war's end, Fortune Island was virtually depopulated, a deserted island.

As you may remember, David, it is a whale-shaped island, its head to the north and out to sea, its finlike tail pointing southwest to the mainland. Most of the northern end, or head, is covered with enormous dunes, as if the sea view had been walled away. The roots of the dunes are entangled with the roots of mummified trees which once stood tall in the sea wind but now are buried and grip the depths of the dunes like anchors. The tail of the whale, the low narrow leeward end, was, in my time, where most of the population, a few fishermen and shrimpers mainly, had little houses along little streets of a village in miniature. A small white church with a steeple that one could see from the heights of Whalehead, near where my grandparents had constructed their own house, was the spiritual center of the island. Out behind it were two cemeteries, one for black folk, one for white, each with a white picket fence not meant to keep people out but apparently to keep our ancestral ghosts in.

I grew up on Fortune Island at a time when the outside world with its school authorities did not seek me out, there far across Pamlico Sound, as other truants on the mainland were sought. It was long before computers, remember. I was, to all intents and purposes, unknown to the mainland world of Beaufort, Moorehead City, and Wilmington, where once and once only the man I then believed to be my father, the Sad Traveller himself—presumably sad with the grief and guilt of the world on his hunched shoulders, but probably what we would call today a manic-depressive, or a bi-polar type—the Reverend Jason P. Cogburn, had taken me on his preaching circuit.

Garcie, the black midwife who had brought me into this world and who continued to watch over me, had taken the mail boat up to Ocracoke Island to be with her dying brother, and so couldn't keep an eye on me that day, and the Reverend Cogburn, whom I always just called the "Traveller," was most reluctantly compelled to take his six-year-old charge with him, where in one church he leaned over me and shouted, "Do you believe?"

How could I believe anything coming from his twisted lips and smoke-blackened crooked teeth? Skinny, in his tight black suit, with his hunched shoulders, he seemed like a hooded snake leaping into the air on its tail, and I shouted, "No!" *No, no, no*, I did not believe what he said, anything he might say, because I knew what no one else there knew, that he had none of the love in him which he preached about so readily, that he had terrified me since my mother's suicide in the sea, and then he slapped me, slapped me, slapped me with his long hard fingers until, crying and half screaming, I lied in his embarrassed, angry, sweating face, shouting, Yes, yes, *yes*, that I did believe, but I did not and could not ever believe whatever it was he wanted me to believe, had never believed, whatever it was, coming from him.

I looked for help, protection, among the congregation; but nobody interfered with the Traveller, for he was the authority on discipline. He set his believers an object lesson on how to deal with their own recalcitrant children, and most especially with a blasphemer, in this case a six-year-old who had dared to say no to belief. Shouts of approval pierced my ears. After all, I couldn't know that this was what they were paying for, what they would fill the collection box with their coins and even their bills for. I had become, before their eyes, an example of the reformed and, finally, apparently, forgiven. But I was never reformed and remain unforgiven and unforgiving till this day.

After the Traveller's sermon (a shouting match with the devil, or, more likely, a colloquy between the devil and himself) I learned that we had been at a church on the banks of the Cape Fear River. I waited outside and could see across to the big city of Wilmington and I remember seeing what a sympathetic church lady told me were Liberty Ships, hundreds of them, it seemed, a mothballed fleet, a long line of gray masts against lines of gray cypress trees, ghostly reminders of the recent war, and that is how I date this event. "No need to cry," the lady said, wiping my eyes with her lacy pink handkerchief. "Praise God, we have defeated the foe."

II.

Congratulations, Ruthie, on graduating from Smith, like your mother and your Aunt Jessie, and now that I'm the proud father of a college graduate and a young woman of great promise, of a daughter who will someday—a day, I hope, far in the future—upon my demise go through my papers—no doubt consigning most of them to the shredder—I want you to be able to make a wise decision about the disposition of your Aunt Jessie's unfinished memoir, excerpted above. She claimed that that part of the memoir represented the earliest memory of her childhood, other than running about on the dunes and getting her toes wet in the sea, so I put it first. I have stuck with what appears to be the correct chronology throughout. It is a personal document, more like an elaborated letter, written to me for the purpose of deepening my understanding of our background. Upon my death, it will pass to you, and you may do with it as you see fit—write a biography (you *are* an English major), or a novel, maybe, or throw it in the fire.

Since your mother's death, there remain on earth but two people this memoir can effect, for good or ill, and they are you and me, and when it passes to you, only you. But you're a woman now, and I feel that you should know what is contained in these pages. With your upbringing, some of it may prove shocking to your sensibilities, but I hope that I am not mistaken in believing that your humanity will manifest itself in understanding and compassion. Your aunt was a great woman. When I think of what she accomplished, against such odds, I am amazed. Of course, your grandmother, my mother after whom you are named, deserves much credit for what Jessie accomplished. But as you will see, your grandfather also deserves kudos for one of the most unselfish acts known to me. Alas, my dear, they are all dead and gone, and finally have nothing to fear.

I felt that the manuscript, incomplete, confused as a house of cards shaken to the table, needed a few words of interpretation and here I try to supply those words, so it is really a double memoir, one to me from Jessie, one from me to you. In love, faith, and trust, I am your father, David Perle, speaking to you from the present, which is, I hope, your distant past.

Jessie Judas, winner of the International Lamarck Prize in Science, the Kyoto Prize for Basic Sciences, and many other awards, died last month, at five o'clock in the morning of March 20, 2003, a cold rain battering the window next to her hospital bed near Chapel Hill, North Carolina.

A nurse told me that her last words were, "It's Hazel." In her delirium, the last throes of the cancer that had eaten much of her flesh away, she was about a half century off the mark, for Hurricane Hazel had struck, killing her beloved Garcie, in 1954, but what she said indicated her recent preoccupation with the past. In the deep subjectivity of the coma that came and went, and under the influence of many drugs, that past must have seemed like a dream, part fairy tale, part nightmare. And so at the end, she would laugh, frown, cry, and whimper, her dying mind still alive with it all.

She was cremated, according to her wishes, and her ashes were scattered from a high dune on Fortune Island to fly over sand, sea, and shoal, into Pamlico Sound west and into the Atlantic east in a maelstrom of salt air. A few of her former colleagues at the University and Duke, and even a couple who had come all the way down from the Woods Hole Oceanographic Institution, and one from the Scripps Institution in California—and I—attended. Adding to the general sadness of the occasion was the fact that you were unable to attend. (Ruthie, will you ever learn to stop taking chances? You are just like your grandmother Ruth—a dare-devil. Please, for my sake, keep off those skis!) Of course Judas wasn't Jessie's real name; it was the name our father had assumed, apparently penitentially, a man who was too hard on himself, as I now see it. Tom Judas' real name was Thomas McQueen. Why Jessie had changed her name to Judas, I had not been able to understand until I read her memoir. It has been hard for me to decide what to think about this confessional piece, written, *in extremis*, when she had nothing to fear, least of all the truth. But I have added a few thoughts at the end of the manuscript with which you might agree.

About six months ago I heard that Jessie was ill, perhaps dying, and I broke off a sliver of time from my work at the State Department, work which had kept me at great distances from Jessie for many years, and went to visit her at her house in Chapel Hill. She was just sixty then—and at her death—and I found her radically changed from the tall, vibrant red-haired woman I had seen only a few years before. Then she had been the eminent scholar of a (to me) obscure branch of science, the author of several scholarly works and one book of personal essays on the academic life.

But on this last visit I was shocked to find a frail, disheveled ghost of herself, her thick red hair become thin and ashen.

We spent a few hours together, reminiscing about our life together as kids in Boston. That was the only life I had known with Jessie, growing up at that Brookline estate my grandparents had built, and which was sold before you were born.

When I was a child, I assumed Jesse was my sister. Later my mother explained to me that she was my half-sister—though, at that time, I could not see any meaning in that minor distinction—still later, the mystery of Jesse Judas deepened for me because she didn't share our name. But what I chose to ignore or took for granted as a child, I felt compelled to ask about on this last visit, time being as short as Jessie's wispy, colorless hair.

"Why Judas?"

"I think our father took the name Judas," Jessie said, "out of guilt for a failure of character—and only once in his life did his character fail him, as far as I know, and for which he paid a high price, not in what others exacted from him for it, but in the price he exacted from himself—he assumed the name Judas, and I for much the same reason, I guess, decided to carry it on."

"Why? What did he do? What did you do? I wish I knew more about the past, Jessie."

"You will."

"But there's no one left but you to tell me."

"And I'll soon be gone. But you'll know all about it."

"How?"

"You'll see. And when you know the whole story, I hope you'll have . . . well, strength and forgiveness."

"Whom shall I need to forgive?"

"All of us—your mother, your father, and me—and me especially." She coughed, waved the subject away.

She looked both imperious and weak. I decided not to tax her with my insistence, and changed the subject.

"Do you remember the time we went to Fortune Island?"

"Do you? You were only about seven. By then there was no one there but the people from the National Park Service—a few public historical buildings—but Ruth and I knew where all the real people and places were. We went to the house where I was born, which really wasn't there, you understand, but was a ghost house, and we walked through it with all its good and evil memories"—she seemed not to be talking to me anymore but simply remembering out loud—"and we went to the cottage where Ruth once lived, and we walked through the rooms where she wrote one of her books and where she began to teach me and possibly where you were conceived. Mind you, nothing on the dunes but thin air."

"An insubstantial pageant faded."

"Yes. Ghosts. I hope to join them soon."

And too soon I had to be on my way, sorry to leave Jessie in such a condition and fairly certain that I would never see her again. Well, we had never seen much of each other. By the time I had entered high school she was already a graduate student. We were fond of each other, but she seemed always mysterious to me, a pleasantly bound but mostly closed book, and anyway more like an aunt than a half-sister, being fifteen or so years older. When I think about it now, Ruthie, I realize that I knew very little about her. But before leaving her on that last visit, she pushed a manuscript upon me, saying, "It's a piece of the story of my life. And yours. You might find it of interest."

And now I know why she and my mother always seemed in league against me when I showed them that I had a certain curiosity about aspects of the past, particularly about my father. Mother and Jessie would glance at each other conspiratorially and change the subject. Their unforthcoming behavior only served to make me more curious, but they were adamant, and I remained curious to no end. There was a secret between them, and I finally decided (for I loved and trusted them both, despite their odd behavior, because, after all, they lavished their love on me) that they would tell me the whole story in due time. I guess that's why I became a diplomat. My talent is patience.

III.

Dear David, over the years I've kept journals, diaries, scraps, and they've helped to keep my memory fresh. The following is for you:

I was born in a ramshackle house on Fortune Island, North Carolina in 1942 with the help of a black midwife named Garcie Cannon and very little else. That area of the Atlantic just off shore from the Banks was then known as "Torpedo Junction." German U-boats—submarines to the unhistorical modern—were sinking hundreds of merchant ships out there on that "stormy moat," as the poet Robinson Jeffers called it. I have been told that the fires of these sinking ships at night lighted the sky for miles. I have been told that I was born by that strange sinister firelight. Perhaps even as I was being born, our father's ship, just a few miles offshore, was torpedoed. He was about nineteen years old then, and had joined the Merchant Marines. Garcie told me that when he woke in the hospital in Raleigh, his hair had turned gray. This phenomenon of shock is called alopecia areata. It must have seemed strange to see such a thick head of gray hair on a man with such a youthful face. Our father, Tom McQueen, had inherited the house from his father and mother, a fisherman and a former schoolmarm, both dead before I could know them. How they came to live on that remote island I do not know, but I've always imagined that there must have been a great love story in it. Who else but lovers would suffer such a life, with no electricity, an outbuilding for cooking, so that the kerosene fumes wouldn't sicken them, and sand so deep and shifting that no car could maneuver it very far without getting stuck up to its running boards? Yes, David, in those days cars still had running boards.

As I say, I was born in that clapboard house with a production of Götterdämmerung going on outside at sea, where our father was being torpedoed into alopecia areata, or so I have come to think of the situation—which, in itself, sounds unpromising enough, but later Garcie elaborated it for me: "You were a long, skinny baby with a lot of red hair and I had to fight to get you untangled from your own cord. Your mamma wasn't strong, and a weakness in her chest caused her to cough and spit up blood." That was Garcie when I was ten or so. And from before that, the Traveller preaching over my mother, her on her knees before him: "You whored your way down from the mountains and across the Piedmont to the cities of sin on the coast—to Wilmington and the shipyards and the only man that would marry you, carrying his misbegotten child, that armed robber who's serving his sentence in Central Prison in Raleigh for trying to rob the payroll of the company that makes Liberty Ships to help fight our enemies. What do you say for yourself? Speak! Can't you speak? Never mind. You have nothing to say. Only pray, pray, pray," and I have an infant's image, whether real or imagined, of my poor mother, her pale skin flushed, coughing and spitting, and asking, begging, imploring, "When will you forgive me, when will you ever forgive me?" And him, drunk: "Never! Only God can forgive you!"

Do I remember this or have I made it up out of Garcie's palaver? I could only have been two or three years old. And one day my mother must have walked into the sea, because she was gone for several days, vanished, and finally her body washed up on the shore, her frail feet and curled toes tangled in green weeds, I have been told, her red hair in dark strands against her iron gray face, like a beached mermaid. Then I had only the Traveller and Garcie, only Garcie really, and she needed a lot of help from me by that time, because her eyes were failing fast, her diabetes winning against the light.

They took my mother's body to the hard sand near the shore, and there was trouble with the mail boat, causing a delay, so she waited for two days in the back of an old station wagon, waited to be taken somewhere for medical examination before being brought back to the island for burial. I went there to be near her and squatted next to the station wagon. I talked to her through the window. The owner of the station wagon came and opened the door and there was a terrible stench from inside and he threw some liquid into the back seat, for the smell, and shut and locked the doors. I waved goodbye when they took her body out in the skiff to the mail boat, even though I knew by then that she couldn't see that I was waving, or maybe I thought that she could see me from some other place. Because of the Traveller, I do not believe in other places any more.

Of course I knew by then that the Sad Traveller, the Reverend Jason Cogburn, wasn't my father—he had made that very clear to me—that my father was an evil criminal named McQueen who was in a prison everyone called "The Wall." I hated my real father as much as I hated the Traveller; sometimes more, because he had deserted me by committing a crime and going behind the Wall and leaving me with the Traveller for a father. I didn't know which one I hated most. I suppose I prayed to God to give me someone beside poor blind Garcie. Because of the Traveller, I don't think I believe in God anymore.

Jessie McQueen. I didn't want that last name. I was ashamed of it. And I was certainly determined never to call myself Cogburn, although the Traveller never asked me to. I was nobody. I belonged to nobody. I lived in the house where I was born, which now seemed to belong to the Traveller, and, when I was lucky, I was treated by him as a step-daughter, and, when not so lucky, he treated me as he had treated my mother. He drank heavily whenever he came home and I was afraid when he did and I would go over to Garcie's to stay with her, unless he demanded that I stay with him, which he sometimes did, when he had grown tired of talking to himself and felt the need of someone to torment.

One day I climbed the stairs to the small attic that was crowded with old damp boxes to see if I could find any of my mother's, or even of my grandmother's, clothes—the Traveller would occasionally bring me something back from his trips—but I was barefoot and in rags most of the time. It didn't make much difference on the island anyway, I guess; but I did need some things badly, and there among the boxes I discovered my father's books. The Traveller had taught me to read the Bible, and there was a dictionary among the books, and so I found a secret life for myself, a life away from the Traveller, away from the world. In the real world I was sinking deeper into my own isolation, but in the world of imagination, I began to expand. I called these books my secret treasure trove, and, handling them, touching them I could touch my father, who had smeared and dogeared almost every page. His mother, my grandmother, the schoolmarm, must have been my father's teacher, must have directed him in his reading. I could feel her hand on the books too. I put my fingers on her fingerprints. I could feel them in the attic with me, my father and even my grand-mother. I could imagine him as a boy of my own age, curled up and reading *Tales from Shakespeare* by Charles Lamb, reading the *Essays* of Francis Bacon, especially the mystery of *The New Atlantis,* which was the mystery of an island like the one I was on. I discovered that Francis Bacon wrote that knowledge was power, and I, being powerless, took that to mean that my only way out of my life of subservience (though of course I didn't know such a word at that time) was through learning, and I set out to educate myself and have never hesitated in my quest for knowledge since.

It occurred to me that day up in the attic, thumbing through those books, that my father must have absorbed some of the things that I was reading helter-skelter and only partially understanding, like Bacon, that in his mind up there in Central Prison at Raleigh behind the Wall he must still possess chunks of Shakespeare, particles at least of Thomas Wolfe—because there was a dogeared copy of *Look Homeward, Angel* and another of *You Can't Go Home Again*. He had underlined passages, and I tried to glean what he had read and to put it into my own mind. There were books of poetry, mildewed but readable, books by Poe, Sidney Lanier, and Walt Whitman. There was one that I read as best I could, and re-read for several years—*Of The Imitation of Christ* by Thomas à Kempis. "To achieve this," my father had written in the flyleaf in a round young hand, "is to achieve perfection." Then how could he have done what he did? How could he have become a criminal? How could he have left me alone? How could he have left me at the mercy of the Traveller? "He that has wife and children hath given hostages to fortune." To Fortune Island!

I found a copy of *Under the Sea Wind*, by someone named Rachel Carson at the bottom of one box. A woman. I didn't know then that women wrote books. It was a very exciting discovery. I was going to read it right away. I carried it out to the dunes with me and discovered that it was all about the dunes, about the little animals that I watched, about the wind and sea. Biology. About my own biology. I went over to ask Garcie about my biology.

"How did my mother and father meet, Garcie?"

"They met in Wilmington, how most men and women meet."

"How?"

"I told you, baby, your daddy was a soft-hearted boy and I guess he done seen a poor gal down on her luck and decided to help her out. Next thing they married and back here and she pregnant with you and he off for the Merchant Marines and he sunk and in the hospital and you born and he back here and off again to do that awful payroll robbery and in prison and the Traveller come tell your momma she need him and don't need your daddy and here we are, you sitting there eatin' grits and me talking up a storm. Now stop asking questions and let old blind Garcie get some shuteye, like I need to shut 'em for the dark, ha, ha."

"But why did my mother give up on my dad? Why did she divorce him?"

"She was a poor, sad, weak creature, more to be pitied, who couldn't do for herself much less anyone else. Without a man she was like a dog with nobody to walk her. She was sick most of her life, child, sick and ignorant and frightened and always needing a man to guide her, to give her direction and protection. Weren't her fault. God just make some of us like that so that the rest who is stronger have some way of using their strength. Some is needy, some is good, and some is greedy. That's the way it works. Your father was strong most of the time with moments of weakness in him—one big moment, you might say. A little of the devil would get into him once in a while, like it gets into you when you go into one of your conniption fits, but he weren't no bad person like you being told by that Traveller. When he got out of that hospital with his hair all gray he was onliest just a youngan hisself, and he got talked into doing something he shouldn't ought to done, thinking it was the only way he had to help you and your mother. He was always the most guilt-suffering boy you ever did see, and I can bet you anything that he is suffering right now."

"What's it like where he is, Garcie?"

"They calls it the Wall, and he behind it. It's a big dark tower, like one of those castles in that Frankenstein movie, but I don't suppose you ever saw that. Don't suppose you ever saw a movie in your life, did you, baby?"

"No ma'am. You know I ain't never been off this island long enough to see anything, 'cepting I remember those Liberty boats I told you about."

"And you never stop talking about them, do you?"

"No ma'am. What if I went to school, Garcie?"

"Just give Garcie another job in minding you. The Traveller is schooling you, according to his way, and nobody argues so far. He don't want you to know some things."

"What things?"

"Don't ask me, he just don't, and he does the payin' around here."

"What things am I not supposed to know? I already know things he doesn't know that I know."

"Like what, pray tell?"

"Like knowledge is power."

"That's a big mouthful for a little skinny blue egg just been cracked open. Go on, now; let me get my nap."

I went walking in the shoal at low tide and looking at the little whelklings in their tubes. I picked one from the clear water and held it in my palmed hands and I remember, I prayed to it: Please, give me someone. I dropped it back with a tiny splash and stopped, listening, waiting. No voice from the blue but the laughter of the black-capped gulls, laughter half drowned in the sea-smelling, soft, salt roar of the wind, and the susurrus of the shifting dunes.

Beaufort Inlet

Drum Inlet

Ocracoke Inlet
Hatteras Inlet
Oregon Inlet

—the ways in and the ways out. Why do they call them Inlets? They are Outlets. Like my mother, who came down from the mountains and across the Piedmont and finally out to sea—those waters, my mother.

If I had understood the word, I'd have known that the Traveller was a sadist. He made me cry whenever he could.

"Look what I've brought back for you from Wilmington," he said one day after his return from his preaching circuit. His black coat hung on a hook inside the front door. He went to it and found something and tossed it on the table, across from his bottle of bourbon. A magazine: "True Crimes." I was about twelve. He sat leering at me as I tried to understand the meaning of the odd gift.

"Go ahead," he said, "look through it." I was sipping coffee. I put down my cup and thumbed through the magazine. "Find an article called 'The Case of the Disgraceful Vets,' he said. "There's a picture of your daddy there, and three others who were involved in that botched robbery." He put a square flat index finger on the page. "That one—Tom McQueen—that's your father. How do you like him in his prison uniform? That's the man your mother loved. That man—not me. No matter what she said, she couldn't make me believe she loved me as she had that man. Damned and evildoers, both of them. And you had better watch yourself or you'll end up a wicked painted woman and a suicide, or like your daddy, a criminal behind bars. I'm watching you, but I can't always be here, so you better watch yourself. It's their blood that's in you. Where do you think you're going, young lady?" He tried, but he was too drunk to get up. "Hey, where do you think you're going?"

I took the magazine and grabbed my book and a blanket and went out on to the dunes on the sound side, found a comfortable place, and read about how my father and his friends had found the police waiting for them when they arrived at the shipyard. It seemed that the wife of one of the robbers had informed on them. The War was still on then and they were called disgraces to the uniform of the United States military and naval services and sentenced to ten years each. I studied the blurry photographs on the pulp paper of the magazine pages. All I could tell from the pictures was that they seemed young, except for my father who seemed old with his pale hair. But I knew that he was as young as the others. I remembered a photograph of him from the boxes in the attic. In that picture he must have been about my own age, twelve or thirteen, and his hair was raveny dark, the way I always thought of him. I understood that he was a criminal and in jail. But I couldn't believe he was really a bad man. I wondered how he'd forgotten what he'd read in *The Imitation of Christ.* Does it just slip away sometimes when you aren't looking? I lost my temper sometimes, so sudden it was scary. I'd yell mean things at Garcie. Once I even pushed her, and I was so sorry afterwards I cried and cried, and finally I cried myself to sleep.

When night comes to Fortune Island, it is like a big hand reaching out from the mainland, its fingers making dark shadows among the dunes, but for a time before that happens, there can be an horizonless silver of sound-water and sky until it darkens and to the northeast the soft steady recurring blink of the lighthouse appears in the dark like a star that you can almost reach out and touch, a star you can make a wish upon. I often empathized with the oyster, that, as it shuts its mother-of-pearl-lined shell, creates its own night, but its stars dim and die while ours spangle the sky.

More and more often, as I grew up, and the Traveller returned from his circuit, I would sleep out on the dunes and stare up, before, like the oyster's, the shell of my mind closed with my eyelids on the pictures they seemed to make.

I had tried the attic for escape but I didn't like the feeling of being trapped up there. What if he were to climb up behind me? There was a little cave, not much bigger than a rabbit hole, which I had dug out, under the back wall of the house, and when it was raining or cold or both I would pile on my clothes and take my blanket and go there to sleep, but most of the time I would sleep with the other small creatures in the sand that walked with the wind. But some of the creatures on the dunes didn't sleep at night—the mosquitoes and sand fleas, "all those danged bloodsuckers," as Garcie called them—and I suppose it was a tiny crab that had crawled into my blanket that night that woke me, caused me to jump up and shake out the blanket. I heard a woman's voice behind me scream and then begin to laugh.

"Oh my God! You scared the bejesus out of me. I thought this place was deserted."

"Don't be scared. I'm just a little girl."

"Not so little, stretch."

"I'm tall for my age."

"Which is?"

"Twelve going on thirteen."

"What are you doing out here so late?"

"I was sleeping."

"Sleeping in the sand? Don't you have a bed at home? It must be three in the morning."

"I didn't want to be in the house with my stepfather. He's drunk."

"Oh you poor kid! Is he mean to you?"

"He's mean as a snake."

The woman frowned. "Does he hit you?"

"He tries, but I can dodge him most of the time."

"What does your mother say?"

"She's dead."

"Oh, I'm sorry to hear that. Well, don't you have somewhere you can go? A friend's house?"

"I can go to Garcie, but he looks for me there. I don't want to bring her any trouble."

"Garcie is your friend? An older woman?"

"She looks after me. She born me into the world."

"Not your mother—"

"Garcie's black. She's too old for any excitement. She was the midwife that helped to bring me in."

"I see. Well, my name is Ruth Perle." She gave me her hand to shake. It was warm and soft, but strong. And that was the way Ruth always seemed to me: warm and soft and strong and firm and brave.

"I never heard anyone talk like you." I said. "You're not from around here, are you?"

"I'm from Boston. Up north. I'm doing some work down here—on the Banks."

"What work is there to do down here—if you're not a fisherman or a boat-builder or—" What else was there?

"Never mind about that now. Why don't you come on home with me and spend the night? Are you hungry? I can fix you something."

"That'd be mighty nice of you. I didn't eat any dinner or supper."

"Well, come on then." Ruth had not let go of my hand, and now she led me off across the dunes, stumbling and sliding and laughing—together! The words of our meeting may not be exact, blown away, as they were, by the night wind, but that was the gist of it. What I couldn't know then was that I had found my someone, the someone I had so long prayed to the sky and the sand and sea to find, prayed to the whelklings, the someone whose voice I had often heard murmuring inside the seashell, the friend from another world.

"Are you married?" I asked her.

"I was. My husband was killed in Korea."

"Mr. Perle?"

"No, no, I never used my husband's name. I was a writer when I met him and I'm a writer now."

"You mean like Rachel Carson? Look, I've got a book by her," and I waved *Under the Sea Wind* under Ruth's nose.

"No, not like Rachel Carson. I'm a folklorist."

"Oh," I said, vaguely disappointed, and wondering what that meant, but also still thrilled at the idea of meeting a real woman writer. "Do many women write books? I never heard of any before Rachel Carson."

"You never heard of Margaret Mitchell?"

"No ma'am."

"Who wrote *Gone With the Wind*?"

"No ma'am."

"Unbelievable!" Ruth exclaimed.

I was vaguely hurt. "I ain't never been off this island, excepting once when I saw the Liberty ships near Wilmington."

"Well, hell's bells, I found myself a Caspar Hauser."

"What's a Caspar Hauser?"

"A little boy who was kept away from the world."

"That's me, then—Caspar Hauser. But I'm Jessie McQueen—at least that's what they tell me, and they've been calling me that forever—well, as far back as I go."

I recognized the cottage we were heading toward. It had belonged, up until a few months before, to an elderly couple who had kept to themselves—almost hermits. There was a light inside, a golden glow at the window.

"What happened to the old people who lived here?"

"The wife died. The husband was taken off to a nursing home in Beaufort." She tugged and pushed at the door against drifted sand until she got it open. "Come on in—what did you say your name was again?"

"Jessie McQueen. The wife died and the husband is in a nursing home because he is so old," I said. "That's biology too."

Ruth looked at me as if I had said something very peculiar. "I suppose it is," she said, "in the larger sense."

"Oh, yes, ma'am, that's biology too. All animals die."

"I'm afraid I know that only too well, young lady."

"Yes, I suppose you do, ma'am. I didn't mean nothing by it. Just things come into my head sometimes and I out and say them."

Later, Ruth told me how I had startled her. She said, "I think I knew then and there that there was something very special about you." Every so often over the years she would remind me of what I had said that night and of its effect on her. "Come on in, Jessie McQueen," she said, in her hearty way, as I remember it, all those years back, those time-eaten years, and I couldn't know then that I was stepping through golden gates into my future, into a life I could never have imagined. As the deck has been dealt, approximately a year to a card, I look back on that moment as the first card dealt, an ace of hearts. I also look back on the vision before me in that little house, with each passing year, more and more, as a kind of Cinderella vision of the magic possible in a world I could not then have believed existed.

Ruth had the place lighted with several soft-gleaming oil lamps—remember, there was no electricity on Fortune Island then—that just kept awake the drowsy colors of hundreds of book jackets, and there were paintings—"prints," Ruth called them—on the walls done in styles that then were as alien to me as would have been a dinosaur or a spaceman; I had never seen anything like them. I had no idea, of course, but I was looking at prints of modern art: Van Gogh, Matisse, Picasso, Braque, all of whom and many more that I have come to consider familiar friends but who then seemed to me to be something from another universe.

"Oh, that's you!" I cried, seeing a black framed photograph dangling crookedly from a nail among the prints.

"That's me and my husband and my daughter. It was taken about ten years ago. Before you ask, my daughter is dead too. She died of polio when she was three. She would have been nearly your age by now."

"I'm sorry," I said meekly. I felt meek before such tragedy, but Ruth just smiled at me and shook her head.

"That shouldn't be hanging there." She snatched the picture from its place and put it face down on a table. "People should be forward-looking. The future is our obstacle course with a pot of gold at the end."

Ruth was a tough-minded woman. If she hadn't been, David, she would never have been able to make the decision, on the spot, as it were, to surrender your father for my future's sake, as you will soon see that she did. But my eyes were still wandering in wonder. A Remington typewriter caught my interest, as a bright bauble catches the eye of a magpie. It was black and chrome and bulky with black keys with white letters on them. It seemed awesome, such efficiency, such power to make words on paper—and there was a half-typed page sticking out of it at the top. I couldn't take my eyes from it, now, even as I heard a cranking noise and music filled the room. I turned on my heel and there stood Ruth, smiling at me and tapping her foot to the music.

"What is that?"

"I thought you could use a little cheering up," she said. "That's Glenn Miller, 'String of Pearls.' Well, what do you think of my humble abode?"

"If you mean this place—well, it's just wonderful! I've never seen anything like it. Our place is just bare boards, straight chairs, a table, and mattresses on the floor. The Traveller—that's what I call my step-father—he don't care about having anything around."

"Why do you call him the traveller?"

"He's a circuit preacher—on the road most of the time—which I'm glad for because I hate it when he's home. He comes home and drinks for a few days and goes off again and that's about all I see of him and I'm glad of it." I looked around. "Could you tell me what that is—that picture?"

"That's a Picasso print."

"What does print mean?"

"Well, it's not a real painting; it's a sort of photograph of the painting. And the painter's name is Picasso. The actual picture was painted back in Nineteen-five."

"So long ago. . . But what is it? It looks like it's full of boxes."

"Do you like it?"

"I guess—sort of."

"That style of painting is called cubism. It does look like a pile of boxes, doesn't it?"

"All different colors—tan, and yellow, and brown. . . But there's a fiddle sticking out of it—part of a fiddle, anyway. And there's a newspaper in some foreign language—what does that mean?"

"It's a French headline. It says—"

"But why is it like that?"

"Because Picasso thought it would be interesting to look at."

"It is—but, you know what? Your whole house is like that—what did you call it?"

"You mean cubism?"

"Uh-huh. All the books and everything—it's like cubism."

Ruth glanced about the room and laughed. "I suppose it is."

"I don't mean no insult. I just mean the books look like they're going to fall over—the stacks of them."

"I'm not the neatest person, young miss. Now how would you like something to eat? How about scrambled eggs and bacon? I'll go out back and rustle us up something. You go ahead and look around at anything that interest you. I won't be long."

The way we cooked on the Island then was in sheds back of the houses. We called them summer kitchens. We used them because the kerosene heat made the houses unbearably hot in summer. The stoves weren't good in those days and fumes could catch up with you, make you sick or even kill you. Ruth took a lamp and went out the back door. I was overwhelmed at seeing so many books in one place. I couldn't get over it. I would have said then that I'd gone dreamy. Oh, I couldn't believe what I was seeing; it was a book with Ruth's picture on the back—*Appalachian Tales*, by Ruth Perle. She did write books! And she was so beautiful too, with her huge almond eyes and her long dark hair, so smart and so beautiful and she was out back cooking me bacon and eggs. I had gone dreamy all right, no doubt about it. The smell of bacon came in first, then coffee, then Ruth with her fresh air smell. We were both hungry, eating fast and not talking much but a "Pass the salt, please," but Ruth finished first, wiping the last of the yolk from her plate with a last bit of bread. She lighted a cigarette—I hadn't seen a woman smoking before—and blew the smoke out with a contented sigh.

"Now tell me about yourself," she said. That's how I remember it—early morning, with the sky lightening outside, Ruth smoking and studying me with those big almond eyes—a word I learned later: chatoyant, her eyes—that looked like they could read your mind, and me, pent up with the story of my life on the verge of exploding from my lips, and a million questions waiting just behind it. Ruth let me ramble on for a long time before she finally stopped me with a question. She was lighting another cigarette and spoke around it.

"Are you really reading that Rachel Carson book?"

"Oh yes. I have a dictionary for the words I don't understand, though I can't find them all. But a lot of it is written like the Bible. You know, nice and simple. It's very beautiful."

"So you're interested in that sort of thing. I mean, the life of animals, sea life, biology?"

"It's funny: all my life I've lived right here and seen these little creatures running up the beach but I never really thought about them—they were just there. Then I found this book, and began reading about them, and, because of the pictures in the book, the drawings, I began to recognize them, and now I go looking for them. I want them to show me how they live. I've been pretty lonesome out here on this danged old island. No kids. No friends. Now it's like I have all these strange little friends. Fiddler crabs, and whelks, and the other day I met a huge ghost crab you could see right through—almost. I talked to him for about an hour. Then he went off about his business."

"What did he have to say?"

"That I'd be better off if I were invisible like him. But in a way I am almost invisible. No one knows I'm here."

"I can see you," Ruth said. "I know you're here. Come over here near the light and let me see your arms."

I stuck out my skinny, freckled arms for her to examine.

"Oh, you've been eaten alive," Ruth said. "I can't tell the freckles from the bites."

"The freckles are brown, the bites are red. I'm always like this except in the winter."

"You poor kid. I'll give you some citronella. Look at my arms." She held out shapely womanly arms with a tinge of dark hair on the forearms for me to observe. "I use citronella. It keeps the bugs away."

I was awestruck. This young woman from Boston knew more about living on Fortune Island than I did. I couldn't begin to imagine what else she might know, but I was to find out in the coming months.

"Miss Perle, I've been wondering, what were you doing out on the dunes so late at night?"

"My time is my own, sweetie—and call me Ruth. In fact, tomorrow I'm going up to Manteo."

"Where's that?"

"Right here on the Banks. Don't you know it? I'm going to see *The Lost Colony*."

"What's *The Lost Colony*?"

"A play by Paul Green—it's about Virginia Dare, the first English child born in America. Jessie, haven't you ever been off this island?"

"What I said, the Traveller took me on his circuit when Garcie was sick or busy or something and I remember seeing Wilmington—that's a very big city—from the other side of the Cape Fear River. I remember hundreds and hundreds of big ships."

"Listen, I have a wonderful idea. How would you like to go with me?"

I was so excited that it choked me. I nodded my head for fear that my voice would crack or come out in a squeal or a screech like an old owl.

"But you'll have to get your step-father's permission."

"Yes," I said, my pipes opening. "Oh yes!"

"Good. Now let's get a couple of hours sleep and then you can run home and ask if you can go. I'll open up that folding cot for you."

I lay in the dark but I couldn't sleep because I couldn't wait; but what if the Traveller wouldn't let me go? I would lie. That's all there was to it—I would lie my red head off.

I would do anything to be able to go on this trip with Ruth Perle. I would not let anything stand in my way. I had to get off this island and see the world. *See the world!* The room was filled with light. Had I dreamed it all? No, it was true; for there was the astonishing Ruth, a reality, preparing for the trip.

In close to half a century, I don't think I've ever been so happy again as I was on that June morning in 1954, not even many years later when I received notice that I was awarded the Lamarck Prize. The joy I felt was like another being inside me trying to burst through my skin. I remember vividly the kinetic sense that my arms moved too fast, my skinny legs seemed to dance to the table for coffee, my head swiveled, not turned, but swiveled, and my heart pounded like a little drum in my chest. I ran across the hot sand of the dunes and for the first time in my life did not notice the heat. I might as well have been a skater on ice, I went so fast, the inner reaches of my mind my only hoveringly physical part, my dream come true. And there was no mean amount of fear. Why should I believe, hope, what would lead me to believe or hope that the Traveller would let me go? But I would lie. I would change my story and lie. I burst into the house and found that my worst fears were unwarranted. The Traveller was gone, off on his circuit once again. There was an envelope on the table—FOR GARCIE. Her money. I grabbed it and ran all the way to Garcie's shack. She had me count the money and read her the note. *Gone for about a week. Enough to keep her fed.*

"Later you take me to Walkup's to get some groceries, hear?" said Garcie.

"I'm going fishing, be back later."

"You watch yourself, now, child, hear?"

When I got back to Ruth's she had a tin tub filled with steaming water. She was naked but for a towel around her hair. I had never seen a woman completely naked before.

Biology again! I lurched toward embarrassment but Ruth's matter-of-factness caught me back.

"Strip and get in there," she said, and I followed her orders unquestioningly but full of questions. "Well," she said when I had stripped, "you're not even a tabula rasa, you're a bas relief of bites, abrasions, and bruises. Let me look in your mouth," and she poked a forefinger around inside my gaping mouth with an intermittent hum as if she were looking for pearls and finding sand; but no, she pulled her finger from my mouth and said, "It's amazing. Your teeth are in pretty good condition. I don't suppose you get much candy, sweets, do you?"

"I don't eat much of anything most of the time."

Ruth said, "I'm going to take a picture of you, so we can check on your progress." And she stood before me with the camera up to her face and the dark V of hair at the bottom of her belly, her breasts crushed together by her arms as she looked for range—and of course I have often seen what she was seeing that morning (I still have that treasured, faded photograph): a gawky, gangly stringbean of a girl topped with a mass of dark reddish hair that looked as though it had never come in contact with a comb. "Pop!" went the flashbulb and, momentarily blinded, I must have jumped a foot off the ground. Ruth, laughed, put down the camera and picked up a lighted cigarette, stuck it between her teeth—and I was laughing now—and said, "Into the water with you, young lady. I hope you don't mind bathing in the same water that I just got out of, but we don't have time for another tubful. Now I'm going to wash your hair and then I'm going to find you something to wear. I've got a pair of bluejeans that should fit you. We'll have to roll the cuffs down, but otherwise . . ."

When we were dressed, Ruth took another photograph of me. In that picture, my hair is combed, and I'm wearing an old sweatshirt with cut-off sleeves that has SMITH

COLLEGE written across the front—the shirt is red and the lettering is gold—the jeans, a pair of Ruth's sandals, just a bit short, for my toes curl over the soles, and I'm proudly holding my first pocketbook, a small brown leather purse with a long thin strap to put over my shoulder. The strange thing is, I was twelve and except for my height I look younger in the first picture; in the second, I look like a young lady. It was the first time it had ever occurred to me that I might be—well, if not pretty, at least presentable in the way that young women ought to be, or ought to have been in the Fifties.

"Now here's our itinerary," said Ruth. I must have looked blank. "This is what we're going to do." And she told me as we trudged across the sand dunes with her logistical haversacks on our backs and cameras dangling from our shoulders. Ruth had explained that she had a tape recorder in a trunk in her "vehicle," which meant car, I guessed. We were heading to Sheriff Walkup's General Store, and working up quite a sweat getting there.

Walkup's General Store was the only store on Fortune Island, and was a good hike from Ruth's place. Walkup was a retired county sheriff then somewhere in his late sixties or early seventies, who had come to the island about twenty years before and opened the General Store, a two-story building the lower floor of which was the store and the upper floor the living quarters. He sold bait and tackle, canned goods, cereal grains, quite a variety of oddments, and was also the Postmaster. His wife was the wooden Indian figure at the cash register. On several occasions I had tried to make friends with her, but she had no interest in children. The most she ever showed me was cold tolerance.

We had to take Sheriff Walkup's skiff out to the mail boat, a pretty white little steamer about fifty feet long with green trim and a red, white, and black smokestack emitting dark, immediately dissipating little puffs against blue sky and white cloud, and followed by a great wing of happily screeching gulls. We climbed into the skiff and Sheriff Walkup began pulling at the oars, puffing and pulling, then stopped about thirty feet from the steamer to wipe his wet forehead with a damp handkerchief.

"I'm getting too old for this," he said; then, brightening, "Lookee yonder, ladies! You see that there feller waiting to get off? That's my new strong back standing there. Don't look like it, does he, in that there seersucker suit and straw Stetson, but I'm gonna have him in dirty work clothes before this skiff has to go out again," and he began painfully pulling at the oars once more while Ruth and I got a closer and closer look at the man on the steamer's deck.

"Look," I said, "he's got a guitar looks like."

"Good God," Ruth said, "he looks good enough to eat."

"He's beautiful," I whispered.

"Watch out, ladies," said Walkup. "He's mine."

We climbed a rope ladder and got aboard the mail boat as the stranger tipped his Stetson in greeting, helped us up with our paraphernalia, and handed down the mail bag, his guitar case, and a battered old suitcase to Walkup. Up close, he looked just as good but surprisingly pale, as if maybe he had spent too much time in juke joints playing that old guitar. We hated to see him climb down into the skiff and row off with Sheriff Walkup. I wished he could come on our trip with us. All duded up like he was, it'd been fun to show him off, like something you'd won at a shooting gallery.

Everyone on board took this adventure for granted, or appeared to, but I thrilled at everything I could touch, smell, or see—the rust on the iron rails, the wake coming from the bow and scudding outward in white foam, the spindrift that dampened my hair, the sudden distance between us and Fortune Island, my home, that seemed so much less important to me now than the invisible place where we were to land, the wild gulls flying in our wake, and the wilder clouds racing across the blue sky. I had probably never felt so alive in all my long captivity. The lighthouse I often saw from Fortune Island, the one that seemed a low, twinkling star to me when I was younger, that always seemed disembodied, was soon looming before me, tall, conical and stark white. But before that, I looked back and saw a Stetson wave goodbye.

On Ocracoke, we squeezed into a pickup truck and were driven to the village, where Ruth unveiled yet another miracle. Behind a building, I think it was a restaurant, Ruth removed a tarpaulin with a "Voila!" to display an old Army jeep. I had never seen one before in my life. It was—exotic! It was dirty and rusty and tough looking as a flat-faced dog, and Ruth had it barking in no time—and bouncing, and bouncing—for I soon discovered that jeeps could go anywhere but they could not go anywhere without bouncing, and I had to hold on for dear life for fear of being tossed ten feet in the air and left on a beach somewhere, forgotten by Ruth, who seemed intent on nothing else but mastering this wild machine. We bounced, jumped, leaped on for fifteen miles, sometimes on the beach, sometimes on the road, sometimes, it seemed, we stayed in the air for miles on end. My first lovely hairdo was in wild disarray by the time we reached the Frazier Peele ferry landing at Hatteras Inlet, where they told us we had to drive our jeep up the planks and on to the ferry first because it was too heavy to lift—the ferry only held three cars: two were put side by side, then the men would lift the third so it would be behind the other two, crosswise. As we made the crossing to Hatteras, Ruth, apparently unfazed, spent some time reshaping my hair. "I don't want you looking feral," she said. Again she could see I was blank.

"Like a wild girl," she said.

"Do I look like a wild girl, Ruth?"

"Not now," she said, smoothing back my hair, pushing here and there. "Now you look like you're ready for Atlantic City."

I pretended to know what she meant, but I couldn't help wondering if we were going to Atlantic City, too, wherever that was.

And then we were bouncing along again and Ruth didn't even slow down when we came to the Cape Hatteras lighthouse, which I was to learn was one of the most famous in the world. "That's the Cape Hatteras lighthouse," she called, dangerously taking her right hand from the jumping steering wheel of the jeep to point at what I thought was one of the greatest wonders that I had ever seen—in fact was one of the greatest wonders that I had ever seen, or almost seen, it receded so fast from view, like a lonely giant peppermint stick. I had to turn my head almost all the way around to face front. Everything was like that with Ruth—whizzbang!

"We're heading up Hatteras to Oregon Inlet," she yelled. I must have agreed. I had noticed by now that disagreeing with Ruth was useless. "Yes," I suppose I said, but then I yelled, "when are we going to stop to eat?"

"When we get there," Ruth yelled back over the growls of the jeep and the roar of the surf.

"Get where?" I yelled.

"Nag's Head," she yelled back. "I have friends there."

It hadn't occurred to me before that Ruth had friends on the Banks—I thought of her as all alone and from far away Boston. The realization that she had friends nearby raised another question in my mind. "But if you have friends, Ruth, why do you live so far away from them? Why do you live on Fortune Island, where there isn't hardly anybody but me and Garcie and just a few others?"

"Because it's the perfect place to write, my Honeylamb. I do my collecting up and down the Banks—like this—and then I bring it back to Fortune Island where there isn't anybody to bother me and I can concentrate and write."

I thought about that for a moment and then I said, "Ruth, am I going to bother you?"

She gave me a quick, disturbed look. "Not you, Honey, never you. Don't you ever worry about that." Then she gave me the warmest smile—at the same time maneuvering on the beach without looking forward. Ruth could do it all.

We crossed Oregon Inlet on a much bigger ferry. In fewer than twenty miles of paved road we came to a populated area. What chance of the flarings and dimmings of the lights of memory brings us back the past and what chance encloses it in darkness forever, I do not know. It seems to me now that we pulled into a big yard in front of a big, gabled house; it seems to me now that the yard was full of children, some younger than I and some older, boys and girls, young men and young women, and that the king and queen of the place, told by graying hair and other signs of advancing age, were in front of the children, or at the middle of the group, or did they appear at the sides of the jeep to help us out? I remember the steamer trunk in the back seat of the jeep being opened and a tape recorder being taken into the house. Greetings, lunch, and hours of taping the voice of our host, as I remember a burly man who told many strange stories of the folklore of the Banks, stories of storms and pirates, and Blackbeard. I especially remember songs, stories and songs all afternoon, Ruth changing reels of tape, taking notes, urging the man on to talk and sing more: and I remember my embarrassment at having to eat with the other children, which was the embarrassment of a stranger who had been isolated for so long at having to socialize with an advanced race of people her own age, fully civilized, knowledgeable young people, whose education had not been neglected to the point of mental infirmity as my own had been. No one actually said, "Are you a dunce?" but I heard it over and over in my mind and I thought I saw it in the eyes around me, but probably not, for everyone was extremely kind, I remember, and one girl who appeared to be about my own age helped me with a personal matter, a biological matter, that had just begun to be a serious consideration in my life.

Then Ruth and I left their house to go to the play, which was long and involved Sir Walter Raleigh, Queen Elizabeth, Indians, and the first English baby born in the new world, Virginia Dare. The image that time has left me is the image of the top of the ship's sail, a rough rectangle of white against the actual night sky, moving away behind the tops of the wooden stakes of the fort, sailing away and to England to get supplies and leaving the remaining colonists on their own—and of course they waited for the ship to return but it never did to their knowledge and they wandered into the woods and were never seen again. I broke down at that image of the sail against the night sky and Ruth took me in her arms and comforted me. I was tired. Emotionally exhausted. So when Ruth asked me If I would prefer to drive back home that night or to go back and stay with that nameless family, I told her that I wanted to go home. I wasn't used to people and the strain of making small talk, and smiling and trying to grasp what was expected of me was too much. I wanted to be alone with Ruth, racing with the moon at the edge of the sea. I fell asleep—even in that bucking bronco of a jeep.

And here I go blank. I only remember that the next morning, or was it the morning after, I woke and found myself back in Ruth's cottage, stretching my skinny self awake on her folding cot, smelling coffee. I lay there and thought about that sail, that tiptop of the sail, bellying the ship away, and the poor people who were left behind and lost forever. I could understand them. When the doctors recently informed me of my condition—terminal—the image of that sail flashed back as if I were there again, watching the play, and wanting to snuggle into Ruth's warm arms, Ruth. Ruth—my friend, my mentor, my mother, my sister, my benefactor, my everything but one.

"I told"—and Ruth named the patriarch of the family we had visited— "that you were interested in biology, and he gave me a copy of *The Science of Life,* by H.G. Wells. She held up a thick tome. "I ought to know more about biology myself, so do you know what we are going to do? We are going to read this book together, and anything you don't understand I will try to explain. If I can't, I'll get us some help."

It took us something like two months to get through that book, with its enormous divisions of geological time making me feel smaller and smaller, like Tiny Alice, finally like an invisible dot, a fractal, and yet, as Ruth made me see, somehow, potentially anyway, more than I had imagined I could be. I began to see the life around me now as moving toward, if not perfection, adaptation, which, I saw, was a kind of temporary perfection, as near as dynamic Mother Nature lets us get to perfection. For things either get better or worse, depending on how you look at them, of course, what vantage point you take, but there is no stasis, no stopping of change; and of course things are ever so maladjusted, because forever trying to adapt themselves to ever-changing circumstances—yes, I saw that too. Not unlike myself. I saw myself as a little unimportant thing trying to adapt myself to my circumstances. I had not seen myself this way before. Before—what had I seen or understood? Nothing, or a blue blank. I had been a container of emotions carried about by the sea wind. I began to sense purpose. If not God's, my own. And my purpose should be partly of my choosing. I came to see that, or I was drawn out to see it, I suppose, by Ruth.

When the Traveller was away, Ruth took me on "field trips." Once we went to Wilmington, where Ruth bought me some clothes at Efird's Department Store, the fanciest store in town. I asked her to take me to the docks to see the Liberty Ships and was heartbroken to see that they were gone. How could I know now that I had ever seen them as my memory told me I had, hundreds of them in a row, and the gray cypresses behind them? Once we went to see the wild ponies on Shackleford Island. They are both of biological and folklorish interest. Once Ruth hired a motor launch to take us to Beaufort, a town not so big as Wilmington but much more beautiful, truly Old South, as Ruth might have said. There they gave a party for Ruth, the famous folklorist, "who has done so much to make the beauty and virtues of the Old North State known to the world through its voice in song and story," as the Mayor said in a speech that seemed to go on for hours. Now I realized that Ruth was not a stranger anywhere she went, but was widely known, unlike my unimportant self, of whom no one seemed aware. This realization didn't spur jealousy—I could never have been jealous of Ruth—but perhaps the first faint glimmers of ambition, the desire to do something important in the world, as Ruth had done: like her, but myself.

I had to introduce Ruth to Garcie. I had seen enough of Ruth in action to know that she would like and appreciate Garcie, and I was sure that Garcie would find Ruth an interesting subject of contemplation. They hit it right off. Garcie told Ruth some wonderful tales for her book.

A point of continuing interest between them was the Sad Traveller himself. I, in my "angel infancy," as Ruth called it, had not realized that Garcie did not like the Traveller. "I takes his money, yes I do, but I would always watch over my little Jessie even without his money. He a religious man? Maybe some, but in a crazy sort of way, too full of hate for me who believe in a loving God."

"Has he ever," Ruth said, turning to me, "has he ever—mistreated you?"

"You mean slapped me around?"

"Well—yes—but—anything else, either?"

"Sometimes. The last time he was home—he was drunk, he always gets drunk when he comes home; he says he needs to relax—I was wearing shorts and he walked behind me and touched me on my backside, but then he acted like it was an accident. I jumped away, and I was burning with shame—"

"And shock."

"Shock—yes, ma'am."

"Has he done that before?"

"No, that was the first time he ever did that, but he's slapped me around a lot of times."

Ruth looked worried. Garcie said, "These things happen to young girls. Can't say how many uncles I had growing up would pat my fanny."

"But it's not right," Ruth said.

"Lots of things not right, young lady."

Ruth conceded the point with a nod. But I could see that she was thinking of doing something and I was sorry that I had spoken out. I didn't want Ruth and the Traveller to get into a fight over me. I was afraid he might stop me from seeing her. I had tried to play down my friendship with Ruth. Garcie said you always come to a fork in the road of life, and then another and another, and on till the end. I didn't want to come to the next fork in the road of my life—I loved where I was, despite the Traveller and anything else that might spoil a moment of it here and now. Ruth told us about a folk singer and guitarist who met the devil at the crossroads and became great and died young. She said he had traded most of his life for a moment of glory, and that that was a mistake. I didn't know what to think about that, but it did make me think, and I guess that was the point. Ruth told us how she became a folklorist. She told us that growing up during the Depression had probably led her into Folklore. She was born in Twenty-nine and, thanks to her older brothers, had heard songs by Woody Guthrie and Leadbelly and others who could be described as folksingers from her earliest days, and, upon entering college, had started as an English major, but, with an ever-increasing interest in folklore, had decided had to change over to anthropology, and, eventually, to the relatively new field of social anthropology—which amounted to becoming a folklorist.

"You mean you had to do all that anthro-business just to listen to people?" Garcie shook her head in consternation. "Well I must be one those anthro-people myself, cuz I have been listening to folks all my days. Finds, in fact, it's hard to get a word in edgewise, most folks telling about themselves until it's running out of my ears. Goodness sake!"

Ruth burst into laughter and couldn't stop until I thought she was going to have a heart attack. But finally she pulled herself together and said, "I'd love to have you make a speech to the anthropology department at Smith, Garcie, it would sure give them a shock." This time Garcie laughed.

By October, Ruth and Garcie and I had become a cozy threesome. We spent hours on end at Garcie's shack, cooking and eating together and Ruth and I listening to Garcie's legends of the Banks, of which she had an endless supply. Garcie did not like to be recorded, but Ruth kept her tales for posterity by making notes on yellow pads. Ruth later told me that listening to Garcie reminded her of blind Homer, and how the Greeks must have sat around the bards, for Ruth said that there were many Homers, and listened to their tales to the accompaniment of plinking lyres. "Garcie may be nearly blind," I said to Ruth, "but you, you're the Homer."

Ruth winked at me and said, "O.K., smarty pants, you got me there."

Garcie knew the inside of her small shack as a clam knows its shell. She knew her life and rolled breathlessly about in it without hesitation, telling one tale after another. She opened up to Ruth as she had never done with me, and so I heard much that I had never heard before. Ruth had a way of prompting people to talk, a subtle way of making them want to tell her things, and she was a good listener, as I had had occasion to observe, focusing her full attention on a speaker, letting him or her know with a word or two that she understood the import of what was being said. Her patience with a speaker was inexhaustible. Her eyes never drifted. It was an art, she said, that she had learned from acting in amateur productions when she was in college. "Don't be an actor, be a reactor," she often said.

I didn't know whether I wanted to be Ruth or just to have her to love. And Garcie could tell that I had found someone who almost replaced what I'd lost in a mother.

"You just crazy about that young woman, ain't you, baby? Well, she mighty nice indeed—mighty nice."

So we had a three-month interlude of pure happiness, or at least I did. But we were flying toward Garcie's fork in the road, or, more properly, it was flying toward us, like a great big black seventy-eight record with an album of booming cacophonous music on it. At its center it was turning at a hundred and fifty miles an hour, like a tornado, and coming at us at fifty at the rim. We had weathered storms before—twice only recently—but nothing like this, nothing like Hazel.

Late in the evening of Thursday, October 14th, 1954, Sheriff Walkup pounded on Garcie's door. "Bad storm coming," he said, stepping just inside, his yellow slicker glistening. "Better get prepared." His general store was powered by a generator, and he had a radio, which made him the unofficial town crier.

"Maybe you all should think about going to the mainland. There's a cutter down by the village picking up now. It'll be there for a few hours. Tom—that's my new man—he can take you out to it. It's up to you."

"We'll ride it out," Garcie said, "like we rode the last two out. But thank you for thinking about us."

"I hope you know what you're doing, Miss Perle," he said.

"We'll be fine," said Ruth, undaunted.

"Step out here and look at those clouds," said Walkup.

"You know I'm blind," said Garcie, but Ruth and I stepped out into a light, windy rain to look. Where had they come from, those dark, iridescent clouds, like malignant brains? They hadn't been there a few hours before, when we arrived at Garcie's.

"It'll be a good night for storytelling," said Ruth. Walkup shrugged and climbed back over the dunes like a goldfish out of water. He knew that the madly-rolling eye of the storm was looking at us, but he had given fair warning. I caught his voice—perhaps words of farewell—on the wind as he disappeared over the top of a dune.

Garcie said, "Ain't nothing but just another storm."

You must remember, David, things were very different a half century ago. Beach cottages didn't have radios, television sets, and newspapers were scarce—no front pages inked in red, green, and white hurricane winds swirling around a blank blue eye—so we sat on talking through Thursday night even as we could hear the wind about us dodging and ramming, missing and hitting, sputtering, cracking, and shockingly booming. We naively thought of it as good atmospherics for Garcie's tales of sunken ships and the ghosts of skull-and-crossbone pirates. Then she told us about the sunken church, inspired by the wind, I guess. It was cursed because its congregation was evil, and it would rise out at sea during evil times, as when a hurricane was on the way, and *that,* said Garcie, was the sound of banshee singing that forecast the storm. "At first," she said, "the storm is outside of you, and then you are inside of it, like old Jonah in the belly of the whale. But we've ridden out a few of them storms before and we do it again, my bet."

It was too noisy for us to sleep, so we sat on until dawn. Then a window broke and water gushed in. When the first wave receded, Ruth and I looked out and saw that everything from Whalehead down was under black or foaming white water, whirling, swirling all sorts of objects in its wake, then the windows shattered and the front door fell in and the debris laden tide filled the room. Except for one shriek, Garcie sat like stone in prayer, water already up to her hips, her body pummeled by broken objects. Ruth and I waded to the door and tried to stand it up, a hopeless task. Then Ruth grabbed me by the shoulder and pointed.

"Oh my God!" she cried. A shrimp boat, about forty feet long, was coming straight at us. The great dark hulk had been beached down by the village for repairs and had been lifted by the tide and now was drifting, without a mind to guide it, toward Whalehead. It was coming right at us when something, a twist of the wind, or a roof beam, something out there in the half-light, caught it and spun it like a top. Then it set off in another direction, its whole huge dark side passing in front of us like a wall that we ourselves were passing, but not quite passing: its bulk slammed into a corner of Garcie's shack and we found ourselves outside, the three of us, boards from the shack spinning around us, careening into us like little battering rams; and now we were up to our chests in whirling water, a maelstrom, and Ruth trying her best to keep Garcie from drowning. She swam and knocked away debris with one hand and pulled Garcie with the other, all the time screaming to me, "Are you all right? Are you all right?"

I went under and came up with a mouth full of salt water. I couldn't answer. I kept drifting away from the sound of her voice. Then I went under for what I thought was good, but a hand pulled me up by my hair and suddenly I was being pulled aboard a bouncing, bucking skiff. The hand laid me in the bottom like a caught fish, face down and vomiting brackish water. When I could look up, I saw Garcie's legs and Ruth's. I tried to get up on a cross bench and was nearly thrown out again, but pulled again by the hand and pressed down until I was sitting in the bottom of the skiff, my back against a man, his knees locking me in place. I had to see who he was and twisted my head to catch a glimpse of my savior—a glimpse of dark hair and pale face and I knew who it was.

Ahead, the dark and chopping Atlantic had seized everything but the second story of the General Store. We were headed for it. It was a good thing Sheriff Walkup wasn't pulling at the oars or we would never have made it, but, as Walkup had said, the new man had a new strong back. He was also a good sailor, for he found back-tows in the whirling water that helped him get us to the store. We climbed through a second story window and I fell to the floor.

I fell asleep and must have slept for several hours. I woke to dismal daylight and rain drumming on the tin roof. Mrs. Walkup, Ruth, and the new man were there, drinking coffee. Where was Garcie? "*Garcie*!" I screamed. "Where is Garcie?" They looked at me, then at Garcie. She lay over in a corner on the floor. "Garcie!" I threw myself on her, shaking her bulk, pulling at the rags that had been her dress. "Garcie, please! Wake up, oh, please! Don't leave me, Garcie—please!"

"Her heart failed," said Ruth, lifting me away and holding me. "I'm so sorry, baby."

I looked around blankly, incomprehendingly. I stared out the window where we had come in. "Where's the water?" I said, as though distracting myself from "where's Garcie?".

"It was a storm surge," Ruth said. "It's all gone back to the sea."

"It was a hellion named Hazel," Mrs. Walkup said. Then she shook her head, "And she stole my husband, little darling" she said to me, and she seemed as uncomprehending as I was, or she never would have called me that. I felt so sorry for her that I took her in my arms and, for a moment, we seemed to do a slow dance together. I wanted to cry for her, and I wanted to cry for Garcie, but I couldn't, I felt like my spirit had left me and all I could do was to wait for it to return. And that was it—the others were in varying degrees in the same condition. I could see that now as my own shock subsided.

Ruth handed me a cup of hot coffee and told me to go over and thank the new man, Tom Judas, for saving my life. "He saved all of us, except for poor Garcie," she said. "He came out in that little skiff just to find us and bring us to safety."

I looked at him. What an odd name, I thought. Judas betrayed Christ. It must be awful to have a name like that. I went over to him and said, "Thank you for saving my life, thank you for saving Ruth, and thank you for trying to save Garcie. It was wonderful what you did."

"The surge brought me right to your door," he said. He was sitting on the floor, still drenched. He didn't look the same. Of course he was exhausted, but what I mean is, that when we first saw him on the mail boat, he looked like he didn't belong; but now he was in work clothes and wet and disheveled as the rest of us and seemed to belong with us, seemed to belong to Fortune Island.

"You're a . . . hero," I said. "Ruth, isn't Mr. Judas a hero?"

"More than a hero, I'd say. A savior."

"Yes—Mr. Judas, you're a savior."

His face, not so pale as it had been when I first saw him, showed a pink tinge of embarrassment, as if, for a second, he'd grown younger, almost boyish. "I was just trying to help," he said, the color fading as fast as it had come, the soberness reasserting itself. "I'm very sorry about your friend. You must have loved her very much."

"Yes, I did. I didn't know how much till now." I looked over at poor Garcie. She looked like a big wet pile of laundry—my Garcie—but Ruth was making her vanish beneath a blanket. "You get used to people, sometimes, Mr. Judas, and you forget how much they mean to you."

He stood and reached out as if to wipe a tear from my eye, hesitated, and dropped his hand. "You're a wise young lady—*Jessie*." I remember just how he said that, with that little break and then my name. Now I understand it, but then, of course, it puzzled me, as everything did, it now seems, in those days.

They found Sheriff Walkup's body crushed beneath the shrimp boat, which had nosed itself into the dunes of Whalehead and stuck. After sending the bodies of Garcie and Sheriff Walkup to the mainland for embalming they were brought back to Fortune Island for burial, Garcie in the black cemetery and Sheriff Walkup in the white, as was done in those days. There had been no time to make repairs, no time and no equipment to pull the shrimp boat out of the dunes, no time to clean up the cemeteries. The picket fences were gone. The stones of the older graves had sat underwater like lagan, keeping their places, naming their dead; but the newer graves had lost their flat markers. No worry, though, the few inhabitants of Fortune Island knew where their dead were buried.

The new graves waiting for their coffins held no puzzle but that of death. First we stood by Garcie's grave, then by Sheriff Walkup's, then I went and said a few words to my mother. I knew where she lay, even if the world did not. What could I say to the ground? Hold her tight? The ground would do that without understanding what it did. I wondered if the Traveller ever came here. I doubted it. And where was he now? He had left the island before the hurricane. He was probably somewhere at this very moment, shouting at people that they should believe, that they were evil and that that was why this awful storm had come. And that horrible man was all that I had left in this world. No, not all. Ruth and Tom Judas had come to join me at my mother's grave, Ruth, my benefactor, Tom, my savior. They just stood by, and that was enough. Then Ruth put her arm around my shoulders, and she never let go, at least not until I was a grown woman and could take care of myself.

IV.

With Garcie gone, the Traveller had to make new arrangements for me. I suggested Ruth.

"That painted heathen you're spending so much time with?"

"She's my friend," I said, "and she's already looking after me."

"Ain't she some kind of Yankee? Ain't she a Jew?"

"She's from Boston. She's real nice. She's rich and she's almost famous. She was the guest of honor at a party in Beaufort. The mayor was there and made a speech about her."

"Fancy that!" He didn't really care who watched out for me, he just had to get his shot glass full of meanness into it. So we trudged over to Ruth's house, him sweating and puffing with a hangover, and me not skipping but wanting to. It turned out just the way I wanted. He offered Ruth money to keep an eye on me when he was away, which was most of the time—he only came home to get drunk out of sight of anyone who might know him for a preacher—and Ruth did exactly what I knew she would do; she rejected his offer of money but told him that it would be a joy to her to keep an eye on me, that he need have no fear that I wasn't being looked after properly and that he could go about his business without hindrance.

Later he said, "Who's that uppity little skirt think she's talking to?" But he was happy enough to have unburdened himself of me on her, and so didn't question the situation any further, except to ask me how much money I thought she had. I told him I had no idea, which was true because I had no idea about money at all at the time. And, as Garcie would've said, that was another fork in the road.

Ruth had already begun educating me. She said I had an excellent brain—truly excellent. She said, "You're like a sponge. I've never seen anything like it. You appear to have a photographic memory and almost total recall." The fact that my brain was what she called excellent was more exciting to Ruth than it was to me. By the end of our first year together, she had me up to geometry and algebra and we were heading toward what she called "trig." Ruth said that it was good for her to go over a lot of this material because she had forgotten it.

"You don't use it," she said, "and it tends to fade away." She unwrapped the textbook she had bought in Wilmington. There it was—Trigonometry! And she had me reading Shakespeare. We acted the plays together. I found that I could remember whole passages without trying. Ruth said that I was 'scary.' I loved *Romeo and Juliet*. "How am I ever going to meet a boy on this island?"

"Plenty of time for that," Ruth said.

Ruth had taught me all about sex, but I couldn't understand where the force of love came from, though I could feel it. I could feel my love for Ruth. Ruth said that biology connected the two. That was my favorite subject, biology. How mussels mated! Those little whelks in their tube—was love involved somehow? If so, I couldn't tell how. It was clear to me that Romeo and Juliet wanted more than sex from each other, but what more did they want? I was learning so much so fast, sometimes it fell into a jumble, triangles and rectangles and arthropods and whelks and Romeo and Juliet and men and women in a heap on the dunes at night.

The times I hated most were the times when the Traveller was home and Ruth had to go to New York or to Boston to see her publisher or editor or on some other business. I would sneak out when the Traveller had drunk himself into a stupor and go to Ruth's—I had a key to her cottage now—and sit among her things where I was happy and could feel her near. But once, when the Traveller was away, and she had to go to New York, she took me with her, and oh heavens was that exciting! And I had thought that New York was so far away but on the airplane it only took a few hours. Ruth let me sit near the window so that I could see the geometry below, and it was just like in the textbooks, everything so different from down there, squared away and clean—the green field, a square house. And we went to the Museum of Modern Art in New York and there were the pictures that Ruth had on her walls at home—the cubists, the impressionists, VanGogh and Gauguin and my favorites the Renoirs with the beautiful ladies who looked like angels. Why did Picasso make ladies so ugly? Why did one lady have two faces? And we went to Radio City Music Hall and saw the Rockettes—the kicking, all in a row. I had never thought of such a thing. I had begun to realize that there was so much in the world that I had never thought of on my lonely island. But now I began to realize how lonely I had been growing up on that desolate dune. How could I have not known? But New York was overwhelming, and I got sick, and I was sick all the way back to Fortune Island, and I didn't feel better until Ruth and I had tea together in her cottage, which felt like home to me.

Tom Judas had worked hard after the storm, saving what could be saved of the remaining dwellings on the Island. He continued to work for Mrs. Walkup and anyone else on the island who needed help. The church had been lifted off its footings, turned over, and sailed off into the sea like an empty ark, so a few of the fishermen along with Tom rebuilt it. He was much in demand. Carpenter, framer, plumber of wells, Tom could do it all. But most of that work was over. Now he was working on Ruth's cottage, fixing it up and adding a room. I thought of the new room as my own, but nobody said so: I just assumed. I spent a lot of time watching Tom work when I should have been studying. With his shirt off he looked very muscular. I liked to watch as his muscles stretched and contracted. He had become tan and even sunburned down his back. It seemed that he was always bending over something, hammering, sawing, or lifting. He glistened with sweat. I wanted him to talk to me.

"I have an excellent brain, you know," I said to him one day.

I couldn't understand why he burst out laughing.

"Do you think I'm funny?"

"No ma'am, I take you very seriously." But he kept on hammering at a plank. I couldn't help myself, but he made me think of biology. He could do so many things with those wonderful hands of his. He could play the guitar like nobody I ever heard before. Blues, he said; he said he played blues guitar, and sang songs that he wrote himself.

You send them out into this lonely life
They get a lonely woman for a wife
And then between them make
A hostage to fortune for the future's sake.

And you should have heard how he sang that one. He hit his guitar like a drum and then twanged it so a cat's fur would stand on end.

I learned he was an expert shot, too. Sometimes when the sea was quiet, when the surf was long and low, we could hear him out on the dunes popping Coke bottles. One day I went out there to join him and he showed me how to do it, how to load the clip in the pistol, pull the slide to get one in the chamber, how to aim and fire. I asked him if the gun was dangerous and he said No, not very, that it was just a little target pistol but don't go and point it at anyone because Yes, it could kill you if you were close up and got hit in the head by it. Always keep it pointed up, he said, away from people. I got pretty good at popping those bottles and he seemed to like having my company. Life had become exciting because I was learning so much about so many things; I, who had been alone with the whelklings for so long. Tom finally finished the work on Ruth's cottage. And it turned out that the extra room *was* for me. Ruth had it all gussied up with girl stuff, fluffy gingham curtains at the window, a bed with a thick patchwork quilt, some drawings I had made tacked up on the walls. I felt like a little rich girl, a princess.

And one day I heard Tom out there on the dunes popping those bottles and I went out to find him. He was leaning against a rock, his shirt off, a cigarette dangling from his mouth, taking pot shots at the bottles. He had told me that target shooting was his form of meditation, that he actually didn't think about the shooting but thought about other things when he practiced. "It's just something to do while I do my thinking," he had said. I often wondered what he was thinking about, but there was something about the way he told me that that indicated privacy, so I didn't ask. I thought that he did a lot of thinking though.

This time I went ahead and asked him.

"About the past, mostly," he said. "Sometimes about the future. Sometimes I think about you."

"Me? What do you think about me?"

"What a wonderful young girl you are."

That's what I was always thinking about him—I mean, what a wonderful man he was. I had to do something. I had to do something to show him how I felt. I was wearing a tissue-thin blouse Ruth had bought me in Wilmington. I knew if I got it wet, it would show that I wasn't a little girl anymore. I ran into the sea and came back to him and stood there, heaving my chest. He could see now that I was a woman, no doubt about it. But instead of reacting as I had hoped, he put his shirt over my shoulders and closed it in front and said, "I want you to come back to my shack with me. I have something to show you."

I didn't know what he had in mind, and, at first, it kind of scared me. But I could see sadness in his eyes, and I somehow realized that he was safe to be with. What had made me forget that for a moment? Myself, I guess. What I had been thinking about had caused me to worry, not anything he was doing. Anyway, when he led off, I followed and caught up and walked along beside him to the shack. It was a good long hot walk and we didn't talk. I had never been in his shack before. It was small, cramped, dark, full of stuff, a real mess, the kind men make when they don't care, when there are no women about.

He put the pistol in a drawer, saying he would clean it later. "But this is what I wanted to show you." He handed me a gold-framed photograph, one of those tinted pictures, of a woman and a little girl of about two or three.

"Is this your wife, Tom?"

"Yes, that's my wife. My ex-wife. She married someone else, but she's dead now."

"And the little girl is. . . the little girl . . ." I looked and looked and then I realized what I was looking at. The woman's hair was bunched in a snood, but I could see now that it was red hair, and the little girl had red hair too. I knew who it was before he said it.

"The baby is you, Jessie."

"And that's my mother. But how— Then you're—"

I stood there staring at him. I couldn't believe it.

"I'm your . . . dad, Jess. I thought . . . it was time for me to tell you."

"But my daddy has gray hair, everybody knows that. You can't be him!"

"I dyed it. I didn't want anyone here to recognize me. After all, I've been away a long long time." He sat at the table, not taking his eyes off me.

I threw my arms around his neck. "I knew it was you! Oh, I knew it was you!" A throb came up from my chest and I began to cry. Tom put his arms around me and patted my back. "Easy. Easy." he whispered.

"I knew it was you all the time," I said, sitting down across from him, "but I was afraid I might be wrong so I never said. I was too scared to think it. But there was something . . . Do you know how I mean, I mean—"

"I understand."

"But it's all coming true. It's coming true. Ruth—and now you!"

"Give me your hand, and let me explain," he said, reaching across the table, and I saw that he had tears in his blue eyes too. Tears for me? The tin roof of the shack began to drum with rain, as if in sympathy with us, and it became like a hollow, but steady rhythm above the noise of pounding water, almost echoing in the small enclosure, and I felt dizzy as I listened to him.

"I was young and foolish and believed I had to do something so that you and your mother wouldn't be dirt poor, and I committed a desperate and foolish act, an act that I have suffered for and have never stopped regretting, that I regret most perhaps at this very moment, when I have to tell you about it. Jessie, I'm ashamed and I want you to know that. And that stupid, youthful misdeed has kept me away from you all these years. It did the exact opposite of what I had hoped it would do. But I want you to know that I have never forgiven myself for it, for doing something that caused you to be without me during all those years when you needed me most." The rain came in bullets aimed at the roof. I was afraid the tin would puncture and we would die just at this moment, when I knew him, had him, could reach out and touch him.

"Your mother came to see me behind the Wall. She said that she had met someone who would take care of her. She wanted me to give her a divorce and sign the house over to her. I felt that it was the least that I could do. I thought you both needed that."

The roar of the rain made his voice seem far away, as if he were speaking to me on the telephone. "Later, I heard that your mom had died. All I could do then was to hope that your step-father, a man of God, I'd heard, would be good to you, love you as I did. I promised myself that as soon as I was freed, I'd come back here and see for myself how you were doing. If you were doing well, I would leave you alone, not interfere with your life, in any way. That's why I didn't want you to know who I was. I didn't want to be known. I just wanted to see. I had to see."

The drumming on the roof was beginning to soften, a cat's purr.

"I want to live with you," I said. My ears heard my creaky voice.

"I can't just take you away from Cogburn. Not just now. There are legal problems."

"Don't you want me?"

"I want nothing more in the world than that we be together, girl. I love you with all my heart."

A thought jumped in at me, sudden as the rain had been. "I've got to tell Ruth. She'll be so . . . so *astounded!*"

"Ruth already knows, Jessie."

"She already knows?"

"I've told her the whole story."

"You told Ruth before you told me?"

"I wanted to know what she thought. Ruth and I have become pretty close, you know."

"Close? What does that mean? Close? Are you in love with her?"

"At this point, let's just say that we're friends."

"I know you're friends, but what kind of friends?"

I had green eyes—*green.* I couldn't help myself. Something had happened. The water was dropping outside. The shower was passing over. "I have to go and see Ruth," I said.

"But wait now—"

"No, I have to go and see Ruth." I'll come back, I said to myself, I'll come back.

"Wait, Jessie, I'll go with you."

"No! I want to see Ruth alone. I'll come back after I talk to Ruth. Wait for me. Don't come over. Don't go away. Stay right here."

"I'll clean the gun," he said, lighting a cigarette. The match flared up, etching his troubled face, his eyes dark hollows under the glinting strips of his corrugated brow. He was exercising a tortuous calculation, but plainly could come to no conclusion.

"Hurry back," he called after me.

"Yes, I'll come back," I said, plunging out the door. Most days it was water but today tiny diamonds dropped from the sky, glittering at every facet. How could the rain be mere water on a day like today? How could anything be what it tried to be? The wet sand jumped under my feet. It was alive! I made it dance but I hurt it too. The atoms in my body were flying apart and crashing together. Something was going to heal, or break. It is just when everything is perfect that it explodes, for nature cannot bear perfection. Only an acceptable adaptation. If today was the happiest day of my life, I was also aware of the sun sinking out at sea. Ecstasy and terror. I punched the air and grabbed it as I ran toward Ruth's cottage. He had told Ruth before he had told me. Something was wrong with that. I wanted them both, I wanted them together, but I didn't want them without me. He should have explained everything to the two of us at once, for the three of us to share. But I knew what it was. I knew how they thought that they knew better. I had begun to see the treachery in grown-up thought, the kindly lies that only confused.

Ruth was working at the typewriter when I burst in. She stood up, seeing my confusion, my tear-stained eyes. For Ruth, I held no mystery. She read me as if what I thought ran across my forehead like the sign in Times Square.

"He's told you, hasn't he?"

"Yes. But he told you first. Why?"

"He wasn't sure how you'd take it. I told him that I thought you'd be fine. Was I wrong?"

"Oh Ruth!" I threw myself against her and she pulled me over to the couch where we sat together while I cried. It was all too much for me.

After a time, she said: "Were you angry because he told me first?"

"A little, I guess. Just a little hurt."

"I know, baby," she said. "It's an awful lot to take in, isn't it? All of a sudden you have a real father. But you suspected, didn't you?"

"I did. I don't know how but I did."

"I think you knew because you could tell that he loved you. You got it a little mixed up, though, maybe, didn't you?"

"I guess." I snuggled in her arms.

"Well, I have some more news for you, too," she said at last. "This is also pretty exciting. I got your high school GED test and your Sanford Binet back. I've brought you well beyond high school level and it looks like you're smarter than I am by a good twenty points. You're a gifted girl, Jessie. And you're going to have to go to school."

I jumped up from the couch. "What do you mean? Away?"

"I can send you to a very fine private school."

"But Tom—my *Dad*—I've just got him. He's here. I don't want to go away now."

"He thinks that if I'm willing to pay for your schooling, you should go. We've talked about it a good bit."

Now this scared me. "What school? Where?" I began to cry again, and Ruth pulled me back into her arms.

"I don't want to leave you, Ruth. I don't want to leave him."

I believed Ruth could do anything she wanted to. Hadn't she been able to get the academic tests that she told me were rarely allowed outside of institutional grounds? Now I was afraid she wanted to send me away. I reached down into my desperation and came up with a counter argument. I sat up straight, facing her. "You can't make me go anywhere, you're not my mother. Are you and Tom—*my* dad—trying to get rid of me?"

"Sweetheart, why would we do that? We love you."

"So you can be alone together? Are you in love? Do you want to get rid of me? Am I in the way?"

I looked at her through my tears and saw that I had hurt her. I threw my arms around her neck. "Oh, I love you so much, Ruth. Please don't send me away."

"Let's just take our time, baby, and see what happens," she said. And that was it. A few days passed, then a few weeks, and there was no more talk of sending me away. I spent the mornings studying while Ruth worked on her book. Tom had taken over Sheriff Walkup's duties at the general store and usually joined us at dinnertime.

Ruth and Tom planned to take me into Wilmington the day before my fifteenth birthday, to celebrate. We had two rooms at the best hotel in town, the Cape Fear. The plan was for Ruth to take me shopping, and to outfit me like a young lady,

"Like a debutante," Ruth said. She was so wealthy she made me feel like an heiress, just being with her. When she told Tom we were going shopping, he decided to tag along.

"I'd like to bear witness to the transformation," he said. And we set out in a gay mood. Being with Tom and Ruth was such fun, I had decided to forgive their occasional hand-holding, the looks that passed between them, which I could never quite understand. That day, at least, they were both focused on me. I had them both in my power, the power of my green eyes and red hair, even the power of my light tan freckles, which I urged to dazzle.

Those silly freckles have all faded away over the years, or have become an occasional brown mole here and there. Years of work in the sun have turned my fair, usually sun-burnt skin brown and creased, all the red has fallen out of my hair, and, as a result of chemo-therapy, much of my hair has been lost. But that day I shined, or so everyone said. The saleslady at Efird's said that I was beautiful.

"Those green eyes. . . she has got to wear mint-green. Let's try this," and she took down a floaty voile dress of mint-green, and, holding it up to my shoulders, said, "and I think white shoes and a white purse." Ruth told me to go into the dressing room and try it on.

I think that was the first time I had ever seen myself from all sides and all the way around in back. Down to my underwear, I studied myself in the mirrors. Tall and thin I was, but I had nice long curves, more of a rump than I had realized, and in profile my breasts looked positively brazen in a new bra. My nose turned up more than I thought it did, but it was kind of cute, I thought, too. The saleslady handed me in a pair of white, open-toed pumps with heels at least two inches high. Of course I'd never owned a pair of high-heeled shoes before. I had to hobble, but I made my entrance. The first eyes I caught were Tom's. A father's eyes say, Look at my little girl. My emotions were turning in my stomach, this way and that, like snakes. I was happy and grateful and hurt all at once. Ruth said, "Oh, my dear, you look spellbinding." That was what she said, "spellbinding." The saleslady said, "She's fit for a grand party." Then I had a vanity attack, but with deep breathing, trying not to show what I was doing, my breasts heaving like that, I got myself back down to the almost right place, to where, I hoped, nothing was showing. "Not too bad, do you think?" I said, my ankles wobbling.

"Now all you need is a bouquet of flowers," said Tom. "I'll get you one before the day is over."

"It must be a special occasion," said the saleslady.

"Her birthday," said Ruth. "Tomorrow she'll be fifteen."

"Fifteen," Tom repeated in a wondering way.

"Fifteen, is it?" said the saleslady. "My compliments," she said to Ruth, "you look too impossibly young to have a fifteen year old. But looking at the two of you, I can see where she gets her looks. But where did the red hair come from?"

"Oh, she's not my daughter," Ruth said.

"Oh, I see," said the saleslady, taken aback. I noticed her curiosity. I suppose we did seem an odd threesome, but, momentarily at least, we were a very happy threesome.

Outside, Ruth told Tom that she was taking me to have a manicure and a pedicure and a permanent wave, so he might as well busy himself elsewhere. He said he would go and get the flowers and a few other things and meet us back at the hotel. I was so excited that I thought I actually saw some of my freckles jump off my arms. Well, I was seeing spots before my eyes, but my wobbling ankles really hurt. It was a hot day and I think they were beginning to swell. Or had my new nylons bunched? I felt so tall, wobbling along beside Ruth in my new heels. She was five six or seven and I swear I was looking down at her.

The Cape Fear Hotel had one of the best restaurants in Wilmington, or so Ruth said. I was proud of my newly-shaped and pink painted fingernails and kept holding them in view of the youngish waiter to see if I could detect a reaction, but I guess he had seen a lot of nails on a lot of girls because he was all polite business. He switched from a soft cultured southern accent to French—especially when he spoke directly to Ruth, who answered him in French, some of which I could understand—if only they had slowed down—coq au vin—and back to "Will the gentleman approve the wine?" Tom knew what to do, which surprised me. He took a sip and said, "Fine" and the waiter poured. Tom had given me flowers to wear and for a birthday present a silver necklace with a locket containing a picture of himself and a picture of Ruth.

"Oh, I just love it," I told him, thinking right away that I might replace Ruth's picture with my own. That made me feel so guilty, I felt like crying. I took Ruth's hand and said,

"I love you, Ruth." Her big dark eyes grew glassy and she turned quickly to say something to Tom. He looked kind of soppy too. Gosh, we were all just looking so sad, I had to do something. "I love all my gifts," I said. "Thank you. Thank you both so much."

"But tomorrow's the real party," Tom said, brightening.

"We're going to show you the town," Ruth said. "There's a fair on the outskirts. Would you like to go to the fair?"

"We'll have a picture taken of the three of us," Tom said, "to mark the occasion." I was so happy that night. I never wanted to leave them, but I couldn't help feeling that somehow Ruth was stealing my dad from me, or was it that Tom was stealing Ruth from me?

Ruth and I had a room to ourselves and Tom had a room down the hall. In 1957, and especially in a good hotel in the south, hanky-panky was frowned on, at least openly. Certainly there were hotels where things went on, but not in the Cape Fear. The unnoticed and all-seeing bellhops kept the nightclerks posted. In such a hotel, house detectives were not uncommon. If progress is movement in a desirable direction, I am dumb to say where we have got to in the year 2000. If I outlast this cancer by a few more years, I'll be content, but I have little desire to see what's coming much ahead. Biology has been my field and my life, but I'm concerned as to where it is going.

Nevertheless, you must have agriculture before you can have high culture and you must have biology before you can have love, so I reach for faith out of thin air, like Shakespeare's poet, or like his madman. But that night Ruth and I climbed into the softest bed I had ever—ever what? It was beyond my dreams. It was a cloud in the heaven I even then doubted, yet that bed made me believe in it. At first, I was like the girl with visions of sugar plums dancing in her head; but I awoke from a sweet, forgotten dream of warmth to find the warmth and then the source of the warmth missing.

"Ruth?" I got up and went to look in the bathroom. No Ruth. I felt a bit frightened. Something must be wrong. I checked the clock, thinking that I'd overslept, but it was just one o'clock in the morning. She must have gone to Tom's room. But what for? What had happened? I put my raincoat over my pajamas and stepped out into the carpeted, ornate hall. One could see through the transoms, light or no light in the rooms. A few were lighted. There was a long dark wall table with a vase of flowers and a straight chair at each end, backs to the wall. Soft night lights—everything white and gold. The thick gold carpet tickled my feet. I came to Tom's door, a few doors down from ours, and I heard voices over the transom, which glowed with soft light. I listened but could not make out what was being said. All I could hear was groans, or maybe moans. Was Tom hurt? I started to knock, but something warned me not to, an instinct, a primitive sense, warning of privacy, secrecy. If they had needed me, they would have awakened me, I reasoned. But what was it? I tried to see through the keyhole, but the key must have been in the lock and I could see nothing but shadow and a blurry wire of light, indicating somehow taboo, privacy, secrecy, saying that what was happening inside was not for me to know. But the moans and groans were growing in intensity, and I was afraid.

I went back down the hall and got one of the straight chairs and brought it back to the door and stood up on it and could just see over the top of the door, through the open transom. Ruth and Tom were naked on the bed, Ruth straddling him and rocking and him heaving, and I felt faint. Woozy. But above all, I didn't want them to know I was there. I got down and took the chair and put it back in its place and went to my room, trying to catch my breath. I threw up my dinner in the toilet, flushed it, closed the lid, and sat there, trying to get things in order. They are lovers! Or was it just biology? Did they have to do this on my birthday? My beloved ones were like animals! I had dreamed of love, but not like that, not like what I'd seen. My heart was not right, and the snakes in my stomach uncoiled and came up through my windpipe and I screamed. I whirled around the bathroom, smashing things. Oh, had anybody heard? I listened. Nothing. I felt trapped. I had to get out into the street, into the cool night air. I dressed myself in my new clothes, heels and all. I smeared lipstick on, and pushed my new permanent into place, took the key, and found the elevator. The doors slid open.

"Down?" said the bellhop, holding the handcrank, and down and out I went, one thought in my mind: "I hate them! I hate them!"

Their naked image was all I could see. I felt like a green-eyed monster. Not wanted, shut out! I wanted to kill them. No, I didn't! I loved them. I hobbled along in my high heels and my Sunday dress feeling like a freak of some kind. What was I doing? Where was I going? Where could I go? Well, the answer to that one came quickly enough. I hadn't gone a block before a car pulled up alongside me. There were two sailors in it. "Where you going, baby?"

"Where are you two going?"

"Just cruising. Want to cruise?"

I got in the back seat. The sailor who was driving said, "Back at base, they call me Devil and him Angel. What do we call you?"

"It's my birthday," I said. I don't know why I said it, it just popped out.

"Okay, we'll call you birthday girl, okay?" Devil had done all the talking so far. Angel sat on the passenger side and looked, I thought, kind of forlorn.

"Here," said Devil, "take a snort of this," and he handed me back a bottle of whiskey in a brown paper bag. "It's a happy birthday drink."

"You don't look old enough to drink," said Angel.

"She looks plenty old to me," said Devil.

Devil seemed older than Angel, who seemed closer to my age. If people really did call them Devil and Angel I could see why. Devil was dark and tough-looking and sounded like a yankee, and Angel was blond and had a sweet face, really angelic, as I could see when he turned to talk. "Don't drink so much of that," Angel said.

The whiskey was like fire and my first impulse was to spit it out, but I gripped myself and swallowed, feeling it boil down into my guts.

"Good, eh?" said Devil. "Happy birthday to you!"

"Oh," I said, pulling the bottle away, "it's like fire."

"Oh, that stuff ain't nothin'," said Devil. "I'm going to drive us out to a place I know where they got a still and a place to drink white lightning—and you can dance there too. Like to dance, Birthday Girl?"

"Listen," said Angel, "how old are you?"

"Eighteen," I lied.

"Are you sure, because you don't look eighteen. I got an eighteen year old sister and she looks a lot older 'an you."

"What you talking about?" said Devil. "You saw how tall she is!"

"But look at her face."

"Looks pretty good to me."

Something like that—because I couldn't tell for certain what they were saying. I didn't realize it, but I was getting drunk, another entirely new experience for me.

"Go ahead," Devil would say, "have another drink," and I heeded his encouragement, ultimately getting down at least half a pint of whiskey. And oh, the warmth, the sweet ease of it! For the time-being the ugly image of Tom and Ruth faded from view, the beautiful, sweet face of Angel turned to me and kept on turning. Then I saw that we were out in the woods and I began to get scared. "You better let me out," I said.

"Let her out," Angel said. "Let us both out. I don't want to go to any still, I don't even drink."

"Aw, come on," said Devil.

"No, let us out!"

"Well, shee-it!" Devil slowed the car and pulled over. "Go ahead, but you're gonna miss one hell of a time." We got out—Angel had to steady me—and Devil roared off honking his horn.

There we stood, out on this narrow country road with a partial roof of rainy-sounding leaves coming from both sides and almost meeting above us in the middle, soft moonlight floating down through the clouds. The soft hoot of an owl made it spooky.

"How far are we from town?" I asked.

"Not far," said Angel, "if we don't get lost."

"Do you know the way?"

"I think so. Come on."

My ankles hurt. I slipped off my shoes and walked in my stockinged feet. To make conversation, I asked about Devil. "Is your friend really bad?"

"Oh, you mean that Devil stuff. His name is Devlin, so they started calling him Devil. He tries to be a tough guy, because he's from Boston."

"I know somebody from Boston. She's my best friend in fact."

"Devlin's going to get himself in trouble with his drinking, though. That's something we all should be careful of, that drinking. I've known it to bring ruin on people, members of my own family, even. I don't drink none at all. Don't smoke, neither."

"Is that why they call you Angel?"

"My name's Johnny Engels—that's where that comes from. What's yours—your name?"

"Jessie McQueen."

"That's a nice name. What's got you so ripped up to-night, miss? You look like you been to a party—did you have a fight with somebody or did somebody walk out on you or did you walk out on somebody else? We saw you come storming out of the Cape Fear Hotel. Shucks, I couldn't afford to check in there even for one night. Heck, a half a night! And you in that beautiful dress—what hap-pened?"

The trees seemed to be moving backwards, with all their shadows and moon-patches, receding behind us. I felt drunk, but clearing up a bit, holding my own, I thought. What makes that night so vivid is that it was the last night, the tail end of my happiness, which already seemed like a long-ago dream.

"Something happened that made me hate the two people that I loved best in the world, that's what happened. Let's stop for a minute, my ankles hurt." I sat down by the side of the road, and leaned against a tree. "Look at them, they're all swollen."

"Sure looks like."

"How old are you, Angel?"

"Eighteen."

"Angel, would you do me a favor?"

"Sure. What?"

"Kiss me."

He made a little tight smile, squinted his eyes, and tilted his head. It was a questioning, good-humored look. "What? Just like that?"

"Like this," I said, and, grabbing his ears in my hands, I kissed him hard on the mouth and held on until he shook me off. "What's the matter?"

I thought any boy would respond with passion, but not Angel.

"Now that's what I mean about the alcohol," he said. "We're going to get ourselves into all kinds of trouble."

"I'm a virgin," I said. "Don't you want me?"

"Oh my, yes, course I do. But you don't really want to do this out here like this. It's because you've been drinking. And let me tell you something. There's nothing wrong with being a virgin. Why, every man wants his bride to be a virgin, and he should be a virgin too, so that they know no other forever always until death do them part."

"Angel, you're a virgin, too, is that it?"

"Keeping myself for the future Mrs. Engels, miss. And I got me sisters and I hope they are keeping themselves too. Expect they are."

"Come on," I said, "walk me back to the hotel."

"But now which way do we go?" Angel said to himself. "See up yonder—there's a fork there."

"There's more glow over left," I said.

"That's probably the town."

Do I imagine all this? Did this interlude develop in my imagination over the near half century since whatever happened on that road that night happened? I remember it almost word for word as if it had happened yesterday, but did I pose the words, did I develop the events? I can't help myself. This is what I remember, and this: that I wanted him so badly that my body ached; that I tried to think of a way to get him to come to my room; that I tried this: "If I'm left alone, I might kill myself. I mean it. I have nothing to live for anymore. I have been . . . betrayed."

"Don't say that, miss." The poor boy looked worried. "Now look, miss Jessie, I can't get into that hotel. There's a desk clerk, for sure, watches everbody comes and goes."

"I could go in first, and you come in and rent a room and then come to my room and sit with me."

"A room in a place like that would cost me my pay, and I don't have much of that left anyway."

"I have money." I pushed twenty-five dollars on him, money which Ruth had given me for anything I wanted—well, I wanted Angel.

"No, miss, I can't take your money."

"Not even to save my life?"

He puzzled.

"Suppose you read in the papers tomorrow that a young girl jumped from the window of the Cape Fear Hotel, then you'll be sorry that you didn't take the money and save her, won't you?"

"Well—I suppose—"

I won; he took the money.

Tangled laundry, my emotions, wet and steamy, and I couldn't pull a shirt from a towel. Tom and Ruth had behaved like animals, and I hated them for it, but I wanted to do the same thing with Angel, in part to get even with Tom and Ruth, in part because Angel was just about the first boy I had ever been with in any old way at all. He was the first boy I had ever kissed. That must seem impossible to some, but I am the only Jessie, wild girl of Fortune Island, and I know it to be true. I wanted to be under that boy and over Tom and Ruth, I wanted to outdo them at their own dirty game and I wanted to know how it felt to be made love to—what biology felt like—and maybe, for a brief instant, I was really in love.

I passed the door of Tom's room, where Ruth and Tom must lay now in an exhausted doze, and went to my room and set what I thought would be the perfect trap. I stripped down to my skin and waited for Angel.

Soon enough came a quiet knock. I opened the door, staying behind it, and let him in. Then, as he stood trying to adjust to the one endtable light I had left on, I slammed the door and slid a chair under the knob. When Angel turned and saw me naked, he stepped back like he'd been shot. He even reached for his heart, as if to be certain that it was there and beating, or maybe to stop it from beating so wildly, to hold it still. I threw myself at him and he fell backwards onto the rumpled bed.

"Oh my Lord," he said, "miss, what are you doing?" I didn't know exactly—several things at once, I'd say now. But before anything could be sorted out, Ruth was at the door, trying to get in, shaking the knob, inching the door open. Angel found his way out from under me and ran to the door, as if for help.

Then I heard Ruth, "Jessie! Why is this door jammed?" And Angel, "I'll get it open, ma'am." And Ruth again, "Who is that? Open this door! Jessie!" And Angel, "I didn't do anything, honest, as God is my witness." And me, "You jerk!"

Then Tom's voice, "Open this door, dammit!"

"Yes, sir. But the harder you push the harder it is for me to open it."

"Who in hell are you?"

"Nobody, sir—just a sailor."

"What are you doing in there?" That was Ruth.

The door flew open. Tom stepped in, saw me, and backed out. Ruth replaced him. "Get your clothes on, young lady."

"That girl is under age," Tom shouted from the hall. "If you've laid a hand on her—"

"God in heaven may strike me dead, sir, if I ever—"

"Or I'll strike you dead," said Tom.

Ruth pushed Angel out into the hall. "Tom, take this boy down to your room and talk to him."

Tom grabbed the young sailor by the arm. "Come on, boy."

"Did he lay a hand on you?"

"He didn't have a chance. But I wanted him to."

"You what?"

"Like you and Tom."

"Tom and I? I just went down the hall to see—"

"I saw you—through the transom."

"Oh, honey, no!"

"You're going to send me away to school so you can have him for yourself!"

"Here, put something on. You don't understand."

"All I need to know, you bitch!"

And Ruth knocked me across the bed with a round-house right. "Oh, my God," she said—"I'm sorry, baby."

"I hate you! I hate Tom! I don't know which one of you I hate the most. I hate you both!"

After due explanation, I suppose, Angel was set free to pursue his quest for a virginal bride. I finally fell into a troubled sleep, awakening several times to find Ruth, pillow-propped, holding me in her arms. Finally I went into a deeper sleep that lasted until noon. When I woke, I realized that I was truly fifteen. Today was my birthday. Of course the big day we, or Tom and Ruth, had planned was not to be. They had been busy arranging for a different kind of day while I slept. Ruth had hired a fisherman who owned a cabin cruiser, really not much more than a motor launch, to take us back to Fortune Island. She'd found Mr. Masefield on the Wilmington docks, advised by others that he was a man who liked the isolation of the island and was always pleased to have an excuse to cross Pamlico and put up on the island for a day or two of fishing.

Tom and Ruth looked sad, maybe ashamed, and I felt horrible, ugly and mean. Ruth had bought me a birthday cake and she held it in her lap in the launch like a precious artifact. She stared at its box, not looking up for the whole time it took to get to the tail-end of the island. Tom talked to Mr. Masefield and smoked cigarette after cigarette. I had never seen him chain-smoke before. Now I can only imagine what he was thinking; then I couldn't imagine at all. Whatever I thought he was thinking was unquestionably wrong, for I was seeing all this through the eyes of someone deliberately misled, albeit for my own good, as others understood that good.

Later, when Ruth thought I was mature enough to understand, she tried to explain to me that Tom, already so guilty, now felt worse than ever, felt that he had let me down in the worse way possible. This was the man to whom I owed my very life.

He had saved me from drowning during the hurricane; had came out to the most isolated area of the island at the height of the surge in that little skiff to save all of us, Ruth, Garcie, and myself, and then had actually pulled me from the flood; had appeared, like a guardian angel, out of nowhere. I owed him my life. Why couldn't I simply accept the fact that he and Ruth were in love, that they saw us as a family, that neither of them would have excluded me for any imaginable reason—that they loved me, Tom in his way and Ruth in hers. But I sat there, with one isolation inside another like a Chinese box of isolations, with sullen pride immingled with fear and watched the waves from the wakes of boats out of sight follow one another, this way and that, apparently pointlessly, and finally the darkness in me spread to the sky and it began to rain and Pamlico Sound roughened and frothed.

Ruth tried again at her cottage. She made coffee and put candles on the cake and lit them and brought it to the table singing "Happy Birthday," but I would have none of it.

"Betrayers!" I cried, melodramatically. "You both want to get rid of me so that you can have each other without being bothered with me." It was the first time I had spoken since Wilmington and I could see that my words came as a great disappointment. Tom shook his head.

"If you only knew," he said.

"You two want to send me away. That's what it is."

"No, no, no, no," Tom said, shaking his head.

"What Tom is trying to say is—"

"You just want to be through with me and have him to yourself."

"Baby, Tom and I love each other."

"Then why did you stop me with Angel? Don't you want me to ever be in love?"

"Because you're too young," said Tom.

"You could ruin your life," said Ruth. "You have a brighter future than you can imagine, I promise you."

"Where were either one of you when I was alone on this damned island? You have no right to try to run my life now."

"Come on," said Ruth, "blow out your candles. Let's try to have a little party together."

"Here's how I'll blow them out," I said, opening the door to the wind and rain. They flickered, and blew out. Ruth said there was no use in my behaving like a brat. She said she was tired and had to get some rest. She tried to kiss me but I moved aside. I went in my room and played possum. Pretty soon I heard Ruth and Tom go in Ruth's bedroom and close the door. I couldn't control my emotions; I felt strange, as if I were watching myself from somewhere up in the night sky.

I ran all the way to what should have been my house but which was now the Traveller's. I was still wearing my mint-green Sunday dress—but it was wet and wrinkled now—and my hair was all in wet ringlets. I had forgotten to wipe the lipstick from my mouth. I burst in the door.

The Traveller sat with bottle at elbow. He looked up from his Bible and said, "Painted woman! I've been back since yesterday. I suppose you were out somewhere with that Jew bitch. Do you know that she paid me two-thousand dollars for you?"

I sat down across from him, panting, trying to catch my breath. "What do you mean?"

"She bought my signature. I signed you away to her in case of my death. Guardianship, it's called."

"Ruth paid you two-thousand dollars for me?"

"What I said."

"She must love me," I said, "at least two-thousand dollar's worth."

"Same as buying a slave, ain't it? Nobody loves a slave."

"She'd never think of me as a slave, I know that."

He took a long drink. "Well, what do you think, think I don't love you?"

"You! You don't love anything or anyone."

"I love God."

"You love being God."

"Well—" he lurched up. "Look at you," he said. "Like a grownup woman, with that paint on your face and that dress—where'd you get that? Never mind, I know. You look just like your red-headed mother, the whore of Wilmington. He leaned with both hands on the table and moved hand over hand around it toward me. I jumped up and moved away. "Come here," he said. "Don't run away. Give me a kiss. A father has a right to kiss his daughter, doesn't he?"

"You're not my father! I have a real father!"

"No, I'm not and yes, you do, and he's a criminal in the Central Prison in Raleigh. Or maybe he's dead. I don't keep up with such people. Or maybe he's done out. Maybe he's been out."

"My father's right here on Fortune Island."

"Sure he is—me—I'm here!"

I was afraid he was going to grab at me, as he had often done of late. I kept moving away from him but then I saw that he had me trapped. He was between me and the door. "Now you leave me alone," I said. But he got a drunken leer on his face and moved toward me. I was being backed to the attic door. There was no place to go but up. I ran up the stairs and looked for something in the dark to hit him with if he came up after me. But he was there already, on the top step. I kicked at him, to keep him from coming up, but he fended off my kicks and kept on coming toward me, looming in the light from below. Then he swung out to grab me or to hit me and I caught the blow on my cheek and fell to floor and he was on top of me, pulling at my dress. One arm was pinned beneath me and with the other I flailed his face, neck, shoulders over and over and over and over and oh—oh God!

Finally, he left me there, broken open, used up. I heard him half fall down the stairs to the main room, heard the bottle crash. In a little while I heard the door slam, then slam again and again, wind-caught. I lay there in the dark and listened to the door slam for what seemed hours. He had ripped my beautiful Sunday dress up the front. It didn't matter. It was just a rag now. Blood has a metallic smell. Biology was not always beautiful, a miracle.

Where was love? Why hadn't it been Angel? I lay there in the dark and reached out on the floor around me, looking for something. What was I looking for? My locket! I felt for my locket and it was there. Oh Ruth. Tom. This was my birthday. I was grown now, wasn't I? The Traveller had his own little skiff and I wondered if he had gone off to the mainland in it, had just decided to leave me here in the attic by myself with nothing but damp books, musty boxes. I reached out and felt around for my father's books that had started me reading so long ago. I just lay there, feeling how worthless I was, and for the first time I could guess at my mother's life with the Traveller, how he must have made her feel, weak sinner that she was. No wonder she threw herself into the sea. I should go down to the shore and throw myself in, for I'm nothing now, less than nothing. I can't offer myself to anyone ever again. There will never be love of that kind in me for anyone after this. In and out I went, sleeping, thinking, sleeping, the door downstairs banging, until a candle-glow of light began to shape and frame the small window at the back end of the attic, a patch of tarnished silver.

Somebody got up and left me there. I had been split in two. I stayed where I was, looking up at the dark insides of the attic, and the other went to the landing. Which was I? The one at the landing left the other on the floor in the attic and descended, going where? Out! Away! But not to Ruth's, not to Tom's. They must never see me again. I was leaving Jessie McQueen in the attic with her books, her father's books, her grandmother's books. I was someone else, a new and different creature.

Him! He lay at the bottom of the stairs, his right leg twisted up under him, as in a wild dance step. I saw that the door was banging still, taken by the wind. He hadn't left; he had been here all night, sleeping off his alcohol, dreaming God knew what horrible dreams, because it wasn't in him to have sweet ones. His must have been full of demons, for he never saw a good thing; everything was sad and bad for the Traveller. I couldn't get out without stepping on him. I was barefoot and doubted if he would feel it. I jumped over him, stepping once lightly on his back, but he caught me by an ankle and kept me there.

"I fell down the stairs," he mumbled. "Help me to the cot. You pull and I'll push with my good leg."

"So you're awake."

"Off and on all night. I'm in terrible pain. I think I broke my ankle."

"Don't you remember what you did last night?" I shouted, kicking him.

"All I've ever done to you is to take good care of you after your mother died. I remember there was a tramp came in here last night that looked like your mother, a painted whore from Wilmington, picked up and assaulted by some sailors, no doubt. I am the man who married Magdalene."

"God, you're still drunk."

"Can't be. Hurts too much. Get me to the cot."

If he had let go of me once I would have fled, but he managed to keep a grip on me somewhere, my arm, my wrist, my ankles, as I dragged him and he kicked with his good leg over to the cot and pulled himself up on it.

"That's better," he said, settling. "Put something under that foot."

I pushed a chair over to him and lifted his bad leg up on it. I felt cold as ice. He pulled up his trouser leg and we saw that the leg was badly swollen and red. "Get me a bottle of whiskey from the cupboard. I've got to kill the pain." I got it.

"Why should I help you? You . . ." I stomped to the door and made it stop slamming.

"Because I'm your father and you gotta honor me."

"After last night? And since when have you been any kind of father to me? I've hated you since before I knew what hate was."

"You keep talking about last night. Nothing happened last night but I fell down the stairs."

"Why are your pants open and half way down, old man? What do you think you were doing up in the attic?"

He took a long chug from his bottle. "I was looking for you. You're never here when I come home. I want you to be here. I demand that you be here, do you hear me?"

"I never know when you're coming home. How am I supposed to know? But you, damn you, you're not going to get away with what you did this time. Look at me, I'm bruises from head to foot. You raped me . . . you monster. . . monster!"

"Don't you ever say a thing like that again, girly, or you'll find yourself in big trouble. I'm a preacher of God, do you hear?"

"Ruth says you're a drunken con-man, a crook who takes advantage of poor stupid people. Why hasn't the church in the village ever asked you to preach there? Why do you have to go and find these crazy little churches in the back woods? That's what Ruth says. And Garcie said the same thing." I was breathless.

"Garcie! An ignorant nigger and a Jew bitch!"

"You talked my mother into divorcing my father when he was in trouble. That's how you got this house. And now you've sold me to Ruth like a slave being sold at market."

"It's for your own good. Suppose I had died falling down those stairs—well, there'd be somebody to look after you."

"But you made her pay you."

"Why shouldn't I get some of the money back that it cost me to raise you up? There's been a lot of expenses. Now I'm in pain." He winced. "The whiskey helps but it's not going to stop it. You got to go to the village and get somebody out here to help me, maybe get me over to Beaufort to a doctor."

"You can't walk out on me this time, can you? You're trapped here."

"You can see that; now get going!"

"I'll take my own sweet time," I said, using a phrase of Ruth's. "The longer you hurt the better."

"A curse on you, girl, a curse on you."

Of course there was a curse on me, and I couldn't have been more keenly aware of it. The girl in the attic reached out to touch what was left of her childhood. The girl down here reached out for a weapon. Possession? Derangement?

Dislocation? Someone else was changing my clothes out in back of the house in the rain. Someone else took my lovely mint-green dress that was nothing now but a rag and stuffed it in the cave at the back of the house, the cave I could no longer squeeze into, the little cave half flooded with rain, the wet blanket, and now my beautiful birthday dress in tatters down that rabbit hole. I must have been the size of a rabbit to have ever fitted into that hole, to have hidden there as I so often did. Someone else put on jeans and a shirt and raincoat and hat and trudged off in the lightening rain toward the village. Jesse McQueen was dead.

Who—whom had I become? Someone else looked out of my eyes. Someone else heard the gulls cry. Another face felt the rain. Someone else returned Mrs. Walkup's wave and someone else saw the General Store, and someone else turned beside it and went on to the shack behind it. The new person knew that Tom would still be with Ruth. The new person knew that the pistol would be in the place, in the dresser drawer, Tom's target pistol, which he had taught Jessie McQueen to shoot. This new person, I, I knew that, if I looked, I would find the pistol, and I did.

How small am I, this new person? Smaller than a snail. Smaller than a bug, to be stepped on. Everyone is gone from my sight. I have no one, no other. They are all gone. Yesterday is gone. Everything is gone but the one thing, the monster. The monster has always been there and the monster will always be there, no matter which tyne of the fork you take. I am an unclean and worthless creature. I know that now. I am removed. I am someone other than who I once was walking with the pistol in my pocket as the rain pauses, stops, and the sun comes out. I am close now. I am near the door.

I pull the door open and step in and shut the door.

"There you are! Did you get some help?"

"I'm here to help," I said. "Just like when I was a little girl and you fell down."

"What's the matter with you? You don't look right."

"No. I don't feel like myself. Myself must have died."

"What are you jawing about, girl. Get me some help."

He raised the bottle to his lips in such a familiar gesture—I had an album of pictures of that gesture, some dating back to my earliest memories. I saw the Liberty ships in Wilmington, the cypress trees behind them. I could still feel the sting on my cheeks from his wet-handed slaps across my face. I could still see the lady, sympathetic, making a motion for me to wipe my tears. I took out the pistol, aimed, and shot. "You raped me," I whispered, with a deep, stranger's voice.

He sat there with a stunned expression on his face, but not what I expected. I saw that there was blood near his left shoulder.

"Why you crazy little bitch, you shot me." He set the bottle in his lap and felt his shoulder. "Damnation," he said, "that smarts something fierce. What is that thing? A twenty-two? Where'd you get it?"

I shot him again. It hit him in the side of the stomach, by the liver.

"Oh my God!" he cried, leaning forward.

I felt faint, dots dancing before my eyes. I went to the table and sat down at his place, where he always sat, where I could look straight at him.

"You better think what you're doing, girl," he said. I could see now that he was feeling a lot of pain. I held the butt of the pistol on the table to steady it, and shot him again. The bottle in his lap shattered. He screamed. His scream just sounded like something he did at his sermons. He was always screaming at people. I pulled the trigger again, and waited. He was quiet this time, his eyes closed. There was a lot of blood all over him. I sat there waiting for something to happen. Then he moaned. I pulled the trigger—pop, pop, pop.

She was almost sure that he was dead, whoever she was. Minutes passed.

Someone was knocking. I had to find myself. I had to answer. Then I heard Ruth: "Is anyone there? Jessie?"

"Hello," called Tom, knocking harder at the door.

"I'm here," I called, suddenly afraid they would leave me alone with the Traveller, "I'm here. Wait. I'll open the door." I felt as if the body I had left in the attic had rejoined me. I was inside of myself again, terrified, horrified, alone. I left the gun on the table and scrambled to the door. Ruth and Tom stood waiting. I spread my arms to collect their reality. Now all of that icy calm I had felt had gone out of me. They told me later that I was hysterical, that I spoke incoherently, that I was sobbing and choking and that my knees went out from under me as I tried to tell them what happened. Ruth told me that Tom caught me up and carried me into the room. If this happened as I have been told, I have no memory of it. Ruth found another bottle of whiskey and made me drink some of it. I remember how I couldn't get my breath, how I was afraid that I might die there and then for lack of air, like a fish out of a tank. Then I heard what Ruth and Tom were saying.

"Is he alive?" I heard Ruth say. "I'll go get help."

Tom said that the Traveller was dead. I distinctly heard him say, "He's dead." Dead, dead, dead. But that's not what I heard him say a few minutes later. I still don't know for certain what to believe about that, because I was sure I heard him say, "He's dead." I am almost sure I heard him say that. I think that's what he said. Between choking and sobbing and gulping air I said, "He . . . raped me. Bruises—look at my arms."

They looked at me with faces filled with horror.

"Oh, no, baby," Ruth said in a whisper, sitting down beside me, hugging me, "oh, no, baby."

"This is all my fault," said Tom. "I've done it again—bringing that stupid pistol to this island. I'm a damned felon. I shouldn't have had the damned thing anyway."

Ruth's face had changed from the knitted brow of horror to wide-eyed amazement. "Your fault? How can it be your fault?"

"I should have got her out of here, Ruth, somehow. This is my fault. All of it is my fault. My poor wife's suicide, the life Jessie must have had with this brute, all of this is my fault, mine, and I'm not going to let her take the blame for what I've done, for my failure—for my mistakes. The blame for this is mine!"

"But Tom—" Ruth started.

"No buts. Please, Ruth, no buts!" He waved his hands wildly in a desperate attempt to explain himself. "Jessie didn't do this. *I* did it. As sure as if I'd pulled the trigger.

You hear?" He went to the table and picked up the gun. "Hear him moaning? He's alive."

Out of some tunnel, I heard my echoing voice: "You said he was dead."

"He's not dead!" Tom yelled, startling the room with his vehemence.

"Then we can get him to the mainland," Ruth said, "to the hospital."

"He'd never make it. Turn away. Both of you. I want to see if he's got a pulse."

"What are you going to do?" Ruth said.

"Turn away," Tom shouted. "Jessie, turn away." We did as we were told.

There was a shot. Ruth was holding me and I could feel her shudder. Then we looked. At first I couldn't see anything different, but then I saw a small black hole in the Traveller's forehead. Tom stepped in front of the body and when he stepped away there was a trickle of blood from the hole. How did it get there?

"See," Tom said, "he was alive. You see the blood? I killed him."

Ruth said, "Are you sure, Tom—I mean, you want to do this, this way? It'll be the end of us."

"Us? What about her? The least she'd get is reform school. This wasn't self-defense. They'll call it premeditated. I don't want to spoil her life. Haven't I done enough to spoil it already? I came back here to watch over her and I've messed that up, but this time I'm going to make things come out right."

"Of course—you're right. Whatever you say."

"I'll probably get second degree. I could be out—well, I won't be in forever. I must have a solemn oath from both of you. You must promise on whatever you hold sacred that you don't know anything about this."

He spoke quickly and softly now, almost whispering. "It was something between him and me and I'll be sitting here holding the gun when they come. If I admit to it, nobody'll look any further. That's the story. You must promise me never to tell another. Do you promise? Do you promise? Do you *swear*?"

"If you want it to be this way," said Ruth, "Jessie and I promise you. Ruth shook me gently. "Your dad's right. Do you hear, Jessie? Do you promise?"

"I promise," I said, Ruth squeezing it out of me.

"We promise," Ruth said.

"There's more," said Tom. "Ruth, I want you to take Jessie and get to Boston as soon as you can. Get Masefield to take you back to Wilmington. He won't be far off. You can find him. He might be asleep on his boat. Get him and get to Wilmington and get to Boston. And don't contact me. Not a word. Do you understand? Not a word!"

"Oh God, Tom," said Ruth, "No!"

"I don't want you to contact me in any way. Do you swear?"

Ruth shook her head slowly from side to side and her big dark eyes were so full of sorrow that I had to look away. She said, in a broken voice, "I—I swear."

"Look," Tom said, "It's not the end. We'll be together again. All of us. Just a matter of time." He got up and took Ruth in his arms and kissed her, then me. He gave me a long look.

"Now take her and go. I want you in Boston by tomorrow. That's the best thing you can do for me. For all of us."

"I'll do it," said Ruth. "You know you can depend on me."

He gave Ruth a rueful smile. "When I feel you're safely gone, I'll go and get someone and tell them—how I hated the son-of-a-bitch, how I shot him, and that's all I am going to say to anyone, ever. Even if they wanted to prove differently, which they won't, because I'll make their case for them, even if they wanted to prove differently, they couldn't."

And, David, that promise cost you your father. Of course, he didn't know about you then, none of us did. But this is why I ask your forgiveness, and why I insisted on bearing the name Judas, because I allowed him to sacrifice himself, and, in doing so, betrayed you even before you were born. But Ruth and I did exactly what your father—and my father—ordered us to do. Ruth gave me pills to take, and she kept me sedated enough to follow her like a zombie, or be dragged by her, until we got off the airplane in Boston. Between the sedatives that Ruth kept giving me and the dreamlike swiftness of the next few days, I was already beginning to wonder if what had happened on Fortune Island had actually happened. When I asked Ruth about it, on those first days at the Brookline estate, all she would say is, "You've had a terrible nightmare, but you're coming out of it." Those words were comforting to hear, even if I didn't quite believe them, and they helped me to remove myself from what I knew to be true. "But Tom—"

"Tom is doing what he believes is right. If I didn't believe he was right, I wouldn't let him do it. I love Tom *because* he wants to do this, because he's the kind of man who would do this. This is his desire, his will, his wish—we have to respect him in this; our respect for what he's chosen to do is our love in action. Now go back to sleep and try to have a sweet dream. Believe me, there is no girl in the world loved more than you."

September on Fortune Island was not an autumnal month, but September in Boston can be nearly winter. The shock of the climatic change marked a change of life. Brookline is a suburb of Boston, so close, so integrated with the city that it might as well be Boston, and that September passed in a flash of adjustment from the tropical to the northern world, and the first snow filled the streets late in November. If sand dunes were white, it would look like that. Down and down the snow came with a raw wind. About a month after our arrival in Boston, Ruth discovered that she was pregnant with you, David. Had our dad known that you were on the way, would he have done what he did? Ruth made no attempt to tell him. The knowledge that you existed would probably have caused him to feel that his hope for redemption had been negated, that he had left stranded yet another hostage to fortune.

The Carolina newspapers gave us the bare outline of what he had done after we had left. He had brought Mrs. Walkup to the house and showed her the body. She had made contact with the authorities. He had told them that he had shot the Traveller for his own reasons, reasons that were none of their business. He had refused to cooperate with the court-appointed attorney, indeed, had refused to say anything except that he had shot the Traveller, had rejected a jury in favor of a judge, had pleaded guilty and was sentenced to fifteen years in prison, back behind the Wall through the gates of which he had so shortly before emerged.

It appeared that he had placed the last brick in that wall without regret. Ruth's letters were returned unopened. But about six months later we received a letter from a priest who had apparently befriended him—a priest, and Tom was not a Catholic. Ruth said that he had probably chosen to talk to a priest because anything that slipped from him should not slip from the priest. Ruth believed that he'd needed someone to talk to, but even so wanted to keep his privacy. The priest wrote that he had written down the return address on the letters his friend Tom had rejected, feeling that he might need to tell someone someday of Tom's fate. It was a bad fate. There had been a riot in the prison, and Tom died, beaten to death, trying to protect a guard.

"He was a Christ-like man," the priest had written, and I remembered *The Imitation of Christ*, which I still thumbed through although I didn't consider myself a Christian anymore than Ruth considered herself a Jew. We had lost whatever it took. Tom Judas was no more. You, Ruth and I were what was left of him, and so we had a duty to him to do our best as he had done his best, mistaken as it might seem to others.

Biology became my subject and I tried to find in it, from the lowliest one-celled creatures to humans, how love progressed. I have been unsuccessful. But that it did progress into power, that it progressed to the point that it defied even the instinct of self-preservation, I have ample evidence. I *am* evidence. I have ample evidence in our dad, David, Tom Judas, that strange mysterious man who sought nothing for himself in life but that rarity, redemption.

V.

The dying woman could not go on reliving those last, horrifying events and the manuscript ends with her final attempt to rationalize them. In other words, Ruthie, Jessie gave up. Judging from a few extraneous scraps tucked in among the pages of the memoir, Jessie had plans to go further and round it out. In her stead, I'm going to try to do that.

My first thought is that the fact that she assumed and kept the name Judas until the end, indicates to me that she could never come to terms with the morality of the situation. I think she was plagued by guilt all her days, probably more so as she grew older and was able to gain perspective on the situation left behind at Fortune Island. For some people, good people, guilt can be a poison in their bloodstreams, and I can't help but think that bearing such guilt all her days must have shortened them, perhaps harmed her immune system and left her open to the cancer that consumed her. But I'm not a doctor or a scientist, and this is only a fancy of mine, I suppose. And yet my instinct tells me that it is possible.

I buck at the thought that a person, even a young person, should go scot-free after killing someone, even if that person deserved killing. What will the new age think, the age of your future? Will it hold a more liberal view? I wish I could come back some day and ask you what you've made of this story. Were they right in doing what they did? Perhaps, Ruthie, you can come to terms with it in the pragmatic morality of some future time. I am left disturbed but sympathetic.

The alternative scenario would have left me with a father—but that's a selfish point of view. And what would have happened to Jessie? Perhaps, with the right lawyer, some claim could have been made for self-defense; but since she left the house, went some distance, found a pistol, and brought it back apparently for the purpose of killing the Traveller—well, that looks pretty premeditated. Of course she may have been in the disassociative state that she describes and perhaps could have been found not guilty for reasons of temporary insanity. There is certainly ample evidence that she wasn't in her right mind. But neither my father nor my mother were willing to risk it. It was my dad's desire above all things to protect Jessie, and he both failed and succeeded. He certainly failed in that he put the pistol within her reach, but how could he ever have dreamed that she would use it as she did. It wasn't even that kind of pistol, scarcely more than a target practice pop-gun. Deadly enough, however. Both he and my mother failed in not getting Jessie away from the Traveller in time. They should have seen trouble coming. Perhaps they had become too involved with each other, too distracted. Perhaps it was the guilt over their involvement that led them to such a desperate act.

They did, however, ultimately succeed in giving her a life undarkened by public censure, but they lost each other in doing it, and my father lost me. Would he have done it, had he and mother been aware of my existence? Perhaps not, as Jessie suggested. But the more I think about the situation, the more the questions ramify. You'll have to answer them in your own way as they did in theirs and as I must seek to do in mine. But, Ruthie, I can't find it in my heart to disapprove of them in the final analysis. They were living the situation, as soldiers live war, and we are placed in the luxurious position of historians. We are given time to think, they had none. They had to act.

Of course I always knew what an extraordinary woman my sister was, but it took this little memoir of hers to make me realize just how extraordinary, and indeed, how extraordinary my mother was.

But Jessie, a lonely little girl on a nearly deserted island, growing without benefit of grade or high school, without even a friend with whom to talk, visited constantly by a monster, and yet becoming what she became, that *is* extraordinary!

I realize now that when we look at someone standing at a podium, receiving an award, an honor of some kind, or we see a picture of them in the paper holding a trophy, we rarely wonder what went into that life, what's behind the public view. Rarely, however, is there rape and murder behind that face, rarely in those eyes such terrible knowledge. But Jessie was too polite not to smile on the night of her triumph, and still her eyes, I see now, shuffling through the photographs of the event, as I couldn't see then, were haunted, as indeed were my mother's, and, I remember, for an instant, she and Jessie looked out over the audience, at me, perhaps, looked for Tom, I am certain, or saw him in me as they chose to, and exchanged a look of the sort that had become a language between them, a language I had never learned to speak.

After the ceremony—I remember this vividly—my mother grabbed Jessie's arm, kissed her, and the two women walked off the stage, half-supporting each other. Jessie was wrong about one thing, though. She needn't have hoped for forgiveness from me—none was required. I know that they all did their best back in a time and in a place and in circumstances of which they were so kind as to keep me blissfully unaware.

III.

THE GOLDEN SQUIRREL

a Fairy Tale

Once, in Russia, back when every czar (a czar was about the same thing as a king) had his own magician, who helped him to run his court, the czar known as Magnanimous the Most (magnanimous means kind and good, and Magnanimous the Most was one of the kindest and nicest czars that Russia ever had) called in his magician, Seymour the Seer (Seer means wiseman or person who sees more than do most, and so understands more) and asked him if he could help to solve a very hard problem.

"What is your problem, Majesty?" asked Seymour the Seer.

"Well, it is this, Seymour," began Magnanimous the Most, shaking his head sadly. "As you know, my darling little son, Prince Leo, has been in China for more than a year now."

"Yes, Majesty," said Seymour. "If you remember, it was I who advised you to send him there, where he would be safe from your enemy, Duke Don, who had threatened that he would steal Prince Leo and not return him to you and the Czarina until you gave up your throne and made Duke Don the Czar." It is sometimes the way with kings and czars, even the nicest of them, that they forget that all ideas are not their own, and Seymour was reminding the Czar of this. But once he was reminded, Magnanimous the Most was always willing to give credit.

"You are right, Seymour," said Magnanimous, "it was you who advised me to send Prince Leo to China, and it was a good plan, but now I must bring him home, for his dear mother, the Czarina, misses him, and is pining away to hold her beautiful golden haired boy in her arms."

"But, Majesty, it is not safe to bring Prince Leo home. Duke Don is still your enemy."

"That is true," said the Czar, "but while the Prince has been in China, I have built a new palace where the Prince will be quite safe and sound. The problem is, how can I get him from China to the palace? He could be stolen along the way."

"Your Majesty is right," said Seymour. "The new palace is safe. But it is also true that Duke Don could send out soldiers to steal the young Prince while he travels home to us. What does Your Majesty think we should do?"

"I have a plan," said Magnanimous the Most, "but I need your help to make it work."

"I will do as you command, Your Majesty," said Seymour the Seer. "Tell me your royal wish."

"Seymour, it is my wish that you turn the Prince into a golden squirrel."

"A golden squirrel? Your majesty, I do not understand. Why do you wish me to turn Prince Leo into a golden squirrel?"

"Let me explain," said the Czar. "I have received a message from my spies in China that many merchants are coming to Russia this autumn in a great caravan to sell their wares. These merchants have the strangest and the most wonderful things to sell. Now one merchant, whose name is Chu-an-loo, is also an animal trainer who is bringing twelve squirrels that have been trained to be sweet pets. He hopes to sell these twelve squirrels, which are the wonder of the

Orient, to the twelve richest men and women in Russia. He hopes that by doing this, they will be ready to buy other wonderful pets from him when he comes in future years. Now, these squirrels are of a special kind that only live in China. They have fur which is unlike the grey or brown fur of our squirrels. Their fur is of a gleaming, golden color—like the fur of a lion—or, I should say, the golden hair of our Prince Leo. And that was the reason that I got this good idea."

"You mean," said Seymour, "to turn Prince Leo into a golden squirrel of this type, and to have Chu-an-loo, the great merchant, bring him into Russia with the other golden squirrels? What a wonderful idea! Duke Don will never know that one of the twelve of the golden squirrels is really Prince Leo, and that way, he won't be able to find the Prince and to steal him!"

"Exactly," said the Czar. "And the Prince will be travelling safely with the squirrels, because each of the squirrels is trained to be friendly, and each can do the most wonderful tricks, so that the little Prince will be entertained as he travels."

"But what about Chu-an-loo, the merchant who is bringing the squirrels? Will he be good to the Prince?"

"Chu-an-loo cares only for money and would sell the Prince to Duke Don if he knew, but we won't let him know that one of the squirrels is really the Prince. I would have you change the Prince into one of the squirrels without Chu-an-loo's knowledge. He will take care of all the squirrels because he is sure to get much money for them when he brings them here to Russia."

"But suppose he sells the squirrel who is really the Prince? We might never find Prince Leo again."

"He won't sell any of the squirrels until he gets to Russia, for that is his plan, and, when he gets to Russia, I, the Czar, will buy them all."

"Excellent," said Seymour the Seer. "My spell will work like this: Prince Leo will be turned into one of the golden squirrels the next time the moonbeams kiss his cheek where his mother, the Czarina, would kiss him if she could, and will turn back into himself the next time he sits upon his mother's lap."

"Can you do it?" asked the Czar.

"I'll begin at once," said Seymour the Seer. And before the great dark night came on, Seymour the Seer had made the magic poem that was to turn the Prince into one of the twelve golden squirrels. When the first moonbeam shone, a long silver ribbon came gleaming down through the singing stars, and Seymour the Seer recited the magic poem, while Magnanimous the Most and his wife, the beautiful Czarina, whose name was Nina, stood by on the balcony and listened. The Czar and Czarina prayed that the magic poem would work.

Seymour the Seer recited the poem like this:

Oh, moonbeam of the night,
Oh, Mega-Gaga-Momo-Moon,
Bring the Prince home safely
To his Mama-Papa and Me-too soon!

and suddenly, far away in China, as the young Prince Leo knelt before his bed to say his prayers—he was going to pray that he might be able to go home to Russia and to see his mother and his father soon again—he was turned into a golden squirrel! And not only was he a squirrel, but he found himself in a large cage with eleven other squirrels.

"What's happened?" he cried. "I'm—I'm no longer a boy, but a squirrel! And not only that, but I am in a great cage with eleven squirrels like myself. I don't understand!" Naturally, he was frightened.

The other squirrels in the cage were all asleep. "That must be it," cried the Prince. "I must be dreaming. When I wake up, I shall be myself again." And so he curled against one of the other fat, golden squirrels, and tried to dream of something else. And in a moment he had a wonderful dream about being at home with his mother, the beautiful Czarina Nina, and his father, Magnanimous the Most. In the dream, he was sitting on his mother's lap, wearing his night-shirt, and his mother was smiling, and petting his long golden curls, and kissing his rosy cheeks. His beaming father stood and watched. But then he woke again and found that he was still a squirrel!

"Oh, my," he said, "I must be dreaming still." But then he saw the Chinese merchant Chu-an-loo come up to the cage, carrying a sack of almond nuts, and began to wonder if, indeed, he had not become a golden squirrel.

"Am I dreaming, Master Chu?" he dared to ask. "Have I become a squirrel?"

Upon hearing the Prince speak, Master Chu burst into laughter, saying, "Ah, it is Confucius, the wisest and the trickiest of my squirrels, who speaks! Are you trying to play a trick on your master? Are you pretending that you are not a squirrel?"

"But Master Chu," cried the Prince, "I am not a squirrel! Really, I'm not! I am Prince Leo of Russia, son of the Czar."

"Ha-Ha-Ha-," laughed Chu-an-loo. "You are surely the prize of all the golden squirrels I own. None but you can play such tricks, Confucius. You alone will make me the richest merchant in all of China."

"But what I say is true, Master Chu. I am not Confucius, the golden squirrel, but Prince Leo of Russia."

Suddenly Chu-an-loo became angry. "Enough of your tricks, Confucius! Behave yourself or I will give you no nuts for breakfast." Then a clever look came into Master Chu's eyes, and he asked, "If you are not Confucius, how do you know who I am, eh?"

"I know because I have been to see your performing animals in the market place. I have seen you there often."

Master Chu-an-loo squinted his greedy, wicked eyes at Prince Leo. But after a moment, the Prince saw that Master Chu-an-loo did not believe him. "No, No," said Master Chu, "you can't fool me, Confucius. And because you have tried to fool me, I am not going to give you any almond nuts for breakfast."

"Oh, please, Master Chu, I am so very hungry. I have not eaten since last night's supper. Please let me have some nuts."

"No," said Master Chu. "I warned you not to play tricks on me. Now I must punish you." That morning Master Chu put only eleven little saucers of almond nuts out, and everyone began to eat but poor little Prince Leo.

"Very well," said Prince Leo. "I do not understand what has happened to me, but, if I am to eat, I must not tell Master Chu that I am Prince Leo. It only makes him angry. I will behave like Confucius, the golden squirrel, until I can find out why I am here. Really, it isn't so bad to be a golden squirrel. Look how bushy my tail is!"

Just then, one of the other golden squirrels came up to Prince Leo, holding a lovely almond out to him. "Oh, Confucius," said the squirrel, "why must you forever be playing naughty tricks and making Master Chu angry? Here is a nut for you to eat for breakfast. I shouldn't give it to you, because you have been so naughty, but it would make me unhappy to see you go without breakfast."

"Thank you," said Prince Leo, "but I am not Confucius, I am Prince Leo of Russia."

"Oh, Confucius," exclaimed the tiny squirrel, "and I suppose that I am not really Ling-Ling, daughter of BimBa, the Great Golden Squirrel, but am instead the Queen of Sheba? Now eat your breakfast, you naughty boy."

"I will indeed, Miss Ling-Ling, and I thank you for it. But you must believe me when I say that I am not Confucius, but Prince Leo. I don't know how it has come to be, but I have changed into a squirrel."

"Well," said Ling-Ling, looking very carefully at Prince Leo, "I do believe that you are telling the truth. But how can this be?"

"Someone has worked a magic spell," said the Prince, "and I think I know who has done it! There is only one man in the whole world who could make such magic and that man is my father's magician, Seymour the Seer."

"Oh, yes!" exclaimed Ling-Ling. "Why, we have heard of Seymour here in China. But why would he do such a thing?"

"Seymour would never do a thing like this unless my father ordered it," said Prince Leo. "My father must have a plan to get me home, and part of that plan must be to change me into a squirrel."

"But," said Ling-Ling, "what has happened to Confucius?" She started to cry, because she missed Confucius already. Even though she thought he was very naughty, she loved him very much.

"Don't cry, Miss Ling-Ling," said the Prince. "No doubt as soon as I turn back into myself, Confucius will return to you."

"Then I must help you to get safely home," said Ling-Ling. "For, if anything happens to you, I may never see my naughty Confucius again."

"Then you mustn't tell the other squirrels, for if they knew who I really was, they might tell Master Chu, and he might sell me to my father's enemies."

"It will be our secret secret," said Ling-Ling in a whisper.

"Good," said Prince Leo. "Now please tell me, what is happening? Why are we in this cage? Master Chu does not fear that you and the other squirrels will run away, does he? I thought that he only sold well-trained pets, for I have seen him in the market place with such animals."

"Yes, that's what everybody thinks, but Master Chu is a cruel trainer. He teaches his animals to do their marvelous tricks by not feeding them unless they behave. We would all run away, if we could. But there is another reason why we are in this cage. Have you not noticed how we go rocking from side to side and up and down? We are in a great wagon which is part of a caravan. We are already on our way to Russia, where Master Chu means to sell us to the twelve richest dukes and duchesses who live there."

"That explains it!" cried Prince Leo. "My father has had me changed into a golden squirrel so that I could be brought home in secret and in safety. He will probably buy me from Master Chu when we get home and have me changed back into myself."

"That must be it," cried Ling-Ling.

"Oh," said Prince Leo, "now I am very sorry that I tried to tell Master Chu that I was the Prince. Suppose he had believed me?"

"If he had believed you," said Ling-Ling, looking very frightened, "he would have sold you to your father's enemies for much more money than he could ever get for a golden squirrel, and then I would never see my darling Confucius again."

Now, unknown to Ling-Ling and to Prince Leo, Master Chu-an-loo had been listening as they talked, and so had come to believe that Confucius, the golden squirrel, was indeed young Prince Leo of Russia. "And now, what I will do," he said to himself, "is send a messenger ahead on horseback to tell Duke Don, the Czar's great enemy, that I have the Prince in the form of a golden squirrel in a cage in my caravan. I will have the messenger tell Duke Don that I will make him a Christmas present—for Christmas is near—

of the Prince, if he will give me a treasure chest full of golden coins. Ha-ha, Ha-ha, ha-ha! All that gold for one very special golden squirrel! Ha-ha, ha-ha, ha-ha," he laughed wickedly. And two days later the messenger told Duke Don what Chu-an-loo had said.

Duke Don, who had a fierce mustache that hung down to his chin and a voice like thunder, cried, "Why should I give Master Chu a chest filled with gold, when all I have to do is to take Prince Leo away from him?"

So, in another day, Master Chu saw that an army was coming toward his caravan. He could see by their bows and arrows and spears that they meant to steal the Prince and not to give him the treasure chest filled with golden coins for which he had asked, so he ordered his elephant drivers to bring the lumbering elephants into a circle and to get ready to fight Duke Don and his army. At this point, Master Chu's caravan was in a very cold and mountainous part of Russia, and it was snowing very hard, so that the land looked like a rumpled white bedsheet, and the sky seemed filled with great balls of cotton. This made it very hard for elephants to see where they were going, and the two great elephants that were pulling the big wagon that held the cage that held the twelve golden squirrels stumbled in the snow and began to slide down a hill. And when the elephants and the wagon came to the bottom of the hill, the wagons bumped against a tree and the cage that held the golden squirrels was thrown high into the air. When it landed, it broke open and the twelve golden squirrels ran off in the snow. At last, they were free!

Prince Leo called to Ling-Ling to follow him, and they started off together in the direction that the caravan of Master Chu had been going. "Come, Miss Ling-Ling, we must go in this direction if ever I am to see my dear father and mother again, and if ever we are to bring your friend Confucius back to you."

And so it came to pass that Prince Leo and Miss Ling-Ling began their long and difficult journey to Moscow, which was, even in the time of which we speak, the greatest city of Russia. It was very hard for the two frightened little squirrels to make their way through the deep snow that had fallen all over Russia. They were not able to go very fast. So slowly, in fact, did they go, that for the first two days they could still hear the sounds of the battle taking place between Master Chu's caravan and the army of Duke Don.

Often, despite their thick golden coats of fur and the bushy golden tails which they could curl about themselves, they were very cold, and poor little Miss Ling-Ling would cry all night. Prince Leo wished that he could cry, too, but he did not want to frighten Miss Ling-Ling. And they were very hungry. No matter how hard they looked beneath the snow for nuts to eat, they could not find any. Being hungry made Miss Ling-Ling cry even more than she had before.

"Oh, I am so afraid that we will never have anything to eat again," she said. And little Prince Leo, who was afraid that Miss Ling-Ling was right, would try to comfort her by saying, "Do not be afraid, Miss Ling-Ling. We will have a wonderful Christmas dinner when we get to Moscow. My father, the Czar, will see to it."

"But I'm afraid we will never get to Moscow, Prince Leo, for, though we can run fast, my legs are very short, and the way is long and cold, and filled with dangers." And so it was.

One night, while they slept in a little hole in the snow, huddled together and shivering and chattering their little teeth, a great bear, white as the snow, sneaked up on them and grabbed Miss Ling-Ling up in his big paws and started to stuff her into his mouth. But Prince Leo bit the bear's foot, so that he dropped Miss Ling-Ling, and they were able to run away. Looking back, Prince Leo saw that the bear's eyes were red, like burning coals in the face of a giant snowman, and he told Miss Ling-Ling to jump on his back, and he ran all the faster, for Prince Leo had always been a mighty runner.

"Oh, we will never get to Moscow," cried Miss Ling-Ling. "We will be eaten by the bears or the wolves or we will starve for lack of nuts. I wish I were at home in China with my father, BimBa, the Great Golden Squirrel, to protect me." But the Prince wiped the silver tears from her big brown eyes and patted her golden coat.

"Don't lose courage, dear little Miss Ling-Ling. For as sure as I speak we will be in Moscow by Christmas and you will have all the almonds that you can eat. And I will be myself again and Confucius will be returned to the world and he will take you home to the Chinese woods and to your father. I will see to it."

So spoke the brave little Prince, but he was very frightened himself. And this will show you that, if you are brave, you will find your way. For, after several more days, the two thin, hungry little squirrels came within sight of the great city of Moscow, with its beautiful domes and turrets that look like giant Christmas candies. And, after another day of travelling, they entered the gates of the city. "You see," said the Prince, "I told you we would get here. Just follow me, Miss Ling-Ling, and I will take you to my father's palace, which is in the middle of Moscow."

Meantime, at the palace, Czarina Nina opened the doors of the balcony and stepped out on it. Magnanimous the Most called to her from inside the room.

"My dear Nina, ever since we learned that Master Chu's caravan was raided by Duke Don's army, you have stood for hours on end and cried on the snow-covered balcony. It is so cold out there that your tears turn to ice. I am afraid you will grow ill. It is sad enough for me that I may never see my darling boy again, but I don't know how I could go on if you, too, were to be lost. Please come in where it is warm."

"Oh, my husband," said the Czarina, "I will never know happiness again, for I've lost my Prince Leo. Do you remember what beautiful golden hair he had?"

"I do," said the Czar sadly, and great tears came into his eyes.

"Here," cried the Czarina to the little winter sparrows who hopped about in the snow. She threw them crumbs of Christmas cake. Suddenly, several little squirrels ran out of nowhere and began to eat, too.

"Oh, look at the squirrels," said the Czarina. "Oh, I wish that one of them were my little boy, Prince Leo." Several of the furry little creatures climbed up on the balcony and began to eat out of the Czarina's hand.

"Oh, come," she cried, "come and look at them. They're so cute. Look, one has climbed into my lap. He is the most unusual golden color!" And suddenly, she found herself holding not a golden squirrel, but her own golden-haired little boy, Prince Leo!

"Leo!" she cried. "It's really you!" And she took him in her arms and kissed him and hugged him to her.

"Yes, Mama," Leo said, and, for the first time during his long, dangerous journey home, he began to cry. But he was crying tears of happiness.

"Oh, my darling boy!" cried the Czarina Nina.

Magnanimous the Most called Seymour the Seer and both joined the Czarina Nina and Prince Leo out on the balcony. "I am so happy," said Prince Leo, "because I have turned back into myself, and I am in my mother's arms. But look at my dear friend, Miss Ling-Ling. She sits with her little paws in prayer for her beloved Confucius. Seymour, can you make him appear?"

Then Seymour recited a magic poem—

Bring back the naughty Confucius
Who loves so much to confuse us!
Let him dance and prance and sing
For his loving little Ling-a-Ling!

and suddenly Confucius was sitting right there beside Ling-Ling.

"This is the happiest day of my life," Ling-Ling said, laughing, as Confucius began to chase her through the snow and away from the palace. "Good-bye, Prince Leo," she called back as she ran. "I am going back to the woods of my father, BimBa the Great Golden Squirrel, so that he can meet my friend Confucius."

Prince Leo said, "Oh Mother, Father, Seymour, Miss Ling-Ling can never make the trip back to China to the woods of her father BimBa. It is too long and hard a trip for a little squirrel to make. Can't we do something to help her?"

And Seymour the Seer said, "Have no fear, my Prince! By my spell, even now she enters the woods of BimBa."

And so it was, for Seymour had changed the park that surrounded the palace into the Chinese woods of BimBa, the Great Golden Squirrel, who greeted his daughter and her friend Confucius just as the Czar and Czarina had greeted Prince Leo, with hugs and kisses. And all was well.

THE HAT TRICK

Jack Clover pulled off his mirrored sunglasses to get a better look at a tall, attractive woman who had just stepped out of a chauffeured Town Car. She was sleek, like a model from a cover of Harper's Bazaar; but middle-aged, with iron-gray hair. It was his ex-wife, Madeleine, a quondam surgical nurse, now married to a famous surgeon. Her wide-brimmed black straw hat tipped and tilted as she spoke to her driver. Jack Clover stepped up to her.

"May I help you, Ma'am?"

"I'd like to see the new—" Madeleine studied him for a moment. "Why, Jack, is that you?"

"Me and Ben Franklin."

"What are you doing in that costume?"

Jack gave her a reproving look. "It's the Fourth of July. Look around! See the flags?"

"Oh, of course."

"Lady, you're smack on Independence Boulevard, also known to buyers and sellers of automobiles as The Strip, the heart and soul of what Cornwallis called the Hornet's Nest. Haven't you heard of the Charlotte Hornets, lady? Where have you been?"

"The question is, where have *you* been? I tried to get in touch with you several times to tell you about Steffie. We tried to find you for her wedding. Is there some place we can talk?"

"I'll take you out for a spin. What kind of car were you looking for?"

"A new Town Car. I thought we'd trade this in."

"Tell your driver to get a Big Mac." Jack ran in to the Tower, the platformed, glass-encased office in the showroom, took a key and a dealer's tag, and was back beside her as her driver pulled away. "Over there," he said, and led her to the new Town Cars. "Shall we go for a drink?"

"I could use a long cool drink. It's blazing out here."

Madeleine was assessing him. "That costume," she said, elliptically.

"I'll take you to Motor City. All the salesmen hang out there. Nobody'll notice the outfit, but they'll sure take an eyeful of you."

"Do I look good, Jack?"

"Smashing! I take it you're also loaded."

"We're well off. How about yourself? You never completed your nurse's training, did you? I always hoped you'd go back."

"I was only there to be with the girls, especially you."

"But you had a real talent for healing, and you were so good with people. That's why I fell for you."

"Talent can do anything. Right now, I'm a blue-ribbon car salesman. I already made nearly a grand this morning, before I even put on my Ben Franklin suit. Guy's been nosing around about a wrecker we had on the lot, and he was waiting for me when I got in this morning. It couldn't have been better if I'd planned it. Today's a big bonus day. If I get a hat trick."

"A what?"

"Three sales. If I get a hat trick I get a five grand bonus."

"Well, I'm pretty sure of what I want. I can be number two."

"You're second to none, beautiful."

Jack pulled the Town Car around behind The Motor City Bar and Grill. "I heard somewhere about Steffie getting married. How'd it go?"

"She was pretty disappointed that her daddy wasn't there to give her away, but my husband stood in for you."

"Your name's Harburg, now, right?"

"Mrs. Morton Harburg." Madeleine looked around the bar as they stepped in. "Half the people in here are Founding Fathers," she said. "It's hilarious!"

"Car dealers aren't very original. But they're very competitive. Watch out for the muskets!"

They took a booth and ordered what they had used to drink together, sloe gin fizzes. "Remember when we used to go shagging out at the old Myrtle Beach Pavilion?" Madeleine asked. "You were a wonderful dancer. Can you still shag?"

"I can still do everything."

"You look a bit drawn, Jack."

"I don't know how. I was in here boozing until the wee small hours last night. But I'm resilient. Good genes!"

"And do you remember the fun we used to have out at Ocean Drive?"

"Old O.D. Did I take you out there?"

"Just who do you remember taking? We used to shag out there someplace. Don't you remember, you used to take me out there on your motorcycle?"

"My first Harley! Sure, sure. I can't remember the name of the place. You said before that you tried to get in touch with me. What for?"

"Well, for the wedding, of course. And then to tell you the good news about your being a granddaddy."

"A granddaddy?"

"Twice, now!"

Jack Clover looked like she'd touched him with an electric cattle prod.

"Why, what's the matter, Jack?"

"Will you excuse me for a minute?" he said, and got out of the booth and went to the men's room. He waited, smoking, while another Founding Father used the urinal, washed his hands, and left. Then he palmed some cocaine and snorted. He put his things away and washed his hands, studying himself in the mirror over the sink. Was he hallucinating? He looked exactly like Benjamin Franklin. But portly old Franklin had Tower Power. He was Buddy Sol's best salesman, but Buddy Sol was jealous of him, of his middle-aged youthfulness and charm, and kept him from his rightful place in the Tower. This emotional roller-coaster dip occupied a second or so and Jack watched as his features reformed handsomely, youthfully. He grinned at himself that prize-winning salesman's grin of his. His blue eyes sparkled. He dried his hands and went back to Madeleine rubbing them together.

"Come on," he said, cheerfully, "let's go for a ride in the country. You want to see how the car does, don't you?"

They drove toward Lake Wylie, Madeleine commenting on the changes in the area. "I can't get over what a big city Charlotte has become. It seems to have happened overnight."

"It just growed, like Topsy. Where have you been?"

"Didn't your grapevine tell you?"

"It's not that good," he said, "and, besides, I've been away a lot, too, up until about a year ago. I've been working in California, and, later, up in Jersey. A good lot lizard can get a job anywhere. How 'bout you?"

"Well, I met my husband in Richmond, not long after we separated, and we moved to New York. We lived there most of the time, but we've decided to come down here for our declining years. A slightly slower pace."

"Only slightly, nowadays. This is the New South, you know. But you don't look a bit in decline." He pointed at a turnoff sign for a Motel-Restaurant. "Let's pull off the highway and get a drink."

"Two sloe gin fizzes," he told the waitress, and pulled out a Kool.

"Still smoke? And you almost a trained nurse!"

"Something's going to kill us, kid. If it isn't cigs, it'll be boredom. So tell me about my grandchildren."

"A boy and a girl. Girl's the oldest, she'll be eight. The boy's six. The girl's named Madeleine, after me."

"What about the boy?"

"Morton. Steffie adores her step-father, and with good reason. He's been just like a real father."

The waitress came back with their drinks. "Sir, I hope you don't mind my asking, but—"

"I'm an actor. I'm playing Ben Franklin. We're shooting out in the woods."

"Oh, how interesting! You're not anybody famous, are you?"

"I'm afraid not, but you'll get a good tip for asking."

The waitress smiled and placed their drinks on the table and scooted off to tell somebody about the celebrities out in front.

Madeleine was laughing. "Honestly, Jack, you never change. You don't seem to grow up at all."

"Want to do a wheelie on my Harley with me, like we used to do?"

"You're not really still riding that thing, are you? At your age?"

"No. In fact I had a pretty bad accident on one a few years ago. No helmet. Cracked my head open. I've pretty much stuck to four wheels since then. God, I can't get over how beautiful you are! You're only a couple of years younger than me. How do you do it?"

"A quiet, orderly life."

"Sounds boring."

"Nothing boring about an active family. We've just bought a house. By the way, you aren't married again, are you?"

"Free as a bird!"

"Just like always. Don't you ever yearn to settle down? At your age, I mean."

"Never think about it. Just keep truckin'."

"Well, as you must have found out with that accident, you can't just go through life doing wheelies. Why not find yourself a nice girl and settle in for the duration?"

Jack shrugged. "I don't like the sound of that duration."

He excused himself, went to the men's room, snorted again, and came back.

"Listen," he said, sitting down, "why don't we check in here for an hour for old time's sake?"

"Are you crazy?"

"You needn't look so flabbergasted. It was just an idea."

"What an idea! My God, Jack, grow up! I've been married to Morton for twenty-five years! Come on, I want you to drive me back to town."

They drove back to Charlotte in silence. Jack pulled the Town Car onto the lot and sat staring at the rabble of buyers and sellers. He didn't move to get out, but said: "Look, Madeleine, I'm sorry. I don't know what got into me."

"What do you think I am, Jack, some motel bimbo? I should have known I couldn't talk sensibly to you. But I thought well, after all these years, you might have changed. At least that much."

"Do you still want the car?"

"Yes, dammit, I'll take the car. It's what I came in here for. What's the matter with you, Jack? I was really glad to see you."

"Me, too, you. I'm really sorry. Come on inside and I'll see how much I can give you on the old car. I'll make it a good deal, don't worry. Dr. Harburg won't be cheated."

"You bet he won't!"

The afternoon sun was beating down on the booming Strip. Jack was melting inside his Ben Franklin costume. Only one more for a hat trick. He went to the Tower and dialed the number of his room at the Alamo Motel. His answering machine gave him his current girlfriend's message, in angry, high-pitched tones: "Jack, you son of a bitch, you said we were going to stay in all day. I know you went to the lot, but I don't give a damn. You had a date with me, today, and you left me here in this porno-video dump to sleep it off by myself. I saw you in Barney's at noon with that tall old broad. She's just right for you, OLD MAN! Goodbye, and I do mean GOODBYE!"

Jack hung up. Buddy Sol came barrelling by, shouting, "Out on the lot, you lizards! I want every one of you out on the lot with the customsuckers. Let's move cars!"

Jack calculated. Madeleine's new Town Car would net him another fifteen hundred at double commission. Three thousand or so for the day wasn't bad. He thought maybe he'd go back to the motel and get some shut-eye, no matter what Buddy Sol thought about it. He could shove his hat trick bonus. Jack knew in his heart that Buddy Sol was never going to let him get Tower Power, any old way. Too jealous! He'd have to move on, get a better spot.

"I take it by your costume that you work here," came a silky young voice. Jack looked at her. For a moment he thought it was his Alamo Motel girlfriend of the night before, but then he saw the difference. Blue mascara, not green. And hair patched orange and black. "I want to test drive that van out there, President Franklin." She pointed.

"Sorry, Benjamin Franklin was never president," he told the young lady, grinning his best salesman's grin.

"Whatever!"

"I'll get the key and the tag," he said. "Go ahead out, I'll be right with you." He went to the meeting room, flicked on a demo-cassette of himself doing a walkaround, and snorted a handful of coke. The walkaround he had done that day won him the Salesman of the Year award. It was used all over the country to train new salesman. Look at that grin! God, how he hated it! He felt like it had been pasted on his face since birth. A good salesman sells himself, not a product. What had he left to sell? He looked like a movie star video. But how long could he keep this pace up? Not another step without the coke. He snorted. Yes, it supplied the energy his body truly lacked. He was lonely. He was aging. My God, he was a grandfather! He left the video running and in a moment appeared on the lot, full of vim and vigor. "You know how to handle one of these?" he asked his customer, who, on second look, appeared to be quite a dish.

"I've driven them all over the country," she said. "I'm with a Punk group, The Living Dead. Have you heard of us?"

"I sure have," he said, "best sounds going." It occurred to him that he would have to learn some of the new music. He was out of touch. "You've got to keep up, Jack," he said to himself. "Keep up, keep up!" He eyed the customer. She was probably a lot younger than his daughter.

"Well, you go ahead and drive then," he told the girl, "I'll watch." He winked, slightly more of a blink and climbed in the van.

"We gotta go cross-country in this, if we take it," she said.

Jack couldn't get over it; he was a grandfather: his granddaughter was only ten years or so younger than this Rocker. How could such a thing be?

"I'll take it out on the highway," said the girl, "if it's O.K. I wanna see how she does in the boondocks."

"Well, we can take her down by Lake Wylie. Do you know where that is?"

"Right on. We've played Charlotte a few times already. My name's Peggy. I'm the singer. The female voice, I should say. Peggy Paroni. You must have heard of me."

"Oh, sure, terrific! You're the bee's knees."

"Hey, thanks! What a cute saying! Say, you're a pretty good-looking guy. I bet all the ladies tell you, huh? But you should ease back on the coke. Dries you up."

"You can tell?"

"I told you, I'm in the music business. Hey, do these seats flatten back?"

"Into a king-sized bed."

"Well, it goes pretty good, blue eyes. You got any stuff on you?"

"Say, young lady—"

"Oh wow! Gimme a break! What're you, somebody's grandpa? Come on, big daddy, you said you knew who I was, or were you just jerking me around with your sales shit?"

"I've got some," Jack conceded.

"Well, let's pull off the road, somewhere, make this thing into a bed, coke up, and have us a little Fourth of July ball. I mean fireworks, Mister President! I can guarantee you a sale."

"What the hell!" Jack told himself, looking at the leering young woman with the two-toned hair through old, tired eyes. "It's the hat trick."

SNOWBOUND

How the free spirit suffers his winter out in the woods is his business, isolated alone in an unused farm house rented from a farmer by a tall strange city man with a beard like a board and a wife who would sleep in it but has left for the winter her husband alone to be hermit at his request, an artist, poet and painter, needing neither wife nor child nor sustenance but vision only, that she go forth to the wicked city and fare there with a former lover while he have visions during long mountain downfall of flakes building to crescendo in white isolation, that there be firewood alone was his matter, that chalk run smooth over blackboard and vision come summoned by white gods of sleet and snow and that that first time should he die then the plan be known as faulted with no firewood and the cold growing in his guts, that he understand what he never understood, the seriousness of his state, and learn to be a man once before claimed by the white tongue, snapped like a spot from large blankness making no orientation: be gone. He feared nothing but the thought of no vision, not the loss of his wife to another, nor the loss of his life, nor the meaning of loneliness, but for the vision forsaking all; was willing and willed that Death in a white coat with bony knuckles knock: his wife in wonder could not love her former lover but was young and thrilled at her husband's exploit, leaving the lover without chance as he regaled her with delights on city nights of restaurants and theaters for always she thought of her strange visionary husband in the mountains alone turning whiter and whiter like a snowbird of some extraordinary kind with wings wide and eaglehead highbeaked proud and coming down in spring with great talons spread arresting her in mid-flight at subway entrance and sweeping off up up and away to his glee-echoing lair high on the spiked cliffs—meanwhile the wise farmer who owned the house had snowploughed his way to the visionary's door and knocked like whitecoated Life and found artist frozen but not dead, who awakened to strains of hospital music and surrendered his soul to it, thanking the gods but not any one in particular for the fact that only a few toes had had to be removed—he liked his nurse, a warm vision in white.

A PRACTICAL NURSE

In a picture perfect neighborhood of a large southern city, a shiny red closed convertible pulled to the curb in front of a beautiful bungalow. A young woman in white got out carrying a small overnight bag and approached the front door. After a couple light, tentative taps, she opened the door and stepped inside. Another small, matching overnight bag sat just inside the door. Next to it was a neat stack of personal effects that looked as if they belonged in it. The young woman sat the bag she was carrying next to it, opened it, and dumped its contents on the rug.

"Hello!" she called. "I'm Lorna Chandler. Your son, Mr. Harry Freemantle, sent me."

From within, a voice answered. "The nurse? Did you lock the door behind you? I didn't like waiting here with the door unlocked. There's a bad element, you know. I don't know why that son of mine has to do things in such an . . . unorthodox manner."

"I locked the door," Lorna Chandler said, stepping into Cora Freemantle's bedroom. She thought the woman propped up in bed would be older, or at least look older. She was beautifully coifed, her silver hair upswept. She wore a pink silk peignoir, and, around a neck gone a bit floppy, a diamond-inset platinum multiple-necklace. Her ears, hands, and wrists, were bejeweled.

"Yes," Cora Freemantle said. "Yes. Good. What did you say your . . ."

"Lorna Chandler."

"Yes. Lorna. Do you mind?"

"No, I don't mind. May I call you Cora?"

"Well . . . Yes, of course. You are a registered nurse?"

"A practical nurse."

"Isn't that. . . I mean—you don't have a degree?"

"I have passed all the necessary examinations."

"But you are quite young. I should think you would be in a good nursing school—something to advance yourself."

"Money."

"Ah, yes, I see. Money. Well, perhaps in future. . . In any case, did my son explain my difficulties?"

"He said you had high blood pressure, several minor and one serious heart failure."

"No, no. That's true, but I can get around ordinarily. But I got dizzy with the high blood-pressure and I fell. Or perhaps I twisted my ankle. But I fell. But the fall wasn't it. The ankle was it. I mean—I can't get about. I can't put any weight at all on the ankle. The pain is excruciating."

"What did the doctor . . ."

"Sprained ankle. Stay off it. See the support?" She pulled the covers back to display her bandaged leg. "Ordinarily, bad heart and all, I can get around. I walk my dog, Suzy Wong. By the way, where is Suzy? I didn't hear her bark when you came in. She always barks. You didn't let her out when you came in, did you?"

"She barked. I guess you were dozing. She's fine, now. Sleeping."

"With her paws under her coochie-coo chinny-chin? Yes, I must have been dozing. You're sure you locked the door?"

"I locked it. You have a lovely home."

"Yes, I think so. Now, you understand that you are to stay with me for the weekend, prepare and serve my meals, help me to the bathroom—well, you understand what I require? My son Harry told you, did he not?"

"Yes, he told me."

"Sit down, won't you? You make me nervous just standing there."

"I'm sorry." Lorna Chandler sat down in a chair near the bed.

"You have things? A suitcase?"

"I left them in the living room."

"Well, there's a guest room upstairs. The maid uses it. She's black. You don't mind that do you?"

"Of course not."

"Well, not necessarily of course not, but good; you take that. This is not a very big house."

"But very nice. I wish I owned it."

"Yes, I think so. I don't need a big house—though I can certainly afford all the house I want—but I won't waste money."

"No."

"My second husband left me this house. When he died."

"Yes."

"Do you want some coffee or something?"

"No."

"Where's your coat?"

"Outside, on my suitcase."

"Well, why don't you see to your things. Take them up to your room. Get settled. Then come back down and make some coffee. I'd like some."

"You'd like some?"

"Yes, I would. After just waking up. What time is it, anyway?"

They checked their watches.

"Nearly noon, Friday."

"Yes. My son was here this morning. I dozed, and here you are—Lorna. Chandler—that name rings a bell. That's an old family."

"Yes, an old family."

"Yes, I recall. Substance. Are you a cousin? Oh, forgive me, dear. I didn't mean—"

"Distant. Yes, a distant cousin."

"No offense. An old lady gets used to speaking her mind. We get tactless, I'm afraid. Compensates for losing our other faculties. Can't see too well—can't walk, etc.—but at least you can say what you think."

"Yes, that's good. Say what you think."

"Yes. Well, why don't you go on and put your things away."

"Yes. Up in the black maid's room."

"Yes, at the head of the stairs."

"Yes. And then you want some coffee."

"I'd like coffee—yes."

"Very well."

"Very well? You sound like an English butler in an old movie."

"I'm sorry. I'll go now." Lorna Chandler rose and left the room.

Cora picked up her bedside phone and dialed.

"Oh, I'm so glad I caught you, Iris. It's about this nurse your husband has sent over here to take care of me—what? What do you mean, you have to run, Mother Freemantle? I'm talking to you. And why do you, after fifteen years of marriage to my son, insist on calling me 'Mother Freemantle?' My name is Cora. What? Wait a minute, I want to speak to you. I don't care about the children—"

Cora looked up to see Lorna standing in the doorway. "Oh, never mind, Iris. Iris? IRIS? She hung up. My own daughter-in-law hung up on me. Rude! Rude! Rude!" She banged down the receiver. "What is it, Lorna? Where's my coffee?"

"Would you like anything with your coffee?"

"What?"

"Perhaps a little wine?"

"Wine? What *are* you talking about? Coffee, that's all. Just coffee. I don't drink."

"Oh. Because there's wine in the kitchen. Several bottles of wine."

"It must be the maid's."

"Oh. She has very good taste. Very expensive. You must pay her well."

"What business is that of yours? I pay her what maids get."

"Black maids? Black domestics?"

"Yes. I don't know where she gets the wine. Oh, bother, of course it's my wine. I have a right to have wine if I want it, don't I? This is my house, isn't it? What am I sparring with you about?"

"I'm your nurse, Mrs. Freemantle. You have high blood pressure. You should not drink wine. You were drinking wine when you became faint, and that led to your sprained ankle. I'm merely trying to do my job."

"Of course. But I will have my wine if I wish it, doctors, nurses or no."

"A glass with your coffee?"

"No coffee. A glass of wine."

"As you wish."

"There you go again, Lorna, sounding like an English butler. Are you deliberately trying to make me uncomfortable in my own house?"

"No, Mrs. Freemantle."

"Cora! Cora! My name is Cora!"

"Yes—Cora. You mustn't excite yourself. It could lead to a seizure."

"You are trying to make me see that I should not have the wine, is that it?"

"I'll get it."

"Don't ignore me!"

"No." Lorna Chandler waited.

"Bother! Go on, then!"

Cora fidgeted in irritation while Lorna went to kitchen and returned almost immediately with two glasses of red wine on a silver tray.

"What is that? Are you having a glass of wine, too? Aren't you on duty, or something?"

"I didn't think you'd like to drink alone."

"That was thoughtful of you," Cora said, sarcastically, "I must say." She sipped her wine. "Is Suzy Wong still sleeping?"

"Yes. Quite peacefully."

She's a Pekinese, you know. No mixed blood. Highly nervous. That's why I was surprised that I didn't hear her barking when you came in. You must get on with dogs."

"I don't care for them."

"How can you say that? Everyone likes dogs."

"Not everyone. When I was a little girl, I was walking with my mother and father—walking ahead of them and somewhat behind a stray dog who, for no reason that I could ever discover, turned around suddenly and mauled me. He bit my hand—there, you can still see the teeth marks. The little ones bark and the big ones bite—like people."

"It's very unfair of you to base your opinion of dogs on an isolated incident."

"It wasn't isolated to me. I was five and it was my hand."

"That doesn't make sense."

"It does to me."

"It's a perverse attitude."

"I guess we are all perverse, each in his own way. The word means nothing."

"I know what perverse means. I was a school teacher."

"That must have been many years ago, in better times. Were there better times?"

"Yes, I think so. I think those were better times in some ways. But these are my better times."

"You mean because you have money now."

"Yes. Money and security. But you weren't even alive during the Depression. You wouldn't know."

"Then why do you say they were better times?"

"Not the Depression. I meant the times before, the Twenties. When I was young and starting out. They were better times—for the world. But these are my better times."

"You married wealthy men."

"I assume that you don't intend to insult me. Yes. During the Depression, when I saw what could be, I decided to marry well, if I could."

"And you could, because you were good-looking and you knew it."

"Yes, I think so. Yes. And I did. I married well, and—"

"And now you are a wealthy woman. You have a black domestic and a practical nurse and, if you wanted, you could have more. Much more."

"I don't like to waste money. I don't need more than I have."

"You could give some away—to your family, say—and make their lives easier. You have it just as you want it."

"Yes, I think so." Cora felt uneasy; it made her heart pound hollowly.

"But you don't care for your children."

"Of course I do, in my own way. What made you think that?"

"Because you didn't marry for love. You married for money."

"I didn't say that I didn't marry for love."

"But you suggested it."

"Give me a cigarette."

Lorna Chandler gave Cora Freemantle a cigarette and lit it. "You shouldn't smoke. It raises your blood pressure."

Cora puffed. "Good! Now that you've said that, I hope you'll allow me to enjoy this in peace."

"Of course."

Cora thought for a few moments. "No, I don't care much for my children. You have insight, I'll say that for you."

"And less for your grandchildren."

"I can't stand the little demons."

"I could tell by the way you referred to them when you were talking to your daughter-in-law. I didn't mean to over-hear—"

"But you did. In fact, I was trying to get hold of my son to ask him about you."

"Oh. Why?"

"Because you seemed—I don't know—I wanted to know something about you."

"But he wouldn't know anything about me. I come from an agency. You'd have to call them."

"What agency?"

"Guess."

"Guess? What are you talking about?"

"No, I mean you'd never guess."

"I'm not in the habit of playing guessing games, young lady."

"The Nightingale Nursing Service."

"Oh."

"Yes, isn't it cute? Do you want to call them?"

"Of course not. I was just curious. Old women are curious, you know."

"Yes, I know."

"You know, Lorna, there's something in the way you speak—I can't put my finger on it—"

"I'm sorry. I'm doing my best to make conversation, to keep you company."

"No, no. I'm sorry, dear. Just an old woman's frustration at not being able to do for herself. Will you get me another glass of wine, dear?"

"You shouldn't have another, should you?"

"I suppose not, but—"

"But you want one anyway."

"Yes."

"You want what you want when you want it."

"Don't be impertinent. But yes, I want what I want when I want it—and I pay a good deal to have it that way."

"You know, Mrs. Freemantle—Cora—you remind me of my mother."

"I suppose that's a compliment."

"Well, in a way. I envy people who can just shut everything else out but what they want, themselves. It's Godlike."

"I'm not sure I understand."

"Let me get your wine." Lorna went out and returned with more wine. It was as if she took no time at all to do anything—so smooth.

"What did you mean by—"

"Oh, I don't know what I'm talking about, I admit it. Most people don't admit it, but I do. Tell me about your first husband, girl to girl."

Cora shrugged. "There's not much to tell."

"But you had children by him."

"Yes, that's true. Two. A boy—my son, Harry—and a daughter, Carol."

"Where's your daughter?"

"She lives in California. I've cut her out for leaving me—old and ill. Harry is the only one I can count on. Besides, Carol has twins."

"You don't care for them?"

"The truth is, I don't care for children. In vino veritas." Cora giggled.

"They have to be tended, watched over, looked after, and loved."

"They're a nuisance."

"They steal your thunder."

"I don't know what that means."

"Children must come first."

"That's a strange attitude for a young woman."

"No, not at all. Yours is strange."

"There's nothing strange about it. What do you know about children? I've had them, and grandchildren."

"I almost had one."

"Almost?"

"When I was sixteen. My mother made me have an abortion. I wasn't married. The boy was gone. Not at all an unusual story."

"Your mother did the right thing."

"Why do you think that? She never loved me. She loved herself. Now I would have had a child to love and be loved by."

"You would have been alone in the world with a child to support. You're young, now, and free. You can have another child when you wish."

"How can you say that? Another child! As if children were interchangeable, like pet dogs, to be replaced!"

"Oh, but you can't replace a dog. Dogs are—almost human."

"Humans are human!"

"Now, now. I understand how you feel, but—"

"But you obviously don't understand how I feel, anymore than my mother did."

"Well, now, calm yourself. I'm the patient here. You should be taking care of me."

"You! You! How can you think of nothing else but yourself? You're a selfish old woman, don't you know that? Don't you realize what you are?"

Cora's face turned red. She struggled to rise, but Lorna pushed her back against the mound of pillows. "Don't try to get up. You'll fall, and it'll be my fault for letting you. You wouldn't take the blame yourself, would you?"

"Are you crazy, young woman? What are trying to do?"

"Take care of you and your hateful little peke."

"Suzy? Where is Suzy? What have you done with Suzy?"

"I'll get her for you. You'd like to have her in bed with you, wouldn't you?"

"Yes. Please get me Suzy." Cora Freemantle began to whimper. "Please bring me my little Suzy Wong."

Lorna Chandler left the room and returned, Suzy Wong hanging from her leash. She swung the dog onto the bed, where it lay, silent. Cora Freemantle screamed.

"She must have got tangled in the leash," said Lorna Chandler, "poor dear. But you can keep her in bed with you, if you wish."

Cora Freemantle could not breathe. "Help. . . I can't. . . She fell back onto the pillows, where she lay, silent as Suzy Wong.

"There's plenty of time," Lorna Chandler said, dialing the phone. "Hello. Can you come over now and pick up Suzy Wong? Yes, Iris, everything is fine. Before I call the hospital, I want this damned little dead beast in your care, where I hope it won't take you very long to discover that it's had such a coochie-coo sad accident. Tell Harry everything went as planned. And, I warn you, don't either of you forget for one minute that this house is *mine!*"

AN EXPERIMENT IN GOVERNANCE

For some very important, and top-secret, reasons of State, the people who decided policy desired a change in the thought processes of the people they ruled, so they brought back the rusty old rack and began to stretch anyone who could not change his or her mind fast enough to suit them. Members of the public entered the Ministry of Thought at their natural height and came out about two inches taller. At last, we have become competitive, cried one of the people who decided policy. We shall become the capital of fashion, for we have some of the tallest models available. The Eureka-like quality of this observation caused the people who decided policy at the Ministry of Thought to completely forget what the very important, and top-secret, reasons were that caused them to bring back the rusty old rack in the first place. It was our intention from the beginning, they said with one voice, to open an international modeling agency: and things looked very promising for the new democracy until the people began to shrink back to their natural height, shrinking cartilage pulled down by gravity, as it were, and the people at the Ministry of Fashion, which the Ministry of Thought was now called, searched everywhere for their original reasons for bringing back the rusty old rack, but found that their drawers and filing cabinets, originally stuffed with strategic schemes, were now stuffed with dress patterns, Butterick having infiltrated the Ministry, which had become little more than a rag-shop. Such are the pitfalls of governance.

THE CODE OF THE BLUE COMMUNE

The Tribe woke that morning to the bright hard sun of the Arizona winter sky. That is—all but one of the Tribe woke to that sun. One slept on, and would sleep on through eternity.

The one who slept was known as Little Lamb. No one knew what his real name was. He had come from the East with some others who had gone on to the West. Little Lamb had stayed. He had stayed because he had fallen in love with Ketchup, the red-haired mystery girl. Some said that Ketchup had come from the East, where she had been a groupie, a camp-follower of rock musicians. Others said that she had come from the West, where she had lived on the Bohemian beaches of Southern California.

Ketchup was a mystery girl, not because she said nothing about herself, but because she told so many stories, many of which were contradictory, that no one knew what to believe about her. It was of no great importance, however, to the Tribe, that both Little Lamb and Ketchup did nothing to clarify their histories. It was an unwritten code of the Tribe, or the Family, as it was variously known, not to ask questions.

It was left to Marshal Tom McCool to do the necessary questioning, and unfortunately one of the two persons who might be able to spread some light on the subject was dead.

"Poor Little Lamb," as Ketchup had put it.

"Poor Little Lamb" had been six and a half feet tall, dark-bronzed faced, blue-eyed, handsome as a star, and heavily be-wooled about the head and face. "Poor Little Lamb" had been an outsized "Christ-figure," according to some.

"He's a land-locked Billy Budd," as one of the Family put it.

"Why would anyone want to insert a ten-inch dagger in his throat?" asked Marshal McCool. "I thought you people were anti-violence, all for love, like."

"We're just people, Marshal." Ketchup threw a pair of pretty, pink-palmed hands out. "We are trying to get away from your kind of violence, but we grew up in your world, and the violence of that world is in us just as it's in you. The difference is, that we're trying to get away from it, in our heads and in our life-style."

"My kind of violence! Look, Miss, I came here to your flower heaven to investigate a murder. Not the other way around, if you please. Now, you say you don't know Little Lamb's real name or where he came from, but people around here say that he was in love with you. I would imagine that you might know something about a man who was in love with you. Isn't there anything you can tell us?"

"Little Lamb broke the code, I can tell you that."

"The code?"

"Yes, the code. Little Lamb had no right to love me. I mean special like that. Here we all love each other the same way. We women are married to all the men, all the men are our husbands. Little Lamb wanted me all to himself. He broke the code. Otherwise there never would have been violence. He made the violence happen. I'm only surprised that it was he who was killed. I half expected him to kill somebody else. He had returned to the standards of your world."

"You didn't return his love?"

"I loved him as I love all my husbands. But he spoiled my love for him."

"Did he break the code right from the beginning? How long has he been here?"

"No. At first he was like all of us. He told me once that he loved our way of life. That was after he'd been here a month or so. He would have been here around six months, now, I guess."

"Now, look, Ketchup, I'm looking for a motive. Somebody put a shiv in Little Lamb's throat. Somebody had a reason for doing that. Money means nothing to you people, or so you say, and I'm sort of inclined to believe you, within certain limits. So why did little Lamb get it? Did one of your people go ape on acid and perform a human sacrifice?"

"We're not lunatics here."

"It can happen, can't it?"

"It can, yes. But that's a whole different thing. We don't go in for the spooky stuff. We're not like that."

"Well, you people have been around here for over a year, and I must admit I haven't heard of any of that type of thing taking place out here. But there's a first time for everything, isn't there?"

"No. Not here. These are gentle kids. Real love children."

"Okay. Let's say, for the sake of argument that nobody went ape on acid or satanism. Money's out—and that leaves love. Or, more accurately, love's angry side, jealousy. Do you agree?

"I don't like to, but I think it must be that. It could be one of the other wives who was in love with Little Lamb and jealous of his love for me."

"I think that it's more likely that it's one of the other husbands. Think about it, Ketchup. Who among the husbands, besides Little Lamb, seemed like he might be on the verge of breaking the code? In other words, was there anyone else who had a special love for you?"

"Well, maybe Mooncalf. Mooncalf seemed not to love Little Lamb as he should. And Mooncalf did come to me more than to the other wives. We held a council once, and he was—well, we all sort of talked to him about it. You know, we rapped it out and he seemed to dig. After that, he was more regular."

"When was that?"

"Oh, a month or so ago. I'd forgot all about it."

"Why wasn't Little Lamb talked to at a council?"

"He was. Twice. But it didn't do any good. He had been divorced by all the wives and ordered out of the Tribe.

"Why was he still here?"

"Well, he just wouldn't go. There wasn't anything much we could do about it. We couldn't use violence to make him go."

"Somebody finally did."

"That's not funny, Marshal."

"I didn't mean it to be."

"Well, we had to feed him. He was a human being. We couldn't just let him starve."

After the questioning of Ketchup—whose real name turned out to be Tania Brady—Marshal McCool called in the young man known as Mooncalf. McCool had seen Mooncalf in town a couple of times: a bearded, curly-haired, lanky kid of nineteen or twenty, with a look of perpetual pain on his face.

"Look, fuzz," said Mooncalf as he stepped inside the kitchen tent which McCool was using as a kind of operations room, "I had nothing to do with this thing. I don't know what that flaming witch of a Ketchup has been telling you, but if anybody knows who killed Little Lamb it's her. Maybe she did it herself."

"That's a serious charge," said McCool, an expression of mild surprise on his face. "Why do you make it?"

"Because Little Lamb was going to leave for the West Coast today, and he wasn't going to take her with him."

"You're saying that she was in love with Little Lamb?"

"Of course she was. Did she deny it?"

"Well, according to Ketchup, Little Lamb was in love with her. She said that he had been making a nuisance of himself and had been expelled from the commune."

"She's a liar! Little Lamb was the most Christ-like person I've ever known. He could never make a nuisance of himself in any way. He was going to leave the Tribe because she wouldn't let him alone. All the other wives and husbands were upset about it. Little Lamb belonged to everybody, but she started everybody fighting over him by trying to claim him all for herself. That's why he was leaving, to help us all find peace again. He was good. A real saint."

"And you think that Ketchup killed him because he was going away without her?"

"Yeah. She begged him not to leave her. She must have lost that temper of hers last night and stabbed him."

"She thinks you did it."

"Sure, she has to blame somebody. She never loved me as she should have, so I'm the goat."

"I'm afraid the goat has already been sacrificed.

"I dig," said Mooncalf, and sulked out, following the line of Marshall McCool's gesture.

The third person Marshal McCool questioned that morning was the Tribe's elected leader, a tall, burly man who was called Father Time.

"I've heard your people refer to your camp as the Blue Commune," McCool said. What does that signify?"

"That signifies under the sky, mountaintop. But what's that got to do with Little Lamb gettin' his throat opened?"

"Nothing," said McCool, "Except by irony. Nature, love, and a man named Little Lamb with a ten-inch dagger in his throat!"

"This don't happen around here every day, you know," said Father Time. He was decidedly defensive, thought McCool, but it did not necessarily read as an attitude of guilt. It appeared to McCool that Father Time was genuinely upset that ill-fame of any sort should come to the Blue Commune.

This followed, thought McCool.

In the past these people had stayed out of the way of the local people and had caused the authorities no trouble. McCool knew that there were drugs all over the place, but why stir up trouble? So long as the local people had no complaints, he would leave the Blue Commune alone.

But now things would have to be different, and Father Time knew it.

"Look, Father Time," said McCool, "I've never bothered you or your people, have I?"

"No, you been straight," replied Father Time, rather grudgingly.

"Well, it comes to this: I can't promise anything, but I'll do my best to see that this thing doesn't blow up too big, if you'll play it straight with me."

"What do you want me to do?"

"Tell me whatever you know about this, naturally. And make it straight."

"And what do we get back?"

"Anybody who isn't directly implicated can get a three-hour start toward the State line. That's all I can do, in a situation like this.

"Living the way you do, the D.A. might be able to lock up the whole lot of you as conspirators, accomplices and accessories before and/or after the fact. And by this afternoon two-thirds of the county are going to be screaming for just that. If you want to get the innocent among you away clean, you'll tell me what you know. Otherwise—there's always the junk, too."

"What makes you think that the whole bunch of us freaks didn't get together and sacrifice Little Lamb to the sun god in an acid ritual?"

"Because he's just lying there in his tent with a ten-inch blade jammed to the hilt through his neck. That means that at least five inches of that blade are in dirt. It might not have happened there, but that makes it look as if it did. And that isn't exactly the setting for a ritual murder. If you people were going to perform a ritual murder, you'd lay your victim out on a rock, wouldn't you? Or hang him on a cross. Something symbolic and comic-bookish, or don't I read your mentality correctly?"

"We're not idiots, McCool."

"You better hope that I keep on thinking you are. Now let's have what you know. For starters, was Little Lamb ordered out of camp, or was he going to leave on his own hook?"

"Neither, exactly. We all agreed, him and us, that if the ideals of the commune were going to survive, it would be better if he went away for a while. Say, McCool, if that blade is still in the ground, how'd you know it was ten inches long?"

"The scabbard matches the dagger. By the way, who owns, or owned, that knife?"

"Everybody. It belongs to the Tribe."

"That's what I figured. Would you mind telling me what you people use a ten-inch dagger for?"

"It's a religious thing, but not the kind of thing—"

"I told you, I dismissed that theory early on. But what did you do with that sword?"

"We cut grass with it."

"You mean pot? Marijuana?"

"Yeah. It grows wild all abouts here. In the summer, when it's growing, we go out at midnight and cut the stuff. The dagger was our official family cutter. Like a religious ritual. Dig?"

"Dig. Where was the knife kept?"

"We kept it right in the middle of the camp, tied to a cross. Anybody could take it."

"What about Little Lamb? Do you know anything about him? His real name?"

"No. He came to us six months ago. He came with friends. They went on. He stayed. He was a saint."

"That's all?"

"That's all. We don't ask questions."

"If he was ever fingerprinted, as seems likely, we'll know who he was by tonight or tomorrow morning."

"And what will you know then, McCool, a name? He'll still be Little Lamb."

"Did Little Lamb stay on here at the Blue Commune because he fell in love with Ketchup, Miss Brady, or for other reasons?

"Not for Miss Brady."

"I've heard from some of your people that Little Lamb was in love with Ketchup. She even said that he was."

"Woman's vanity."

"And the others?"

"You the one said they had comic book mentalities."

"You mean you people gossip about each other just like the people out in the big bad world?"

"We are human here, too."

"All too human, apparently. Father Time, I am becoming disillusioned with you flower people."

"We're only trying, McCool. That's more than the rest of you do."

"What's your real name, Father Time? Your mother didn't christen you that, did she?"

"My name is Father Time. Furthermore, I have never been arrested. Neither have I been in the army. There is no way of ever identifying me as anybody but who I am—Father Time. So you might as well give up on that right now, McCool."

"Okay, for now. But as soon as I decide to know, I'll find out."

"How? Nobody in this camp knows my name. What are you going to do? Are you going to beat me with a rubber hose? Come on, McCool, I don't think you're the type. Forget it, I'm Father Time, that's all."

"Watch it, you might be Father Time in the State Pen for withholding evidence. Don't say I didn't warn you. Now, what about the dame, Ketchup? And what about this kid, Mooncalf?"

"Ask me."

"Was there anything between them?"

"Mooncalf dug her. What can I say?"

"He was in love with her?"

"Yeah, I guess."

"Was it—how do you people say it? A special thing, out of the code?"

"Maybe. Yeah, I guess."

"How did she feel about him?"

"He was only a kid to her, nothing. Just one of the husbands."

"He's turned on her now. He seems to despise her. He appears to have worshiped Little Lamb."

"That's natural, ain't it? He'd come on like he dug Little Lamb so nobody'd think he did it, wouldn't he?"

"Sounds good. Go on."

"Well, he comes on now like he hates Ketchup so's nobody thinks his loving her was a motive."

"He accused her of doing the job."

"He don't think anybody'll believe that."

"Why not?"

"'Cause no woman would have the strength to drive that knife through a big man's neck and five more inches into the dirt."

"Well, you're quite a detective, Father Time, as well as a male chauvinist pig."

"I told you, we aren't idiots."

"So your bet is that Mooncalf was in love with Ketchup, and was afraid that she'd go off with Little Lamb, and, maybe in a fit of jealousy, killed him."

"I ain't saying that."

"But you are, by implication. But how do you account for the fact that Ketchup said that she was being annoyed by Little Lamb? If she loved him—"

"She's a smart girl. She would say that now, so as to stay clear of the trouble."

"Disown the whole thing. Is that it?"

"Makes sense, don't it?"

"Take a guess," said McCool suddenly, "how many people have you got in this camp?"

"You mean how big is our tribe?"

"That'll do."

"Don't know, exactly. Maybe seventy-five."

"And in the summer you go out at midnight and harvest that pot? All of you?"

"Yeah, so what?"

"That's quite a haul, isn't it? Father Time, you ain't gonna sit there and tell me that you people smoke all that pot. You sell it, don't you? You deal? Give it to me straight. Now let's have it. Who deals?"

"Okay, so I do the dealing. So what?"

"In other words, you lead that pack of comic-book people out to those fields in the moonlight and with your magic dagger start the harvest celebration, then the tribe goes to work and brings it in by the bushel. You do the diviying. The kids get a share to keep them happy and stupid and you store the rest away, for the benefit of the tribe, only not really for their benefit, but to sell."

"I sell it to buy us all groceries. We've gotta eat like everybody else."

"Can it, Father Time. You sell enough stuff to supply the Army, Navy and Marine Corps with food for a century. I was told that you haven't been in camp for a few weeks. Where have you been?"

"All right. I've been in Mexico. and then in New York. Why bother to ask if you know?"

"Just wanted to hear you say it. You picked up heroin for pot money in Mexico and took the heroin to New York where you supplied dealers. Say yes."

"I ain't saying nothing else till I talk to my lawyer. You're a fink, McCool."

"And you're a Brady, Father Time. The New York police sent a copy of a certificate of marriage between a Miss Tania Armstrong and a Mr. Timothy Brady out here when you people first started the Blue Commune. The local citizenry wanted to know what kind of people were moving in among them. The report I made to the Chamber of Commerce dispelled a lot of fears. Just a married couple and a bunch of harmless hippie drop-outs.

"Now, Father Time, tell me what really happened? Did Little Lamb and Ketchup get too close while you were away making deals? Those people that Little Lamb came here with—New York dealers? West Coast dealers? Were Little Lamb and Ketchup going to split out with the profits? You plunged that knife into Little Lamb's neck, Brady, and you and that fire-topped wife of yours decided to put it onto the kid, Mooncalf."

"That's right, Marshal. Now just sit tight while Tim puts some rope around you." Tania Brady held a hard, cold object to the back of McCool's neck. Tim Brady's face broke into a large cheerful smile. He said: "Good girl."

"So," said McCool, "he runs a knife through your boyfriend's throat and the next morning you help him get away. You people of the Blue Commune have a strange code. Only the gutter-rats of the underworld know how it works."

"Shut up, McCool," said Tania; "you think I'm going to let you have Tim, because of what happened with Little Lamb! Yeah, I went for Little Lamb, in my fashion, but he's dead. I've been with Tim a long time; I ain't gonna cross him for the Establishment. Come on, Tim, tie him up."

"There are two other men from my office here. As soon as they see you take off they'll be after you," said McCool.

"Sorry, McCool. Their car has four flat tires, and we'll take yours. How are they going to follow us? Run?"

"You've got a smart girl there, Brady. Maybe too smart. Keep an eye on her, or you're liable to end up like Little Lamb."

Suddenly McCool heard a scream and the sounds of a struggle behind him. Brady, who had been trying McCool's legs to the rungs of a chair, leaped to his feet, a horrified, stunned look on his face, and wavered uncertainly.

McCool dove, ramming a shoulder into Brady's midriff. Brady's chest came down on McCools's back. McCool heard the breath heave from Brady with a woosh. He sounded like a crushed bellows.

But McCool's left leg tangled in the loose ropes, and he was jerked to the floor like a roped steer.

Brady staggered backwards, clutching his stomach, his chest heaving. His eyes darted wildly from the sprawled McCool to the struggle that was taking place behind the lawman. McCool got to his feet, keeping his eyes fixed on Brady. Whatever was happening behind him had Brady plenty scared, and that was enough for McCool. McCool desperately tried to kick free of the rope that entangled his boot. Brady was coming at him now.

McCool stepped sideways, dragging the chair with him. Then, just as his boot slipped free, Brady was on him. The impact of Brady's short, cracking uppercut sent McCool sprawling. For an instant, he lay stunned, panting. He was able to lift his head in time to see Brady's heel vanish beyond the tent flap. He rolled over on his stomach and saw Tania Brady being slowly and methodically choked from behind by Mooncalf, who held the cheaply bejewelled scabbard of the ritual knife across her milk-white, slightly freckled throat.

The girl was still conscious, her fierce blue eyes rolling wildly, her throat clicking for air. Half of Mooncalf's face was buried in her fiery mane; the other half, the part that McCool saw, had gone mad, the tender boyish mouth torn down like a jagged scar, the eye a glinting coin.

McCool scooped up the pistol that Tania had dropped and, in a continuous motion, hooked the fingers of his free hand over the scabbard, and sent the pistol glancing off Mooncalf's temple.

McCool yanked at the scabbard, and Tania Brady dropped to the floor unconscious between himself and Mooncalf. With the speed of a cat, Mooncalf let go the scabbard. McCool reeled backwards. Mooncalf kicked out, knocking the pistol from McCool's hand. Both went for the pistol. Mooncalf got it, and ran from the tent. McCool was on his heels.

Fifty feet away, McCool's Chevy, with Brady driving, was pulling off, heading for the town road. Mooncalf stopped short, whirled about, and caught McCool running, clipping him across the side of the head with the pistol. McCool's momentum, plus the blow, sent him sliding belly down. He looked up, drunkenly. Mooncalf raised the pistol in a straight-arm aim. He fired six times.

The shots echoed, whining back from the hills that surrounded the Blue Commune. They drummed against the clear, cold sky.

By the third shot, McCool's eyes were on the car. With the practiced eye of an expert marksman, he picked up the uneven line of punctures. He had counted to the third when he saw the fourth appear, a black pock on the car's white side.

The first shot smashed through the rear fender; the next, higher, through the rear door; the third hit the window of that door, turning it milky; the fourth and fifth made a tight group at the top of the car.

The Chevy swerved and ran off the dirt road into a ditch. It sat rocking for a moment, then came a small puffing sound, and a long delicate whisp of flame rose from the hood. Suddenly the car vanished inside an angry red cloud.

The sound of the explosion rocked the Blue Commune.

Leading him back to the tent, McCool casually took the empty pistol from Mooncalf's limp hand.

The two troopers who had accompanied McCool, joined the denizens of the Blue Commune who were already gathering about the smoldering car. McCool didn't have to look. He knew. He had watched as the sixth bullet turned red on Father Time's right temple. Why did you do it?" the Marshal said, eyeing Mooncalf doubtfully.

The boy, his downy face gleaming in the midday sun, breathed heavily several times, then said, in a shaky, quavering voice: "Don't you see? I loved Little Lamb and love is the most important thing in the Blue Commune."

LAST EXIT TO EAST HAMPTON

I will get off the 4:19 in Easthampton at 7:15
—Frank O'Hara

"Entre nous, Roger and I visited some friends out on East Hampton, and there was a wealthy and beautiful chatelaine there, sans man, whose name I have conveniently forgotten, and Roger took up with her, because, *I* think, she looked like Truman Capote, blond and a little plump, and the next thing I know I'm soloing it with my Martini very dry and feeling like a dipstick in the sand. Roger and I are always together and I could not understand such isolation as had befallen me. After all, I was being dumped for a female—well, maybe. But just as I was reaching the blue dog black funk basement on the down elevator, a woman wearing an amazing diamond choker passed on some interesting and distracting gossip. Apparently, Bergdorf's had appropriated Augustus John's portrait of Tallulah, to whom *adieu*, which cheered me I can't tell you how much; and, after swallowing the last of my Martini very dry, I sighed happily, and said, Oh well, we still have beaucoup de music classique et moderne. There was a band all in gold. The diamond-choker lady elbowed my ribs, indicating the door, and so I saw Roger leaving with the beautiful lady (maybe). Absolutely horrid of him, of course. Still, I tittered anyway. Later I took a dive in the pool to cool off. You know how it is. These people are harder than they look, like a roll of Krugerrands you put in your fist to make your hand strong when you punch somebody's lights out. Oh hell, life is beautiful, don't you think?"

THE ORPHANED

By midnight, people lay about on the floor, some drink-drugged, some plain drugged. Harry Goldfarb, director of the Oh-No Soho Gallery, appeared at the door with big Denise, a performance artist, arm over shoulder, covered with blood. He had several dent-like cuts on his forehead, dripping in gouts. It seemed that Denise was having one of her bad trips. She'd wanted out. Harry had tried to help her down the long, iron-covered, loft stairway, she'd thrown a fit, and they'd both gone tumbling down. One of Harry's female assistants popped up, joined them, and tried to soothe Denise. They tried to hold her still, but Denise flailed on. Jimmy Whistler went over and took Denise by the shoulders and tried to pin her to a wall. But in her madness she was very strong and broke loose and slapped him back and forth across the face with both hands, nearly unhinging his jaw with the first blow. He got her back in his grip, and held her there. Then she went loose and slid down the wall into a sleep or coma or God knew what oblivion. Harry and the assistant tried to wake her. Someone patted her face with a wet towel, and Harry fed her coffee. At last they got her on her feet. She was docile now, whimpering and pathetic. Harry led her out the door. He must have taken Denise all the way home. Neither of them came back. The place was a bloody shambles. Some Opening!

When Jimmy woke, scenes from the night before returned. He had poor Denise and her bad trip on the brain.

He remembered the early days, when Denise and he worked together—how she had got her landlord to rent him his first place in New York, in the Village—all of it was alive in his mind, bits and parts of his hangover.

Maybe it was just sentimentality, nostalgia—but he decided to find a place where he could get a couple of quarts of cold beer and take them up as an offering to good old Denise in what was probably her hour of need.

She lived in an ancient musty building. Jimmy climbed four flights of stairs and banged (cheerfully, he thought) on the door. Denise moaned from within, and called: "Who's there?"

"It's me, Denise; Jimmy."

She let him in, and lowered herself down on the floor, on a blanket, where she slept. She had her B.A. in Oriental studies, and it was her little resultant vanity to sleep on mats. She'd slept on a bamboo mat in the house where she'd got him his little room. She had used to play the recorder (the instrument, not the machine) and would play herself to sleep at night. She'd play until she dropped the wooden instrument in her lap, and, if she left her door open, as she often did, you could find her there in the morning, sitting up, mouth hanging open, holding the musical stick, like a child whose thumb has dropped out of its mouth. But, though she still slept on the floor, she no longer lived as she had in the old days. Her little shoe box of a room had been kept in fanatic order; its books, on neat shelves, floor to ceiling, had been arranged according to size and content; the pens on its neat desk neatly placed: a place for everything and everything in its place. This room looked like a small storage room for used books, bags of garbage, and other superfluities, and one in which all the shelves had broken and everything had caved in and commingled. It was fortunate for orderly eyes that the only light fixture was broken and ended in a frayed and dangling cord. The place was shadow-lit and dreary, the room of a drinking and drug-taking anchorite. Denise sat in the middle of this devastation like a big, pale statue of Sorrow. She wore only a shabby pink slip, most of the fluffy tops of her big breasts exposed, showing blue veins. Her hair, which was thick, black, and kinky, was in wild disarray. Her feet were dirty, and the little toes black from sticking out the holes at the sides of her sneakers. (Jimmy thought she must have bought her sneakers with holes in the sides.) The sneakers themselves, the crumpled black skirt, and the blood-stained army fatigue shirt, which she wore the night before, lay on the floor near her feet. She held her knees in her hands. She looked like a woman who didn't care what happened next, sad as an old salad, just beat. A kind of young, frumpy Gertrude Stein. Jimmy put the beer down on the floor by her feet, and said:

"Here, kid! Here's something for the morning blues. Want some?"

"Oh, man," she said quietly, groaningly, "I'm so ashamed."

"Oh, come on now. What's this? Come on, let's have some beer."

"No, man . . . no . . . it was terrible last night . . . ."

"What're you talking about. You got a little high, that's all."

She shook her head, slowly, side to side.

"Oh, Jimmy . . . Jimmy . . ."

"No. Really, Denise, you didn't do anything—" then he gave her a big, stupid smile, and added—"except freak out, fall down the stairs, and knock my jaw off its hinges—" and then he made a face and said—"As a matter of fact, your conduct was . . . *deplorable!*"

She couldn't help herself. It started with a faint, blossoming, impossible-to-suppress smile, and then all the tension she'd been building up exploded into laughter, and every time she looked up at him, she exploded again. While the latest of these seismic fits was in diminuendo Jimmy opened one of the beer bottles. He wondered if what she had been on last night was still working on her. When her laughter had subsided, he stuck the bottle in her face, so that, before she could think about herself too much, she was tasting and swallowing. When she finished drinking, and put the bottle down, she looked at Jimmy seriously, and said:

"You mean you aren't angry with me?"

"Of course not. Why should I be angry?"

"I hit you."

"Oh, come off it, Denise. Drink some more beer. It'll help unscramble your brains."

She took another drink, then handed him the bottle.

"Look, kid," he said, "what are you trying to do with yourself? If it sends you away to the badlands, you should skip it."

"All my trips aren't bad."

"It looks to me like most of them are. Why push it? You're going to wind up in a bad way."

"I don't care. I don't care about anything. I just want to see something beautiful. Sometimes I see beautiful things."

"Doesn't look like you've seen anything beautiful lately, huh?"

"No, not lately."

"Then give it a vacation, why not?"

"Yeah, yeah, man; I will."

"Denise—you know, baby, you've got to take care of yourself a little . . . ."

She didn't say anything for a time. Then she shrugged; said: "I saw my mother, who had big boobs like mine, lean over a table so they fell free away from her body"—she got up and walked to a little table, on which books were unsteadily stacked, and demonstrated, placing her hands on the table, arms stiff, leaning forward and letting her breasts drop free beneath the slip—"like this, in such pain as I could never bear to see again. And six months after she'd died, my father—father—was killed in an auto wreck—"

She stopped abruptly, and, distorting her face, her eyes squeezed shut by a smile so tight she looked like an exaggerated comedy mask, trying to hold back the tears that were flying from them anyhow. She went back to the blanket and threw herself down on it, face away, without a sound.

Jimmy's own drink-agitated nerves allowed for it, and he felt the rising damp himself. He wiped his eyes on his sleeves, and sat on, waiting, trying to feel as little as possible.

About ten minutes later, Denise turned about, solemn, but dry-eyed. She said:

"Pass me the beer, please."

Jimmy did, and she drank, and then she lit herself a hazardous cigarette, blew smoke, and smiled.

"I guess I can't do anything right," she said.

"Don't feel bad, kid," Jimmy said, "I can't either. None of us can. But we have to try, don't we?"

"What for?"

"Why not? If it don't matter, it don't matter either way, do it?"

She smiled.

He added: "Otherwise it do matter, don't it?"

She laughed. "You're a witty guy. I always liked that about you. You know what Auden said about wit?"

"What?"

"In his experience, he said, wit required a combination of imagination, moral courage and unhappiness. All three are essential: an unimaginative or a cowardly or a happy person is seldom very amusing."

"So you think I'm unhappy?"

“Aren’t you?”

Jimmy shrugged. “But seriously, kiddo, one has to figure out what one’s about. I remember in my downer days I used to say I was a puppet. It was true. I was living out my father’s life for him. I was even afraid of my mother, because I knew she’d have told me I wasn’t my father; and, though she didn’t know it, what that meant to me then was, or would have been, that I wasn’t myself, either; that I had no self, in fact. See what I mean? If I’d been myself, there could hardly have been any question as to whether or not I was my father. When you have a self, you’re not afraid to take advice—even from parents.”

“Well?”

“Well, this. If we don’t find, or even make up, some kind of authority for ourselves, we’ll wake up at death-time to discover that everything has been pointless. I saw that, when I thought I was going to die. I was sick, Denise, pneumonia. When you were away. That’s why I’m determined, now, to become my own father. In this bloody world where no one else is willing to be your father, you have to become your own father; then you’ll always have someone to look after you in your hour of need. Let me recite you a poem I wrote. It’s called ‘The Orphaned’ . . .

When the mood comes upon him to die
of a loneliness deeper than death,

he must speak to himself like a parent
in a lecturing voice, but with love.

He must be his own father and mother,
and at night when he looks up at heaven,

where nothing of earth seems to live,
and the range of all things is so great

as to startle the love from his breast,
he must think of his father, the Rock,

and his mother, the Dead Sea, and of
the message he brings from the sun."

"Oh, Jimmy!"

"See what I mean? Be your own daddy and momma, then you'll be all right all right. Be Big Momma."

"I dig, Jimmy; I dig."

"Good. Why don't you start right away. What would be the first thing your momma and daddy would make you do this morning."

"Stop drinking."

"Well, now, let's not be extremists. What's the second thing?"

"Wash my face and brush my teeth."

"Good. Why don't you do that."

"Because I don't really feel like it."

"Good. Then don't. I mean, if that's the kind of momma you are, I guess you're just going to have a dirty kid—right?"

"Right!"

"Good," Jimmy said. "Pass me the beer."

"You haven't cured me, you know, with your poem and your shitty jokes." She winked at him.

"Yeah, I know," he said, lifting the bottle. "It takes a lifetime."

THE KAISER COMES TO ORLANDO

You are having another one of your crazy nightmares and a big gaping mustachioed mouth is chasing you up seven post-Great-War decades of the Twentieth century. You're keeping ahead, but you come to a red light, and you have to stop because beyond is nothing, or heaven, or hell, so you mark time, waiting, and the gaping mouth is catching up to swallow you, you who have pledged allegiance to the Moose, and you collapse your dry knees like folding chairs, you break and bend them until you are under the kitchen table and, when you look up and out, you are back there again and they are charging at you across no-man's-land, spiked helmets and long thin bloodguttered bayonets, and in Orlando you go to the V.F.W. and live in a house where the sun burns back blindingly off the flung newspaper, its date a liar making you nearly a hundred, and you look up from your muddy trench, your long, bolt-action Springfield, its stock tangled under your trenchcoated arm, barrel aimed out toward them over sandbags, and with your free hand you pat your pet rat. Little black clouds form and vanish. You think they are like exploding eight balls. You hear *FIRE!* And your nerves jerk the trigger, while still petting the traitorous rat that scurries off. *OVER THE TOP!* You hear things crashing about you: the table, sugar bowl, coffee cups, a whole sideboard filled with dishes . . . And now a Great Power is holding you down and it is the cartoon face of the Hun, the fat rat-face and mustache of the Kaiser. He wants to eat you as he would a Belgian baby. Then you awake voiceless in England, a fire-breather, your elephant-nosed, goggle-eyed gas mask tangled, your sucking-for-breath, mustard-gassed lungs collapsed. Then you awaken in another hospital, in Orlando, Florida, seventy years later, and you are surrounded by strangers who say they are your family—they are strangers, of course, because you are still too young to marry, as Mother says you are, still too young for such responsibility, only a beardless boy from Hoboken in a slouch hat and brogans, an apprentice leatherworker commuting to Brooklyn, no scared-to-death doughboy in the Argonne and Belleau Wood, no Alzheimer's patient in a hospital bed in Orlando. And look, no jaywalker you! The light turns green for you to go!

HAYDN'S HEAD: A PASTICHE

for Jack O'Brian, columnist, New York Journal-American, who tipped me off

We are aboard the Orange Blossom Special, returning to New York from Florida, and I am hopeful that Tweedledum and Tweedledee, as Johnny calls them, a couple of bad eggs in plaid suits, are not.

"Odds are we've left them shaking their fists on the station platform, Pug," Johnny says, mopping his brown brow with a white silk handkerchief. He gears his seat back, loosens his tie, tips his Panama over his eyes, and acts like he hasn't got a worry in the world. I act like I am watching the midnight Miami lights recede, but what I am really doing is watching the window for reflections. I expect to see Sam the Elephant's bonebreakers appear at any second.

Most all gamblers have a specialty—cards, craps, horses—but Johnny Belmont will bet on anything. I have first heard of him a year ago, when he places a spectacular bet on the presidential election and loses to all concerned. He is in deep trouble until his rich family steps in. But they are very much put out, because he has bet on Stevenson and they are an Eisenhower family. So they warn Johnny that they will not rescue him again. At least this is the version I have heard outside of Lindy's restaurant, in that vague area of the environment around Broadway and Fiftieth Street which Damon Runyon has dubbed Jacobs' Beach in honor of his ticket speculating pal, Mike Jacobs. On Jacobs' Beach you meet the sporting crowd—scalpers, bookies, touts, mobsters, and journalists such as Walter Winchell and, until he passes on in '46, Runyon himself.

But it is at Hialeah that Johnny and I have become pals. The Florida sharks do not know that Johnny is a black sheep without a red cent; so, with his good looks, his classy manners, and his family name, he has been able to borrow large amounts of hay from Sam the Elephant, who is called such because he does not forget so easy. But Johnny has been having the world's worst losing streak, and has tried to get on the good side of Lady Luck by placing some bets for me. Unfortunately, Sam the Elephant has heard of said bets; and, because he does not care from which individual he collects, has decided to hold me partners with Johnny when he calls in the bets.

We are tap city when we step off the Special at Penn Station—unless you count Johnny's lucky two-bit piece, which he never spends. But Johnny thinks we can get a stake at the Hotel Bon Chance, a gamblers' haven in the West Forties. I figure he means to check us in and flip his quarter into wealth. But I am worried that some of Sam the Elephant's boys might be keeping their eyes out for us there. Johnny laughs kind of grimly and says that we will have to gamble on that because the Bon Chance is the only place he can think of where he can raise a stake.

It looks like we are going to have to hoof it through a cold November rain, which is pouring out of buckets. It does not matter much to me, because I am not a dude, but it matters to Johnny, who is a clotheshorse. We have had to leave all our clothes in Florida, and he only has this one tropical suit left, which is on his back. So he shakes his head, and says: "Pug, I'm not going to let this suit get soaked."

I follow him through the crowd and up to the Lost and Found, which is open all night in those days, and it is now about midnight, as our trip takes us about twenty-four hours, and he tells the busy clerk behind the counter that he has lost his black umbrella. The clerk hustles off and is back in no time with three such. "That's it," cries Johnny, and takes the one that happens to be the best of the lot.

As we are walking away, Johnny says, "You know, Pug, one could get anything that way." He stops and looks at me with his green eyes bright like two Go signs. "Think of something, I'll bet you a belated C-note that they have it—that the clerk will hand it across to you."

There is nothing like a wager to cheer me up, and I need cheering. "You're on," I say. "We'll make it for the first C-note one of us gets."

"O.K.," says Johnny. "But I choose the item. It can't be anything with an I.D., and it can't be anything too unusual—like a zither. Fair enough?"

"Fair enough," I say, wondering what a zither is.

"Say a plain square box—a cardboard carton or package wrapped in plain brown paper and tied with twine—O.K.?"

"You're on."

"You ask for it. I got the umbrella. The clerk might remember me." On the 5-yard line from the Lost and Found desk, Johnny says: "I'll wait here." In two minutes I am back, carton in hand.

"I owe you a C-note," I say, dangling the package from a finger by the twine. "The bet's good," I add, and say that I will now return the package.

"Wait a minute, Pug," says Johnny. "How about another C-note on what's in it? Let's say on whether it's animal, vegetable, or mineral."

I say, "It's bigger than a breadbox, that's for sure."

"Takers?" says Johnny.

I shrug. "Takers," I say. "So where do we open it?"

"Not here," says Johnny. "I'll tell you what, Pug. We'll take it with us to the Bon Chance, and open it there. Then I'll have a boy re-wrap it and bring it back here to the Lost and Found. What do you say?"

"I suppose you want I should carry it?"

"And I'll keep us dry with the umbrella. Come on."

The Bon Chance is a few blocks uptown from Penn Station. Cats and Dogs of rain are bouncing knee-high as we turn off the avenue. On the next corner is a Yellow Cab stand, or used to be in those days. I duck to look into the first cab in the line and there as usual is Sleeping Bill, who could make a claim to being the worst hack in New York, as he never takes a fare. Actually, it is his own car, done up to look like a Yellow Cab, and he is no hack at all, but a bookie. I tap his windshield but he is asleep at the wheel. I think he has been so since I left for Florida. Anyway, he's in the same position he was in when I left.

In a block or two on this numbered cross-street the pedestrian traffic has thinned down to Johnny and me. Ahead, through the watery dark I see *BON CHANCE* come and go in nervous green neon winks. I am looking at this sign, and thinking about a hot bath, when a dark, shiny limo sprays up beside us. The back window on our side is rolled down and there is the head of a white-faced, dark-hatted woman in it. She has thin red lips and big white teeth through which she hisses something at us, which I cannot make out due to the fact that the rain is doing drum rolls. A big boy in a chauffeur's uniform comes around from the other side. He is waving a revolver which has a silencer on it like a rolled-up racing form. He believes that action speaks louder than words, because instead of explaining himself he hooks a couple of thick fingers into the twine on the box I am conveying and tugs. I tug back. He then swings at me and misses, but corrects himself by bashing the big silencer down on my knuckles. Only now does he decide to make himself clear.

"Let go, you fat swine!" he cries, adding insult to injury. But before I can be offended, Johnny has collapsed the umbrella and batted it down on the pistol, which splashes into a jumping lake at the rear end of the limo.

"En garde!" cries Johnny, stabbing the guy several short ones. The big guy lets go of the twine, and slips in the rain just as I step in with a right cross. He falls against the limo and keeps on going down toward where the pistol has submerged, slapping at street water, grabs up the pistol, aims, and pulls the trigger.

Because of the silencer and the noise of the rain, I don't know if I have been shot or not, but then I realize by the look on the big guy's face that the pistola is waterlogged.

Johnny and I have jumped away when he has had the pistola pointed at us, so he has a head start when he ducks around the limo. The door slams and the limo speeds off, making a wake like the Titanic.

"What the hell . . ." says Johnny, looking after the limo.

"It is this dumb package," I say.

"Did you see the plates?" says Johnny. "They were diplomatic. Let's get to a room and see what we've got here."

There is a new night clerk at the Bon Chance, a straw-haired, freckled kid with a Southern accent. This is a break, as the old clerk would have sold out his mother to Sam the Elephant or any other shark for the price of a warm beer. It won't help much if Sam the Elephant's boys are looking hard for us, but it is anyway worth the ink to register under a couple of phony names, so we do. A kid who looks like the younger brother of the yokel behind the desk shows us up, carrying the package by the twine, like a suitcase.

In our room, Johnny offers to flip the kid double or nothing for the tip, neglecting to state the amount involved, and the kid eagerly takes the bet. Johnny then offers to let the kid owe him "the ten spot." But before the kid has about-faced, Johnny has flipped him into serious debt, which he immediately cancels, on the condition that we get top service, to which the kid gratefully agrees.

Johnny orders sandwiches, coffee, cigarettes, cigars, razors, etc. He also needs a bottle of good Scotch. He sends the kid away with our wet clothes. In those days, you can get a good steam press all night, even in a cheap hotel.

"Well, now, Pug," says Johnny, ripping open the package, "let's have a look at this."

I go over to the table on which the kid has placed the box and look into it. Johnny is pulling out a lot of excelsior. There is something round and gray down in the middle of the box. Johnny pulls more excelsior out, reaches in, and jerks back like he's been stung. I see it now and let out a whistle. It is a human skull.

As soon as it sinks in what we have here, we do a thorough search of the box for identification of some kind—"Provenance," Johnny calls it—even checking inside the skull, but discover zero. We pack the bony head away; and then, while we bathe and shave, we discuss the nature of things as they stand.

We ask ourselves: Who are the foreign couple in the limo? Why do they want this old skull? Should we call the police?

Johnny says, combing his dark hair down over his forehead and cutting a part in it, "Do the chauffeur and his lady know that the package contains a skull, rather than something else more valuable? Surely an ordinary human skull can't be worth much. Surely not enough to induce armed robbery."

Comes a rapping at our chamber door.

"Who is it?" Johnny calls.

"Bellboy. I got your clothes and a wagon full of food and drinks."

When the bellboy goes, Johnny says, "Get dressed, Pug," and pulls on his pants.

I am tying my tie in the cloudy mirror over the dresser when there is a second knock at the door.

"What now?" Johnny calls over the transom. He thinks it is the bellboy again.

"Please," comes a wheezy reply. "I am Professor-Doctor Albrecht Schmitt with my daughter, Agnes. We have rooms down the hall. I must speak with you."

"It don't sound like anybody Sam the Elephant would know," I say.

"Nor like the chauffeur from the limo," says Johnny. He opens the door a crack and peers out. Then he steps back and opens it wide.

This gent has a couple of inches on me and I have a couple of pounds on him, making us two barrels, but his weight is then as old as mine is now, and he has never been a lightweight boxer as I have before I lose my last match in the late 40's and begin consoling myself with pumpkin pies.

He has a gray, yellow-streaked walrus mustache, and thick, silver-rimmed specs. His daughter is taller and a hundred pounds lighter, a honey-blonde in powder blue who looks like a wicked witch has chased her out of a fairy tale. She eyes Johnny like he is Prince Charming.

The old gent extends a thin manicured hand. "I'm Professor-Doctor Schmitt," he repeats. Gray moths flutter behind his specs. "I see you have opened our package. We were on our way up from Washington with that skull when we suspected we were being followed. You see, it is a valuable specimen, and there are those who would stop at nothing to possess it. Research is highly competitive. You

Americans have a phrase—*it's a jungle*." He gives out with a nervous cackle.

Johnny lights a Fatima. He says, "It hasn't got a name or a number on it. How do we know it's yours?"

The Doc looks stumped. The gray moths look like they are trying to break out from behind their glass cages.

Johnny purses his lips, lifting his little black mustache, and blows out some Turkish smoke, giving Agnes the once-over twice. She looks at him with big sad blue eyes. He cracks a smile. "Maybe you can tell me how you lost it—?"

"Oh, no," the Doc almost stutters, "it wasn't lost. Just as we were leaving the train, we became *certain* that we were being followed. But we hoped we had lost our pursuers in the crowd when we came upon a row of lockers. Unfortunately, neither of us had an appropriate coin—"

"We had to work fast," Agnes breaks in. "In a moment's inspiration, my father saw the Lost and Found, and we deposited it there."

"Then," the Doc picks up, "we waited nearby to make certain that our pursuers had not seen us turn in the package."

"You can imagine," says Agnes, "our surprise when we saw—you, Mr.—"

"Morris," I say. "Pug Morris."

"—Mr. Morris, pick up the package."

"You were not at all what we were looking for in our pursuers," says the Doc.

"Sorry," I say, as I am pulling the ring from a Prince Albert.

"No, no," says the Doc, kind of flustered. "I did not mean—"

"Frankly," pipes Agnes, "we thought you might be some sort of confidence tricksters who preyed on Lost and Found patrons."

"If that should prove to be the case," says the Doc, kind of shrugging, "I'm certain that we can come to terms–"

This time I break in. "We picked up the package on a lark," I say, around my stogie, which I am busy lighting.

"We're gamblers," Johnny says. He explains the bet.

"I see," says the Doc, when Johnny has finished. "We followed when you left the station, and saw the assault on you. We should certainly have helped, for those who attempted to steal the package from you were assuredly those who pursued us from Washington, but I'm getting old, and the rain was beating down, and we had fallen too far behind to be of any assistance."

"They must have found us," says Agnes, "and then seen you ahead of us with the package, passed us by, and attacked—"

"We saw you turn in here," says the Doc.

"We told the clerk we were friends of yours and wanted rooms on your floor," says Agnes. "We've been drying off and making ourselves presentable."

"Now," says the Doc, "if you'd please be so kind as to give us our package . . ."

Johnny grins, and says: "We still don't know that the package is yours. Maybe it belongs to the pair who jumped us."

"Yeah," I say, "and maybe everything you've told us is a load of—"

"Pug!" says Johnny.

"—baloney," I say.

Schmitt's face falls. He thinks for a moment, and says, in a much more businesslike manner, "We haven't much time, gentlemen," reaches into a breast pocket, pulls out a fat wallet, and takes a couple of bills from it. "Will a hundred—er, two hundred—one each—be satisfactory?"

"Mister," I say, "we lose more than that before breakfast."

But Johnny takes the two bills, stuffs one in his pocket, and, handing me the other, says, "Here, Pug, get change, and call the cops."

I start for the phone, but the Doc cries, "Stop!" When I turn back, he is holding a .30 Mauser, with its little black eye looking right at me. "Put your hands up and hand me that box," he orders.

"Which is it, Professor?" says Johnny in his usual cheerful way, his hands half up, talking through the smoke from his dangling Fatima.

"Agnes," says Schmitt, "get the head."

Now we are all startled. Someone is at our door again.

"We are very popular tonight, Johnny," I say.

"Infamously, Pug," says Johnny.

Neck on neck, Johnny knocks the Mauser to the floor and I catch the Doc on the chin with a light fast uppercut.

Schmitt has gone down across the coffee wagon, taking a few items with him. In short, he has made a good deal of noise. Plus which, Agnes has screamed.

"It could be the Elephant's boys," I say.

Johnny grabs up the Doc's Mauser, looks sharp at Agnes, finger to lips, and steps to the wall by the door so he will be behind it when it opens. He nods at me.

I stay put and call, "Come in!"

It is the chauffeur and the pale-faced lady from the limo. The chauffeur is holding the revolver with the big silencer on it. The gat looks dry and newly oiled.

I back up some toward the table with the package on it, drawing them in. They bite, and step in, eyeing Agnes and the Doc's unconscious bulk.

"Where's the other—?"

But the chauffeur has got curious too late. Johnny jams the Doc's Mauser into his back.

"Well," says Johnny, "if it isn't my fencing partner! Drop it."

The chauffeur drops the big revolver with a thud. Johnny kicks the door shut behind him, steps around in front, and kicks the gat to the side.

"Who are you two?" he asks, pleasantly.

The chauffeur clicks his heels. "Colonel Ivan Lensky," he says, "Soviet State Security. This is my associate, Frau Yeva Von Heller of Austria."

"KGB," says Johnny. "How interesting. My uncle is Wild Bill Belmont."

"OSS," says Lensky. "I have met him. A double-dyed conservative McCarthyite reactionary."

"That's Uncle Bill," says Johnny, smiling.

"Who are you talking about?" I say.

"Spies!" says Johnny.

"We already know Doctor Schmitt and his daughter," says Lensky. "Who are you?"

"Not-so-innocent bystanders," says Johnny. "Gamblers who made a bet on a live lark and wound up with a dead head."

"That head is important to Frau Von Heller and myself—to the governments we represent. We are prepared to offer you two thousand dollars. I have on my person an instrument for that amount. Payment cannot be stopped."

"Two *grand,*" I say. "That might keep the Elephant from our door, Johnny."

"Elephant?" The Colonel looks intrigued.

"An Americanism," says Johnny. He looks at Agnes, who frowns, and at the Doc, who groans, and at me, who shrugs. "Make it five thousand," he says.

"Ah," sighs Lensky. "It so happens—"

"That you have another instrument for five thousand," says Johnny.

Frau Von Heller says: "We represent the rightful owners."

The Colonel waves a hammy hand at Agnes and the Doc. "These two are frauds."

"No," cries the Doc, looking up from the floor, "don't give it to them! You would be betraying your country. It doesn't belong to them and you cannot put a money value on it. It's priceless!"

Now come more knocks. It is like a convention.

"House detective," comes a voice. "Open up!"

"No deal," says Johnny to Lensky and Von Heller, who have closed ranks. Lensky whispers something in Von Heller's ear.

"Shut up, you two," I say. "And behave."

"Open up!" says the dick outside the door.

"Get your father up," Johnny says to Agnes.

A key is inserted in the lock.

"He's got a key, Johnny," I say. "It's the house dick, all right."

Johnny shoves the Mauser in his belt at the small of his back and drops his coat tail over it. He pulls open the door, a ring of keys jangling on the other side of the lock.

"What the hell—" says the house dick. He is long and thin in a worn blue suit and looks at us from a long thin yellow face, sour as kraut. "Why didn't you open up?" he asks, scowling.

"There's been an accident," says Johnny. "We were busy."

"What's going on in here?" says the dick. "Folks down the hall say they heard noise and screaming. You realize it's two in the morning?" He gives me a hard look. "Hey, wait a minute. Ain't you Pug Morris?"

"You got me," I say.

"You ain't registered, Morris. Who's he?" he asks, spotting the Doc.

"He's my father," says Agnes, rising from the floor where she's been trying to get the Doc up. "He fainted and knocked over the tray and the lamp and I cried out. He's been suffering this condition for some time, but I'm still terribly upset and was caught off guard when it happened. I'm sorry we disturbed the other patrons."

I notice now that Frau Von Heller has her big black hat off. The house dick has stepped in close to get a good look at the Doc, and Von Heller and Lensky are edging toward the door.

"You're not leaving?" says Johnny, like a disappointed host.

"Duty calls," says Lensky. "I hope you and Mr. Morris will reconsider our offer."

"Ah!" cries Von Heller. She has dropped her hat. It is pretty obvious to everybody but the house dick, who has his back to her, that she has scooped up the big revolver with the hat.

"Keep your powder dry," I say.

She touches her pale cheek with a red nail, says, "Yes, it's still raining," turns on Lensky's arm, and the pair step out of the room; and, I hope, out of my life, but I doubt it.

"Everything here all right then?" asks the dick. "Want me to get a doctor for your father, miss?"

"No," says Agnes. "It isn't serious. And my father's a doctor."

Schmitt sits up and shakes his head. "I'm getting too old for this work," he says.

"I'd better help Father to his room," says Agnes.

"I'll help you with him," says Johnny.

"Wait a minute," says the dick. "Don't I know you, too? Ain't you Johnny Belmont?"

"Clarence Feathergale," says Johnny. "It's on the register."

"Feathergale! Well, Feathergale, *I'll* help the young lady and her father. The Bon Chance don't want no lawsuit on its hands."

"I'll be back when Father is comfortable," says Agnes, "to explain."

Johnny pushes the door after them, leaving it ajar.

"That dick has us pegged," I say. "He'll tip the Elephant's boys for sure."

"Maybe not," says Johnny. "Maybe he doesn't want any trouble here on his carpeted beat. In any case, we'll have to gamble that he doesn't. We can't walk out on a situation like this, Pug. That young lady needs help, and maybe our country needs help—and maybe there's enough money somewhere in this situation to pay off Sam the Elephant and to get us a new stake."

"So what makes an old skull so valuable?" I say.

Johnny snaps his fingers. "Pug," he says, "maybe it's not *what*, but *who*."

This gives us something to think about while we straighten up the room. We set the wagon up, put what is unbroken back on top, and I fix us a couple of drinks. I call down for the boy to clean up the mess on the rug and bring us some fresh sandwiches. When he has gone we finally put some food aboard. I am several meals behind.

As I'm swallowing the last corner of the last sandwich, Agnes taps and steps in.

"How's your father?" says Johnny.

"All right," she says. "He's resting. But he really shouldn't be doing this."

"Doing what, exactly?" says Johnny.

"This kind of work—for the government."

"It's on the level, then?" I say. "Listen, Miss Schmitt, I am really sorry that I have to deck him, see, but I want to make sure that he comes loose from that Mauser."

"He understands," she says. "He shouldn't have drawn the gun. It was an act of desperation. Oh, why on earth did you pick up that package! How did you *know* about it?"

"We didn't know," I say. "It was just a wild bet."

"Then, you really *are* gamblers?"

"You do not know the half of it, lady," I say. "We are even now being chased by loan sharks who will bite off our legs if we do not paddle."

"You're not criminals?"

"My name, Miss Schmitt," says Johnny, "is Belmont. I come from a long line of generals and statesmen. A good third of my family is in government—the other two-thirds are in money."

"Then you're . . . patriots?"

"Black sheep, but true blue," says Johnny, with plenty of pride, "and with wounds to prove it."

"Johnny made a hero of himself fighting Hitler," I say. "That's how come he ain't in Korea. War wounds. And he has the medals to prove it."

"Well," says Agnes, impressed. "Perhaps you'll fix me a drink. I'm a little unsteady."

I fix the three of us some Scotch and soda and we settle down to hear what she has to say.

"Do you know anything about Austria?" she begins.

"Nope," I say.

Johnny just sips his Scotch.

"It's divided," she says, "Into the American, British, French, and Russian zones. Vienna is in the Russian zone, but the Inner City is administered by each power in turn for a month, and patrolled day and night by groups of four soldiers drawn from the Four Powers."

"Sounds complicated," I say.

"It is," she says. "There are hopes for reunification, even plans ongoing. But things *can* go wrong."

"Well, what has this got to do with the head?" I say.

"My father and I are agents for the forces in and out of Austria who oppose Communism. That skull may become important—even more important—if reunification fails.

You see, it is the skull of one of the greatest composers who ever lived—an Austrian named Franz Josef Haydn."

"What did I tell you, Pug," chirps Johnny, beaming. "It's *who*." He leaps up and digs the skull out, palms it, and says, like an actor: "Alas, poor Haydn! I love his music!"

He sits down with the skull in his lap.

"Then you may know," Agnes goes on, "that Haydn died in Eighteen-nine. Austria was at war with France then. A battle was advancing into Vienna. Haydn was buried in the middle of that battle. The local prison chief, a man named Peter, was an amateur phrenologist—"

"What is that?" I say.

"One who studies the conformation of the skull to divine mental faculties," says Johnny.

I guess he can see that I have missed him.

"They study the bumps on your head to see what you're like," he explains.

"They would think that I am pretty complicated," I say, "what with all my bumps."

"Extremely complicated," says Johnny.

"And so," Agnes picks up, "in the middle of all the confusion of the battle, the prison chief, Peter, had the body exhumed, and the head cut off. He stripped the head of all flesh, studied the skull, and finally pronounced that Haydn had the bumps of music fully developed."

"And what if he hadn't?" asks Johnny, smiling. "Would this Peter have cancelled his season ticket?"

"I don't know," says Agnes, laughing. "Anyway, he had planned to return the skull, but had taken too long in his study of it, and now felt that returning it was too dangerous. Instead, he had an ebony, glass-windowed box made, which he had decorated with a golden lyre. The skull was placed in this box, on a white silk cushion trimmed with black.

"But Peter lived in fear of being caught with it, and later passed it on to a man named Rosenbaum, who was secretary to Haydn's patron, Prince Esterhazy. Prince Esterhazy was, of course, unaware of all this, until he decided to give Haydn a more dignified burial than the one he had during the war; and, in course, had the coffin brought to him at Eisenstadt, the capital of Burgenland, in East Austria, where Haydn had lived under his patronage, and opened. The Prince was horrified to discover that there was only a wig where the head should have been. He investigated, and traced the decapitation to the prison chief, Peter. He was furious, and sent the police to Peter, who confessed his deed, and that Rosenbaum now had the skull. The Prince demanded that the head be returned. Rosenbaum returned a skull. The Prince had it examined and identified as the skull of a twenty year old man. Haydn died at Seventy-seven. Now the Prince had a search made of Rosenbaum's house, but it did not yield any result, as Rosenbaum's wife, the singer Therese Gassmann, had hidden the skull in her straw mattress and lay on her bed during the search.

"It was Frau Rosenbaum who was behind Rosenbaum's refusal to return the skull. The glass and ebony display case containing that gruesome relic you're holding had become the highlight of her famous musical evenings.

"Then the Prince tried bribery. His emissaries promised Rosenbaum a huge sum if he would deliver the skull. Whereupon the besieged Rosenbaum bought the skull of an old man from a Vienna mortuary. This skull was much closer in phrenological detail to Haydn's, and was accepted as the original and interred with Haydn's body.

"On his deathbed, Rosenbaum bequeathed the real skull back to prison chief Peter, who in turn bequeathed it to the Society of Friends of Music in Vienna, who owned a great number of Haydn relics. But Peter's wife gave it to her doctor instead, who presented it to the Austrian Institute of Pathology and Anatomy in Eighteen-Thirty-two. They supposedly passed it on to the Society of Friends of Music, to whom it was originally willed by Peter.

"In Nineteen Thirty-Two, Prince Paul Esterhazy—direct descendant of Haydn's patron—promised to build a magnificent tomb for Haydn, if the head were restored to the body. But, while the authorities were still discussing the matter, the Second World War erupted. As a result of new political divisions after the war, Haydn's skeleton lay in the Soviet Zone while his skull rested in the International Zone. All of this is public knowledge; but of how the skull was stolen and taken to the Soviet Zone, then retrieved by agents of the Western democracies, nothing has been made public. The world in general still believes the real skull to be in the possession of the Society of Friends of Music, in Vienna. Both the democracies and the forces of Communism would like to claim the genius for their own, but neither can, until skull and skeleton are reunited. No price can be put upon the propaganda value of such a coup."

"And this is the real head?" I say.

"Yes," says Agnes, "and the Communists know it. If they get it, they will have Haydn."

"How did it get to the States?" says Johnny.

"That remains a classified secret," says Agnes. "But it's my father's job to get it back to Vienna."

"Why didn't they send it on a battleship?" I say.

"Classified," says Agnes. "But let me say this much. It's not generally realized that the skull in Vienna is a fake, as I've said. So everything has to be done—unobtrusively."

She studies us for a moment, then says: "The head is priceless because you can't put a price on propaganda value, but there *is* financial value attached to it. The authorities are offering twenty-five thousand dollars to anyone who is of assistance in recovering the head. So, if you'll help us, you wouldn't be doing it for nothing."

I look at Johnny. His green eyes are very bright.

“I can explain a little further,” says Agnes. “There are two other skulls being pursued right now—bogus skulls—one in Europe and one in Asia. They are meant to confuse the Communists.”

“Two phonies,” I say, “and we have the real one. Just like three card monte, eh, Johnny?”

“What do you want us to do?” says Johnny.

“There’s a freighter leaving at four this morning from Pier Ten. We want to be on it and at sea before Von Heller and Lensky or anyone else knows. If you and Mr. Morris could get us safely to it . . .”

“Why not a plane?” I say.

“The Captain is our associate. The few other passengers will have been closely screened and will present us with no problems. It’s all been arranged, you see. We were supposed to go directly to the ship from Penn Station. Your intervention—”

“Threw your plans off,” says Johnny. “Of course we’ll help. Pug, would you wrap up Maestro Haydn’s head, please. Here, let’s have one more drink for the road, then we’ll go down the hall and collect your father and see how we can get safely to Pier Ten.”

In a few minutes we are standing in front of Doc Schmitt’s door. Agnes raps on it lightly, calling:

“Father! Father!”

When no answer comes, Agnes opens the door.

The Doc is stretched out on the carpet. He faces the ceiling, open-eyed.

Agnes runs over and shakes him. “Father! Father!” she cries. She looks back at Johnny, her face twisting with grief. Johnny goes to her, bends down, feels the Doc’s pulse, listens for his heart, but it’s all automatic, as the old man’s eyes keep staring up, like he’s looking through the ceiling at the stars. Johnny takes a shoulder and turns him over.

"He's been stabbed," he says.

"Not shot?" I say.

"There's a slit in the back of his coat, not a hole."

"Stabbed in the back," I say. "The dirty cowards."

"But why not shot?" says Johnny, like he's talking to himself.

"Noise," I say.

Johnny gives me an impatient look.

Agnes falls across the Doc's body in a dead faint. It must be delayed reaction. Johnny carries her to an easy chair, gets a damp towel from the bathroom, and pats her cheeks and forehead. Pretty soon she opens her eyes, which look bigger and bluer and sadder than ever. Johnny perches on the arm of her chair and puts an arm around her shoulders, which are shaking. She buries her face in his chest and in ten seconds his suit is wetter than it got in the rain. Finally she pulls back and says: "I shouldn't have left him alone . . ."

"Shouldn't we call the cops?" I say.

"No," says Johnny. "They'll tie us up and we've got to make that ship." He thinks for a minute, then says: "We've got to leave things as they are—for the time being. It's what your father would have wanted, Agnes."

"Yes," says Agnes, wiping her eyes. "He would want me to carry on with the mission. I must pull myself together—for him. What time is it?"

"Nearly three," I tell her.

She says: "And the ship weighs anchor at four o'clock this morning."

"Won't it wait for you?" I say.

"No," she says, shaking her head. "It's to leave without us. The Captain is to assume that we've failed."

"And if you fail," I say, "it will be our fault. Maybe this will cure you of making these wild bets, Johnny," I add, feeling pretty bad about the whole thing. "Now maybe we have even hurt Uncle Sam."

Johnny says: "This must have happened a few minutes ago, when Agnes was in our room. That means that Lensky and Von Heller aren't very far away. Pug," he says, "take Agnes back to our room. Give her a drink. I'll be right along."

"What are you going to do?" I say.

"Place a bet," says he.

"A bet!" I am disgusted—almost.

"Go along now," he says, and I can see that he means business. "But leave the head here."

I have almost forgotten that all this time I am holding the box. I shrug, put the box on the bed, help Agnes to her feet, and take her out. She is pretty shaky, poor kid.

In the hall, she says: "I can trust Johnny, can't I?"

"You can trust us both," I tell her. But I cannot figure out what Johnny is up to.

In our room, I fix two drinks and hand one to Agnes.

"I guess he's right," she says. "The main thing is to get the head to the ship." She threw down her drink like she needed it. "We can call the authorities about—about my father once that's done."

"Sure," I say, pouring her another drink. She is beginning to get back some color. I jaw with her for nearly twenty minutes, and I am beginning to worry about Johnny, when in he comes, carrying the box.

"Listen, Pug," he says, "we've got to be careful—"

I interrupt him with: "What have you been up to?"

"Calling us a cab," he says. "I got the cab stand to tap Sleeping Bill. He'll be waiting out front."

"All that time!" I say. "And why didn't you call from here?"

"I didn't want that house dick—or anyone else—to know that anyone from this room was going any place.

Now stop asking questions," he says, "and keep sharp." He looks at his watch. "We better get a move on, if we plan to make that ship."

What makes me edgy as we step out of the elevator is that the lobby is deserted. The yokel night clerk and his kid brother are nowhere in sight. But, as we are halfway to the front door, the house dick appears from a room behind the desk.

"Checking out?" he says. "Trying to skip on your bill?"

"We'll be coming back," says Johnny.

"Then," says the dick, "let's have your keys."

Johnny checks his watch. "We haven't much time," he says. "We better pay him."

We go back to the desk. I, for one, feeling kind of sheepish.

"What's the tab?" says Johnny, pulling Doc Schmitt's hundred dollar bill from his pocket.

"Ten G-s," says the dick. "You boys owe Sam the Elephant ten G's."

"Can't stop now," says Johnny, turning us about.

"Oh, yes you can," says the dick, pulling a gat. "Now, if you two and your lady friend will just step back into the office for a minute . . ."

Behind the desk, the dick does a quick frisk on me and Johnny. I guess he thinks he is too much of a gent to touch Agnes. He puts his own pistola away and holds Doc Schmitt's Mauser, taken from Johnny, pointed at us.

He orders us into the office with a jerk of his gun hand.

Who should be waiting for us there but Tweedledum and Tweedledee, our bonebreaking friends from Miami, the bad eggs in plaid suits.

The night clerk and his kid brother are sitting on a small couch, looking meek and mild.

The dick is behind us, blocking the door.

Tweedledum says: "We was just on our way up to see youse. Tanks for coming down."

Tweedledee says: "Mr. Elefanti wants his ten G's, Belmont. I hope for your sake that you have scored well during your brief stay here at the Bon Chance."

Johnny says: "I have, indeed, boys. As a matter of fact, we were off just now to collect a large sum. How about giving me an hour?"

"You must be nuts," says Tweedledum.

"Let's break his arms," says Tweedledee.

"Let's break his knees," says Tweedledum. "Then he can still deal from up his sleeves and make Mr. Elefanti's money back, but he can't run, see?"

"Pug," says Johnny, "we haven't got time for this right now" and I know what he means.

I grab Agnes by the arm and slam back with the box, knocking the Mauser from the dick's hand, as Johnny is making two stabs with his umbrella to the soft round bellies in plaid.

We jam through the door, I lose my grip on Agnes, and she falls. I pull her up, and we beat it out of the hotel to Sleeping Bill's phony Yellow Cab. But Sleeping Bill is not ready for our getaway. He is—sleeping.

Johnny pulls him out of the driver's seat, stuffs the C-note into his pocket, and we leave him standing there. I think he is still asleep as Johnny steers us out through the flood like we are in a motor launch. We head for the river, downtown.

At corners we are making huge wakes of water, which blur the night lights outside so they seem to run crazily down the windshield and windows. But through the back windows I can see headlights that are staying with us.

It is just like this when a shot smacks through the back window between Agnes and me and goes out the front by Johnny's ear, and Sleeping Bill's old car kind of faces one of these steel pylons, that are holding up the West Side Highway. Johnny is a smooth driver and pumps cooly on the brake, coaxing it, but Sleeping Bill's car has made up its mind. At the last second Johnny finds some traction and pulls the wheel sharp. The car leaps, avoiding a head-on, and slams into the pylon sidewise, on my side, back by the gas tank. Then we hear a puff.

"We're on fire!" cries Johnny. "Get out! Out!"

Now the three of us are running in deep water over slippery cobblestones.

I hear Sleeping Bill's phony old cab blow apart. Well, Johnny gave him a C-note, and the car was worth maybe only fifty bucks.

Up ahead of us is coming a police car, siren squawking. The cops in the car don't see us in the rain and the dark. They pass right by us.

I look over my shoulder and see that the Elephant's boys have negotiated a U-turn and are now heading off from whence they came.

Agnes says: "There's the ship! Follow me!"

Aboard, Agnes takes charge. "This way," she says, leading us through passageways. "Cabin A," she says. When we are at Cabin A, she opens the door and walks in ahead of us. We follow her into a good-sized stateroom, I guess you call it.

She crosses the room and turns around to us. Now she is not like Agnes at all. She is like some altogether different person. It is all in the look on her face. I get a cold chill up my back.

"Good morning, gentlemen," comes a voice from behind us.

I turn around and there are Von Heller and Lensky. He is holding his pistola with the silencer.

I am certainly confused. I look at Agnes. She is holding her daddy's Mauser.

"I'll take the package," says Agnes.

"What is going on here?" I say. I must admit I am by now feeling pretty stupid. I look at Johnny, and I am amazed to see that he is smiling. He sees that I am mentally in a bind and is good enough to answer my questions before I ask.

"We are rounding up secret agents, Pug," he says. "Uncle Wild Bill would be proud of us."

"What does he mean?" says Lensky to Agnes.

"I don't have the slightest idea," says Agnes.

"How did she come by the Mauser, Johnny?" I say.

"That falling act she did at the hotel. These two women—not to call them ladies—are aces at scooping up guns."

"But Agnes," I say, sadly depressed, "your father—"

"Doctor Schmitt wasn't her father," says Johnny.

The hatch now opens behind Von Heller and Lensky.

Two men with pistolas in their mitts step in.

"F.B.I.," says one.

"C.I.A." says the other.

"You might as well hand over your weapons," says Johnny. "There's a Coast Guard cutter blocking your way out to sea."

The feds go around the room collecting from Von Heller, who has a nice little pearl-handled automatic of her own, and Lensky, and Agnes. When the F.B.I. agent is taking the Mauser from Agnes, Johnny says:

"Agnes, I've been meaning to tell you all night that you have beautiful legs. Would you mind lifting up your skirt so that I can get one good look at them before you go?"

Agnes gives Johnny a grim little smile, shrugs, and lifts her skirt. On her right thigh is a scabbard with a long knife in it.

"That's what killed Schmitt,' says Johnny. "Oh," he adds, "thank you, Agnes. I shall never forget them."

* * *

It is a week later and we are sitting in a couple of beach chairs by the pool of Sam the Elephant's Miami Beach hotel. It is a glorious day and there are beautiful ladies stepping all around us and the noise of the diving board and splashing and palm fronds waving over our heads.

Sam the Elephant is in his gold bathing trunks and has a gold towel over one hairy shoulder and is wearing dark shades over his eyes and smoking a huge Havana cigar and sipping occasionally on a straw which draws up something green inside it. Johnny has been telling him the story, as follows, which clears things up for me too:

It seems that Agnes planned to slip away from Schmitt, with the head, at Penn Station, and catch the limo in which are waiting Von Heller and Lensky. The three were then going to drive to the freighter. The freighter was a Communist ship. Agnes, however, has been suspected of being a double agent. In Washington, she has been ordered to pose as Schmitt's daughter, but Schmitt has been warned not to trust her. Agnes, of course, does not know that Schmitt suspects her. Then Schmitt's inspiration about the Lost and Found, plus Johnny's bet with me, messes up her plans.

Later, she dumps Schmitt the hard way, with a knife, when the house dick leaves her alone with him, calls some contact with the freighter, and explains what has happened. She leaves word for Von Heller and Lensky to meet her at the freighter, and that she has a couple of suckers who will help her make the pier without interference.

Then she comes back to our room to tell us the story of Haydn's head, to make enough time elapse before we discover the body so that we will think Von Heller and Lensky have killed Schmitt. Also because the story will help convince us that she is in danger and needs help.

We go and find Schmitt, with me, at least, thinking what she wants us to think, that Von Heller and Lensky have paid Schmitt a visit. But Johnny doesn't think so. What troubles him is that Schmitt is stabbed in the back. Why should Lensky need to use a knife when he keeps waving around a revolver with a silencer on it? And why in the back?

That's when he thinks of Agnes. He sends me off with her to our room, but he keeps the head with him. He's afraid she will use the shiv on me, take the head, and scram.

When I asked him how come he knows for sure that she has a knife, he says: "It was a logical deduction, Pug, from the circumstances—besides, I felt it on her thigh when I put her in the chair." He guffaws.

"What about me?" I say. "She wouldn't tackle you, Johnny, because you had the Mauser. But suppose she used that pig-sticker on me?"

Johnny says: "Why would she? She wanted to keep us with her. Besides, I had the head." Then he laughs and says: "I just had to gamble that she wouldn't knife you, Pug old boy."

I say: "Thanks a lot!"

Then Johnny puts in a call to uncle Wild Bill Belmont, in Washington. He says: "I took great pleasure in waking him up at three in the morning," gets the dope on the situation, and sets the trap at the pier.

Sam the Elephant is delighted with the whole story. He is also delighted that he will get his ten G's when we get the reward, which is to be within a month, from what we are told. But it is our nerve, says Sam the Elephant, which delights him most, the way we have come down to Miami and walked right in on him with our tale. Also, he is a great patriot, he tells us, and appreciates what we have done for our country. He is going to stake us until our money comes, and we will have the best.

He is laughing as he heaves himself up and waddles off, laughing and shaking his head.

A waiter comes out and passes him, bringing a telephone. It is Wild Bill in Washington has something to say.

Johnny is all smiles at first, but then he frowns.

"Wait a minute," he says, "are you sure?"

But I have already heard a click.

Johnny hangs up, looks at me, and says:

"Pug, we've got a problem."

"What's that?" I say.

"The head was a fake. The real skull has been with the Society of Friends of Music in Vienna since Eighteen-Ninety-five. The authenticity of the skull in their possession has been proven beyond doubt."

"A fake," I say. "Does that mean we do not get any reward?"

"I'm afraid not," he says. "It seems that Schmitt knew he was carrying a fake. He was under orders to do everything he could to convince Agnes that it was the real thing, and she believed it. And so did we."

"But, Johnny," I say, "now we owe Sam the Elephant the ten G's again—"

"Plus," says Johnny, "five hundred expense money."

"Not to mention," I add to the list of our woes, "our hotel bill."

"We better get packing, Pug," says Johnny.

"So it looks like we are on the run again," I say with a sigh.

I am not overly interested in history, as I have a tendency to think that it is all in the past; but, for what I guess are obvious reasons, I stay interested in the subject of Haydn and his head. I follow it in the newspapers.

They finally get his head and the rest of him together in Nineteen-Fifty-four in Burgenland. In Nineteen Fifty-five there is such a thing as an Austrian State Treaty, which is signed by the Four Powers. So it seems that nobody takes over Haydn's country, which joins the U.N. in the same year. All this is very interesting to me, because I feel like, in a little way, I am a part of it. Also, when I think of it now, it brings back the days when Johnny and me were always on the run. Being on the run was a lot of fun if you ran with Johnny Belmont.

WORLD'S STRONGEST MAN CALLED UPON TO LIFT SLEEP

Life is movement. Once you stop moving, you're dead. Choose life.
—Eugen Sandow

The world's strongest man was in the great tradition of Sandow, and so was intelligent as well as strong. He thought in terms of leverage and balance, not merely brute power. He would size things up, then think out a strategy for a lift. He resented being thought of as a mere freak of strength. He had studied engineering. This, he admitted, was to be his greatest challenge, and he thought for a long time before taking it on. The proposition posed many questions. Sleep has no handles. How do you get a grip on it? How do you train for such an event? Do you practice with naps, as you might with dumbbells for a barbell lift? And how many naps would be the equivalent of one sleep? Indeed, how long is a true sleep? And what of rem sleep? Do dreams and nightmares add to the weight? What does the average sleep weigh, and where can be found its specific gravity?

He asked himself, "Are they asking me to lift the sleep of the world, or of just one person?" The rules must be made clear.

His manager said not to worry, that lifting sleep sounded like a leadpipe cinch. "All you do is wake everyone up."

But the world's strongest man replied that it would not be an easy task to wake everyone up at once, all over the world. It took more than sheer brute strength to be the world's strongest man; you had to have brains as well. You had to understand exactly what you were getting into.

"You don't just lift things," he said. "But you have a point," he added, after a few minutes of thought. And he thought, Lifting sleep is the same as waking the sleepers. So I must find a way to wake everyone at once: and he decided to shake the Earth until everyone was awake.

"That's my angle," he said. "I've got it." He had decided to push against the sky and run until he turned Earth's rotation backwards, causing such an uproar that everyone would wake up at once, thus lifting sleep the world over. He began pushing against the sky and running, digging his spikes into the soft earth, and lifting his knees like pistons.

Then the world's strongest man's wife shook him and said, "Wake up, dear, you're having a nightmare." And he knew that he had lifted sleep from at least one person. Then the clock radio went on and he heard people talking, indicating that there were more from whom sleep had been lifted.

"I think I've done it," he said, running about the house and pushing the sky in front of him.

"We've overslept," said his wife. "You must hurry off to work."

"Yes," he said, grabbing his briefcase, and he heeled out the front door—forgetting the car, which waited in the driveway, and down the block of suburban houses, and into the slow rise of the mountains, pushing the sky as he vanished into the distance.

IV.

MARIJUANA AT MONTICELLO

a Comedy in One Act

SETTING: THOMAS JEFFERSON's empty study at Monticello.

AT RISE: We hear low, indistinguishable voices off stage. Sounds of people milling about.

TOUR GUIDE: (*voice-over*) Stay together, please. Many believe Thomas Jefferson to have been the greatest of the Founding Fathers. A liberal in the classic, not the modern sense, he did not believe in big government. That government is best, he wrote, that governs least. In fact, he considered government service not as a career at all, but as a duty, in the sense that the legendary Cincinnatus of Rome considered it. You will remember that Cincinnatus left his farms to save Rome and returned to them as soon as possible after the crisis. Jefferson did not even state that he had been President of the United States on his gravestone, nor that he, along with James Madison—and with Ben Franklin's input—wrote the Constitution of the United States. He was proudest of the fact that he founded the University of Virginia. A man with a profoundly enquiring mind, he considered his work in education to be his truest legacy. An architect, lawyer, writer, farmer, inventor—his accomplishments are numerous, outside the field of politics. Nothing was lost on him. A gourmand, he did not consider it to be a minor point that he brought the French fried potato back from France to his homeland. He was a connoisseur of wines. A self-taught chef. Truly, a man for all seasons. As tall as Lincoln, he was a handsome, red-headed man built like an athlete. Now, follow me. I'm going to take you into his study—

JEFFERSON: *(Enters, wearing work clothes, smudged on clothing and face with dirt, sweating. He goes to his bookcase and searches for something. Mutters to himself.)* Cannabis. Cannabis. (*There is a soft knock on the door.* SALLY HEMINGS *steps in.*)

SALLY: Am I disturbing you?

JEFFERSON: No, no, my dear. (*He extends his hands to her and she crosses to him. They clasp hands and then he takes her in his arms and kisses her, a long, passionate kiss. He releases her, feigning annoyance.*) Now you've made me forget what I was looking for, you vixen. Should I pursue you through the house like a hang-tongued hound?

SALLY: A red bloodhound after a black bunny? You sweet-assed man, you mastermind, what are you after? It's not me, when you're onto an idea.

JEFFERSON: I've been planting an exotic, a plant with extraordinary properties. It produces a narcotic affect, quite pleasant, when smoked. I have reason to believe it could be of enormous medicinal value. It's called Cannabis. (*Continues looking in bookcase*)

SALLY: Pot! You been planting pot?

JEFFERSON: No, no, my silly. I've been planting it on yonder hill. (*pointing out window*)

SALLY: Thomas Jefferson. You mean to say you don't know?

JEFFERSON: Know what, my dear? What are you on about?

SALLY: Why, you can't plant marijuana on yon hill. The D.E.A.—

JEFFERSON: The what—who—?

SALLY: The D.E.A., the Drug Enforcement Agency. They fly helicopters and light planes over here all the time. They'll spot your pot and raid Monticello. They break down your door and make you lie facedown on the floor and handcuff you from behind and drag you off, you big fool!

JEFFERSON: These . . . er, helicopters—sun-drawn seeds? You've become quite the scientist. Exceeded the teacher, for I must admit I have not heard of them before. What books are you reading?

SALLY: Never mind that, Tom. The D.E.A.'ll—

JEFFERSON: Are they some secret band of terrorist sent by the mad old king? Are the English still after revenge for the Revolution? We have many friends in Parliament, but there are always diehards. Should we raise an armed militia? It was for such types, and others—primarily, for those in the government of the United States who would attempt to reduce the dream of freedom that is America, that I and the others made certain that the citizen could retain his weapons of defense. I feared a tyrannical taxation, which is the first tool of tyrants in their attempt to subjugate their subjects. Next is open force. (*He ponders*) So, the Brits are at it again. Call out the militia!

SALLY: No, Tom, not the Brits. Parliament doesn't pay any heed to the mad old king anymore.

JEFFERSON: Who, then? And why should this D.E.A.—did you call them?—why should they care what I do? What possible difference can it make to anyone, that I am experimenting with Cannabis? I have experimented with things all my life. It is the nature of the mind to explore. How is it any of their affair?

SALLY: They are a government agency, Tom.

JEFFERSON: Is this a nightmare? Are you telling me that the government of the United States of America would have anything to do with what a citizen does on his own land and in the privacy of his home, barring, of course, some criminal activity?

SALLY: But growing marijuana *is* a criminal activity.

JEFFERSON: How, confound it! It is an interest of mine, and it has become a pleasure, like my wines, like my French fried potatoes. What in heaven's name are you on about?

SALLY: They have made a law against it.

JEFFERSON: Why that would be exactly like making a law against opium. Why would anyone do that?

SALLY: There is a law against opium—the same law.

JEFFERSON: Opium is against the law? Why? It has marvelous properties.

SALLY: They don't want people to use drugs.

JEFFERSON: Who are *they*, that they should tell the people what to do? Perhaps it's time for another revolution. Next you'll be telling me there's a law against wine, the first miracle of Christ.

SALLY: There will be—between Nineteen-Twenty and Nineteen Thirty-three. It will be called Prohibition.

JEFFERSON: (*astounded*) Prohibition! To prohibit? The United States Government is in the business of prohibiting people from ingesting wine and good stout and bourbon whiskey and of all things, opium. Why?

SALLY: It's not good for us.

JEFFERSON: Who are they to say what is and is not good for anyone? The people decide that, individually. There is nothing *malum in se*, evil in itself, about any intoxicant. Life is difficult, one escapes it from time to time. It is perfectly normal. One does it in reading a book, watching a play, in conversation over wine, in watching a sunset. Prohibition? That is merely *malum prohibitum,* an evil because it is called one. And by whom? Let him who does not enjoy wine do what he does enjoy. I enjoy wine. What is it to him? (*goes to a sideboard and pours himself a drink, drinks it, then pours both of them a drink and hands one to her.*) I must admit to shock. This has happened since my retirement?

SALLY: This and much more since I was free.

JEFFERSON: I had not the power to set anyone free, my love. There is another example of the evil of law, what tyranny it becomes when unrestrained. How people give their freedom away for a false safety. Life is not a thing to feel safe in.

SALLY: A security blanket.

JEFFERSON: Yes, yes, that's very good. Yes, life is not a security blanket to feel safe in, it is a thrilling adventure, dangerous and doomed, but it offers the opportunity, once in the universe of eternity, to test one's metal, to see if the stardust can hold its own.

SALLY: You're wonderful with words, Tom. But you must go out and deracinate that pot.

JEFFERSON: Never! I stand on my Constitutional rights. After all, I wrote them. This government has its priorities misplaced. Every person has as much right to do as he or she desires to do as does the government, which is only another group of persons, somewhat less talented than the average artist or scientist, mostly middle-brow lawyers. The government is here to see that we do not hurt one another and are not hurt from the outside. We are here to see to it that the government doesn't hurt us. Have you not heard me say, my dear, that when the candidates tell you they have a plan, you should tell them that you already have a plan. It's called the Constitution of the United States of America, and proceed to inform them that they are not James Madison, et alia. The purpose of the Constitution is well known. It's purpose is to keep out subsequent plans by politicians, including candidates. Its purpose is to make the government leave the citizen alone. This is called freedom and is highly valued by all enslaved peoples, though not so highly valued as it ought to be by those possessed of it. Freedom allows for invention, invention creates wealth, wealth is a syrup one pours into pies, causing them to expand their crusts, crack, and ooze rich juices that drip . . . all over the place!

SALLY: That's all very well, Tom, but, as to the drugs, they would say that they cause violence.

JEFFERSON: How? Oh, I've been in a taphouse brawl or two. I might not look it today, but I was quite accomplished in the art of fisticuffs when in my youth.

SALLY: I love your muscles, my dear. No, but that isn't what they mean. There are those who shoot each other over the drugs. Dealers and the like.

TOUR GUIDE: (*voice-over*) Right this way, now—into the garden.

SALLY: They'll see the pot out there.

JEFFERSON: Let them. I told you, my dearest, I planted the Cannabis in the ground, not in a pot. Why do you keep insisting—?

SALLY: Tom, pour me another drink, please. I need one.

JEFFERSON: It's particularly good Amontillado. (*pouring*) We had a boy at the University of Virginia, I heard, an extremely intelligent chap name of Edgar Poe, who wrote a wonderful tale called the Cask of Amontillado. I enjoyed it immensely. (*handing her a glass*) Do you know, speaking of intoxicants, this young Poe was said to have experimented with all manner of them. I was so interested. I wanted to have him come for a visit but I was never able to locate him. Bit of a bounder, I'm told, but I can't help think that anyone who can write like that must have the stuff. Dropped out, unfortunately, after only a year. Money problems, gambling, or something.

SALLY: My dearest, you don't seem to understand the danger you're in. The D.E.A. plays rough.

JEFFERSON: Rougher than the Brits? I doubt it. And we sent Cornwallis on his way. Now, there again, is an example of what I mean. Taxation, the tool of tyranny!

SALLY: That's how they pay the D.E.A.

JEFFERSON: What? You mean with our taxes? I remember old Ben Franklin used to say, there are only two certainties in life, death and taxes. I always liked that one. But how do they extract such taxes?

SALLY: From income.

JEFFERSON: Tyranny, tyranny, tyranny, and the end of wealth. For a man of spirit will not work for under fifty percent of his labor's worth.

SALLY; Poor Tom, you ain't seen nothing yet!

JEFFERSON: No, no. "Haven't" and "Anything."

SALLY: I know, precious baby, I know.

TOUR GUIDE: (*voice-over*) Someone has planted marijuana in President Jefferson's garden. Marijuana at Monticello, can you imagine? But wait! What's that? There are Apache helicopters overhead. You can see the rockets and the machine guns. They are an American fleet. I can see the flag-emblem of the United States of America—and, something else—what is it?—D.E.A. Oh my God, people, run for your lives!

SALLY: Tom, Monticello is being stormed. Where can we hide?

JEFFERSON: Hide, nothing! Hand me my long-rifle. I'll take my stand for *liberty!*

CURTAIN

THE MOVING FINGER

The Moving Finger writes; and, having writ,
Moves on: nor all your Piety nor Wit
Shall lure it back to cancel half a Line,
Nor all your Tears wash out a Word of it.
—Rubáiyát of Omar Khayyám
Edward FitzGerald

Sad, suffering a mild depression, I went to Coney Island one winter day to walk along the beach and see the sea, when I came upon what I took to be a huge sandbox, four boards, at least twenty feet each, joined into a square, brimming with wet sand of a somewhat different shade than the rest of the beach, a sort of olive drab, and I immediately saw in this square a frame suitable for writing. It was a cold windy day and there was nobody about to bother me as I focused my attention on what I would write on this beautiful big page that looked up at the sky. I decided to write my sins for God to see, or perhaps for low-flying airplane travellers, or balloon people, anyway somebody up in the flowing clouds. Of course, one of my sins is that I am always looking for a way out, so I was counting on a high tide or rain or snow to wash my sins away before anyone got a good look at what I'm made of, deep inside. I decided I would tell the absolute truth about myself and my many misdeeds. I would attempt to do what Jean Jacques Rousseau meant to do in his Confessions, but did not succeed in doing; I would attempt to be perfectly honest, absolutely honest, come water or high hell. And so, having a tendency to hyperbole, another of my many sins, I went to great lengths to defame myself, mixed emotions rocking my heart, forcing me to stop several times in order to throw up on the beach—not of course, in my beautiful frame. With first thoughts best thoughts in mind, I did not want anything I scratched in the olive drab slurry to be smudged or lost to the sky by being covered with nervous vomit. And I told of my misprisions until the huge page was covered. I signed my confession at the bottom and placed my address and phone number below my signature, then threw the stick down and surveyed my work. Confession is good for the soul, I had always heard, and there it was, my masterpiece, the truth and more than the truth about me. The work had taken most of the afternoon and the sun began to set out at sea. I was exhausted with all this truth-telling. I looked once more at my huge page of sins, and walked on along the shore where the tide was rising, soon to wash away all that I had written. Tired as I was, I felt new life surging through me, an exhilaration, for the worst was said and done and over. I slept well that night for the first time in weeks. I rose from my bed feeling like a new man, buoyant, weightless, with a new life before me, free of the terrible burden of my sinful past. I resolved to live in a new way, clean, straight, honorable, fruitful, with malice toward none. The sandbox had turned me into a child again, and I whistled my way through the day. That night I turned on the evening news to see what sins had been committed by the rest of the world that day, when one item caught my attention. A man had written a full confession on a cement slab at Coney Island. The slab had been intended to hold a concession stand. The phone rang, and I realized my voice mail was full of messages. Most of them were crank calls, many containing improper suggestions. Some gave me the news that I was in the papers, on TV and the net. One was from the police, another from the DA's office. I was to be called before a Grand Jury. Several others from various priests and ministers—You need spiritual help, they claimed. A psychiatrist offered me his couch and a lifetime of psychoanalysis, free of charge. The contractor who had laid the cement slab offered to reconstruct my nose but opined that he would settle for a law suit and a nice chunk of money. Several lawyers offered to fend off any lawsuits that might be brought against me, thus relieving my anxiety about the contractor. Finally, my girlfriend left a message to say that she was breaking off with me, a truly corrupt and perverted personality.

DEEP-SEA DRIFTER

Before my body began to swallow my soul, before it began to *try* to swallow my soul, I was like you. I pushed myself up from all fours and took my first infantile steps. I could see my feet. Soon I could run and play. I was like any little boy. But then a rare glandular condition began to act upon me—a genetic condition, the doctors told my mother—and I began to become what I am: a man who weighs over a thousand pounds, over half a ton.

We lived in Brooklyn until my father died. Fortunately, he left us a lot of money, Mother and I, and, after his death, Mother moved us to Saga Bay, Florida, to an isolated beach house. It's a good thing we had money, because she had to hire a number of professionals who possessed the knowledge and equipment to transport a six-hundred pound twelve-year-old from Brooklyn to Florida.

The house in Florida had to be rebuilt for me—doors and halls made wider and special lifting and turning equipment installed. Two vans, with equipment for lifting, were kept on the property—two, in case one failed in an emergency. I already suffered from high blood pressure, sleep apnea, respiratory problems, and incipient diabetes. I was of course threatened with stroke, blood clots, heart disease, and, later, the likelihood of cancer.

There was a hospital within reach; but, as I have said, the house was isolated, and, with its private beach touching the Straits of Florida, it was a likely target for hurricanes.

Why had my mother picked such a place to move us? Because I had already become a curiosity. People liked to come and look at me, perhaps to guess what I was. In a few years I had completely lost the shape of a human being. It wasn't long before I had reached my present weight of over a thousand pounds. I couldn't keep track of myself. Large parts of me, as big as you, sprawled this way and that. The little skeleton inside of all this adipose tissue could not lift it. My body was utterly useless to me; I was its prisoner. Speak of being buried alive!

It has been decades since I could move as I do now. I fly with my cape rippling behind me. You who are of average size cannot begin to imagine how wonderful I feel. I feel the ecstasy of a superhero. This miracle has occurred because I tried to save my mother's life.

But my body had also tried to kill her, just as it was trying to kill me. At first and for some time she had summoned medical people to help her with me, and we were known at the hospital and to others; but, as I reached new proportions of sprawl, Mother took to drink and with alcoholism came increasing eccentricity, sometimes bordering on madness. Mother was—perhaps is—an ectomorphic type, thin and nervous, always high strung. In time, she would sit by my bed, drinking her cold gin and tonics, and talk, and the more she drank the stranger her talk became.

My air passages closed by degrees and I found it increasingly difficult to answer. But I began to understand that her grief over my condition had turned to guilt, to deep shame. Some time ago, I can't say exactly when, people stopped coming to the house, and we were left to our own devices. She continued to wash me, rub oil and antibiotic lotions into my creases, but less and less often, until, finally, she just sat by me and drank.

Eventually, it seemed, everyone forgot us. Mother said that people were too busy with their own problems. Perhaps somewhere in her mind, unrecognized by herself, was a desire that I should die. Perhaps there was a desire to be rid of such a literal weight. She was only middle-aged and still attractive in her way. She told me so. I impute no evil intentions to her. She loved me and I broke her heart.

Then one day I did break her heart. She dropped her drink and gasped. *What's wrong?* I said inside myself. She fell out of her chair and lay beside my bed. Pushing hard, I pivoted on my stomach until I could see her. My eyes are mere slits. I can scarcely see out of them. But I saw that she was blue and surmised that she was having a heart attack. It was useless for me to try to find a phone of any kind or any alarm system that she may have had installed, utterly useless. There was only one way for me to draw attention to our plight.

I had heard of wonderful things being done by people in desperation—mothers lifting cars away from children, mountain climbers cutting off their own limbs to free themselves from rocks—and now I know these stories to be true; for desperation allowed me to do the impossible, though it took an unspeakable amount of time and Herculean effort. It took hours—I could tell by the changing light—but I crawled down an unremembered hall and out an unremembered door and heaved myself down unremembered steps and onto an unremembered beach. There I became lodged in the sand. Someone must see me, I thought, a creature so huge. At last I had found an advantage in being myself. And someone did.

The effort had rendered me unconscious. When I woke, I could hear that a crowd had gathered. Immediately, I tried to tell the many-voiced crowd that Mother lay dying inside the house, but, of course, nothing would come. Then I realized that the crowd was asking itself what I was. I posed the question—*Are you people crazy?* It was almost impossible for me to realize that these people could not recognize in me a human being.

Then I heard the voice of authority. "It's a leatherback. You can tell by the leathery cape down the back, instead of the usual carapace. As to its color, I'd say it's an albino. Yes, the more I look, the more certain I am. It is Dermochelys coriacea, largest of all living turtles. They grow to 800 pounds as an average adult, maybe 2,000 pounds as a record-setting lunker.

"It's also the fastest-growing and heaviest reptile in nature, the fastest-swimming turtle, the most widely distributed, and highly migratory reptile, and the only one that can be called warm blooded. In this and other respects they seem halfway to mammals."

You idiot! You madman! My mother is dying! Inside! Inside!

"Being an albino, this is a very rare find, and it's very likely that the Marine Institute, if they are summoned, will take it away for study. As a member of the Green Party, I think that would be wrong. Born free, it should go free."

"What should we do?"

"Push the poor creature back into the sea," commanded the expert.

And so it was that the well-meaning but misled crowd pushed me down to the sea. It was terribly painful, being dragged and shoved on the hot sand that felt like ground glass until my underside was raw and bleeding. I screamed from deep inside—*I am not a turtle, you fools! I am a human being! Mother is dying inside. Please save her. Help! Help me! You'll drown me! I don't know how to swim. You'll kill me! What are you doing? Are you people mad?*

Can you even begin to imagine my terror?

It must have taken an hour to get me into the surf, an hour in which I realized the full horror of being myself. Why my heart didn't stop, I can't imagine. But then something wonderful happened.

The sand grew smooth, soft, and slippery. It grew cool and wet. Water splashed my face, as it might another's upon awakening, as others splash their faces in the morning, but, of course, much to my relief, the sun was going down, down and setting in full red splendor. I felt small before the hugeness of the sea and sky.

Then, suddenly, I was adrift. I floated. The crowd cheered. I moved my arms and legs freely for the first time in years, and I knew the Zen of swimming, the healing salt of the sea filling my every cracked crevice, cleansing my every abrasion. I guess I doggy paddled—or turtle paddled—and soon I lost my fear of the water, of drowning. I washed this way and that, exulting in my new freedom. I was caught in the current. I realized that I was probably in the Gulf Stream, being propelled north. The water whirled me about, and on shore I saw an ambulance drive to the front of our house. I realized that someone had discovered my mother. At last there was help. At last something was going to be done for her. Across the susurrus of the sea I could hear the siren and knew they were rushing her off to the hospital, perhaps to be saved and, I hoped and prayed, to go on to live a normal life without me. Perhaps I had saved her by bringing so much attention to the house. For once in my life, perhaps, I had achieved something, and now, as I whirled and whirled, slowly learning to direct myself, I was free of my imprisonment—an imprisonment that you of normal proportions will never know—and could look at the beautiful, splendid horizon, a spangle of stars appearing overhead.

Come thirst, come hunger, come starvation to make me nothing but bones, a tiny skeleton, come sharks with death in their teeth, come what may, I tell myself, for when I speak I speak only to myself and to Mother, who can no longer hear me for the sounds of the sea.

POUR LES OISEAUX

Fabliau, France, 1929, the year of the Phoenix—a gleaming white city rising like plumes on a cocked hat, in a semi-circle from the sea. Its port-section slums are famous for vice, crime, and an exotic mixture of birds—my kind of town! I'm a private dickybird. I flew here from the States seeking an exotic English chick, name of Song Sparrow. She knows where the eggs are hidden, and I'm going to find out. She's been smuggling guano in from South America. I'm pretty sure that it goes through Fabliau to the Italian Mafia—what they do with it, hey, don't ask me. Ever since the Crash, people have been pulling some pretty crazy deals. Guano is fungible. These days it can buy just about anything, including the goose who laid the golden egg. I know it'll buy me an Old Crow in any of these wormy waterfront nests. The barkeep's a big ugly-looking condor, one of the last of his breed. Is he a displaced Californian, I ask myself in pidgin. But I say it in his beak in plain American, that Peruvian parakeets and Hartz Mountain canaries can understand. The ugly old condor is as laconic as he looks and comes back at me with an owlish "oui" that's packed with innuendo and sarcasm. I slug down my Old Crow, swizzle-worm and all, and order another, take off my feathered Alpine hat, that I picked up on the wing, and place it on the bar, a kind of challenge. He can take it or leave it. He leaves it. He probably figures I got a quiver full of new-fletched arrows under my feathered boa. He's no dumb dodo. I'm looking for an English bird name of Song Sparrow, I tell him. He holds his long dirty wings out like what's it to me and I get a whiff of his wingpits. Fold 'em up, Pollution Pits, I tell him, as I take a gander at the rest of the roost. A couple of old ducks sitting down at the end of the bar, quacking on about the Crash, a middle-aged bird in a tux who looks like a penguin, soft but there's something cold in his eyes; a Brooklyn bird name of Robin, with big, red breasts, a couple o' gay birds up the other end doing some kind of mating dance. But no sign of the real Song Sparrow. Now I got a little red light inside, tells me when there's danger, and on it goes. How do I put it? There's something reminds me of reptiles—no, dinosaurs. Yeah, that's it! These birds look too innocent, like they're hiding something—their real nature, which is definitely saurian. There are winged dragons afoot, and why didn't the canary sing, as Sherlock might not have put it. Then I'm pecked from all sides. It happens so fast I can't tell the pecking order. All I know is I'm getting the bird. It was at that moment, as I saw my life flap by me, that it first occurred to me what a worm I really was. Bob White, this is your life, I said to myself in disgust. Then I heard a distinctly English bird call, a sort of Oxonian chirp, and I found myself in a large cage. Sing, cooed the beautiful, copper-eyed Song Sparrow, who had emerged from her condor costume. I want you to turn canary, she told me, and sing your heart out, like the Hartz Mountain whistleblowers. I said, Sure, why not? I should die for twenty-five pounds of guano a day—and expenses? I'm no sapsucker. We know that the passenger pigeons are bringing the stuff in, I sang, but we don't know how you're getting it out. We fly it out, she tweeted, in stork sheets. She eyed me sideways, giving me the once-over, and then hopped forward and planted one on my beak. That was when I decided to quit being a Hawkshaw. I'm folding my wings, I told her. Let's you and me take off. She dipped her head in agreement. Then we picked up a couple of pieces of straw from the floor and went looking for a good old Anglo-American tree to build our nest in, leaving Fabliau and all its smuggled guano behind us.

Cage closed!

AN ACTOR PREPARES

The actor must use his imagination to be able to answer all questions.
—Constantin Stanislavski

Jimmy Whistler, a struggling actor, and his widowed mother, Fay, superintended an upscale apartment building, named The Mondrian, in Greenwich Village.

His neurasthenic girlfriend, Phyllis, called Jimmy in the middle of August to tell him that her parents were coming East from Seattle for a visit—just a week-end—and she wanted him to go with her to show them around. In fact, she wanted Jimmy to play husband, which is what those two poor deluded people still thought him to be—their never-met son-in-law. The father, of course had been in and out of New York often, in the past few years, being, as he was, a pilot for a major airline, and having had, for a time, a regular run between New York and Seattle. About a year and a half ago, he had been switched to a run between Seattle and Tokyo, and that had saved Jimmy and Phyllis a great many headaches. Before that, when in New York, he'd tried to meet Jimmy several times, but Jimmy had always somehow avoided the encounter. Phyllis had met her father uptown several times, but had told him that her "husband" was called away, was sick, had to work, was drafted—any lie she could think up to save Jimmy the meeting and still not make her father suspicious. But this time her parents had written:

“We are coming East to see a few shows, but more especially to meet Jim. We sincerely hope that nothing will happen to make that impossible.”

“You’ve just got to meet them, Jimmy,” Phyllis said. “I don’t think they believe me when I tell them about you anymore. Please, just this once.”

Jimmy couldn’t find it in his heart to refuse her. But, on the other hand, he didn’t like the idea of pulling off such an imposture. He was an actor, not a liar. He didn’t want to lie to a couple of (probably) nice people, to make them think he was their son-in-law. Phyllis shouldn’t have told them that they were married in the first place, but surely she should have told them that they weren’t, by now.

The fact was that they were hardly even seeing each other nowadays. Jimmy had always considered Phyllis more of a friend than a lover, though that had been part of their relationship for a while, the result of Jimmy enjoying her intellectual companionship, and his affection for her, but she was not Jimmy’s type when it came to amorous affairs. Phyllis was careless in the extreme about her appearance—she’d let her teeth go badly, though her parents would have been delighted to send her to any of the best orthodontists; she did not eat well, and she experimented with some of the lesser drugs, so she was undernourished and sallow of complexion. She loved getting clothes at the Salvation Army and other thrift shops and often wore a hodgepodge of odd garments. Many things had conspired to cause Jimmy to want to keep his distance from dear little Phyl, for whom he otherwise felt a great warmth of genuine affection, perhaps even a touch of love. She had a wonderful witty quick mind and a charmingly skeptical view of life. She said it was “a bullshit world,” and that she could prove it anytime she liked.

That was the situation. Well, that was the half of it. As if things weren’t complicated enough, Jimmy’s “in-laws” were coming to New York on the same weekend that Fay had invited her sister, Jimmy's Aunt Myrtle and her husband, Uncle O'Toole, as Jimmy had always called him, to visit. It was going to be a busy weekend.

Fay worked very hard on their super's basement apartment all week. She had polished the furniture, put up new curtains, waxed and rewaxed the rubber-tiled floor till it was gleaming—in short, she had prepared it for the inspection of her fastidious big sister, Aunt Myrtle, and for the enjoyment of her equally fastidious brother-in-law, Uncle Albert O'Toole. It was Fay's intention to show her lace-curtain Irish relatives how well she was doing—and, indeed, the apartment looked very pretty, entirely satisfactory for that purpose. By Friday afternoon, she had a roast pork in the oven, three pies baked, hors d'oeuvres on a platter on the table, drinks mixed, etc., and was in the process of getting herself dressed to receive her visitors.

Jimmy, too, was getting himself dressed in his best bib and tucker. He'd accumulated a few clothes in the past year, and was now able to make himself fairly presentable in a well-cut, good-fitting suit, a chocolate shirt, cream-colored tie, and a new pair of oxblood loafers. He was slimmer, now, than he'd been for quite a time, and he had a good tanning machine tan, and his hair, like the Washington Square grass of that summer, was bleached, with strands of bright gold running through it. He had gone to college on the G.I. Bill, majoring in drama, and was now appearing with an off-Broadway repertory company. Jimmy was dedicated to the art and craft of acting, and couldn't help but feel that this weekend presented him with a challenge, even if there was a lie involved. After all, acting was lying, of sorts, wasn't it? For now, his dilemma had no horns.

Fay and Jimmy had discussed the situation, and decided upon a plan of action. Since Fay had no intention of meeting Phyllis's parents and palming herself off as

Phyllis's mother-in-law, Jimmy would tell Phyllis's parents that his Mother was away, visiting her sister in New Jersey, and that he had been unable to get in touch with her in time to have her back in New York to meet them. It was a frail story, but Jimmy thought he'd be able to bluff it through. Furthermore, he'd tell them that he'd volunteered to help keep the house that she superintended in good shape while she was away, and that would give him an excuse to spend some time with Fay and Aunt Myrtle and Uncle O'Toole. A lot would depend upon what Phyllis's parents wanted to do; and, of course, upon what Aunt Myrtle and Uncle O'Toole wanted to do.

First, Jimmy was to wait and meet and greet Aunt Myrtle and Uncle O'Toole when they arrived at five, then he'd make some excuse or other and leave and go over to pick up Phyllis, and, from there, go uptown to the hotel where Phyllis's parents were staying, and meet them.

At ten minutes after five the doorbell rang, Jimmy pushed the buzzer, asked who was there, over the speaker, and heard Uncle O'Toole, his voice full of static, say, "Jimmy? Is that you, Jimmy? Uncle O'Toole here. How do we find you?" They were in the lobby. Jimmy went upstairs and led them back down.

Nervous laughter.

Confusion.

Hugs and kisses.

"Say, this is a pretty fancy building," said Uncle O'Toole.

"What a lovely apartment!" said Aunt Myrtle.

"Do you mean you get this apartment free?" asked Uncle O'Toole. "Do you get tips, Jimmy? Well, let *me* give you a tip. Save your money. Ha-ha!"

"What lovely curtains!" said Aunt Myrtle.

"What smells so good?" asked Uncle O'Toole.

"Fay, you look lovely!" said Aunt Myrtle.

"You're lookin' good, Jimmy," said Uncle O'Toole. "Lost a little weight?"

"Do you get a salary here, too?" asked Aunt Myrtle.

"Quite a deal you've got here," said Uncle O'Toole.

They all sat down and had a couple of drinks together; then Jimmy excused himself, saying that he had to go over to the docks (his day job) to pick up his pay check, and that he'd be back as soon as possible.

He grabbed a taxi out on Seventh Avenue and scooted over to pick up Phyllis. When he got there, she was all aflutter. She was worried about how she looked, but Jimmy couldn't remember the last time he'd seen her looking so nice. She had her fine, pale hair in an upsweep, and was wearing a pretty teal suit. She wanted to know if she looked nice, and he told her that she did.

"Oh, this is such a lot of bullshit," she said nervously. "If only I didn't have to pretend with them."

Jimmy's sentiments exactly. Then she donned her tan raincoat and picked up her little native-American beaded pocketbook, and spoiled the whole thing.

"Haven't you got another purse to carry?"

"What's wrong with this one?"

"It looks like you picked it out of an ashcan somewhere in New Mexico," he said.

"Well, it's the only one I've got," she snapped angrily.

When they got out of the subway in the midtown area, Jimmy stepped into a store and bought a plain black pocketbook for her.

"But what'll I do with this one?"

"Put it inside the black one."

"Bullshit!" she said, as she did so.

Jimmy stopped her again, taking his handkerchief and wiping off some of the excess rouge from her face. He hadn't noticed it in the house, but out in the daylight she looked like she had a target on each cheek. Ordinarily, she never wore makeup, and, surprisingly, for a girl who could paint pictures, was considered by some to be a serious artist, she had developed no skill whatever in the use of makeup. Jimmy, on the other hand, had been taught to do theatrical makeup. He stood, dabbing at her with his handkerchief, trying to tone her down a bit, while she cursed and complained, full of impatience.

"To hell with it!" she said. "Come on; let's go!"

"Well, you don't want to look like you're ready for a war dance, do you?"

"To hell with it! It's just a lot of bullshit."

The poor little thing. She was more nervous than he was, and he wasn't exactly calm.

Her parents were staying at a good hotel in the upper-midtown area. At the desk, Phyllis called their room. They were told to come right up.

Jimmy felt embarrassed getting into the elevator. The incongruity of their situation struck him. He disliked himself for feeling it, but Phyllis embarrassed him. She hadn't stood still for his treatment, and her makeup was smeared. The black pocketbook he'd bought her in such a hurry seemed far too large and awkward for her (still, it was an improvement over the beaded Indian one that was contained in it). And Jimmy could see, now, that her pretty teal suit had black cat hairs all over it; and her stockings hung loose and twisted on her thin legs. Some of the upsweep of her hair had come tumbling down, and despite the cool evening, she had beads of nervous sweat on her forehead, corrugating her face powder. Little Phyllis was not beautiful, but had she had the instinct for adornment of a primitive, she could have made herself appear quite attractive. But the instinct for adornment was completely missing from her personality. Makeup was missing from her makeup. Looking at her, Jimmy wondered what her parents would think. Here he was—tall, well-built, and, by most accounts, good-looking.

Would they think he was some kind of fortune hunter, taking advantage of their little Phyllis? Some kind of rogue? How could they ever understand how it was that Phyllis and he had got together? How could they understand the tenderness he felt for her, his admiration of her gutsyness and her artistry? How, perhaps, theirs was a case of friendship gone too far?

The elevator stopped: they got out and found the appropriate door and knocked.

"How do I look?" Phyllis asked.

"Fine," Jimmy said. "You look fine."

The door was opened by a round-faced, good-humored-looking man of medium height, wearing a grey pilot's uniform. He had a ruddy complexion, blue eyes, and close-cropped salt-and-pepper hair. He was holding a cocktail glass in his hand.

"Daddy," Phyllis said, and threw her arms around his neck. Then she pulled away and turned to Jimmy, saying:

"Daddy, I want you to meet my husband, Jimmy. Jimmy Whistler."

The pilot, smiling, extended a hand to Jimmy. Jimmy took it and shook it.

"So you're my son-in-law, are you?" he said; and Jimmy thought for an instant that he doubted it. "Meet your mother-in-law, Jimmy." A slim, attractive woman stepped forward.

"Mummy!" Phyllis cried, and threw herself into her mother's arms as she had into her father's. When "Mummy" had disengaged herself, she came to Jimmy, put her arms around his neck, and planted a kiss on him.

"My, Phyl, but your husband is a handsome young man," she said, and then to Jimmy: "I want to welcome you into our family, Jimmy. Do you realize that you and Phyl have been married for over three years and this is the first time I've laid eyes on you. Well, I certainly like what I see."

Jimmy felt crummy. How could he have ever got himself into something like this?

"Have a drink, Jimmy?" asked the pilot.

"Yes," he said, "please."

"Canadian Club?"

"Fine."

"Soda?"

"Please."

"Ice?"

"Please."

"Well, Phyl. . ." said the mother, holding her daughter at arm's-length and looking at her, "you look just fine. Married life seems to agree with you."

"Yes," said the father, handing Jimmy a drink, "you look well, kitten. You know," he said, speaking to Jimmy, "Phyl was a sickly little girl. She had one thing after another. Not like her sister at all. Her sister was a regular little butterball. But Phyl looks like she's putting on some weight, now, too, dear," he said, addressing his wife, "doesn't she?"

"Yes, she looks wonderful."

"I bet," said the father, "that you make her eat; don't you, Jimmy?"

"Yes, I try." It was true; but Phyllis was anorexic.

"Oh, I can see it," said the mother.

"Why don't we eat now?" said the father. "Let's go down to the restaurant and we'll all have a nice dinner. How's that sound?"

They went down to the hotel dining room and ate. The mother had fried shrimp, and Phyllis and the father and Jimmy had Lobster Newburgh. Jimmy was so nervous during the meal that he choked. All he could think of was getting away from these good people before he tipped his hand.

They weren't unusually inquisitive, but naturally they had a great many questions to ask of the young man whom they thought to be their son-in-law. That was what they took him for, it seemed. And they seemed to like him, too. Jimmy wondered how Phyllis was going to explain this away in years to come. She'd probably tell them that they'd got a divorce on the grounds of mental cruelty and Jimmy's stock with them would hit bottom. Even now, that future time troubled him. Being an actor, he liked to be liked.

Phyllis was ecstatically happy. Jimmy could see that she was very proud of having got herself married, in their eyes. Probably she never thought the day would come when a young man whom she could claim as her husband would sit at a table with herself and her parents and please them so. For her sake, Jimmy was very attentive to her, and tried to show the parents that he loved her, which, in fact, he did. But he felt that the whole thing was not only preposterous, but sad. He knew in his heart that he wouldn't be with Phyl much longer, and this seemed an awful crime to commit near the end of their time together.

They left her parents that night with the understanding that they would meet at ten the next morning and that they'd take a tour of New York together, and, later, Saturday evening, they'd all go to a play, and afterwards have a few drinks and a snack somewhere. Phyllis knew that Aunt Myrtle and Uncle O'Toole were at The Mondrian, so she didn't object to Jimmy taking a different train and going straight there. When he kissed her goodbye on the subway platform, she thanked him for going to meet her parents, and said: "Wasn't it really nice? I mean, they're real squares, but aren't they nice? Do you like them, Jimmy?"

Jimmy said that it was and that they were and that he did.

"Oh, Jimmy, why can't we be really married?" she asked wistfully.

He felt like a criminal.

When he got to The Mondrian, there was a party in full swing. Fay was dancing with Uncle O'Toole, and Aunt Myrtle was engaged in a monologue about her grandchildren. They were three sozzled sheets in the wind. Jimmy sat down, nervously exhausted, but relieved to be at home, and let Aunt Myrtle chatter at him while he drank a good stiff drink.

Aunt Myrtle was only about two years older than Fay; but Fay, who'd kept her figure, looked about twenty years younger. Uncle O'Toole, who referred to himself as "a tough guy from Joisey," was a lean, dapper man in his late sixties. He did not have the same settled appearance as his wife. He was a wiry, energetic man, full of fun.

"Let's go out somewhere," he said. "This is Greenwich Village, ain't it? Let's go out and get a look at some characters, whatdaya say?"

"Now, O'Toole," Aunt Myrtle put in, "we can't afford to spend—"

"What the hell, Myrt!" said Uncle O'Toole. "You only live once, right Jimmy? Whatdaya say, Fay? Shouldn't we go out and see the characters?"

Uncle O'Toole won the day, or the evening. Jimmy took them out to a place on Seventh Avenue where beer was served in pitchers and a banjo-band played Gay Nineties music. They loved it. They sang with the band and drank the beer until none of them could talk or walk normally, and then Jimmy took them home in a cab. Fay gave them her bed and she took Jimmy's and Jimmy left them all there, puffing and snoring, and went over to Phyllis's to sleep. He set the alarm, and next morning, bright and early, he was there when they came to.

Uncle O'Toole leaped out of bed as full of energy as he'd been early the day before. Aunt Myrtle seemed groggier, but came around fast after an eye-opener. Fay had a hangover, and felt sick. She spent some time in the bathroom, throwing up. Jimmy felt like he was sleep-walking.

Aunt Myrtle wanted to know if there was much of that "mess-sin-ation" around Greenwich Village.

Jimmy gathered that she meant the mixing of the races. "About as much as anywhere," he told her, never having thought much about it.

Uncle O'Toole said:

"I don't approve of that; do you, Jimmy?"

Jimmy told him that he had nothing against it. "I wouldn't go out of my way to marry a black woman," he said, treading where the ice was thin, "but if I fell in love with a black woman, and we wanted to marry each other, I'd marry her."

"You *would*!" exclaimed Uncle O'Toole, shocked. "But suppose you had a daughter," he said, explaining the problem succinctly, "you wouldn't want your daughter to marry one, would you?"

"Well," Jimmy said, "it looks like if I had already married one, and I had a daughter, I couldn't offer much of an objection to my daughter marrying one, too, could I?"

"Mmmm," said Uncle O'Toole, thoughtfully. "I see your point."

"You're not going to marry one, are you?" asked Aunt Myrtle, genuinely frightened.

"I haven't been asked."

"My God, Fay," cried Aunt Myrtle, "Jimmy isn't thinking of marrying a colored girl, is he?"

"He's only teasing you," Fay said.

"Oh," said Uncle O'Toole, "I get it," and laughed.

Aunt Myrtle said:

"Well, for a minute there, I thought my poor sister was going to become the grandmother of a pickaninny. And me the great-aunt of one. You mustn't do that to her, Jimmy. I know you've got some weird ideas, but she's had a hard enough life as it was, with your father." The thought inspired her. "Oh, what a strange man your father was! I wouldn't have put it past *him* to marry a colored girl."

"Now let's leave him out of this," said Fay. "He's gone to his rest. Let's not talk about him when he's not here to defend himself."

"Well, I was thinking of the life he led you. My dear Albert has never treated me in such a way. He's worked hard all his life. He always supported his wife and children; didn't you, dear?"

"Yeah," said Uncle O'Toole devilishly, "but sometimes I think maybe old Elliot had the right idea."

"Oh," said Aunt Myrtle, turning red, "to say such a thing!"

Jimmy left them there to hash that out, while he went uptown with Phyllis to meet her parents. When he got back from taking a scenic cruise around Manhattan Island, from looking at the "ant-like" people from atop the Empire State Building, and from climbing into the Statue of Liberty's head, the same discussion was still underway back at The Mondrian.

"Why did that man wear his hair like that?" asked Aunt Myrtle.

"He looked like a girl," Uncle O'Toole said.

"Why do you live over here?" Aunt Myrtle wanted to know.

"Was he queer?" asked Uncle O'Toole.

"I'd like to see a lesbian," said Aunt Myrtle.

Next thing Jimmy knew, he was coming out of a theatre on Forty-sixth Street, having just slept through a Rogers & Hammerstein revival. Years before, his coach, Dr. Zolauf had introduced him to them at Carnegie Hall.

"You've got to be carefully taught," came to mind.

Phyllis and he walked hand in hand, ahead of her parents. Phyllis said:

"They really love you, Jimmy."

He'd been turning on the charm. Once, in drama school, he played the Hairy Ape, and he felt suddenly swept with nostalgia for the part.

Then he was at The Mondrian again, sitting at the table, and Aunt Myrtle, now thoroughly sloshed, was saying:

"Let's go out and see if we can find a lesbian bar."

"Let's go out, Jimmy," said Uncle O'Toole. I want to see some Bohemians."

Jimmy took them to the White Horse Tavern.

"This is where Dylan Thomas drank himself to death," he said.

But it cut no ice with Aunt Myrtle. Far as she could see, it was just a dump. And who was this Dylan Thomas and where did he get such a funny name?

"He was a famous Welsh poet," said Jimmy.

"Famous for getting drunk and not supporting his wife and children," Uncle O'Toole said, showing a dumbfounding knowledge of modern literature. "I heard all about the bum." This turned several poetic faces in the crowd. The White Horse was a shrine to the Welsh poet.

"Your Uncle O'Toole knows just about everything," said Aunt Myrtle with pride and conviction. "Go ahead, ask him about something."

Jimmy sat, dazed, smiling, his head nodding approval, his mouth in a frozen smiling rictus.

Phyllis's parents left on Sunday afternoon. "We are so glad to have you in the family, Jimmy," her mother said. And to Phyllis: "You take good care of our son-in-law, Phylly, do you hear?"

Aunt Myrtle and Uncle O'Toole left on Sunday evening.

"See you all of a sudden," Uncle O'Toole said waggishly.

“We’ve had a wonderful time,” Aunt Myrtle said, “even if I didn’t get to see any lesbians.”

Exhausted, embarrassed, and ashamed, but having completed the greatest performance of his life, and one that he vowed would have no encores, Jimmy collapsed on his bed at the Mondrian. It had been an epiphany. Now he thought he knew the difference between acting and lying. He hoped he did.

MANHATTAN SPLEEN

What's madness, but nobility of soul
At odds with circumstance? The day's on fire!
—Theodore Roethke

I. PARANOIA

Well, all right. I speak my mind, which gets me into trouble sometimes. It's like my friend. One night in Manhattan, he was stabbed in the back because he said something to somebody and had to have his spleen removed. I stopped going out after dark. Yes, the spleen. It was formerly believed to be the seat of passions, a vascular gland-like ductless organ near the stomach, or the generator of melancholy—the spleen, or just spleen: what I felt after the unfortunate incident involving my friend; what Baudelaire felt about poverty in Paris, the Parisian poor—Paris Spleen—or how he felt about life in general, or how I felt about life in general after the incident involving my friend. The gay blaze of Manhattan lights dimmed. After "recovering" from the incident, my friend had to take many medicines, could not live the same free and relatively happy life he had lived before. No more could I. Yellow light flooded a yellow room. I slept fitfully, many nights I slept not at all; would switch off the light at dawn and stare out my hotel window at the glow of a Manhattan morning. My friend finally died and I continued to hide in my room, not afraid of what lay outside my small domain but utterly disgusted with it, with the East side West side Island. I grew enormous from compulsive eating and lack of exercise. I became constipated, gaseous, and nauseated. Then I could not get food delivered, for no delivery person would come near to the door of my room for the mephitic odors that emanated from it, and I grew thin and finally wasted away to a mere ghost of former self. My unpaid rent mounted until it became impossible for me to pay such an amount, even with all the checks the government sent me. I lay dreamless in dirty sheets until the door was broken in and I was taken away. Doctor, this is how it all happened, how my hatred, my spleen, grew boundless as my body vanished.

II. A Third Avenue Fit

Hey, you there! I have assigned myself the duty of following the first person who passes by. I am out of work, homeless, maybe mad—well, not quite, though some have claimed it: I live in a cardboard box behind the Port Authority building and get my out-patient disability checks at a flea-bag hotel on West 48th Street, where I used to live—and I need this job. Furthermore, I see all persons as making an arc, like a rainbow, in their travels, and so can expect to find a pot of gold at the place where my subject stops, and that pot of gold will be my pay. There goes one. I must be vigilant that I am not noticed by my subject, who seems to be window shopping. I have brought along a notebook and write down the fact that my subject seems to be window shopping, along with other details. I have a person of indeterminate sex in sight—short hair, slacks—who appears to be meandering down Third Avenue, looking in the shop windows. I stick like glue, like SuperGlue, in fact. Well, long tendrils of glue, such tenuous tendrils of glue that they cannot be discerned stretching between us. The subject has taken an outdoor seat at a cafe. The subject is ordering food. The subject is being greeted by a passerby. The passerby is of the same indeterminate sex as the subject—business suit and flats. The passerby is taking a seat at the subject's table. It is at times like this that I wish I had become a lawyer. The passerby is ordering. It is at times like this that I wish I had become a dentist. The subject and the passerby are sharing a carafe of wine. It looks dark from here, probably a red, perhaps a Burgundy, or maybe a Merlot—without my binoculars I am unable to detect the year of vintage. It has begun to rain. The subject and the passerby are undisturbed by the rain because there is a red and green striped awning over them. I am disturbed by the rain because I am standing catty-corner from them in the open. My writing is becoming blurry with raindrops. Of course, I have no umbrella. I am getting drenched. It looks as if subject and passerby are good friends. Their gesticulations indicate an intimate knowledge of each other. Their laughter indicates a jolly relationship. They are eating something unidentifiable. I wish I could record exactly what they are eating, but perhaps I can check with the waiter later. I'll put down crab. It looks as if they are preparing to leave, getting out money or credit cards. Yes, one of them, the subject, is signing for something, and the other is pushing out bills. Three, I think, which would mean, at fifteen percent— Uh-oh, they are hailing a taxi. I have no money for a taxi, being unemployed. And there they go. I have lost them. To whom should I report this failure? You? You there!

"Come on, pal," said the first cop.

"Let's see what they say at Bellevue," said the second.

III. Out-Patient

The letter had an official look about it. I decided not to open it until I could sit down in the safety of my room, among familiar things, furnishings that offered confidence by their familiarity, advanced age and state of decay. I took it up to my room, gripped between thumb and forefinger and at left arm's length, as if I held the neck of a rattlesnake. People in the old rattling elevator watched as my hand shook and caused the envelope to rattle some mysterious and ominous document inside it. My aunt had served my unsuspecting uncle with mailed divorce papers across the breakfast table one morning long ago. But I was already divorced, twice, incompatibility. My aunt had blamed my uncle for being unfaithful—and there was a question of money. I had never cheated on my wives, nor was money a problem. My crime had been my nervousness, which my wives asserted had caused them to become nervous wrecks themselves. And it was true that, as far as I knew, their nerves had been good until I married them, at which point they began to show signs of neurasthenia—impatience, tooth-grinding, insomnia, etc.—in point of fact the exact same conditions I have always suffered from. I dropped the letter on my cot and looked at it. It had landed address-down. I went to my closet and got out my vademecum that I had acquired at a flea market for fifty-cents, a slender walking stick of good birch with silver tip and handle, a device not only useful for aid in walking—I have a bad knee, acquired by banging it against another knee in the subway—but a handy tool of protection in case of an attempted mugging, like the one that killed my friend. Fortunately, I had never had to use it in the latter capacity. It was sheer luck that I hadn't been mugged by now, by which I mean by middle-age. With the silver point of my walking stick I gingerly flipped the letter over, leaned the stick against the cot, and myself over to study the return address. My eyes were rheumy and I couldn't make out anything of the return address but some printing that suggested the blurred word *borough*, or *buro*, not clear at all. But, come to think of it, it suggested some dangerous department of government, did it not? I went to my desk, where I keep a pair of reading glasses and a magnifying glass, put the reading glasses on, being careful of my ears, and brought the magnifying glass back to the cot with me—but did I want to go on with this? Suppose it was a death notice, or suppose it was some official message involving an expense, a tax I had neglected to pay, or an assessment of some kind—what then? I stepped back from the cot and whacked the handle of my stick down upon the offending letter. It lay crinkled and bent in half, like a pale yellow claw gripping at the aggressive but escaped stick. Fear rose up through the floorboards, through the musty worn carpet, through the smooth soles of my smooth, thrift-shop patent leather shoes, and began to vibrate my legs, my torso, my whole body. My heart pounded until I could see it through my glistening shirt, heartshaped, leaving my chest, pounding more and more rapidly, thundering, now, in my ears. Fear had made it impossible to breathe. Something clanged in my head, a death knell, accompanied by the tintinnabulation of my mad fear. The roaring of my blood, the clanging in my head, the thundering of my room, made it impossible for me to think. I could only feel—hatred! Hatred for this pale claw that had intruded on my solitude, my small, ordered grace of life, and I beat at the letter, but it only bounced about on the cot as if jovial at the condition to which it had brought me. I remember nothing else, but I have been told that the landlord saw me from the door setting fire to the cover of the cot. I still don't know—was the letter from this institution?

APPALACHIAN TALE

Played the devil's fiddle, stomping to it, shaking it out, full of corned blood, his boot down down down! Days before the corn, his old bitch Lucy lay by his piston heel. Said later she smelled it, stayed by it, waiting for the meaty bone; said later never done him no harm at all; said later not even a ghost of evil but Lucy got it, old bloodhound bitch like red clay, wrinkled old lady hanging from her own bones—could make her moon-howl, pointing his wild bow—do that at dances. Devil in a Baptist, playing the fiddle. Gradual as the mountains, he found out how the devil got in. Fiddle under his spiked, gray chin, corn jug thumb-hooked and cradled on top his elbow—capful for Lucy—then stomp stomp stomp: music through Blue Ridge pines! Could choo choo it so's you see smoke and steam, hear that wheezy accordion whistle; could conjure with it up a trainload of places or turn you back home to the station of pines and blue smoke mountains, bring musical rain, or put the devil in your heart, winking and drinking and stomping. Everybody loved him and his Lucy, including said devil, as the corn dropped down into his right big toe. Said it hurt to stomp. But it don't stop the fiddler. Don't nothing stop the fiddler! He was one thing else than music; he was a man. Take more'n corn going through, dropping down in my right big toe, says at the May dance, everybody seeing him stomp, ouch ouch ouch on his big red gray spiked old corned face. Devil got in through the corn, slick as silk; got down in my boot, but

I'll stomp him out; give old Satan a headache—stomp stomp stomp! But that corn went to killing him. His bow was flying! Went on like this, folks say, a tad's five year, him stomping the devil in the corn and the devil stomping back. Said now he couldn't play no more if he don't get rid o' that old devil. Takes him a broad wood chisel out back on a stump, sets his right foot up, sets that chisel to his toe, and strikes down with a good hefty hammer. When he pulls back his foot, that devil in the corned toe stays on the stump, says looka me, I'm off! Has brought him some fireplace soot and some gingham. Sticks that foot in that black soot, to staunch the blood, and wraps it in gingham rags. Said never done him no harm again, quiet as a bone, and he goes back to stomping in peace, rid of the devil. But first, he throws that old corned toe to Lucy. Says: I knowed you always wanted it. Now mind the nail, Lucy; don't let the devil get you, you drunk old droop-skinned hound bitch, cuz I love you. And Lucy goes to lickin' that toe, pops it in, and goes to grinding up that devil in her old ground down chops. And next time we see them, the fiddler and his drunk bitch, they both full of corn, and ready, now, for the dance!

STAR VANISHES

George Jean Nathan (1882-1958)
Leading American Drama Critic

Gene Seer stood before the window of a bookstore in Grand Central Station. In the window, plain as day, he saw himself, through spectacles, admiring his own creation—*Abishag: A Biography of Star Kirkland.* Hollywood legend blamed George Jean Nathan's bad, and, some said, misconceived, review of "Abishag" for Star vanishing. But she had been more than a little crazy since childhood, when she was dimpled Baby Stella, of whom Charlie Chaplin had quipped, when she sat on his knee and peed, "Tinkle, tinkle, little star!"

In the mirroring window of the bookstore, Gene Seer saw Grand Central's cavernous room and imagined what romance it must have held in Star Kirkland's day. But the shabby present imposed itself. Even he was not too young to remember how the big Irish cops used to chase the bums from the station, and now the city dumped them in it, calling them the homeless. And those young thugs, what were they doing? They were taunting that poor old bag-lady! Gene Seer, possessed of righteous chivalry, stepped into the fray.

"Leave the lady alone," he commanded.

"They've stolen my bags!" she cried. "Get my bags!"

A young ruffian threw a shopping bag. It slid up to their feet, its contents ejected behind it like the fuel of a

NASA rocket. Another boy threw another bag with the same result. "High hat old bitch! Call us red-caps! We ain't no reds!"

"She's an old lady. Pick on somebody your own age!"

The old lady was already refilling her shopping bags.

* * *

Gene Seer took two steaming paper cups of coffee from the counter man and handed one to the old lady.

"Let me pay you," she said. She put her cup on the counter and fumbled in an ancient sequined handbag.

"Are you hungry?" asked Gene Seer.

She handed him a dried brown newspaper clipping. "Can you break this?"

Gene Seer pushed back the knotty hand. "It's on me," he said.

"That's very good of you." Her checkerboard tongue flickered silently in her mouth; then she said, "I hate waiting for trains, don't you? But the Twentieth Century's Limited." She put a hand to her chin, a bony finger on her lips, tipped her head, and smiled a little dark void of a smile to show that she had made a joke.

Gene Seer, needing uplift, said, "I just came in from East Hampton."

Disappointment at her failed joke colored her face in pastels. She changed the subject. "Why did those red-caps behave so rudely?"

"They aren't red-caps, you see. They misunderstood you. They thought you were insulting them. Look," he said, eyeing his watch, "I have to leave now. I don't think they'll bother you again."

He took her hand, pressing a ten dollar bill into the clipping she held, and let go as if he felt something uncanny. Oh, the germs! Now he'd have to go to the lavatory and wash.

* * *

The old bag-lady looked at the enormous room of Grand Central Station, reflected in the window, and pitied the poor, homeless people who sat idly about in it during this period of economic depression—Hoover's fault!—but consoled herself with the thought that Roosevelt would soon set things right.

She thought she had better move on. Though she wasn't costumed as Abishag, as she was on the cover of the book in the window, still, someone might easily recognize her, one of the ten most famous women in the world.

Was the Twentieth Century Limited? she asked herself, laughing. But seriously, should she board now? And her bags, her bags! Where were those red-caps? She looked for tip-money and found, folded together in her purse, a ten dollar bill and a newspaper clipping headlined STAR VANISHES. She replaced the clipping, holding out the bill for a tip for the red-caps. Oh, but why should she go back to Hollywood, anyway, after what the "American Mercury" had said about Abishag? Perhaps she should go on to Washington instead; lend her services to the New Deal, at least until George Jean Nathan recanted.

A FABLE

It seems there is a place where beggars and poor people go to tell tales, and the mostly riding moon will park to look and to listen in the dark to the tales as they are told by the poor beggar bards of the hobo jungle, a place lonely as life, at the end of the track, in a cul-de-sac of starred, campfired night, in a turntabled copse in the dark ragged green of smoke-stunted oak and rope-strong weeds, where birds bivouac: and of all beggar bards who sang a sad ballad there, for the folk, or chanted a moon-watched tale, the most famous because most magical was the hobo bard the Pinkertons called "The All-Seeing Eye," because of his blind, superhuman vigilance, and the mooncalf folk called "O'Shay the Irish Shaman" for his gift of curative power, uncanny control of events, and for divining the deep, hooded meaning of things beyond their poor eyes and plain powers to see.

Now O'Shay rose up and loomed before them, above them, his flame-mapped face red and changing as the cat-o'-nine-tailed fire, his great, blind eyes like those of the horse of his inner-eye (a carp-eyed stallion), his hair a red, swimming flame dowsed by the cool waters of the moon. O'Shay, though blind, was free, though poor, was proud, and did not like to see the poor folk bowed by that boulder, Care, nor bullied by the railroad dicks and afraid in their camp at the end of the track underneath the parked moon in the starred, turntabled copse where he loomed now, watching their weak eyes with his strong, inner one, and knowing that they needed a hopeful tale to be told that the Depression be lifted, courage restored, and the parked moon set free to ride the night into dawn, and new hope for them, crying: "Pride's the subject of my moon-watched tale. Now listen to O'Shay, poor people, and see what you think—stop, look, and listen with the fascinated moon.

"There was a white stallion that lived when you were but babes of scuttlebutt at heaven's height, nay, that full, silver moon itself unborn of the great, swaying sea; a stallion of clouds and spirit that came finally to gallop the great plains of the North American west; a pale, proud, bellows-nostrilled, carp-eyed king of a horse, that could blow back the floozy wind from Manitoba down to the plains of old Mexico; that could whinny across the west to call a brood mare from her happy home to him a thousand miles away in the night; that spoke in trumpeting tongues of his freedom, stamped, and neighed pride from his great, rampant heart; who hammered hope with his hooves to the ranging mustangs of the plain.

"A maverick king, he! And this is the best part, for the horse was blind like myself, and nothing daunted, unconstrained, for he saw with his four, steamed, cow-catcher hooves, and his ears that could hear the baby-breath sigh of a willow on an unborn wind; saw, too, and best, with an inner eye like my own, and had powers, like myself, gifts of nature, with which he could divine the treachery of humankind, and thus keep himself free, and wear no man's hot brand.

"For he wore no man's brand; and that was a heartache to all rich ranchers who had heard of the white stallion: his freedom mocked their staked, barbed wire; and they offered gold for his capture—pots of rainbow gold those rich ranchers offered the buck who captured the stallion; gold, gold beyond a poor cowpoke's wildest dreams, fifty thousand dollars in gold bullion to the buckaroo who brought in the phantom of the prairies, fifty more to the bronco buster who broke him—fifty thousand in gold, one hundred thousand in gold bars to do both! They came from the stretched limbs of the continent—wranglers, roustabouts, beggars and poor people like ourselves, all with mad schemes to capture the blind, white stallion, keen on the trace of gold."

Here O'Shay's brick jaws mortised, his lips ringed teeth, and his dark sockets fixed face after face, saw! And yet they knew O'Shay was a blind man and could not see the mad excitement they felt, hearing of gold, could not see how they stood who had sprawled or hunkered down on their heels here, could not know, therefore, how ready for pursuit they were, how each in his mind saw a fleece-white phantom flee his grasp, as O'Shay took pause from his moon-watched tale, and they cried out to him, suddenly, as one many-voiced, to go on.

"Mad men with mad schemes!" cried O'Shay. "For they knew, the earthly fame of the phantom being, by now, widespread, that all the ordinary methods of capture had been tried and had failed. No, a ghost must be caught in some other way. Hence these mad or tragic traps. One loon dreamed of speeding hoopsnakes that would ensnarl the steed's cow-catcher hooves, another's gold-frenzy fancied a fast balloon. The supernatural horse and the idea of gold had made them mad. Not all, some had sounder brains and better schemes. A wrangler, a strong man who knew his horses, had staked out an arroyo which was a haunt of the white steed. He pitched camp and waited; and happenstance his patience was rewarded when, like a mirage, the pale, maverick king, with his own remuda of mares prancing and curvetting behind, galloped up to drink, stamping and snorting. The wrangler climbed a rise, and, twirling an Indian-charmed lariat of rawhide interwoven with shot-gold wire which he had bought from a Kiowa shaman, roped him, looping the golden noose neatly around his neck. The white stallion whinnied, rose rampant, and snapped the charmed, magic lasso as the wrangler might have snapped a golden thread; and the still-noosed stallion and his mares vanished in white dust. But this was the closest that any man had come."

O'Shay stopped his story here, drank from his flask, wiped his mouth up his sleeve, and looked intently out at the poor people, who had begun to suspect that he was not blind at all, so seeing seemed his ragged, flame-valanced sockets. And now they felt that he could see them fingering their necks, golden-noosed now, like that of the white stallion of his long, tall tale; fingering their necks and feeling the golden noose tighten, as they pulled from the shaman, and snap, freeing them. Suddenly O'Shay laughed, and the rubber-necking, neck-rubbing folk shook: but then there seemed to have been no laughter there but merely the bark of dogwood flame from the heeling fire or the sudden gold caw of a blackbird, bivouacked nearby.

O'Shay frowned, now, and said: "Having heard how the wrangler had failed, the rich ranchers upped the purse to a million; but before any could claim it, he must represent them, having won a competition for horsemanship from among the finest cowhands and vaqueros to be found; and then, having conquered all men, must conquer the white stallion. The competition involved every trick or skill of wrangling science and art, and lasted a twelvemonth. A vaquero triumphed, and had fine mounts stationed at mile intervals from a wheel's hub out for a hundred hot miles, the hub the arroyo where the horse had escaped the noose, the fine mounts the posed spokes of a great wagon wheel. The vaquero waited at the hub of the wheel for the white phantom until it appeared, and the pursuit was on for a hundred miles, mile on hot mile, with fresh, mile-new mounts, for the vaquero hoped to exhaust the phantom. But the great vaquero could not exhaust or overtake the white steed, who taunted him with his easygoing gait; and, after his hundredth horse had dropped, could only report that the golden noose still hung from the phantom's neck. News of the hunt's failure spread up and down the plains, told by range riders on lonely duty tours, at starred, campfired night, until word reached a famed trapper up in Manitoba, one who had trapped every kind of animal. His name was Hawkeye Red."

O'Shay paused here to take a swig from his flask and to consider the beggars and poor people, who were amused by the blarney of their shamrock shaman, who again managed to relate himself to the pacing white stallion. A few friendly hoots were heard, with which, O'Shay, scrunching a flame-snake of brow in a dark wink, returned to his tall, romantic tale.

"Hawkeye Red," he said, "left his cold northern home and journeyed far southwest to find the white phantom, or to find out where he might be found. Then he methodically began work on his great trap. He gathered the strongest oaken lumber that could be found and built a great stable in the arroyo where the horse was golden-noosed, and in it placed the most beautiful young mare that the rich ranchers possessed among them, a doe-eyed, blazed-faced bay with black mane and tail. Ringbolt-tethered, high-strung, frightened, Bonny-Pru would be the bait. Now he set the trap doors, cleverly contrived to clap shut behind the white stallion when, or if, he entered, trapping him. After making sure that the trap would work, Hawkeye Red and the rich ranchers went to a vantage point to wait for the phantom. Under the riding moon, Bonny-Pru pulled, kicked the oaken planks, and whinnied for her freedom across the dappled night, until her fearful, fearsome cries were borne as on an unborn wind to the white steed. The man-watched moon rode high as the hours passed, and nearer and nearer he galloped with all his magical might toward her in her trap, and his. At last he came to the dark and looming stable; and, though the great, mouthing doors gaped open, paused, galloped away, circling wide the foreboding building; then, though he knew this was a trap, galloped in to the distressed, stable-trapped, ringbolt-tethered damsel mare who cried out for a brave champion like himself. The trap doors shut! Silence! No sound whatever from inside the stable. The rich ranchers whooped high for their victory; but, somehow, Hawkeye Red, now rich, felt let down by success.

"All left their vantage point and approached the stable. But, nearing it, the doors split, splintered like kicked glass, spilled, filled the spiked air, and up and over the heads of Hawkeye Red and the rich ranchers rose the white stallion and his damsel mare like two wide-winged, magical, legendary birds. Hawkeye Red shook his head in unbelief, turned, dazed, to see them, bullets that followed the riflings of infinity. In a moment of wild, unholy desperation, he ran to his horse, reached for his rifle, aimed, and fired. The rifle exploded, but from the breech, not the muzzle, blinding him. And in that first blind instant he saw the horse of his mad pride go free, the white phantom rise rampant and neigh, like a musical muscle that flexes and sings, and vanish from the land, with his blazed-faced bride, Bonny-Pru, by his side, never to return again."

The poor people were on their feet, now, whinnying, and galloping in place, for O'Shay had turned them into happy horses who would wear no man's brand, who applauded their pleasure with hoof-clap hands and tongues that rode the roofs of moon-watched mouths.

"Hawkeye Red," he said, "regained his vision, but saw no more with his outer eyes, but with a strong, inner one, and lived to tell the tale at the end of a track, in a cul-de-sac of starred, campfired night, in a turntabled copse in the dark, ragged green of smoke-stunted oak and rope-strong weeds, where birds bivouac."

And he set the moon free.

WHAT I DID ON MY SUMMER VACATION

This summer I flew to Trieste to visit with Joyce, then journeyed on to Prague to see Kafka, who was cryptic. I made a pit-stop in Paris to have a drink with Beckett, caught up with Thomas Wolfe, who had stayed over from the Oktoberfest in Hamburg, and roared around town for a few days, then flew on to Casablanca to have a drink at Rick's and hear some good piano. I met with Graham Greene in Saigon (though they call it Ho Chi Minh City now) and he explained how the quiet American was going to cause trouble. I made the big leap from Dirty Dick's to Sloppy Joe's because the Literary Travel Agency had screwed up my itinerary, but soon found myself chugging through the Chunnel and into Poet's Corner at Westminster Abbey, where I ran into a raging Dylan Thomas. Well, he hated the States but loved Third Avenue, so he said he would help me paint London red, white, and blue. Next morning we had vanilla ice-cream in our beer for our health's sake. Later that afternoon Caitlin kicked the stilts out from under his house, so I thought it was time to leave them there, fighting in Laugharne, and get on to the relative peace and quiet of Ireland, where I visited with Pat Kavanagh, who had come to regard comedy as the "ultimate sophistication," which ordinary people, "do not understand and therefore fear." Pat believed that in tragedy "there is always something of a lie—comedy is the abundance of life," etc., but I had to leave him there, laughing at himself, and life in general, and catch the train on to Heathrow. I landed in New York, where I was met by Walt Whitman, who was holding up a disheveled Eddie Poe, who greeted me with a wet kiss. I got a manly hug from Walt. Then I flew back down to Asheville to present Wolfe's hometown with his latest, *You Can't Go Home Again,* which he gave me in manuscript (much edited by Max Perkins) and then drove back to the College by the Lake; and here I am again, grading papers.

A MAN OF CONSCIENCE

The night can sweat with terror as before
We pieced our thoughts into philosophy,
And planned to bring the world under a rule,
Who are but weasels fighting in a hole.
—W.B. Yeats

This happened in London, although it could have happened in Dublin or New York or any major city of the world. It could have happened in some backwater as well, but it happened in London, not far from Piccadilly Circus. But where it happened is of no real importance—when is more relevant, but that will become clear in the telling of it. The story derives from a Scotland Yard confession, to which the author was privy before his retirement.

It was early evening of a cold November day. The pavements glistened under falling heavy mist and traffic sounds were muted. Two men were walking down a street. The man following came up behind the man ahead. The man ahead felt the barrel of a pistol in his back. He was told to keep walking and was ordered into a dark doorway.

"This was a trick," he said in a hushed voice, back over his shoulder. "I was told this was a meet for the cause."

"Get down those stairs."

The man ahead did as he was told and at the bottom was pushed through a door. Inside, the room was dark but the man behind switched on a light. It was a dank basement room of ancient drooling bricks, criss-crossing pipes, dust and cobwebs, deep below the street. There was a table. A few chairs. An old desk. Little else except looming shadows. The man ahead saw a rat stand up and look at him in a far corner when the light went on. Then he was struck a stunning blow to the back of his head. He couldn't think. He fell to the cement floor and as he fell the Uzi he kept in an inside pocket of his trenchcoat was ripped away. Minutes passed. Then consciousness returned.

"Awake?" said the man with the guns. He held the Uzi in his left hand and a long-barrelled Webley in his right.

"Yes." The man on the floor looked around. As he took in this filthy empty room he was filled with unease and at the same time outrage.

"Where am I?" Then he realized that he was bound hand and foot with duct tape, could not move. "Where am I? Who are you? What's this? Who are you? What *is* this?" His head was clearing. "Obviously, you are not the man I was supposed to meet."

"I am the man you were supposed to meet—inevitably. I'm your punisher. No, your redeemer. We are Napoleon and Wellington at Waterloo."

"Punisher? My what? Is that what you said?" Then he felt outrage become rage and raw anger. "Who in hell are you? Some kind of maniac?"

"Of course, we are both maniacs, living in a mad insane-simian world. I told you, I'm your punisher."

"My punisher . . ." he muttered to himself, "my punisher." Then, he looked up intently and saw, for the first time, a tall thin man with a salt-and-pepper mustache, a sharp pointed aquiline nose and eyes pale as ice-water. The man's demeanor portrayed no emotion, only purpose. Now the bound man felt a thrill of uncontrollable fear as he looked at the neat gray overcoat and the gray fedora downward slanted over the cold pale eyes.

"My punisher? For what? And who in hell are you to punish me? Some kind of damn fascist cop? Where is this place? How did I get here? Oh, yeah, I remember. You stuck a gun in my back. Why did you have to hit me so hard? My brain's scrambled."

"Better now?"

"I can see straight, but you've given me a thudding headache. What's this all about? I can see your intention isn't robbery, so what is it?"

"As to where you are, this is Purgatory. You are on your way to hell."

"What then, are you some damn loony representative of the Church? An agent for the Vatican or something? I don't have to tell you, do I, that I don't believe in hell?"

The tall thin man spoke slowly, with supreme confidence, "Oh, oh, I assure you, you're going to hell, whether you believe in it or not."

"You know it, then?"

"It? What?"

"Hell."

"I'm a veteran of several wars as are you. I've had your file for some time. You've sunk from soldier to terrorist."

"Hell—ha! Now look you, enough of these crazy metaphysics. Who are you and—"

"I'm not being metaphysical. Quite the contrary."

"What are you talking about?"

"I mean that I've been thinking about you for a long time. And I guess there's a hell. If you exist, there must be a hell to swallow you up. Maybe not in the earth, but on the surface of it. And that's where you're going."

The bound man thought that perhaps he was dealing with a real lunatic. This was no ordinary stick-up or assault or kidnapping that one in his business might expect. He thought he'd better go easy here. He felt that he was dealing with a fanatic. "Now look," he said, "just explain to me why you have me tied up in this room? Tell me who you are. Explain!"

Dreamlike, the tall thin man said: "Who you are. Who I am . . ."

"Damn maniac!"

"Yes. I used to think you were the maniac. Maybe you are. But it won't change anything. I'm—" he searched for the right word— "implacable. But I know who you are. You, in particular. But I know who you all are."

The bound man struggled in the tape and tried to sit up straight. "All right. I think I've got it now. Oh, damn, I've got a headache. Damn, my head aches! You must be some kind of agent . . . CIA, FBI, MI5—something. This is an interrogation. You want information . . . is that it?"

"No."

"No? Look, maybe I can help you. Give you some information. I know plenty. What is it you want?"

"At first I thought I wanted you dead. But as I thought about it I realized that would be no punishment for you. It would only set you free."

The bound man felt apprehensive. He couldn't figure this guy out. "Revenge?"

"I suppose so. But the more I thought about that the less important it seemed. Anyway, revenge must be taken in hot blood. There's satisfaction in that. There's no satisfaction in what I'm going to do. Indeed, I've condemned myself to a life of misery. You've brought me to this."

"Not revenge? Not revenge! What then? What are you going on about? What do you mean, condemn yourself to a life of misery? Why?"

"I'm a man of conscience."

"Conscience?" The bound man thought as fast as he could and said, "Look, are you some kind of madman, or what? Is there any water here? Got any aspirin? I feel nauseated. How long was I out?"

"Ah. I wonder."

"Now what's that supposed to mean?"

"I've been thinking about you for a long time. About this day. Suppose we say . . . suppose we say that I'm the husband of a secretary whose hands were blown off, opening one of your letter bombs."

"Are you?"

The tall thin man put his revolver on the table, fished in the desk drawer and brought out a bottle of brandy, a tin of aspirin, two glasses. "No," he said, as he stepped back and leaned down to the bound man. "Open your mouth. And yes." He took out a few aspirin and put two on the bound man's tongue, then poured brandy to wash them down.

"Now what's that supposed to mean?"

"It means that it might be the case, but it's no longer the major reason. It means, as I said before, vengeance must be taken in hot blood. I am not your punisher. I am your redeemer." He became more excited as he spoke, his voice trembled and rose in heat and volume. The single overhead light made the creases in his face seem to jump and rearrange themselves as he paced back and forth in front of the bound man. "It means that right after your plastique blew my old father to pieces in Dublin I wanted to kill you. In hot blood! I wanted revenge. Vengeance! Who wouldn't? But I cooled off. It means that after my friend Izsak, the great Olympic runner, had his legs severed by a blast of machine gun fire in an airport. . . . It means that I wanted revenge for Izsak! It means that I wanted to kill you. In hot blood! But I cooled off. It means that after my thirty daughters ranging in age from nine to ninety were blown up in a hotel ballroom in Paris—I wanted to kill you! In hot blood! It means that after eighteen Christmas holiday travellers in Vienna and Rome were blown apart at the airports, I wanted to kill you. But I cooled off. I cooled off."

"I don't know what you're talking about. I had nothing to do with Rome, Vienna, Paris. Thirty daughters in Paris?—you're completely mad!"

"Am I? Have I become mad? Might be." The self-called Redeemer shook his head as his voice lowered. "Ask any psychiatrist, madness is contagious. If I'm mad it's because you're mad. If I'm sane, you're sane, too. If we're both sane then there must be evil. If there is evil, there must be good. I've thought of all this. Finally, I don't know what to make of it, but that neither one of us is a civilized human being. And if human beings can be civilized, how does one account for endless wars? Isn't the human race a bunch of monkeys fighting over banannas and nuts? And I'm not a philosopher, I'm a . . . "

"Go on, what? What are you?"

"Can't make any difference, really. I've been a soldier."

"Ahhh. Now we're getting somewhere."

"Oh, well, we're not really getting to anything in the sense that you mean. Who hasn't been a soldier? A political killer? In a world where *you* exist, everyone's a soldier."

"What do you mean, *my* world?"

"As I said before, I'm a man of conscience."

"Couldn't you loosen this?" he asked, holding up his bound wrists. "I haven't got any circulation. My legs are asleep. You're not a torturer are you? You seem civilized."

"Seem civilized. *You* seem civilized—whatever that can mean. But it's a good question. I think the answer is that I'm about to become a deep torturer."

"Then why did you give me the aspirin and the drink? That's not the sort of thing a torturer does. That's the act of a humanist."

"Oh. . . I wanted your full attention. You can't pay any attention to me when you're suffering."

The bound man shook his head. "I don't understand you, I admit it. Deep torturer. What does that mean?"

"It means redeemer. It means I'm not out to punish your body."

"Then loosen these bonds."

"Perhaps. Even at this moment, I'm not certain which of us is mad."

"What do you mean, deep torturer?

"Redeemer. Redeemer! It means that I've thought and thought about it. I mean . . . look at the weapons you choose. The weapons of a terrorist, bombs and sprayed bullets. You are a terrorist. You are my terrorist and I am going to redeem you." He picked up the bound man's machine pistol from where he had put it on the table and waved it back and forth with contempt.

"My Uzi?"

"Yes. Look at it. Sprays venom. Now look at this." He takes his long barelled Webley revolver from the table, aims at the terrorist's head. "One shot." He cocks the revolver. "I am accurate. If I kill someone, it is my intention. I am not careless about murder."

"You don't mean to kill me, or you would have done it by now."

"I could hit you between the eyes at the distance of a city block."

"Meaning?"

"Meaning that I don't spray venom like a spitting reptile." He spat on the Terrorist's machine pistol and threw it into the dark corner where the rat had stood at attention. "Meaning that I'm selective. I choose my victim."

"You sonofabitch!"

"Pointing my pistol at you was a wanton act. It was almost an act of torture. You see, I can tell the difference. I've still got enough humanity to possess a conscience. I know that what I just did was wrong, pointing my pistol at your head, cocking it. Oh, I've thought about it for a long time. No, I'm just a simple soldier. At first it was vengeance. But I cooled off. I thought about it. I asked myself what kind of human being . . . no, sub-human . . . could send letter bombs through the mail to blow off the hands of secretaries. I have access to files. I know your ilk. I know you, particularly. You're . . . your family's quite wealthy. You, dear boy, are a spoiled brat!"

"I have a cause!"

"You have a vanity!" the self-called Redeemer shouted. "You have an arrogance. You have a will to be constrained by no political system, nor any conscience. A terrorist kills to feel infantile power. If you got what you want, it would pall immediately. Immediately you'd want something else. Then and there. What you want is . . . is obedience! Power over people. You are a great ape in a jungle. You are what civilization was meant to conquer."

"I want to help in the struggle against fascism!"

"But, my boy, you *are* a fascist. Your life is telling other people what to do. It's a disease in an adult, a mental illness. You see, every baby is born a fascist. Every baby wants what it wants when it wants it. And this is as it should be. And every baby will use every means at its disposal to get what it wants. And what parent, late at night, has not been the victim of a torturing baby, who uses its shrill cry to make you move and move quick. Babies are fascists—one in the same. And you, my boy, have simply never grown up. You see, you're that thing most to be feared . . . a willful child with a machine gun or bomb." He walked over to the dark corner and picked up the machine pistol, came back and held it under the terrorist's nose, pushed it into his face.

You see?" He went back to the table and dropped it there, picked up his Webley and said, "A man's weapon. The weapon of a skillful, selective, mature human being."

"You're as crazy as they come."

"Admittedly. As I told you, I'm not a philosopher. I'm a soldier."

"Not a torturer, or so you say. Loosen these tapes."

"Why not?" The Redeemer took out a switchblade, snapped it open and cut the Terrorist free.

"Oh, God, I'm like putty," the Terrorist said, rubbing his arms and legs to get the circulation going. He tried to stand but his knees would not cooperate.

"Oh, you're a helpless victim. How does it feel?"

"Not so helpless in a few minutes. Let me get my blood flowing."

"The thing is, you're like an infant. During the course of growing up, you never acquired a conscience. No, you've been deprived. When you commit an act of terrorism, apparently it doesn't trouble you that you've made handless or legless or sightless, or lifeless, another human being."

"What about you? You're a bloody soldier. You've wounded people. Killed them."

"Yes. Troublesome, isn't it? I've thought about it. As I was preparing for this I thought a good deal about it. The only thing I can come up with is the fact of randomness."

"What about your bloody bombs? What about Dresden? Hiroshima? Nagasaki? London? Bunch of sonofabitching soldiers doing that, wasn't it? There were innocents in those cities, weren't there?"

"Oh, God!"

"Don't call Him in on it now."

"Yes. That's a terrible question."

"Nothing selective there, eh?"

"Yes, it amounts to the question—don't you think—of whether we're all mad or sane, and, therefore, evil, and that, then, there must be good, too. Doesn't it amount to that?"

"Look, you damn bastard, I'm no bloody philosopher, either."

The Redeemer saw that fear had receded from his victim's eyes. "Crawl back, over there," he said, indicating direction away from himself. The Terrorist saw resignation in the pale eyes of his captor, some kind of loss, and sadness.

"Stay on the floor. Back! Maybe the answer is that evil is who initiates . . . who starts the thing."

"To hear you talk, babies start it."

"It's that we're wild animals, not yet fully human. No, I've got to stay with my point. My only sanity is my point."

"Which is?"

"That people have to suffer for the crimes they commit—for the evil they do. That they can't suffer unless they have a conscience, and they can't develop a conscience without suffering. That that's what I mean by deep torture. I think the difference between you and me is that I have a conscience. It does seem different to me—that if a man tries to kill me, in defending myself, I kill him—than if I were the one who decided to do the killing first. That does seem different to me. The secretary didn't try to kill you."

"I didn't try to kill her, either. I didn't know she existed." The Terrorist was exasperated. With the impetus his freed limbs gave him he grabbed one of the chairs and sat, while the Redeemer followed his movements with his gun.

"You didn't care," said the Redeemer. "You haven't got the imagination, the empathy required. No, you see, there's the point. You just meant to inflict pain, death, upon someone, anyone. That's your power. Yes. Yes. That's the point. You were the initiator."

"So I'm the bloke without a conscience, is that it?"

"That's it."

"Your point! Your point! Oh, I get your point, all right. It doesn't make a hellova lot of sense. *My* point is that we're in a war here so—the war of the apes.

"But you are permanently out of the war. You may get your circulation back, but you are not going back into circulation. No, not you."

"You mean you're going to hold me prisoner? You said before that you didn't intend to kill me."

"I don't. That's why I'm going to have to be very careful."

"You do intend to torture me then?"

"I'm going to have to inflict pain. But I would do what I intend to do without inflicting pain if I could."

"Damn you! What is it you intend to do?" The Terrorist thought he could lunge for this lunatic. He waited for the right moment.

"When you leave here," said the Redeemer, "and you will leave, you will be a changed man. You will begin a lifelong process of learning remorse. I'm going to make you grow up, laddie buck. You're going to learn what it is really like to share this planet with other members of your species. In your mind, which will gradually develop a heart, a conscience, you will be deeply tortured for the rest of your life. Because you have never understood what it is to see yourself in another being—sympathy—empathy. You've been locked in a cell all your life, laddie. But I'm going to lock you in so tight and for so long that you'll scream night and day for the word of another human being. For the sight of a face. For the grace to move with another in a dance. Even now, I can hear your *cri de coeur*. It is sweet to my ears."

"What in hell are you going to do?"

"I'm going to lock you in your body. All by yourself."

"What? What? What?"

"I'm going to cut your tongue out, so that you'll never be able but to vomit sound. I'm going to hold this pistol next to your eardrums and fire it, so that you'll never hear the sound of a voice again. I'm going to use my thumbs on your eyes. I'm going to castrate you. And I'm going to break your elbows and knees, and I'm going to see to it that you live. And for the rest of your days your punishment will be . . . isolation."

"And you, you bastard, you call yourself a man of conscience?"

"Oh, I know, I know. I've thought about it a great deal. I've thought it all out for a long, long time."

"You can't do it! You haven't got it in you, to do a thing like that. You're just trying to frighten me."

"Yes. I can do it because I hate your kind beyond reason. But, at first, I thought I couldn't do it unless—"

"Unless?"

"Unless, after I'd done it, I killed myself."

"My God, you mean to do it, don't you?" The terrorist was dizzy with this talk. One minute he thought his captor a garden variety nut case whom he could overtake and the next, some horrible philosophical maniac whose black whirling nonsense was seeping into his own reasoning.

"Yes, I mean it. But then I thought. . . then I thought that would be cheating."

"Cheating what? God?"

"No. Myself. My conscience. You see, if I want you to suffer remorse, then I have no right to escape it. That's what I meant when I said earlier that in condemning you, in . . . acting as your therapist, in awarding you the gift of a conscience . . . well, how could I run out on my own?"

The Terrorist realized then that only one chance for him existed. He lunged at the Redeemer in desperation.

In a reflex action the Redeemer jerked the trigger of his cocked Webley and a red hole appeared between the Terrorist's unbelieving eyes.

"Oh no—Oh God!" the Redeemer cried, as the Terrorist fell to the floor. "O no, O *God*!"

Later, out of that place, in the icy splash of mist, still shaken, he walked the streets without purpose or direction, among average people who were just trying to live.

THE MAN WHO SOLD WORDS

for Selah

It wasn't until she had almost given up hope that she saw the man who sold words. She had been moping by the playground fence, where she first met him, thinking of how it would be when she told her father that she had all the words she needed for Scrabble and could play with her mother and father and big sister, when her eyes, casually following the dreamy flight of a blackbird, passed him by in their sweep, and returned to the mystic point of recognition.

He was standing high on a green hill, between two silver-barked and green-leaved maples, waving to her, pointing at the open gate to the right of her and circling a hand in the air, indicating that she should come out of the playground and up to him, there, high on the hill. She knew she was not to leave the playground, but she knew too that she had to disobey this time, just this once, or the man who sold words would go away. Already he had turned his back and was walking down the other side of the hill. How many hills would he go beyond? Even now, she could see only his wild, gray head bobbing, bobbing down, downwards, beyond the bright hill's green horizon, gone! She hiked up the shiny shoulder-strapped leather pocketbook her father had given her for her fifth birthday. It was heavy, filled with coins from her piggy bank. She might have counted out the change she would need, but there had been no time, and she had dumped the whole contents of the bank into the bag. She ran among the children, bumping them, her heavy pocketbook banging her hip, the backs of her legs, nearly knocking her down, tripping her up. But she ran as fast as she could—through the side gate, across the walkway, around and outside of the fence, up the hill, floundering and sprawling, visions sweeping by, breathless, unnoticed.

* * *

A full moon hung over the heads of the police and parents as they fanned out. The little girl's mother had gone several small hills beyond the playground, and was coming down a hill, when she saw her, huddled in sleep, against a tree. She did not see the man. She heard him. Her flashlight was full on her child and she was about to call out when she heard a grunt, a sort of snort. She flashed her light from her daughter to the place where the sound had come from, registering, in the back of her mind, metallic glitters of coins, glassy glimmers of bottles, and writing—words, misspelled, crazy jargon, written in large deep letters all over the ground, beneath the trees. Then she saw him, a rag man, a fat scarecrow. He opened redrimmed eyes into her flashlight, and said, his pink tongue squirming drunkenly in his mouth, "Egypt!"

"That's only eleven points," said the mother, breathlessly, taking in the scene with increasing relief. "Besides, it's a proper noun." She looked into the moonlit space at her daughter, who sat with a kind of anticipatory surprise registering on her little, round-eyed face, and then at the other, who wore something of the same look as her daughter. Her daughter had mentioned him, she now remembered, but she had been too busy to heed the child. She had idly thought that the child was referring to a fairy tale, or—

Yes, she *had* heard of him, the man who sold words.

BAD TRIP

I noticed what beautiful teeth the young man had. Mine are missing or turned to coffee, red wine, and smoke. The hitchhiker had a seabag stencilled with my name. I have an unusual name and it could not have been sheer coincidence. I was going west—he said west was fine with him. The Mojave highway was empty for as far as I could see. I stopped the car. He tried to open the door, but I had them all locked. I shot him, then unlocked the doors and pushed his body out into the roadside sand. I got out and rolled him out of view, down a sand dune, and buried him, dust to dust. Well, I might as well have done so, even if I didn't. What I did to him was nearly as bad, maybe worse. I let him live and become me. So most of my life I have been living inside a much younger man. It was quite an adventure, being young. He ran a lot, ran long distances and very quickly short, marathons and dashes. He got embarrassing erections on buses, hanging on to the strap, and would have to face away in a twisted posture, but the rest of him, being loose, not stiff, he could contort and hide his secret lust. In middle age, he was big-voiced and positive, sure of everything, in a way I find impossible; I, who doubt all. I have many photographs of him. Lifting barbells. Boxing. He is always glad to pose. Myself, I hate having my picture taken. It is certain to come back to me as an old fart, grinning stupidly at the camera, as if to say, "I am still like him, like that hitchhiker." But I am not just like him, not at all like him, inside or out. I miss him but I don't want him back. I would rather crawl forward and under; for, now that I think about it, he never was so hot, never the number he thought he was.

A BOWERYMAN'S CHRISTMAS

Jack Reilly didn't think it was exactly an inspiring place to spend Christmas Eve; but, what the hell, his back was aching. Besides, the joint was decorated prettily, with paper chains across the ceiling and over the dark, desilvered mirrors, and that snow that sprays out of aerosol cans puffing out of the oddest places. Sprigs of red and green here and there. It was O.K. He'd been in worse places. Danang, where he lost his dangler, and he was just out of a Veteran's hospital that was almost as bad as this. He limped across the slimy tile floor, his hip on fire, careful to avoid the potholes, and dragged himself on to a rickety barstool. Ready, now, he was, to celebrate Christmas 1966.

The bartender, a man who looked as if his head had been stuffed with hair, so profusely did clumps of it grow out of his nostrils and ears, said, "Merry Christmas," and asked him what his pleasure was.

He looked up and down the bar. He noticed that several of the men along the bar were drinking large glasses of sticky-looking red wine with small glasses of beer, which were used as a sort of chaser. Judging from the look of the men who were drinking this combination, it was cheap and highly functional. He ordered it.

He sat swilling the stuff, warming up a bit, and read the signs behind the bar:

WHISKEY 70¢
BIG BOY SHOT $1.10
EYE-OPENERS
MON.-SAT. 8 TO 9 AM 80¢

EAT AND DRINK WITH CONFIDENCE

And on a large piece of ragged cardboard, in a green crayon scrawl:

COVER YOUR COUGH!

No sooner had he read that than he took a gulp of wine that went down the wrong way. He had a spasm. The sticky stuff seemed to lock his throat shut. He sucked for air, but it couldn't get through. His bronchials were like bent tubes. He got panicky. He thought if he couldn't get some air he'd collapse, maybe strangle to death. He leaped off his barstool, feeling that his chest was about to explode. Then somebody banged his back, and air suddenly found its way through the tubes, into his lungs; filled them up, grey balloons. He stood shaking in his black, spit-shined Marine Corps issued shoes, thanking the bird who'd clouted him. But when he'd got his streaming eyes back in focus, he realized that his guardian angel had gone. He looked about, embarrassed by his fit, and saw that nobody had paid him any attention. The fit had been worth no more than a slap on the back in passing. This realization calmed him down, and he climbed back on the barstool and sipped his beer, meekly.

At three in the morning Jack staggered into the street. He walked a little way through the snow, which was now ankle-deep, passing doorways where men slept in heaps of five and ten, looking like speckled monsters of many arms and legs, and—worse—heads. Hydras of degradation, pus in their veins instead of blood, reeking, crawling with vermin. He wasn't going to throw himself on top of one of those human mattresses. He wasn't that far gone, no! He was a United States Marine. He had his pride. He kept on trudging through the ice-bottomed snow until he came to the Salvation Army Mission.

He stepped inside, but a sign read *NO ROOM*, so he went back out. In a way, he didn't care where he went—he was so drunk. But that attitude was qualified by a few things. One, he wasn't going to throw himself on one of those heaps of flesh. Another, he wasn't going to go crawling up to some woman. He'd had it. He was sick to death of the whole crazy lot of them. He was sick of dealing with them, of dodging them, of running after them, and of running away from them. After all, he had nothing to offer them. No, he'd foxed them this time! No women! No women!

A red-white-and-blue neon sign blinked through the blinding snow. *FREEDOM FLOP.*

"*Flea*-dom Flop." He expelled a bitter laugh. He climbed up the narrow metal stairs of the flophouse, his shattered hip aching; his head shrouded in some kind of black lace hood, and brig-stepped, dragging his leg, to the screened-in desk.

Behind it the clerk bobbed up.

"How much for a room?" he slurred.

"Merry Christmas. Ain't got no rooms left. Got a dorm pretty empty."

"How much?" He was counting his change. He'd bought a pint of the red stuff from nose-hair just before he'd stumbled out into the street. He had about two dollars and a half in change, not counting his mustering-out pay which he kept in a wallet with his Purple Heart—he felt for it—ahh, there it was—for the future, to give to somebody he did not have.

"Two seventy-five," said the clerk, the screen filtering few impurities from his breath.

"I only got two-fifty."

"O.K., two-fifty."

He dumped his change under the opening of the screen, and the clerk slid a key back. He looked at it, wondering what he needed a key for, in a dormitory. It had a wooden stick attached with number 88 painted on it. The clerk jerked his thumb and said:

"Upstairs."

"O.K." He followed a red arrow that pointed up another flight of stairs. He climbed up this vomitus flight with great care and with what was left of his strength, and, following the red arrows, turned into the dormitory, an enormous, gloomy room.

He stood there a minute, trying to figure things out, muddled. Then he began to get the picture. There were rows of small, metal army cots, the unoccupied ones covered with moth-eaten army blankets, and next to every cot was a small wall-locker with a number painted on it. It reminded him of Parris Island.

He walked down one of the narrow aisles between the cots and found 88.

He dumped himself on it, as he had dumped himself on many military cots before. The room was cool, but not cold; and on one side of him a man lay naked, his thin blanket having floated to the floor. He was a geezer with gray hair all over his body and a deep, half-healed cut on his forehead. His legs were swollen and gouty, one being very large and red and unwholesomely soft-looking. He snored and spasmodically coughed in his sleep. He looked the right age to have been a Second World War Vet or maybe a Korean Vet. From other distances of the enormous room other coughing fits echoed cavernously, seeming to answer in response, like a code, punctuated by the comma of an occasional fart. What were they trying to say in their troubled sleep?

Jack got up and pulled off his cold, wet clothes, down to his skivvies, stuffed them into the bottom of the locker, and got into bed and lay on the springy cot. The damned thing was like a hammock; his ass bounced on the floor, hurting his hip. He wrapped the blanket around himself, shivered, coughed, and broke the seal of the bottle. *Glug,*

glug, glug, glug, it went, "down the old hatch." He lay there, shivering, curled in a little ball, his blanket wrapped around him, his bottle in his mouth. For the moment he was numb and it was sweet—carefree, cozy, and warm—like being a baby. Nothing to do but dream, maybe of beautiful women.

The VA hospital had given him pain-killers that didn't work. But all those bloody pills he'd taken still wouldn't let him drift right off, as he'd hoped to. He lay there and listened to all the lonely sounds—the screeching springs, the stirrings and shiftings, the elongated farts, the coughing, the occasional moan, the gibberish of sleep-talk—and then he heard something else, someone either reciting verse or reading the Bible in a low, trance-like voice that was somehow familiar. Someone perhaps from long ago and far away.

He listened. It was biblical. "Pilate, therefore, willing to release Jesus, spoke again to them. But they cried, saying, 'Crucify him, crucify him!' and he said unto them the third time, 'Why, what evil hath he done? I have found no cause of death in him: I will therefore chastise him, and let him go!' And then they were instant with loud voices, requiring that he might be crucified. And the voices of them and of the chief priests prevailed. . ." This seemed to be a natural break, and the low voice vanished from the fetid air.

But he had placed it. It came from number eighty-seven, the cot on the other side. It was the low, funereal, Cotton-Mather voice of Burden. He had heard Burden go into these fits of scripture-recitation before, years ago. He threw his legs over the side of the cot and reached over and tapped where he thought Burden's shoulder should be.

"What? What?"

"Burden? Is that you?"

"Yes, yes; my name is Burden."

"It's Jack Reilly, Burden. Don't you remember me?"

Burden braced himself on an elbow. Jack could see him now, a gaunt man. His hair was shaved close. His face was thin, cheeks sunken, his black eyes dazed. He seemed not to quite know where he was. He said: "I'm sorry, friend. I don't know any man by that name. But peace be with you." Then he flopped back on his cot and vanished in his blanket.

Jack said: "Burden, listen. I used to know you in Danang. We were in the same outfit."

"Danang?" Burden rose up again.

"Yeah," said Jack, "I was a buddy. Remember? You were the corpsman, the medic, that saved my damn life when they blew off my dick! Remember?"

"No, friend. I'm sorry. I've had a hundred and twenty-five shock treatments. I don't remember any Danang. But if you say you're a buddy, I believe you. God bless you, friend!"

"Burden, do you want a drink? I've got some rot-gut here."

"No, thank you, friend. I do not drink. I am an angel."

"An angel?"

"Yes, friend." Burden sat up and reached out to him, gripped his shoulder with a bony hand. "I am an angel, and I say unto you that death is near, and that you must ready yourself for it. It is very close at hand, friend."

"What do you mean? What are you talking about?"

"Death. I look into your eyes and see black holes and listen to your voice and know that Death has been following you."

"Stop it, you lunatic!" Jack pulled free of him and got back on his cot, got on the far side of it, near 89, the naked cougher.

In a moment Burden whispered over Jack's shoulder:

"How bad was it for you?"

"You're cracked!" Jack yelled back.

"No, friend, it is you who are mad. I warn you to be saved, for Death walks close at your heels."

"Go to sleep, you crank! You crackpot!"

"I will sleep well, in the arms of my God. Whereas, friend, you can't afford to sleep because you killed so many."

Jack looked over his shoulder and saw that Burden had risen, was waving his arms about, working himself up to a full-scale sermon. He saw that Burden had a huge scar in his side. Why wasn't it bleeding, Jack thought. It was so deep. Jack pulled his blanket up over his head.

"Death . . ." Burden had begun, but Jack stuffed his fingers into his ears. Yet even with his eyes squeezed shut, Jack had a vision of Burden, an after-image, a cross of pale flesh against the darkness. Then he was shaken awake by the clerk of the night before.

"Hey, fella," the clerk said. "Let's go. I gotta clean this place up."

Jack was out on the street and three blocks away before he remembered Burden. It was a nightmare, he thought. He remembered a Burden in Nam, a Lieutenant Burden, not a Navy corpsman. Surely, there was no Burden. It was just another of his nightmares, wasn't it? Catholics have evil dreams. But his mustering-out pay was gone, along with his Purple Heart. Where did they go? Stolen? Were they ever there? His shrouded mind couldn't guarantee it. Did he ever have them? Or was that too, a dream? It occurred to him that it must be Christmas day.

Here he was, trudging along through the crusty, sooty stuff the snow had become, and with no idea of where he was going. Where *was* he going? He felt hot to his own touch, feverish. Hell! He'd been walking in his sleep, maybe, or in a daze, because he just now felt himself awaken!

What he needed was a drink, a hair of the dog, the fur of the dog. He wouldn't be able to assess the damage until he had had a few—maybe many a few. But he was tap city: desperate hands searching pockets full of lint and loose tobacco. And he was still waveringly drunk from the night before, or the night before that, the night before Christmas. Surely, soon some good Samaritan would cross his palm with silver and wish him a Merry Christmas. He had to sit down. His hip felt like shards of broken glass. He found in the deep doorway of an empty store, a newspaper bed that had been spread by a previous homeless tenant; and so he eased himself down upon it as the news came up to him from between his legs.

As he sat in relief from the grinding pain in his hip, he leaned closer to the front page of the newspaper to see what it said. There was Christmas holly at the top of the front page—green leaves and red dots, berries—but then the black date told him that it was Christmas 1967.

It was sinking in—he shuddered with realization. Today was an anniversary. He'd been on the Bowery for a year! Now, for an instant, he understood. From the cave of his doorway refuge he watched the snow gently falling and building up out on the street, wet then white and then whiter and thicker, all in a minute.

Was he seeing the snow or was it the fog in his head? He struggled to think. These were not the same clothes he was wearing when he came to the Bowery. These laceless, scuffed old boondockers were not his spit-shined shoes. When was it that he had been discharged? Wait! How old was he now? "Merry Christmas," he yelled, and fell back in a stupor of dreams, some good, some bad.

V.

GRAVITY FLOW

One snowy Friday evening, Jimmy Whistler took the Hudson Tubes, boarded a rickety old Newark bus for a half hour ride, and walked up Baldwin Avenue toward the house he thought of simply as "Baldwin," a big, gray, peeling, Victorian house, full of turrets and gables, with a large, sittable porch, and a short, overstuffed lawn, buttressed with a foot high wall of stone; a rooming house his parents ran, where the fallen came to rise and the risen came to fall; where nothing and everything mattered; where the incurably but, it was presumed, safely, mad were "mainlined" from gloomy institutions like Vineland for the hopelessly sad and sometimes mad and even bad, to build a little life the state was duty-bound to finance; where some committed suicide and others made incessant wars on phantasmal enemies; where the dipso- and the tulipomaniac smiled different visions from the porch; where all was well and well was ill; where life was crazily life, and death death.

For some, it may have been the dawning of the Age of Aquarius, but for Jimmy's parents there was nothing really new about the onset of the Sixties. They had been practicing a dressed-up, permanent-waved and clean-shaved version of Hippiedom ever since their son, Jimmy, could remember. Their knockabout life-style had been initiated with the Crash of Twenty-nine and developed to a fine art during the Depression and the War, the best years of their lives. They had taken the job of superintending Baldwin while Jimmy was in the service. His mother, Fay, collected the rents, kept the books, and did the cleaning, as usual, while his father sat at the kitchen table, amid the debris, wearing one of his ancient, handsome, tailored suits, smoking a king-sized Chesterfield, and guzzling cheap sherry. But on this particular visit, there was a surprise for Jimmy.

"Where's Dad?" he asked, shaking out his coat and settling down for a cup of coffee in the small kitchen.

"Your father's moved out," answered Fay.

"Moved out! Where's he gone? Why?"

"I don't know. I don't know what's the matter with him. I think it's all those pills he takes. Or maybe he's getting senile. He's nearly ten years older than I am. He'll be seventy, you know."

"He's not senile. Far from it. If he's anything, he's hopped up. Is he drinking?"

"He hasn't stopped since your last visit."

Fay sat down with Jimmy. He was glad to be there, in that tiny place. Everything looked very clean and pleasant after his new place on the Lower East Side, a dump on Pitt Street, truly the pits. He had recently moved in there with his new girl friend, Phyllis, who was a speed-freak artist, too hyper-active for housekeeping.

"He's been working on this new scheme of his," Fay went on, "about getting the Bishop to back him in a chain of charity stores."

"Yeah, he told me about that."

"What do you think of it?"

"It's crackers."

"Well, anyway, he says he has to be alone, so he can think. He says I'm a nay-sayer. But it isn't that, Jimmy; it's just that I don't see how he can do anything when he's taking all those pills and drinking all the time. How can he go to see a Bishop when he's drunk?"

"He *would*."

"Oh, I know he would. That's what I'm afraid of. Besides, that isn't the only reason he left. It's because he wants to be alone so he can drink. And do you know how much those pills of his cost him last month? Nearly a hundred dollars. I saw the bill, and I saw him take the money out of his cash box. He's not working at all, now. And there's only a few hundred dollars left. He had it up to nine hundred dollars when he was managing the Angels' Own Store. He was robbing them blind. That was the most money we've ever had at one time, and now he's spending it all. I don't know what we're going to do. He's too old to get another job. And I've got all I can do to run this house. It's a good thing we get free rent and his social security. Here, look at this—"

It was a note, scrawled in Elliot's large, aggressive hand.

"*My Angel,*" it said. "*I am leaving without saying good-bye because I don't want to wake you so early. But I'll be back tomorrow evening. Love and kisses from Casanova.*"

"Casanova! Gee, that doesn't sound like Dad. Was he drunk, do you suppose?"

"I suppose so. But it was a nice note to get. It really cheered me up. He left it yesterday morning. He spent the night here. He came up to get his heavy overcoat out of the cleaners, and it was snowing so hard I talked him into staying. He doesn't look well, either, Jimmy; he's getting gray in the face from drinking. And did you notice his eyes the last time you saw him?"

"No."

"His eyes are all mixed bloodshot and yellow. And do you know what it's from? I found out. I caught him taking some new pills, things I never saw before, and when I asked him what they were, he looked so guilty. Finally I got it out of him. The last time he went to the drug store to fill his prescriptions—he's got about twenty, you know, and they're all expired or faked—he asked the clerk if there was something he could take to . . . you know, to be able to make love. The clerk told him this bottle of pills would work. All they are is iron tablets—I read the label—but he's been taking them by the handful. They're turning the whites of his eyes yellow. That's what I think."

Jimmy couldn't help laughing, and Fay began to laugh too.

"I think that's why he's gone down to that hotel apartment house on Broad Street to live," Fay said, turning serious.

"You mean the Magdalena? That dump?"

"That's it—the Magdalena. I think he hopes he'll find some woman in that place who'll stimulate him." Then she laughed again. "But I don't think he will."

"Oh, Mom, I think he'll come home when he gets tired of it. This is just another binge."

"I don't know," Fay said, "he's got this bug in him about going some place. He's been talking a lot about Denver, and about the old days when he had money. He's been saying that he wants to go back out to Denver before he dies."

"He always says that when he's drunk."

"But I think he means it this time. I think he'd like to take the money and go out there. It's only that he doesn't want to leave you here in the East. He'd never go anywhere unless you went. He loves you so much, Jimmy."

"I know, Mom. I love him, too, but Jesus, he has a strange way of showing it."

"But what would we do out there? I don't know what he could ever do, at his age. It's just a dream of his. Another of his crazy dreams." They were silent for a few moments. Then she asked, "Do you miss Vera?"

"It's peaceful without her. I can write."

"I never liked her—you know that."

"I know. But let's stay off her, Mom."

"She calls sometimes, asking about you, but I don't tell her anything."

"Well, don't. She used to lay in wait for me outside the bookstore. That's why I quit. It's got to be a clean break. If I went back to her, it would just be the same old thing. She was always nagging at me about being an actor. But I don't want to be an actor, I want to be a poet. I've just won a prize. I'm beginning to get somewhere."

"But, Jimmy, poets don't make any money, do they?"

Jimmy changed the subject. How could he tell her he was going to be a bum? Bum. Beatnik. Hippie. Whoever didn't work in a factory or an office for a lifetime, and then retire, and be old, and be dead. Elliot was downwardly mobile. Fay was upwardly hopeful, but feckless. They had been hippies since the Twenties but they didn't know it, and would not have found it possible to have seen themselves that way. Fay would have said, "We always dress well," but they had been running away from bad checks for as long as Jimmy could remember. And yet Fay looked askance at Jimmy for being a poet, as had his former wife, Vera. How can you love someone who doesn't love what you love? Who despises you for loving it, and despises it as a rival? Jimmy being a poet was the one thing that those two, Vera and Fay, could agree on—both against it, against the only thing that really meant anything to him. Around him the world was coming apart at its seams; the Cold War seemed to be building to some terrible climacteric; but he didn't care. He knew others might disagree with him, but he felt that it was a rotten time to be young—a time when a few fools with bombs could subsume into politics every other noble human endeavor. At times he didn't care if the world blew up, although he doubted that the fools with the bombs had even the courage for a full-scale exchange. But he could take no chances. He had to write one lightening-struck poem before what may or may not come. For Jimmy, it seemed a time of double doom. Beyond that amorphous-end-of-the-world threat that seemed to permeate the air they breathed, there was a more definite, immediate, and frightening one.

It was obvious to even the casual observer that Elliot Whistler was killing himself; and, if he died, Jimmy's sense of duty would demand that he take care of Fay, an ignorant, and, as Elliot would have said, *negative* force. This prospect represented doom to Jimmy's dream of being a poet; this was the secret fear that led him to live as if nothing mattered and every day was his last. He needed time to come to grips with his work, and Elliot's self-indulgent life threatened Jimmy with Fay's negative proximity. Elliot stood between them like a guard at a gate, whether Elliot realized it or not, protecting Jimmy from Fay's destructive capacities. Fay did not simply dislike, but *hated* everything she didn't understand, and she did not understand poets or poetry. Jimmy feared Elliot's death and Fay's proximity more than he feared an atomic Armageddon. Elliot's death was doomsday.

Jimmy left Fay and took the bus downtown to see his father. He arrived at the Magdalena just in time to be put to work. Elliot was moving. "I've been hoping you'd call so I could get you to come over and help me carry my bags. Otherwise I'd have to pay somebody. Do you want a drink?"

Jimmy said he did. He always loved having a drink with his dad. "What's that you're wearing?" Jimmy asked.

"What?"

"That. . . *tie*. It's got a hula dancer on it!"

"Oh, you mean Sweet Leilani. I got it at the Angels' Own. It's really something, eh?"

"But, Dad—my God! It's a piece of *trash*. I never saw you wear a thing like that."

"Well, how about this?" said Elliot, his eyes gleaming as he flashed a huge fake diamond ring under Jimmy's nose.

"Oh, Dad! What's the matter with you?"

"The matter! Why, my boy, I've never been better! Bright-eyed, bushy tailed, and free as a bird!"

"Your eyes are like two boiled eggs!"

"I don't believe that the ladies would agree with your assessment. Not by a long-shot," he said, winking.

He went into the closet and reached up on a shelf and pulled down a little pinch bottle of whiskey. From where Jimmy was sitting, on a cardboard box packed with some of Elliot's things, he could see a whole row of pinch bottles, at least ten little soldiers, lined up and ready in formation. Elliot poured Jimmy a hooker of booze and Jimmy swallowed it. It was damned good to be out of the cold and the snow.

"Well, Dad, where are you moving to?"

"To where are you moving?" Elliot corrected, and told Jimmy that he had found a room around the corner, on Kitchen Street, in a house where they had lived twice before, once, when Jimmy was a baby, late in the Depression, and once later when he was about five, near the end of the war. It was the house they had been living in when Jimmy had started kindergarten. He remembered when Fay had forgotten to come and get him on his first day, and he had had to find his way home by himself. He was terrified, and, in his terror, had forgotten the address of the house, which Elliot had drilled him in. He could only remember the fact that the house in which he lived was the only one on the street that had shiny, curvy brass handrails siding its front steps. With that information a nice lady was able to bring him home to his befuddled mother.

"But why are you leaving here, Dad?"

"It's too expensive, keeping an apartment," he said. "I can get a room over there and if I want to boil water for coffee, I'll use an electric plate. I'll eat in restaurants, or up at Baldwin. You can fix this electric plate, can't you?" Elliot handed the contraption to Jimmy, who looked it over.

"Yeah. It'll only take a minute," Jimmy said, seeing there was a wire loose. "Dad," he said, "why don't you go home to Mom? She's lonely up there all by herself." He took out a pen knife and started fiddling with the gadget. He wanted Elliot to remain the guard at the gate.

"No, my boy," said Elliot. Jimmy could always tell that Elliot was drunk when he started my-boying him. "No, my boy; like Garbo, I want to be alone. My head is steaming with plans and I don't want any interference. Your mother is a nay-sayer. *I* am a *yea*-sayer."

"Dad, you know, she loves you so much. She's awfully lonely." If Elliot stepped aside, Jimmy would have to take his place. The prospect sent a chill of fear up his spine.

"I love her too; but I can't live with her. You should understand that. How many times have we offered you a free room at Baldwin, and how many times have you refused it?"

"I knew she wouldn't let me concentrate—let me do my work, study, write. She'd always be calling me to *eat*—interrupting me. She doesn't understand what I'm trying to do. She doesn't understand extended concentration."

"I read some of your poetry, you know. I don't understand this modern poetry. I like Poe and Kipling and Tennyson—'Crossing the Bar'—but it seemed to me you knew what you were doing. Look, I have a typed copy of 'Crossing the Bar' here in my wallet." He showed Jimmy a creased, stained piece of paper but did not unfold it—tucked it back in his wallet. "I want you to read it at my funeral, if I ever die." He laughed.

Jimmy shook his head. "The thought of living with her scares me to death, Dad—it would kill my chance to work—she's always interrupting; she won't stick to any agreement—but it's different with you."

"No, it isn't. That's just what I've been trying to tell you. I have my dreams, too. Do you remember Tennyson's 'Ulysses'? 'There's still some noble work toward the end'—or something like that?"

"Yes, that's it. But you'll go back when you've got all your plans made, won't you?"

"We'll see. Do you want another drink?"

"Sure do."

"All right. But don't get drunk. I want you to move me."

"Don't worry, Dad; I won't." But Jimmy did. They both did.

Fortunately, Kitchen Street wasn't far to go, just up the block and around the corner. When Jimmy saw the house he was disappointed, because those beautiful, shining brass handrails he remembered so gratefully were green and tarnished now. The place had become a fleabag for derelicts, drunks, and prostitutes. One of the places from which Jimmy had started out in life. The small apartments of the Depression and war years had been redivided with plasterboard into tiny compartments. It was just a flop house now, not that it had ever been anything so special, really, he supposed. But he could still remember Mrs. LaSalle, the fat lady with the pince-nez who used to own the joint. Now in her apartment—the very apartment where Elliot had written the letter to the President of the United States that resulted in having Mrs. LaSalle's son released from a prison camp—there was a horrible old virago, gin-soaked and toothless, with a nasty-snouted barking bitch of a terrier in her arms. Elliot asked her to show Jimmy the room in the basement that he had rejected.

"What do you think of it?" Elliot asked.

It was the only basement room; the rest of the basement was used for storage.

"This looks better to me than being way up on top. Suppose there's a fire? Down here you'd be safe. It's all cement."

"But I like it better up there, even if it does cost a little more."

Jimmy saw what was on Elliot's mind. There wouldn't be any company down here. Upstairs, everybody kept the doors open and wandered through the halls. Jimmy thought, how ironic it was that all during his own early years Elliot always wanted a basement apartment and now he had to be up near the roof.

"O.K., it's your pick."

He hauled Elliot's bags up to the chosen compartment, on the fourth floor. But he was still sober enough to be thinking about safety, and he said to Elliot: "This place is a firetrap, Dad. Promise me you won't stay here very long. Promise me you'll go home to Mom as soon as you get your plans made."

"We'll see," Elliot said. "We'll see, my boy; we'll see." He looked haggard and gray of face, as Fay had said, but he was still a handsome old rake.

They drank together all afternoon.

The snow stopped falling toward ten o'clock in the evening, and Jimmy decided it was time for him to get back to New York. He had obligations, responsibilities. Work to do.

"Why don't you stay here and spend the night with me?" Elliot said. "The snow's deep out there. Your feet'll be soaked by the time you get to New York. You can go in the morning, can't you?"

"No, Dad. I've got to go. I've got to go." Jimmy was drunk. Could hardly walk. But he had things to do. He had things he just *had* to do. Just like Elliot. They had to do whatever it was they thought they had to do.

A week later, at Pitt Street, Jimmy looked into a half-filled beer bottle that had been left opened and standing out and counted six dead roaches floating atop the stale, flat beer. He was disappointed because he could have drunk the stuff. He had no aversion to warm, stale, flat beer, and had learned to put a head on it by dropping an Alka-Seltzer tablet into it. But he wasn't about to drink any beer that had six dead roaches floating in it, bodies like boats and legs like oars raised up, so aimlessly. The place was filthy. In order to write, he needed some order!

He went out and bought some roach spray and sprayed the walls, up and down, back and forth, until there were billowing clouds of poison closing on him from every corner. It was bitter cold out, but Jimmy knocked the cardboard out of the windows and let the air suck the poison out from under his nose. Then he blocked the windows again and started in the kitchen. But before he began in the kitchen he turned to survey the carnage. Roaches of all sizes and shapes were swarming over the walls, dropping with small, ticking sounds and rocking on their curled, chitinous backs, flicking, flailing, their feelers drooping. What a rout!

Across the Hudson in Newark, Jimmy's mother woke and heard a radio report of a fire on Kitchen Street while she was having her coffee. The report didn't frighten her, because the number of the house given was across the street from the rooming house in which Elliot was staying. Still, she was a bit concerned; so just to be sure she picked up the telephone and dialed the number of the superintendent of Elliot's building—the drunken virago with the snapping terrier in her arms. The line was dead. Then she went back to the radio and dialed around the stations, looking for a further report on the fire. At ten o'clock there was a bulletin the purpose of which was to correct the address as formerly given. The announcer's voice now numbered the house where Elliot lived, and apologized for the error.

Fay was struck with fear. But only six dead; six, and the house, as she understood it, held thirty, at least. He must be among the survivors. There was no way she could reach Jimmy immediately—he had no phone—so she called her sister, Myrtle, who lived nearby. Had she heard about the fire? Myrtle said that she had, on the morning news. "That wasn't where Elliot was living, was it?" Myrtle asked cautiously. Fay told her that it was.

"Oh, my God, dear! Did you call there?"

"They don't answer!" Fay was weeping.

"Now, don't you be afraid, Fay. He probably wasn't even in the house. You just stay there and we'll be right over."

On the radio came a report naming two of the dead; but not Elliot.

"Oh, please come—yes. I can't get ahold of Jimmy. I don't know how to get him. He's over in New York somewhere with his hippie friends and I don't even have his new address. Have you heard anything? They say six are dead. Oh, Myrtle, please come over—hurry!"

Fay dressed and went and knocked on Moe Golden's door. Moe was a taxi driver who lived in a hall room upstairs, a sickly, kindly little bachelor, who considered Elliot his friend. Fay told Moe what had happened.

"Oh, gees," said Moe, "was Elliot in there?"

"I don't know."

Moe's face, all bones and up-pointed chin, the sallow face of a man who had never been well, twisted with sudden fear, adjusted, resolved itself. "Come on," he said, "let's go down there and find out." When they got to the house it was still smoldering, hours after the time it was estimated that the fire had started. The big old house was roofless and nearly wall-less. Fay and Moe stood on the street with the others and looked into the cubicles, where, it seemed now, only insignificant lives could have been lived.

Jimmy had only been up for an hour, having slept late that day as a consequence of having been up so late the night before, murdering roaches. But, "Oh, blessed rage for order," he was in a room that had been swept and mopped. The stove (even its permanent stains) was glittering with the cleaning he had given it. And he was celebrating these surroundings with an early glass of cheap sherry of the type he called gasoline and a cup of black, instant coffee, when there was a rapping at the door, *rat-a-tat-tat.*

"Telegram for Whistler!" a voice called.

Jimmy went through the usual telegramaphobic reactions of persons unused to getting wired word of things. Then he read it.

JIMMY. CALL YOUR MOTHER. AUNT MYRTLE.

He sat down. Maybe it was the roach-murdering spree he'd been on, but he'd had an eerie feeling since getting up. He'd been doodling on a poem, and had got it completed, just before Fear with bony knuckles knocked. He'd tagged the poem "Oncoming Company," because it was about such things—eerie feelings, telegraph messengers—

Swings pendulously now
that dark, that bleak o'clock
of place, the held in hell
ingrowing grave, the sea
of flooding tides, the fell
oncoming company.

Jimmy had a fit of the creeps, gulped his gasoline, went out, made the call, and Fay told him what was up.

"Oh, now, listen, Mom; don't get excited. He probably wasn't there."

"No, Jimmy—no. He would have called me by now. He wouldn't let me worry like this."

"What have you done?" he asked. "Did you go down there? Did you check the hospitals?"

"Everywhere. Moe's been so good. He drove me everywhere. They've got a refuge set up for all the people who were burned out. Moe drove me there, but your father's not there with the rest. Then a fireman called me and said I should check at the morgue. So Moe drove me down there. He went in and looked. He said Elliot wasn't there."

"Thank God!" Jimmy said. "If he isn't there and he isn't with the others he must not have been at the house last night."

"But where is he, Jimmy?"

"I'll come right over. Stay put."

"I will. I'm waiting for Aunt Myrtle and Uncle O'Toole. They should be here any time. I don't know what's keeping them."

Fay's family consisted of two sisters, one a couple of years older than Fay, Jimmy's Aunt Myrtle, and one a couple of years younger, Jimmy's Aunt Brenda, and Aunt Myrtle's husband, whom they referred to as Uncle O'Toole. Aunt Myrtle was a housewife who had raised five children, and Aunt Brenda was the widow of a suicidal butcher, a domineering woman. Fay had them, and she had Jimmy, and that was about all she had.

"O.K. I'll be right over. Now don't you worry. Dad'll show up and we'll all have a drink together."

Jimmy hadn't heard any report of the fire—just what Fay had told him—so he didn't know how much to make of it. He did figure that if Elliot wasn't in a hospital, wasn't at the refuge, and wasn't in the morgue, he probably hadn't been in the fire—there seemed small chance, considering the time, of any more bodies being discovered—probably had not gone to the house at all that night, but had been off at one of his other secret places, somewhere with some crony of his, drinking. But Jimmy was sure Elliot would have called Fay, no matter what, had he known about the fire and had he had a few of his wits about him. He wondered if Elliot could have been dazed and gone wandering off somewhere.

Jimmy went to the Hudson Terminal to take the train through the tube to Newark. On the train, across the aisle from Jimmy, a man unfolded his Daily News. The headline read:

SIX DEAD IN BLAZE IN NEWARK.

When he got to Baldwin, Aunt Myrtle and Uncle O'Toole were there. Fay was already going into a kind of shock: she was unnaturally calm, very unlike herself. While Jimmy was on his way over, she received another call from the fireman with whom she'd spoken earlier.

The Fire Department had compiled a list of the tenants of the house and had checked them out. The count was complete: all living tenants accounted for and six dead bodies added up to a full house. Was it possible (the voice was trying to be gentle) that a mistake had been made? Did Fay have any male relatives? Was there some man who could come down to the morgue and check—just to be sure?

"I tell you, he wasn't there," said Moe. It was clear that he was reluctant to press his (and Fay's and Jimmy's) luck with a second visit. Finally, Jimmy and Fay got him to take them to the morgue. His small, collapsed face was running with tears as he started the motor of his taxi. Aunt Myrtle sat on one side of Fay and Uncle O'Toole on the other, in the back. Jimmy sat up front with Moe. They stopped to look at the house, which was on the way to the morgue.

As Jimmy looked up at the ruin, with its blackened, still steaming timbers, and the great, jigsaw holes torn out of its walls, its roofless top, he remembered again the day his mother had forgotten to get him at school and he was brought home by the strange lady, and he remembered those jaunty brass banisters, which were black and crumpled now like the old horns found occasionally among the refuse heaps at the city dump, and how they had shined once, like beacons, when he was a child.

Aunt Myrtle waited with Fay and Moe while Uncle O'Toole and Jimmy went into the morgue. Jimmy could see Aunt Myrtle, round, plump, in her early sixties, sitting in the back of that idling, question-mark of a cab, hugging Fay to her, and Fay, after thirty years of marriage, just her frightened little sister again. The worst part was that Fay was not resigned, as he was, now. Part of her was still convinced that it was all some kind of mad nightmare mistake. "I know—I just *know*—that he's alive. Suppose he were to go home while we're here?" she said.

A man in a black suit rolled them out one at a time, each time pulling the sheet aside like a magician pulling aside his cape to display a bunch of flowers, or a rabbit. After the second time Jimmy began to say "Voila!" silently, to himself.

Some of the bodies were burned terribly, literally roasted; others didn't show a mark of pink, or even a scratch, despite the fact that the roof had blown off and then caved back in on them (all of the victims had been living on the top floor). These unmarked were victims of smoke inhalation. Only one of the victims was young, about thirty; all were men; the others were old, showing emaciated, debauched bodies. Elliot's was the last they saw.

When the man in the black suit pulled the sheet aside, there he lay, stark naked. He had a big pink hand up over his heart in a familiar gesture. There was a triangular, second-degree burn on his chest. His bristly hair seemed pale.

Jimmy knew that it was Elliot before the sheet had been removed. He could tell by the feet; those big pink feet were sticking out. Jimmy had seen them when he came in, but was glad when the man in the black suit led him in a different direction. Jimmy leaned down at Elliot's side and touched his hair. He wanted to kiss him, as he had done so many times before, even the last time he had seen him, when he'd moved Elliot's things up into that firetrap, but Uncle O'Toole and the man in the black suit were there.

Back at Baldwin, after a long tearful interlude during which many drinks were consumed, much to Jimmy's consternation Fay asked Uncle O'Toole, not Jimmy, what should be done. This foreshadowed the future for Jimmy, this was how it would be if he and Fay were to live together. After many a few, that prospect seemed more impossible than ever. Jimmy chose to ignore them. He drank, smoked, and listened to the radio—"Twilight Time." His mind went passive, tuning out a conversation that seemed neither practical nor interesting. It was the best he could do in the circumstances. There was an empty room waiting to be rented in the basement of the house. He woke up several times on top of the bed in that room, rejoined the gathering, a sort of wake, really, and pleasantly rejected it once again for the quiet comfort of the bed. Each time he returned to the gathering, it seemed that there were several more people present, each time night and day seemed to have reversed themselves. Oblivion rapidly followed, but, by all reports, he was walking and talking among the others, then he drew to a consciousness of cars, and a kind of slow motion hustle and bustle, and umbrellas and complaints. The rain came down like silver nails in his father's coffin. Then he was being asked if he would say a few words and he read from his father's crumpled copy of "Crossing the Bar" by Tennyson.

"Sunset and evening star,
And one clear call for me!
And may there be no moaning of the bar,
When I put out to sea,

But such a tide as moving seems asleep,
Too full for sound and foam,
When that which drew from out the boundless deep
Turns again home.

Twilight and evening bell,
And after that the dark!
And may there be no sadness of farewell,
When I embark;

For tho' from out our bourne of Time and Place
The flood may bear me far,
I hope to see my Pilot face to face
When I have crost the bar."

Swaying on his feet, he stumbled over the words and got through the reading. But it didn't matter that it was a bad reading, because this was all a dream anyway, wasn't it, a nightmare, from which he would awaken, *the* nightmare, the recurring nightmare that had plagued his sleep for months, if not years?

Fay hung like a broken doll between Aunt Myrtle and Uncle O'Toole. Sometime soon now they were going to turn her over to him and that moment would represent the end of his life, the end of his poetry, the end of his dreams. He began to do a little St. Vitus dance, a drunken man preparing to run for his life.

When they got back to Baldwin and the crowded little apartment, booze appeared from every side. Soon Fay had the radio blasting Chubby Checker's "Peppermint Twist."

She shook like a Shaker. Really, she was hysterical. Overheard comments from the relatives caused Jimmy to think of Dylan Thomas's line, "After the funeral, mule praises, brays. . ."

"She's better off without him."

"He left her nothing."

Pale-faced Moe Golden seized Jimmy's arm. "Your father was a great tipper," he said. "A real mensch. You know what is a mensch? A human being. Someone of consequence. Someone to admire. Someone of noble character. Jimmy, your father was a real mensch, so don't listen to these gossip ghouls."

"An old reprobate," corrected somebody. "A spendthrift with nothing to spend. A bum!"

"Well, Jimmy will take care of her."

"Not him, he's just like his father."

Desperate to get out, Jimmy lurched toward the door, but in the hall an ancient apparition croaked condolences and Jimmy invited him in. The apparition was one of Baldwin's mainliners from the madhouse. Jimmy had already grabbed his hand in a half-shake, half-supportive motion that enabled them to stagger back across the room and into chairs. Now they began to pump hands, so joyful were they to be firmly seated.

It was his old, moth-eaten and stained-stiff pajamas and robe that had caused Jimmy to take the old man for an apparition. Actually he was a handsome old duck in his eighties with tufts of white hair flopping wildly about on his head. Jimmy saw big, gnarled hands, and great, plumbeous eyes. For a moment it seemed that he had been delivered back to his father. But no, Elliot's spirit was gone from the air around them and Jimmy felt that not only he but every one on Earth remaining had lost an opportunity, a possibility, whether to know a good man or a bad didn't matter. But here was another, tenuously clinging to life's most important goal beyond survival, the manifestation of the spirit. Sobbing Jimmy of the crying jag could have taken him in his arms and danced him around the room, but his old legs would have broken and Jimmy's would have stumbled with drink and with rising sorrow.

A few lost days later, Jimmy emerged from the Bowery at Cooper Square, where stood the grim edifice of Cooper Union, and read the Con-Ed clock with blurry eyes. After ten, time for church; but he wouldn't go. He decided to borrow some money from his friend, Ralph, and get an eye-opener.

When he got to the door of the building his friend Ralph superintended, one of the few renovated apartment houses in an otherwise dilapidated neighborhood, there stood Ape, the plumber, buzzing furiously away at Ralph's bell. Ape was a short, powerfully built man of about forty who, as a result of his proclivity for the more kinkier forms of sexual activity, preferred to frequent the more Bohemian bars, where Jimmy and Ralph hung out, rather than the sort of blue-collar joints where you might expect to find him.

Ape told Jimmy he didn't look so good, and Jimmy told Ape he was O.K. He didn't want to tell him that he had buried his father on Saturday, nor that he was blank on most of what happened since standing in the freezing cold at the gravesite.

Ape said he had an emergency job to do, something overflowing into a flood in a tenement on the Lower East Side, and that he was trying to get Ralph to help him, his regular helpers being gone for the weekend. He said: "But as usual Ralph ain't nowheres ta be found. How 'bout you?" he said, inspired. "Would ya like ta pick up a couple ten bucks say?"

"How long will it take?"

"Oh, nuttin'—a few hours. Do it for me, Jimmy. I really need somebody. I'm in a fix."

"Is it going to be hard? I don't feel so hot."

"Nah, nah. Listen, movin' a few stones, dat's all."

"O.K.," Jimmy said, and Ape changed a bit. He looked Jimmy over, said:

"But, do ya feel O.K.?"

Now Jimmy wanted the money, so he wound up selling Ape on the idea of using his services, and on the idea that he was fit as a fiddle.

Off they went in Ape's overburdened pickup truck, through the sloppy, winter streets. They climbed out on East Third, and Ape yanked his huge leather bag of tools out of the back of the pickup. It had a long leather strap on it, so that he could stoop, put the strap over his shoulder, and stand up, hauling it up with him. He asked Jimmy to carry it. He had pipe, hoses, and shovels to carry. Jimmy threw the strap over his shoulder and heaved upward, but the bag did not budge.

Ape shook his head. "O.K.," he said. "I'll bring it. I don't want ya should bust sumpin." Up came the bag, and he walked with it and the pipe too.

The constipated building was a few doors down the block. Too bad that they couldn't get the truck any closer, but there was a vandalized car in the way. The trouble was in the basement, directly below a bodega. Above the store there were five human-infested storeys. The Rat and Mice Arms, Lower East Side, Manhattan, New York, New York, U.S. of A, North America, the Universe. A lovely place to bring up children.

Ape dumped his load of iron and leather on the side-walk and pulled open the cellar doors.

"Phew! Multitudes of foul-smelling molecules did a death-dance up their nostrils. Jimmy's stomach flip-flopped. He thought of the Rolfe Humphries translation of the

Aeneid. *Now, said the Sibyl, summon up your courage, for you will need it.*

Ape descended. Jimmy followed. *Before the threshold of hell they passed, and avenging Cares, pale Disease and melancholy Age, Fear and Hunger that tempt to Crime, Toil, Poverty, and Death—forms horrible to view.*

"How long has this place been backed up?"

"Couple days."

"A couple of days?

"Yeah. I had so many udder jobs, I couldn't get back to it."

"It's a wonder the Health Department hasn't been here."

"Hey, dis is New York."

The filthy ooze was a foot deep and jet black, anaerobic. "If anybody upstairs has a case of typhus, we've had it."

"Ah, I wade around in dis stuff all da time and I'm all right." Ape handed Jimmy a pair of rubber boots. "Here, put dese on."

They stood high up on a peak among peaks of the mountainous islands of rocks and gravel and mud that Ape had dug out on his previous visit. Sweat broke out on Jimmy's forehead as he pulled on the boots. His shirt and pants stuck to his skin. Outside was a cold winter day, and it was cool here, but humid, clammy. How the hell did he get himself into these things!

Ape put him to work at pulling up and stacking more of the slimy stones while he pumped some of the mephitic semi-liquid out from under them.

Each time Jimmy plumped his gloved hands into the ooze to catch another slippery stone he thought of the possibilities of infection. Bacterial, protozoan, parasitic metazoan—words from books kept coming into his head. Passages! "It is inevitable that these infections, so common to the alimentary tract of man, should be found in great numbers in the feces, and even in the urine." Talk about the alimentary tract! He was wading around in the intestinal tract of a slum tenement.

"What are we trying to do here anyway?"

Ape was wrapping up some hoses in the cellarway.

"Gravity flow! Dat's what we're after. Gravity flow! We gotta get dis shit runnin' out into da sewers. Dere's a block under dem stones somewheres. Dat's what's stoppin' it. We gotta find out what it is and get it out outta dere."

"What could it be?" Jimmy asked, using his interest as an excuse to stand up straight for a moment. He felt like vomiting.

"Never can tell. A few tings get trowed down da terlet and dey gadder up and make like a heap. Da pipes into da sewers is eight inches, but from what I can makeout, dat drain you're clearin' is like one o' dem Roman drains—just a concave brick jobber, see, so it could happen. Den again a heavy flow might of moved a loose brick outta place. Hard ta say. Sometimes dere's bio-foulin'. Dat's like when plankton forms up real t'ick. Hard part's findin' it. Rest is easy."

Not for another hour did Jimmy get the bright idea of tearing off the tail of his shirt and tying it over his face like a mask, stuffing the bottom down his collar. It relieved him a bit. He wished that he could pull it up over his eyes so that he couldn't see what he was digging in. He thought of Aeneas in the Infernal Regions, his only object being to see his father. He imagined how it would be if his father materialized. He'd be all dressed up, spick-and-span, neat as a pin, sitting at a little table on top of one of those mountains of slime, watching. His mother would be there, and she and Jimmy would dig together while his father watched them, kindly but superior, indulging their blessed rage for order. Well, unlike Aeneas in his Infernal Regions, he wasn't going to find his father down here. *O, how willingly would they endure poverty, labor, and any other infliction, if they might but return to life!*

"Here it is!" cried Ape. "Like I tought, it's a brick jam."

Jimmy crawled along a ridge of a slippery mountain of detritus and got shakily to his feet beside Ape. There it was. A half dozen or so bricks had fallen apart and melted down into a red stopper. It had caught eggshells, sanitary napkins, bits of glittering glass, a thing that looked like a skinny black snake but turned out to be a coathanger, and doubtful stuff packed in layers, packed in strata. *Here is the judgment hall of Rhadamanthus, who brings to light crimes done in life, which the perpetrator vainly thought impenetrably hid.* Ape picked up a shovel and gave the red stopper a couple of tentative taps, then one clanging blow, breaking it to pieces. "Woo-ish!" it went. The sewer was hungry! What an appetite!

"I'm gonna turn on da water," Ape said. "I wanna wash dis out so's I can see how bad da damage is. Just be a minute."

Jimmy sat thinking and dreaming, of Anchises and Aeneas. *Have you come at last, Anchises said, long expected, and do I behold you after such perils past? O my son, how have I trembled for you as I have watched your career! O father! your image was always before me to guide and guard me. . . . Then, he endeavoured to enfold his father in his embrace, but his arms enclosed only an unsubstantial image.* He rested his head in his arms. He could feel it burning through his shirtsleeves.

Suddenly a little stream of water, relatively clear, trickled down the Roman canal. Jimmy remembered what he'd read in Da Vinci's Notebooks, about man being only a passageway for food. Would that he were only that, and have some peace. He would have forgiven any man his meanness—his bloody devilish cravings—in the mood he was in. He watched the water purling away. No doubt it'd soon be carrying away nice loads of human excretion, the lost parts of bodies, dead cells, hairs, bits and parts of burnt energy, the stuff left over after the day's work, after the argument, the loving in the small bed while the kids slept fitfully nearby. Yes, there goes love. Off it goes, the domestic sewage, off to join the industrial waste, off to form the municipal sewage, to join the storm runoff, and there all to be wed and to become the combined sewage; off they go, through flush tanks and diverting weirs, through siphon spillways and sewage-treatment plants, through bar racks and fine screens and skimming tanks, through settling tanks and scum collectors, through grit chambers and sedimentation tanks, through trickling filters and activated-sludge units, through oxidation ponds and the centrifuge, through heat coagulators and into the incinerators, where, at last, all our loves go up in smoke. And the outfall works drop pure water, cleansed, unsullied by any particle of humanity, by any watery history of the human condition, into the swaying receiving waters of river and sea. Out of the water we came, onto the land, and into the sky we go, and the smoke of our loves will crowd out the light of the sun, one dark day.

ON SITE

Maddie let herself in, went to the refrigerator and put away her chicken sandwiches and a sixpack of root beer, and was about to prepare the model home for display—turn on all the lights, straighten up, whatever was needed—when she noticed that the back door was sitting slightly ajar. She tried it and it creaked open. It was a metal door and it had been jimmied. She could see the dents where something—a crowbar, maybe—had done its damage.

She went to the kitchen phone—there were only land lines, cell phones were just then coming in—and called Yoblonsky, Deer Run's developer. He said he'd get hold of Roy and send him out. He told her to wait for Roy, not to do anything until they were sure what had happened. No police. Not yet, anyway. Roy himself might have had to jimmy the door for some reason. Or Joe. So she should wait for Roy before she did anything. Then Yoblonsky said maybe she better look around the house, see if anybody was sleeping—or hiding—in it. He'd hang on.

The sun was blazing outside, but it was dark, shadowy, and cool in the house. She heard the faint, reassuring hum of the air conditioning unit. Maddie was nervous, though she doubted anyone was there. She turned on all the lights and looked around. On the rug in the master bedroom lay a used condom. There was another one in the toilet, floating. There was a half-empty can of beer on the window sill. In the living room there was the roach of a reefer on a tin paint can lid, stuck to it. She made her report. "No, there's nobody here now. Yes, I'll wait for him." She hung up.

Maddie had nearly quit smoking, but she went through her purse nervously looking for a cigarette, found an old crumpled pack of Kools down at the bottom and went out to the back deck. This lone model home, the first of what was to become Deer Run, sat just inside the apex of two black asphalt country roads like a little, if effete, fortress; tall grassy fields rising up to her from either side. This hill-top acreage, a plateau, had once been a Carolina cotton field but lay ploughed and raw now for development.

Suddenly she felt surrounded by camouflaged marauders. They were out there, everywhere, fifty or a hundred yards away, down the sides of the tall-grass-obscured hills, too distant to see clearly, but close enough to be felt. Why was this new model home, her car, herself, of such—she felt it—malignant interest? The locals in front, down the slight valley to the singlewide shacks couldn't see her from back here on the deck—or could they?—and the ones she now studied from the back deck were hidden down behind a thick stand of tall pines, trees deep. She lit one of her crumpled cigarettes and immediately realized that she had left the front door unlocked. She ran in through the house to the front door and closed and locked it. Then she unlocked it and opened it again. She pushed the lock on the outside glass front storm door. Now she could see out at what was coming, and she could hear Roy or Joe or the police or whoever.

She looked down the long meadow to the locals' singlewides out front—a little shantytown down there from which smoke rose from what smelled like barbecued pork. A powerful wave of rockabilly music hit her, thumping, wild. Had it just begun? Then there was the roar of a motorcycle. She saw no sign of it, but thought it must be somewhere across the road in the deep field grass between herself and the shantytown. Then it emerged right across from her, out of the field, two of them, two helmetless wild-haired white males on motorcycles, and she ducked back out of sight, puffing her bent cigarette, scared.

The two pivoted in dust and took off roaringly up the highway, along where Roy, the contractor, and Joe, his helper, had put lot-markers. They ran up on the grassy side of the road and deliberately knocked down as many markers as they could hit, finally vanishing around a distant bend, wild-haired, tiny and hateful. Were they the ones who had left the condoms? Did they have women in here? Or were the condoms some kind of threat to her, Maddie, the lone female agent on this isolated site? Should she fear assault? Robbery? Rape?

When Roy quietly said, "Yoblonsky wouldn't like you to smoke in here," Maddie nearly jumped out of her beautiful skin.

Next she was sitting on the couch, and Roy was looking at her, concern on his rawhide face. "Are you O.K.?"

"Yes," she said. "Where did you come from?"

"Pulled in around back. Came in the back door so's I could see it. Yoblonsky called me. Joe's gone to get us a new door. A stronger one, I guarantee."

Maddie toured Roy around, pointing things out. He shook his head. "Well, looks like some of them old boys done had them a party las' night. I 'spected as much."

"You expected it?"

"Oh, it's juss a new toy to 'em. If we'd've put up a couple of houses they probably wouldn't be interested—but just one, standing out here in the old cotton field all by itself—it's like bait. I doubt they do it again. 'Specially with the new door I'm gettin'. Steel! That other one was just tin. It done give 'em temptation, ignorant country boys like they is. I called the sheriff, anyway."

Two officers in two cars showed up. One, the County Sheriff, fat, kindly, middle-aged and soft spoken; the other, an emissary from the local police department, young, military, and hard. Maddie thought they were calm to the point of indifference. The Sheriff said, "I don't think they's anything to worry about. You go ahead and put up a good heavy door, that'll be it."

"But I'll be out here alone," Maddie said, "and I have a night shift coming up."

"Nightshift?" queried the Sheriff.

"Into the evening, when it's dark," said Maddie.

"Hell, lady, comes with the territory," said the young cop. What he meant was, if you women can't take the heat, stay out of the kitchen. Maddie didn't like his self-satisfied young military male face. He was about her son's age, and wore a wedding ring. She didn't envy his wife.

Roy reassured her after they left. "They just a bunch of old country galoots down there," he said. "Squatters, really. They ain't out to harm anybody. They just too stupid to know better." Of course, Maddie thought, Roy and Yoblonsky were partners and didn't want to lose an attractive agent just before the Grand Opening.

But then Joe arrived with the new door, and it did look much sturdier than the other one, much more solid and safe. Maddie asked him about the locals.

"Do you know them, Joe?"

"Yes, mam, I know some of 'em. Ain't none of 'em got a job. Some say they dealing drugs, but they juss a bunch of rednecks. Don't you let 'em make you scaret."

"Yoblonsky's going to throw 'em all out," said Roy, "as soon as he picks up the options on those fields. Do you want me to go and have a talk with 'em?"

"No, don't do that," Maddie said, "they'll think I put you up to it. They'll come after me even more. Just let it go. I'm all right. I'll be fine."

But she wasn't. Every time Maddie was on duty, something happened. First, some of the women from down the hill came up, herding many small, dirty children before them, and wanted the grand tour. Maddie couldn't refuse. The women, an unsightly lot, were foul-mouthed, tattooed, and tough as nails, in their country way. The children, some nearly naked, ran all over the house pulling at things and fingering the white painted walls. The women only laughed, cursed, and refused to control them. For whatever reason, they made their dislike of Maddie plain. Maybe it was her fashionable clothes, her cultivated speech, her BMW parked out in front, the door of which had been mysteriously, deeply scratched.

Then, another day, several of the men rode up on motorcycles and asked to look at the house. They were patched with tattoos and seemed to be either skinheads or to have tangled shoulder-length hair. Maddie had the screen door locked and told them through it that she was on the phone with her boss. She asked them to come back later. They rode off with Rebel yells, laughing, gunning their motorcycles.

Another time two of them drove up in one of their junk pickups, parked out in the field near the house and sat there all afternoon, drinking and smoking, at the edge of the temporary vegetable patch Roy and Joe had planted for themselves. Roy and Joe had put up two tin bucket-headed scarecrows to protect their little garden, but the scarecrows had no effect on the birds of prey in the pickup. Maddie was afraid they would stay until dark, but finally in late afternoon they gunned the pickup's motor and rolled off drunkenly, leaving, from what Maddie could see, a serpentine pattern in the tall grass. "Yip, yip, yipee!" she heard a distant, cracked voice finally call.

One afternoon when the truck was parked in front of the house, Maddie called her mother for moral support, and her mother had told her to get out of there, right this instant. But Maddie couldn't leave. She couldn't allow herself to be intimidated—her husband would laugh at such fear; he was, after all, a war hero—and that was exactly what they were trying to do, intimidate her; she saw that now as plainly as she could see their distant shanties down the hill, behind the house and out in front of it, half-buried in valleys of tall field grass, from which thumping music welled up ever more intensely, as if they were doing a war-dance around her, nerving themselves up for an attack, and sending up smoke signals to each other. Then there were telephone calls with no one on the line when she answered with her formulaic "Hello, this is Deer Run Subdivision, the best in affordable country living," or rather someone who never responded to her greeting, just breathed and snickered. Sometimes it sounded like a child's laughter, sometimes like a woman's, sometimes like a group of men, and once a dog was made to bark into the phone.

* * *

Maddie didn't tell her husband, Van, an exclusive-lake-property realtor and developer, to whom she was trying to prove her middle-aging independence, about any of this. When he called home from Atlanta, where he had gone on business, she told him everything was fine, fine, fine. He was content. He was busy. Not long now, he said, and he'd be home. I love you, he said, and when he hung up, she cried. She couldn't help it. She needed help, but she didn't want to ask for it. And then it came to her, how to get help without asking.

She went downstairs to Van's gun cabinet and unlocked it. There it was, that new special—what-do-you-call-it?—pump-action shotgun that he had taken such pride in showing her, and that she had mocked him about. "Stupid macho stuff," she had said. Maddie hated guns. Van was a hunter. Maddie loved Van but she hated hunting. She admired and respected Van, the way he faced up to the world. He had been a hero in the Viet Nam war, a pilot, shot down and five years a P.O.W. She had waited. Maddie felt herself to be a very lucky woman, perhaps undeserving of her luck, her husband, her family, her affluence. Perhaps it was just guilt, but she believed Van suspected her of being overly timid, or housebound, which she was not. This job at Deer Run was her first in twenty-five years. She felt that she had to prove herself. She remembered what Van had told her about how the boys in the jungles of Viet Nam had sent home to their friends, families, whoever would help them, for a pump-action shotgun as a more effective weapon in close quarters than the carbines that had been issued to them. They'd saw off the barrels and when someone jumped out at them just feet away, a shotgun was what they needed.

Van had pointed out that the new shotgun's stock had a compartment in it, in which were the maintenance instructions. She opened the hinged compartment and pulled out the little rolled booklet. How to load, how to fire, how to clean, it was all there. Van had a shell or cartridge drawer under every gun in the cabinet. She pulled one out and there they were, boxes of shells, twelve gauge. She inserted them as per the booklet.

* * *

On site, she waited until late afternoon, or, as her tormentors called it, evening. They called anything after high noon time "evening." She ignored the phone when it rang, ignored the pick-up truck that sat out on the road in front of the model home for hours on end with two beer-swilling locals in it, ignored the crazy laughter, the blasting music, like drums before an attack, emanating up from the cement block-propped singlewides of the little shantytown down in the field, ignored everything and read the booklet on the gun; then she went out back, determined, slamming the door. She pumped the gun, and started with the scare-crows in the vegetable patch.

The gun made a tremendous report, ringing afterward and echoing on down the hills. Actual crows reached wildly up for the sky. The gun had quite a kick, but Maddie pumped and fired again, and blew the tin-pail-head off one of the scarecrows.

The sky was shot with red, as if there were a fire over the horizon, blazing up. Then, above that, it was pink, then violet, and finally black with the oncoming night.

Maddie pumped and fired again, beheading the second scarecrow. It was her territory now. It was just as Van had said, all you have to do with a shotgun is to point it. She heard the pick-up pull away with a screech of spinning wheels. She heard the music from down the hills fall silent. It was the quietest she had ever heard it out there, except for the tremendous echoing boom of the gun.

NOTHING FOREVER

The end is where you start from.
—T.S. Eliot

"Nothing Forever" is constructed almost precisely backwards, although a more useful key to opening the story's meanings may be the metaphor, the trope, embodied in "AND/OR."
—C. Kenneth Pellow
Editor, Writers' Forum

Young fell forward and the pistol fell from his hand. He had been leaning on the stone wall of the bridge and he toppled over into the river and was carried off to the sea. Probably eaten. The body never washed up.

The dark sky was starry but unfriendly that night, huge beyond humanity. Young leaned against the moist stone wall. The pistol dangled from his left hand. A little less than half the world was left-handed. He belonged to the left-handed part. He looked and he saw his own left hand with the pistol in it. The hair on his hand was neither dark nor light. Now it was the hand of a murderer. This had not been true only a short time ago, the flick of a page back. The flick of a page forward and here he was—a wave had become a particle. Someone thought him up. Things have to be observed to be. Now you could see him standing with the pistol in his hand. Something thought the metal of the pistol up. Something thought everything up, observed it, and there it was, like the river out there, flowing under the stone bridge, like the gleaming wet stones near the water. He could see the lighted buildings down near the bend of the river. What dreams were being dreamed in them? Where he was, it was too dark for anyone in the buildings to see him, but he was there, waiting to die, neither dead nor alive, now falling forward.

Young felt an eerie déjà vu of being a child, but with the gladness gone out of it. It was the gladness that mattered. Without it, nothing mattered. These things were with him as left the house with the mangled body in it and made his way to the bridge, this being a child but without the qualities that bring the child joy.

Gladness, hope, optimism. These words were in solution in his fluids from birth. Once, he would have loved this starry sky. It would have led him to a grand future. Young was thirty-five. Nearly every morning of his life he had seen a hopeful, open face in his mirror. Now there was forever nothing. Now the stars did not know of their own existence. They had not yet formed senses, nor, more, a mind. They did not exist. Nothing of the panorama of the night existed. Nothing forever.

If eaten, he did not know it. Did the fish enjoy him?

Why did his horrified self walk to the bridge? Why the pistol?

Well, he was a soldier. The pistol had been issued to him. The bridge was somewhere between France and Germany. Alsace: a place that no longer existed.

But Young had been stationed there for quite some time. He was not an ordinary soldier. What then?

Well, he had been an investigator. The Young who no longer existed had been a policeman of sorts. The optimist. The poet of gladness.

He had found an evil man. Banal: it has been said since Hitler.

To Young, the man's cause was small. Look at the size of the sky! A little political cause, temporal merely, for which the man had killed many people. Bombs on innocent heads, exploding letters in innocent hands. It made Young sick.

Isn't there a way of understanding these things?

What are small, evil things, anyway? Do they occur because we observe them?

ORs, part of the great AND. Everything is explained then, in the AND. The AND is the end and the all, a sort of heaven with explanations. Young had comforted himself in this way for years. ORs and the AND. It was a way of explaining the ugly parts of life, the big fish eating the little fish, the fact that he had become a soldier, and then a very special kind of soldier, the kind who dresses in mufti and carries secret weapons on his person, the kind who lies about what he is.

At twelve, thirteen, fourteen, fifteen. . . he began to wonder back. Somewhere in there he began to wonder back to the sky, to the sky's beginning.

Spring and green grass and flowers again and he lay on his back in a field and studied the sky. Graffiti said God was dead. But what was this then? The chemistry of his optimism could not accept graffiti's dictum. Something meant all this. But why would life be made like this, with everything eating everything else? It was horrible. In school they fed insects to the frogs. In National Geographic people ate one another—long pig. What kind of being would have made such a place, such a situation? An evil one? These thoughts shocked him. He looked at the grass and then at his hands. Fine hairs were beginning to show on the backs of his hands. But it was a beautiful spring day. New flowers everywhere. The ground was soft from an earlier rain. The grass was cushiony. The sky blue. White clouds. Faces? Things? ORs. ORs in the AND. Not God but AND. No need to know now. Know in the AND. Then everything will be resolved. Goodness will answer any question.

So, later, it was not hard to be a soldier. Soldiers were ORs. War was an OR, not the AND. Young concerned himself with the OR-world. Someday his questions, his doubts, would be answered. For now, he functioned without doubts. They were for later, and then to be resolved.

He attended West Point. He liked mathematics and became an engineer. He wanted to build things—bridges. He liked bridges. He wanted to build bridges between people too. He wanted the world of people to be connected by bridges of good faith. Soldiers had become peace-makers and peace-keepers. Peace is our Profession, it said on the side of SAC bombers. So he took the examination for West Point and did very well indeed. He was very intelligent, and he was not without an active imagination. Bridges between stars. They would have to be very flexible, yes, he agreed with a fellow cadet who had laughed at his good-natured fancy.

All bridges should be flexible. Stress and strain. Sturm und Drang. The trees bend with the wind and do not break. Where was the stone bridge that he came to then? It had not been observed by him as yet—it did not exist. But in its non-existent state two armies clashed for its possession. It had been strafed, bombed, and strafed. Displaced Europeans had jumped from it, into the river where he was going, even then, before the bridge existed. The bridge was an OR that appeared to him only on the night of his death, when he wandered to it, wounded, and seeking a way out. Others who had crossed it or gone under it had never seen it before. Rats lived near it, Young had noticed. Once, people hid under it, from the bombers, the strafers. Once, people lived under it, from the dislocation. It had appeared to all of them for the first time once, even its builders, appeared out of nowhere in a century that no longer exists, was observed by someone, somehow, somewhere, even before it was there. On paper, presumably. And with only the history of the hand drawing it.

Young loved order. The military just suited him in this. Life on the parade field. Nothing so aimless now as that spring day way back when he was child, a growing boy. Now he liked everything to have a point, a purpose. Time and motion.

Young played soldier with his brother. They marched with broomsticks on their shoulders. They copied the movies. Left flank, right flank, ho! It was fun. In one movie, a particular favorite of the brothers, there was a battle over a bridge. Two armies clashed. Planes dropped bombs and strafed. It was very exciting. Young and his brother built the little bridge in the park near their home out of bits of wood and pebbles. They made it span a tiny rivulet of rainwater from a puddle, and, late in the afternoon, when it was time to go home, they dropped rocks on it and smashed it down. The bridge in the movie was in another world. Older men, uncles, big brothers, went to it and came home, or didn't come home. Stars were hung in windows. You could see them all over town. Then, pretty soon, they knew where the places were. They kept track.

Young was growing up. He would become a soldier.

But he would never meet an implacable evil, no, and he would never kill such an evil in cold blood. No, not like the different fishes, stonefish, sharks. No, he would never torture a man with many wounding shots, never make the man beg to die. Only the enemy did that. You saw it in the movies.

He would never torture a man into admitting his evil.

"Say how empty you are! Tell how you have wasted your own life along with the lives of others!"

That would be taken care of in AND.

Young could not imagine hating anyone so much that the gladness of his chemistry could turn into a toxic grief. Young could not imagine being sick to his cells with hatred. Young saw the sky one spring day or other.

Young suckled warm milk from his mother's breast and learned love.

Young was conceived in love, a twinkle in the eye of eternity.

SUBJECTS IN MIRROR

Not on its reflecting surface, but in the depths of the mirror, the "scenes" appeared. I turned away, then back, incredulous, aware of the tricks the mind can play. Friends, relatives, lovers, even barely-met workmen, the electrician who came to do some wiring, the plumber who came to fix the pipes, the cable man, the woman from the next apartment who had lost her keys, and some I did not remember or recognize, all stared into their own eyes, into their nostrils and mouths, picking and probing—even the baby-sitter with her young lover behind her, watching her own young lust, whom I thought to have been so innocent. And then there was somewhere else, a room not recognizable, a previous place, the mirror apparently having travelled, and a strange, beautiful woman, her long, fair, platinum-streaked hair unravelled to her narrow waist, over her bare bronzed shoulders and breasts; and oh that scene was worse than the earlier scenes, with those unabashed, secret performers, most of whom I thought I knew, for nothing moved but the woman's jade eyes, up and down, back and forth, even more lustful for herself than any man might show himself to be, had he been watching her. And I realized now how sickeningly full the mirror was, a mirror of disturbing and disgusting emotions; and, as I watched the self-love burning in the beautiful woman's eyes in the mirror that had given up its secrets, my throat ached and I began to choke with tears; and that was when the mirror broke, and I withdrew my bleeding hand, which had been reaching in to touch what was in the terrible, honest mirror.

MANSLAUGHTER

Mutter trug das Kindlein im weißen Mond . . .
—Georg Trakl, "Sebastian im Traum"

I.

A disheveled Tod Mitchell sat at the head of his large dining room table, drinking beer from a glass mug. His mother, Spring, had arrived at her son's Brooklyn apartment a few minutes before, and had brought along her new boyfriend, "Butsy" Suddeth, a short, red-headed, handsome man some years her junior. Spring got up from the table, leaned down and then grabbed her son around the neck, kissed him on the cheek, and said breathlessly, "I still can't believe it! It's just wonderful!"

"I got up about nine with a terrific bloody hangover," Tod said, "and I was just having a Heineken's—trying to get my head together—when the phone rang. Well, when I heard the voice the thought flashed through my mind: What's Jerry," he looked at 'Butsy,' explaining, "that's my agent, what's Jerry doing calling me on a Saturday morning? I was still in a fog. 'Well,' he says, 'I've sold your novel.' I didn't think I'd heard him right. He had to say it a few more times before I could take it in. He says: 'I've got you an advance of five grand'—which is really pretty good for a first novel—'and I've got some film people interested.'" Tod looked at them. "That's a big deal!"

"I can't believe it," said Spring, sitting back down, shaking her head.

"But it's true, Mom. It's really true! I'm supposed to start work with an editor at Triumph next week. But there isn't a lot to do—just small changes."

"Well, you've worked hard enough for it, I must say. You deserve a lot of credit."

"I can't wait to tell Gracie. She'll faint, just watch and see."

"Where did you say she went?"

"To Macy's. She went up to do some shopping. I wish she'd call so I could tell her. She'll just faint when she hears." Tod turned to "Butsy."

"Want another drink, er . . . "

"Fred—Fred Suddeth, but everybody calls me 'Butsy' on account of I smoke cigars all the time. Boy, I really walked in on something, didn't I?"

"Looks like you did, Butsy—it's going to be a party all day—all night—all weekend, maybe!" said Tod. He got up from the table and went to the kitchenette for more drinks and kept talking. "Bourbon or beer—or both? See, Mom was supposed to come over yesterday, er—Butsy—but she never shows up when she says she will. Hell, I got depressed waiting for her. I was supposed to be working—writing. But she said she'd be over, so I didn't work."

"I just didn't have the energy, Tod."

Butsy smiled, glancing at Spring and said, "I guess not." Then he looked at Tod and explained, "We went out dancing Thursday night, so on Friday we—" At that instant Spring kicked Butsy's shin under the table and gave him a "be quiet" look. She didn't want him saying too much about what they'd been doing.

Tod put a pitcher of beer and a bottle of bourbon on the table and said, "Well, that's O.K., but why didn't you call? I could have gone ahead with my work. I waited all day for you. It got me all off my schedule for nothing."

"I wasn't sure whether I'd come or not."

"Well . . . Well, never mind. It's a happy day. One of the best of my life."

"What's your book about?" Butsy said.

"It's about my mother and my father and me, growing up absurd. It's called *Walking the Edge.*"

"I don't know nothing about books. But I can tell you this—your Mom sure is a good dancer."

"I know. I don't think she's ever going to grow old—or up."

"I don't want to grow up," Spring said. "If you grow up you grow old and I don't have any intention of growing old." And, as if to add emphasis to her declaration, she said, "Let's put some music on, Tod."

"Anything to please," said Tod. He walked over to the record player in the bookcase, shuffled through a few albums and put on an old romantic Harry James. "Can you believe it?" he said quietly, almost to himself, "I'm a novelist!"

"And don't forget that five thousand dollars!" Spring called over to him, "But, you know, you don't seem all that excited about it."

"I'm still in shock, I guess."

Butsy was reminded of a time when he too, had been in shock. "I was in a movie once," he said.

Spring, whether she meant to contradict, or just add to Butsy's comment, said: "Butsy's' a jockey."

"*Used* to be a jockey," he said. "Mostly nowadays I just play the nags."

"Butsy's a sporting man," Spring said.

"Yeah, that's it. You got some Mom here, Tod, and a good little drinker."

"She's a sport, all right," Tod conceded.

"Oooh, all this attention!" Spring said. "I love it!"

"I met your Mom a few months ago, over in Jersey, at a bar—a nice place, you know—and she was behaving like a perfect lady. That's what I said to myself—that's a perfect lady."

Tod was amused by Butsy's impression of Spring and said, "Oh, she's not always such a perfect lady. Are you, Mom?"

"I hope not," she said, smiling.

Butsy didn't quite get the joke and said, "Hey, you shouldn't talk like that to your mother."

"Butsy's Irish," Spring said to Tod.

"She kids me about being holy. So O.K., that's the way I was brought up. Anyhow, she's Irish herself, ain't she? She told me that she wanted to be a nun when she was a little girl."

"She wasn't cut out for a nun," said Tod.

Spring stood up and downed her beer. "Let's drink to that!" she said. "Let's drink to that and then let's dance. Come on," she said. "I want to dance with my son, the author." Spring held out a hand to Tod.

They were good dancers, but unyielding to each other's desire to lead. Butsy sat, amused, curious, humming, and puffing on his cigar as they stumbled about. As the dance ended, Butsy applauded and Tod bowed to his mother. He sat back down, wiped his brow, and drained his beer mug.

Butsy got up and danced Spring about the parquet floor, occasionally puffing at his cigar. He danced in the style of an earlier era, doing deep dips, and whispering in Spring's ear. Tod watched until the dance ended, then went to the refrigerator in the little kitchenette and brought back more beer.

Butsy began to hum, and then to croon "The Christmas Song." "Chestnuts roasting on an open fire . . ." That's one colored guy had a beautiful voice, that Nat Cole."

"You have a beautiful voice," Spring said. "Doesn't he, Tod? Butsy's a real crooner."

"I wish Gracie would call," said Tod, distracted. "What time is it, anyway?"

Butsy looked at his watch and said, "It's noon. Hey, what do you think of this watch? It's digital. How much do you think it cost?"

"I couldn't guess," said Tod.

"Nothing. It got stuck on my wrist." He laughed.

"Butsy! Listen, why don't you go and get us some food," Spring suggested. "If this is going to be a party, we need some cold cuts."

"Sure, is there a deli around here?"

"Straight down the hill, Butsy, two blocks," said Tod. "But I should do the buying. You're my guests. Trouble is, I haven't got any money." He laughed. "Flat broke."

"Tapped out?" Butsy asked.

"Tap city."

"Don't worry. Butsy'll buy," said Spring.

"Sure," Butsy said. "I hit it big at the track last week. I'll get some more beer, too. Back in a jiff." He got up, put on his jacket and went to the door, giving them a little wave as he closed it behind him.

Tod said to his mother, "Where did you find him?"

"Do you like him?" she asked.

"He's O.K." Tod said, and shrugged.

"Sort of common, eh?"

"I don't think of people that way, Mom. But he's a thief, isn't he?"

"Oh, he just picks things up. He does it more for the game. But he sure is a comedown from your father, isn't he?"

"I'll have to admit that."

"I miss your father so." Spring was silent for a few moments. "I was just thinking the other day—it'll soon be his birthday. He died five years ago. Where does the time go? You're so much like him, Tod."

"Not much, really. He was a gentleman."

"You're a gentleman."

"I can act like one when I have to. He didn't know how not to be one, anymore than he knew how to stay sober for thirty days in a row."

"I loved him but I never understood him. Tod, you don't mind me going out with men, do you?"

"Absolutely not, Mom. You've got a lot of living to do. I want you to do it."

"Then you didn't really mean what you said."

"What?"

"What you called me on the phone. A whore."

"Of course I didn't mean it. I'm Irish too, you know. But don't you remember what got me started?"

"I know."

"You didn't call me or let me know where you were for three months. I was going crazy with worry. I called the police. Missing persons. The hospitals. Everyone. The Fire Department! And all the time you were shacked up with some guy who told you that calling me meant that you loved me more than you did him. It's crazy. Naturally, when you finally did call and told me how things stood I was upset—angry—by God, I was furious! What did you expect? There you are, sixty-six years old, and vanished somewhere in the wilds of New Jersey—"

"Sixty-four!"

"O.K., *sixteen*! My sixteen-year-old mother vanishes one day, only to turn up three months later, to say that her boy-friend—of whom I've never heard—told her not to call me. A stranger to both of us!"

"I know. I was wrong. I just didn't want to cause any trouble."

"Cause trouble! Think of the distraction! I couldn't write! How do you think I felt?"

"Well, let's get off that now."

"Why? Just because you want to? It always has to be your way, doesn't it? To hell with me!" Tod sat silent, staring into his beer mug. It was an old argument.

"Tod, let's not fight. This is a big day. You've sold your novel. Think of it! My son, the novelist!"

"And here I was, pretty newly married, and I couldn't even invite my mother for a visit because I didn't know where she was. It played havoc with my nerves."

"You're not the only one with nerves."

"And I think Gracie lost the baby because of what happened."

"She lost the baby because of Billy Shaw and all that upset. And that happened because of your drinking."

"Well, who taught me to drink? It's the only thing I ever saw as a kid. You and Dad! Parties and dead soldiers!"

"Other people survive their parents without becoming drunks."

"Yeah, if they've got something else. What the hell did I have? I never went to school. No brothers or sisters—thanks to your abortions—or even any friends. I was just locked up alone with you two and your drinking. Kept with you so you wouldn't have to worry about me. Not even let out of those dismal apartments to play on the street. I played under the table with your feet kicking at me. At least you could have sent me off to school in the morning."

"You know we moved too often for you to go, to keep regular. We were in and out of town in a week."

"There *were* laws."

"Oh, we did get into trouble. Do you remember the time when the truant officer came to our door to check on you, and Dad was standing across the street—" She smiled at Tod.

Yes, Tod remembered, of course he remembered. It was a funny memory they shared. "Dad just left the house, going somewhere—" he said.

"He was going off to his territory to sell," Spring said. "And when he saw this nice-looking man at our door—"

Tod laughed. "He came charging back, thinking the man was your secret lover—"

"And you should have seen the look on his face when I introduced them. 'This is Mr. Whoever-it-was, the truant officer—'"

They both laughed until they were interrupted by the ringing of the telephone. Tod jumped up and ran to the phone. "That must be Gracie."

He looked back at Spring and shook his head, no. "Hello," he said. "Oh, Jean. No, I thought it was Gracie. Yeah. She's gone shopping. Macy's, Manhattan, I think. You're home early. Half day, today? Yes, sure, come on down. We're having a party. Yes. I have some wonderful news. Wait till you hear. O.K., 'bye."

"What's she doing home at this hour?" Spring said. "I thought she did some kind of counseling or something on Saturdays."

"She does. But it was a half day today."

"Is she getting adjusted to being a widow?"

"I suppose so. She seems all right."

"It's easier at her age. She's young."

"I don't know. Being a widow at twenty-five must be different from being one at sixty-five but who can say that it's easier?"

"That's probably right. You're very wise for such a young man."

"I'm not such a young man and I'm smart enough, at least, to know that I'm not very wise."

"There you go, always taking exception to everything I say. Isn't there anything about your old mother that you like?"

"Why, I like everything about my not-so-old mother," he said, and gave her a hug.

There was a knock at the door and Tod went to answer it. He held the knob, turned back to her and said, "Except that she tells me one thing and does another. She tells me she'll be over on Friday and makes me give up a day's work—which makes me get drunk, which gives me a hangover—and then she shows up on Saturday with a stranger in tow." He turned away from her and opened the door to a pretty, young brunette.

Jean Shaw was an upstairs neighbor. She stepped into the room with familiarity and said, "Hi, Tod. Oh, hello, Mrs. Mitchell. I didn't know you were visiting. How are you?"

"Jean, you know I like you to call me Spring. I'm fine. How're you?" Spring got up and gave the young woman a hug.

"I'm lucky today. I got off early."

Spring sat back down at the table. "I don't know how you can stand it, being with children all week and then again on Saturday." she said. "I know I couldn't bear it. I remember—"

Tod recognized the direction of his mother's often-repeated story, and changed the trajectory: "Sit down, Jean. Want a drink? A beer?"

"Sounds good."

Spring took up the thread of her story, "Well, I had six little sisters and brothers and one older sister who refused to do a thing. We were very poor. Our father had died at only twenty-nine—and Mama worked as a cook in a girls' school and was away most of the time and it fell to me to take care of all those kids—and I used to say to myself: Spring, I'd say, when you grow up don't you ever be such a fool as to get married and have children. I even thought I might become a nun."

"But you didn't. You got married and had me." Tod lifted his mug to Jean, smiled at her and tilted his head toward his mother with an expression of "here we go again" on his face.

"Well, yes. I fell in love with your father. That's what kind of fool I am, as the song says."

"Thanks a lot."

"Well, I didn't mean—"

"Of course not," said Tod. "How do you think it makes me feel every time you say that? I've heard it all my life."

"You know I don't mean . . . That's just the way I chatter on. I don't mean anything."

"You don't think about the way you make other people feel."

"Oh, let's get off me. Tell Jean the news."

"Yes, what is it, Tod?"

"Tod sold his book," said Spring.

"Oh, Tod! How wonderful! Where's Gracie? I bet she's in seventh heaven."

"She doesn't know yet," Tod said.

"No," said Spring. "She's been out all day."

"Oh, I've got to stay and see her reaction. I know she'll be in her glory. She always believed in what you were doing and she loved that book! So did I. And so did Billy. We knew how good it was."

"So did I," said Spring.

"You!" Tod knew that she'd never read a word he'd written.

"Well I did. Of course I did."

"I don't know how you could have. After depriving me of any education whatsoever, you told me I couldn't be a writer because I didn't have any education."

"Well, I didn't know anything about those things. I had to leave school in the sixth grade to go to work in a mill. You should have asked your father. He was the big brain. He went to college."

"Yeah, Dreiser's mother didn't know anything about those things, either. He had to teach her to read. But she said that he could be or do anything he wanted to be or do. She didn't constantly put him down in order to exalt her own feeble ego. Vanity! All is vanity!"

Spring turned to Jean and said, jokingly, "Let's ignore him. He's drunk."

"Let's do. Until he cheers up."

There was a knock at the door and Spring got up to answer. "That must be Butsy," she said. Butsy came in, an enormous load of groceries in his arms. There was a young delivery boy behind him, pushing a loaded shopping cart.

"What's all this?" Spring said. "Where have you been so long?"

"What's it look like? I've been shopping," he said, leading the boy. "Come on in, kid. Push it in here."

Spring said, "My God, what did you get?"

"I got some of everything. I mean, this is a party, ain't it?" Tod helped Butsy and Spring unload the cart and passed a few cans to Jean.

"Stuffed artichoke hearts!" said Spring. "Canned lobster! Crabmeat!"

"How did they get in there?" said Butsy. " I don't remember payin' for them."

"Butsy, you didn't!"

Oblivious, Butsy turned to the delivery boy. "Here kid, buy yourself a chocolate cigar," he said. The delivery boy thanked him and left, pushing the cart ahead.

Butsy called after him, "More where that came from, kid."

"Sure I did, Spring. I got plenty to spend—easy come, easy go—and I don't mind spendin' it; but those supermarkets are a bunch of crooks. You think I should pay for lobster at their prices when the lobsters are running all over the ocean? Look!" He took two small glass jars from his pockets and said, "Butsy's got the magic touch."

To Tod and Jean, Spring said, "Butsy's got light fingers." Then, to Butsy she said, "What do you think Tod and Jean must think of you?"

Tod said, "I'm with Butsy. The supermarkets are a bunch of crooks. They take us, we should take them. More power to you, Butsy!"

"Me too," Jean joined in.

"There, you see?" said Butsy. "They think I did right."

"But suppose you got caught?" said Spring.

"Hell, I been lifting stuff all my life and never got caught yet, besides, they only warn you the first time. Gimme a drink, will you, somebody? That hill's a hot climb."

Tod led Butsy to a chair, got him a fresh beer and said, "Butsy, this is a friend of ours—Jean Shaw. She lives upstairs. Jean, Fred Suddeth, a friend of Mom's."

"Nice meetin' ya," he said.

"Same here—er . . . . "

From over in the kitchenette, still putting away groceries, Spring called, "Call him Butsy."

"Yeah—call me Butsy. Everybody does."

"That's an unusual name."

"Because—see—" He fished in his breast pocket, found a half-smoked cigar, and began to light it.

"Ah! And what do you do, Butsy?"

Spring called again from the kitchenette, "Butsy's a jockey."

"*Was* a jockey. Now I'm a sporting man. Anybody can see I'm too old to be a jockey—and too fat. She's always building me up to her friends. What do you think? Something wrong with what I am?"

"Not that I can see," said Jean.

"Hey, I like this one. You I like. Good-lookin' too."

Spring came to the table and said, kiddingly, "Watch out there." Whether she meant it for Butsy or Jean, was unclear.

"You better watch out, Spring. Butsy is very handsome—in a rugged, red-headed way. My husband, Billy, was a red-head."

"That right? Oh, I'm old enough to be your father."

"*Grand*father, you mean." said Spring.

"I wouldn't say that." He leaned over toward Jean and said, "She's always tearing me down."

"I thought she was always building you up."

Butsy said to her, "Well, like this, see: building up what I do, tearing down what I am."

Tod plopped down beside Butsy and nursed his beer. He looked distant and rather gloomy. He said, "I know the feeling."

Jean looked at Butsy and said, "What *do y*ou do, Butsy? What's a sporting man, anyway?"

Tod said, "Butsy's a gambler, I think."

"Spring, you got a sharp son here."

"Nothing sharp about it. You said you were flush from the track."

"Did I? I get a few drinks, I forget."

"Butsy, did you stop off along the way? I think you stopped off and had a few somewhere. All that shopping should have cleared your head."

"Well, I hadda, Christsake! Oops! Shouldn't take the name of the Lord thy God in vain. I mean, here I am all of a sudden sitting around with a guy who writes books—me, who on'y reads the headlines and funnies and sports pages of the Daily News. I'm nervous."

"You? Nervous?" Spring said.

"Yeah—me—nervous! I'm human, you know." Butsy looked over at Tod and said, "All the way over here from Jersey I'm thinking: I got to behave very elegant now because I'm meetin' Spring's son who is a writer. And I got nervous."

"You're not nervous now, are you?"

"Nah. Not so much now. First thing I see you drinking beer I say to myself: This is a regular guy."

"I told you my son was no snob."

"But *you* are." Tod was clearly feeling his drinks. Numerous old battles with his mother were being reviewed in his mind.

"Aw, no," Butsy said, "don't talk unpleasant to your Mom. Look, Tod: I know I ain't got no education; but that don't mean I haven't learned nothing. And one thing I know is: a mother is the most wonderful thing in the world."

"Bravo!" Spring applauded. "I told you he was an Irishman."

"Hey, look at the Irish mug on her! I'm nuts about your Mom, Tod. She's what I call a lady."

"Well, thank you," Spring said, smiling.

"And you too—" Butsy said, looking over at Jean, "what'd you say your name was?"

"Jean."

"That's a pretty name. Hey, seems to me like I heard your husband was dead. Did I get that right?"

"Yes, he's dead."

"I was with him," Tod said. "It was an accident."

"Yeah? What kind of an accident? Oh, listen, I don't mean to make you talk about it if—"

"No, it's all right," said Jean. "I've got to get used to it."

Tod said, "We were out drinking together. Billy was my best friend. We'd been drinking all day . . . I tried to get him to come home but he didn't want to quit. Finally, I got him into a subway station, but he darted for a car and the doors closed behind him before I could get on. Next morning he was found dead at Coney Island. He'd apparently fallen down a flight of iron stairs from the elevated."

Tod looked at Jean, sorry for a moment that he'd told the story. He said, "Jean, are you—"

"No, I'm all right. That's what happened." She looked down into her beer glass, then, looking up, she said, "He had red hair, too, like yours, Butsy."

"Mine is all full of grey."

"He was a musician," Tod said.

"A classical musician," Spring added.

Butsy said, "Classical. Gee, I'm sorry."

"Come on, let's cheer up," Jean said, pushing her chair back from the table.

"I've got an idea," said Spring.

"What?"

"Let's surprise Gracie," she said. "We can get the place all spruced up—"

"A real party!" said Tod. "And thanks to Butsy we've got everything we need."

"We should decorate the place," said Jean.

"Yeah, like Christmas!" Butsy joined in.

"That's it," said Jean. "We'll get out the Christmas decorations—chains and lights and everything and really make it look like a real celebration. Then when Gracie walks in we'll all—you know, jump up and shout: Surprise! Surprise! Hip, Hip, Hooray! Tod's book's been sold!" She jumped up and down, caught in excitement and flushed. As she calmed down she said to Tod, "Ah, Billy would have loved this so much. He thought you were a fine writer, Tod. He really loved that book."

Tod looked at her. Jean grabbed his hand and said, "Oh, this is a great idea. Come on, let's get started."

"I'll do the dirty dishes and clean up," said Spring, "and you start hanging the decorations. Don't forget the lights! I love bright, pretty lights!"

"What should I do?" said Tod.

"Nothing," Jean said. "What do you think the party's about? You're the one who wrote the book. You and Gracie. You can watch and supervise."

"I'd never have done it," Tod said, "if it hadn't been for her, you know."

"She always believed in you," Spring said.

"She must be a great gal," said Butsy. "Hey, what should I do?"

"You keep Tod company," said Spring. "Show him some of your card tricks."

Tod said, "She's the only person who ever helped or encouraged me."

"Amazing Grace," said Spring. Tod thought he heard a tinge of sarcasm in her voice. "Let's get busy," Spring said, jumping up. She went back to the kitchenette and began cleaning out the sink, rattling silverware and pots.

Jean went out the door, saying, "I'm going upstairs to get our Christmas decorations. We've got everything. *I've* got everything."

Butsy pulled a deck of cards from an inside pocket, broke the seal, and methodically shuffled them while he puffed on his teeth-clenched cigar and watched Spring admiringly.

Tod sat at the table, and stared off in space.

Butsy sat opposite Tod, but ignored him. He was busy with his cards and watched Spring as she worked in the kitchenette. "Ain't she something?" he said, impishly, perhaps to himself, perhaps to Tod, "Ain't she something?"

After a few minutes Jean came back into the apartment, carrying a large cardboard box of Christmas decorations. She put it down on the table and got to work decorating the room. She left the door ajar and in a moment, quietly, a stooped, gaunt, once-beautiful old woman slipped into the room. She leaned on her cane and asked, in a cultivated British accent, "What's this? It isn't Hogmanay yet, is it? I feel like Rip Van Winkle."

Tod, snapped out of his momentary reverie, got up and shook the woman's hand, putting an arm around her shoulders. "Sophia," he said, "I've had wonderful news! My novel's been accepted."

Sophia Bennett lived in the basement of the old brownstone apartment house and was a writer, herself—a poet, in fact, and was a good friend to the younger couple.

"Really?" she smiled.

"We're going to have a party," said Jean, coming over to greet Sophia. "Oh, you know Tod's mother, Sophia. And this is Mister—"

"Butsy, just call me Butsy. Do you live here, too?"

Sophia looked across the room to Spring and nodded hello. "How do you do, Mister Butsy? Yes, downstairs."

Spring answered Sophia, "Mister Suddeth. That's his nickname—Butsy."

Tod led Sophia to the table and helped her to a chair. She looked at Butsy and asked, "Suddeth? What an odd name! Is it English?"

"Well, Irish-American," said Butsy. "Are you a Brit?"

"Welsh—so you see, you needn't be defensive," she smiled and said. "Jean's Irish too. We are all Celts here. Well, congratulations, Tod! How wonderful for you! Now tell me about it. I can imagine how happy Grace must be."

"She doesn't know yet. She went off to Macy's before I got the news."

"We're making a surprise party for her," said Jean.

"Would you like a drink, Sophia?" Spring said.

"Yes, a whiskey, if it's available, and soda—no ice—thank you, Spring. You must be very proud of Tod. This is certainly his red letter day."

Spring went off to the kitchenette to fix the drink, and called back, "I certainly am!"

"She was telling me all about him on the way over from Jersey," Butsy said. "I was sort of scared to meet a writer until she told me what a regular guy he was—how he was a shoeshine boy as a kid—like me—and had been in the Marines and all. She said how he never had no education to speak of, how he educated himself. We're from the school of hard knocks, ain't we, Tod?"

"But Tod is a very well educated man," said Sophia. "He went to University."

"On the G.I. Bill," said Tod.

Jean called down from her perch on a chair where she was tacking up Christmas lights, "Sophia's a writer, too, Butsy—a poet—"

"And," Tod said, "an actress. She once worked with Leslie Howard on the stage. Do you remember him?"

"That English actor who was with Bogart in 'Petrified Forest.' Sure, I know all Bogie's movies. I started to say before how I was in a movie. It was 'High Sierra,' where I did the fall for Bogart. You know. When he rolls down the mountain. That was me rolling."

"Really," Sophia said. "Were you a stuntman?"

Spring chimed in, "He's more of a story-teller. He's making that up."

"Well, I did do some stunt work. I told you. Before I was a jockey."

"That's very interesting," said Sophia. "What do you do now?"

"He's a sporting man," said Spring. She handed Sophia her drink and sat down with the others.

"I'm a gambler," he said.

"I like to gamble," Jean said.

"Ah, Monte Carlo," Sophia said, with a flutter, kidding them a little, "when I was a young thing!"

"Not me," Tod said. "I want something I can count on."

"But Tod," said Sophia, "you've gambled all along. You've gambled on yourself, and your very life! And look, you've won!" The old woman was obviously very happy for her young neighbor. She had spent many evenings with Tod and his Grace, drinking, reciting poetry together and discussing his novel-in-progress.

"Yeah," said Butsy, "that's a way of looking at it!"

"Three cheers for Tod!" said Sophia, raising her voice and her glass.

And they all joined in, "Hip, hip, hurray! Hip, hip, hurray! Hip, hip, hurray!"

Sophia wasn't satisfied. "And three more for Grace, his amazing wife!"

II.

The long day's light had drained away. Now the apartment was illuminated by lamps and Christmas lights, which reflected on the brightly-colored ornaments and baubles that hung alongside chains of popcorn and glittering tinsel. The decorations lent the room a harsh, garish appearance, or so it seemed to Tod, but maybe it was just because his unexpected happy excitement had drained away like the day and his submerged but growing worry about Gracie's absence played at odds on his nerves. They had been drinking and talking for long hours. Music from the Big Band era filled the room. Jean and Butsy were dancing. Spring and Tod moved around them, struggling a little, trying to feel who would lead. Sophia looked on and tapped the floor with her cane.

Spring stopped suddenly and said, "Enough!" She turned away from Tod and sat back down at the table with Sophia.

Tod followed her. "Too much," he said.

Spring looked at the other couple and said, to Jean, "Isn't Butsy a wonderful dancer!"

"He certainly is," said Jean, "he's a dream!"

"I wonder where Grace is," Sophia said. "It's getting dark outside."

"Yes," said Jean, "and we've been at it for hours. Isn't anybody getting hungry?"

"Let's bring out the food," said Spring. "Gracie can eat when she gets here. She won't mind if we don't wait for her."

Tod said, "I'd like to wait for her. She can't be much longer."

"She won't mind, Tod. Help me, Jean. We'll make a nice crabmeat salad."

Spring and Jean got up, went to the kitchenette and began putting together the cold cuts and salad.

"Your Mom just can't wait for anybody, Tod. I'm always running after her. When I say, 'Why can't you wait for me?'—you know what she says? 'I'm an individual.' I don't even know what she means. She's really something! Ain't she something, Tod."

Sophia looked at Butsy and said, "Why?"

"Why what? Butsy asked.

"Why do you run after her?"

"Because I'm crazy about her. What do you think? She's a free spirit. Don't like to be pinned down."

"That's a bit irresponsible, isn't it?" Sophia said.

"Hey, wait a minute," said Butsy. "She don't have to answer to nobody."

"She doesn't *have* to, but shouldn't she? I know of several times when Tod has stopped working because he expected a visit from his mother and then she didn't show up." Sophia hit a sore spot. And she knew Tod well enough to know that it was true.

"That's her business, ain't it?"

"No. If you make an appointment and someone stops what he's doing because of it and then you don't meet him or call him up and explain, I'd say it had become his business. Tod is a writer. His work requires concentration and good work habits. It requires self-discipline, and that sort of thing is very distracting and weakening. Too much interruption can damage a work, or even damage the writer. I know. I write myself. And I wouldn't allow anyone to do that to me. Tod's patience amazes me."

Butsy looked over at Tod and said, "Is this old dame a good friend of yours?"

Spring had heard this little exchange and came back to the table and said to Sophia, "If I ever do that, it's between my son and me, and I'll thank you to mind your own business."

"Huh-oh," Tod said.

Sophia was undaunted. "Tod," she went on, "is a good son. I know how unhappy you sometimes make him, Spring. I've seen him put his very important work aside and sit in expectation of one of your visits, then you not show up. You don't seem to understand what it does to him."

By now all the drinks Spring had polished off during the afternoon were rising and carrying her to greater heights of . . . who knew?

"Who are you?" Spring went on. "You have no business here anyway, you old drunkard."

Even Butsy seemed to think some cheer should be restored. "Don't get sore at the old dame, Spring. What a temper! Ain't she something?"

"No! She can't talk to me like that in my son's house."

"Nevertheless, Mom, she's telling the truth. Suppose I had been working today. You had no way of knowing I wasn't, but you barge in anyhow, without any warning, and even bring company. I waited for you all day yesterday. And nobody showed up or even called. This has happened a thousand times."

"I've explained that."

"Your Mom explained that," said Butsy. "Remember, your mother is the best friend you'll ever have. I know my mother is."

"I don't know about your mother, Butsy, but mine has been driving me crazy ever since I can remember. That's what my novel is about—my playboy father and my merry widow mother. They were both so damned gay! Except when my father was staggering around for weeks on end in his shitty undershorts and my mother was screaming at him until I thought my eardrums would break. They were irresponsible, that's what they were! Selfish and irresponsible!"

Jean was listening and suddenly said, "I'm not so sure you have any right to talk about anybody being irresponsible, Tod. If you had been more responsible, maybe Billy would still be here." Then she was quiet and began to cry. Sophia and Spring gathered around her and tried to comfort.

Sophia said, "She's just had a little too much to drink, I think."

"Naw," Butsy said. "She *needs* a drink."

"Mister Butsy," Sophia said, "I wonder if you would be so kind as to go to the liquor store for me. If you would get me a pint of whiskey—I'd like to go to my own apartment." She waved out a bill from her dress pocket.

"Do it, Butsy. Get it for her," Spring said.

Suddenly, Jean stood up from the table, still crying. She pointed a finger at Tod and cried, "He killed my husband! He took him out and killed him!"

"You know damn well that isn't true, Jean!" Tod was hurt by the accusation, even though he knew she knew it wasn't true and it was just the booze.

"It is true! Billy had a wonderful career ahead of him, and now he's dead!"

"You know as well as I do that Billy was an alcoholic. He was reckless. He was picked up by the police where he had fallen many a time. He was always bruised and banged up from falling down somewhere."

"But you had him stay with you and drink that day and then you let him get away and die—"

"I was too drunk—"

"Well, isn't that irresponsible?"

"Well, aren't you drunk now? Didn't you ever drink with him? It just *happened* to happen when he was with me."

"Is that how you explain it to yourself?" She was calming down a bit now.

Tod hesitated and said, "No." No, he thought, he could never explain it to himself.

"She's just upset, Tod," Spring said. "She doesn't mean what she's saying."

"To hear you," Sophia said, "nobody means what he or she is saying. I can assure you that *I* generally do. But Jean doesn't *know* what she's saying."

Tod put his arm around Jean, and tried to make her look at him. "You know Billy's death wasn't any more my fault because he had gone out with me than it would have been your fault if he had gone out with you. You know that, Jean."

"He never died with me," she said quietly. "Somebody's got to be responsible for something!"

"Here, have another drink," said Spring. "Now drink it slowly."

"She should have some coffee," said Sophia. "Tod, why don't you recite a poem? It'll get her mind off it. Tod's a wonderful reader."

"Oh, I don't want to hear any of that," said Spring. "This is supposed to be a party."

Jean looked at the others and tried to dry her eyes with her sleeve, "No, let him," she said. "I like to listen to him recite. Billy always said Tod was a wonderful reader of poetry."

"I don't feel like it," Tod said.

"Please, Tod. I'm sorry for what I said. I don't know what comes over me. Billy loved to hear you read."

"It's boring," Spring sighed. "It's very boring when you are trying to have fun."

"Well," Sophia said, "it *is* his party. Recite something for us, Tod."

"Yeah—O.K. I've got just the number for this occasion." He went to the bookcase and pulled out a volume. He thumbed through it it and began:

"This is by Poe. It's called 'To My Mother—'"

"Is this going to be insulting?" Spring said. "Because if it is—"

"I don't see how anybody can be insulted by this. Why be defensive? Do you feel guilty?" He began to read:

"Because I feel that, in the heavens above,
The angels, whispering to one another,
Can find, among their burning terms of love,
None so devotional as that of 'Mother,'
Therefore by that dear name I long have called you—
You who are more than mother unto me,
And fill my heart of hearts, where Death installed you,
In setting my Virginia's spirit free.
My mother—my own mother, who died early,
Was but the mother of myself; but you

Are mother to the one I loved so dearly,
And thus are dearer than the mother I knew
By that affinity with which my wife
Was dearer to my soul than its soul life."

While Tod was reading, Butsy quietly opened the door and entered the room. He waited there, bottle in bag in hand, listening, and puffing on his cigar.

"Now that's the right way to talk to your mother," he said.

Sophia got up and went to meet Butsy, saying to Tod, "Thank you for that good reading, Tod. It was lovely!" She took the bag from Butsy and turned toward the door, tapping her cane.

"Your change," Butsy said, and handed it to Sophia.

"Please keep it for your trouble. Good evening. And congratulations again, Tod! I knew that wonderful novel would be snatched up by somebody." The door closed behind her.

"Keep it for my trouble!" said Butsy. "She gave me a tip, like I was an errand boy! The nerve of the old dame!"

"Sit down, Butsy!" Spring said. "That poem was beautiful, Tod. Thank you."

"What for? I don't think you understood it, did you?"

"Now don't start on me again, just when I thought you'd stopped."

"You know," Butsy said, "that poem makes me think of how I haven't called my Mom in a long time. I think it's been a year. She's nearly ninety. She won't be around much longer."

"Now don't go getting sentimental. Let's have some fun, for God's sake! Put the dance music back on, Tod! I just love to dance, don't you, Jean?"

"I loved to dance with Billy. He was a wonderful dancer."

"How 'bout me?" Butsy said, looking at Jean.

"Butsy is a wonderful dancer," said Spring

"And red-headed, like Billy."

"Hey, Spring, is she flirting with me? Are you flirting with me, girly?"

"The vanity of men! You old fool, she's young enough to be your granddaughter!"

"My daughter, maybe. Don't forget, I'm a lot younger than you are."

"Oh, thanks a lot. But you aren't *that* much younger."

Butsy sat down at the table and said, "I can't stop thinking about my mother. It comes to me sometimes that maybe she's dead already, and I don't know it."

"Doesn't your brother live with her? Spring said. "He'd tell you if anything had happened to her."

"Maybe not. I'm the bum in the family. They don't care what I know. The last time I saw my brother, I tried to put the touch on him for a few hundred—he's a contractor and he's got the money—and he wouldn't give me a dime. He tried to throw me out, but I bopped him one on the nose. I broke his beak for him, that's what I did. No; maybe he wouldn't tell me."

"I thought you were a jockey, not a boxer," said Jean.

"I fought feather weight in the Golden Gloves before I was a jockey."

"Was that before you were a stuntman?" she said.

"Yeah. But suppose Mamma's dead?"

"If you want to, you can call her up from here, Butsy. The phone's over there."

"Gee—thanks, Tod—but no. I'm afraid she might be dead. I don't want to know."

"That's just the way I felt when Billy was missing," Jean said.

"I was home, drunk, asleep," Tod said, thinking of Billy. "I didn't know until the next day. He was still alive, in intensive care, when I went to see him. Unconscious. He died a few hours later. I didn't want to know, either, when he died."

Spring said, "When my husband was missing—in the fire—I was glad when he wasn't immediately identified. There was a chance, then. But I knew he was dead. Tod finally identified him at the morgue."

"He was living in an old fire trap rooming house in Newark," Tod told Butsy and Jean. "It was filled with derelicts and drunks like himself. Six of them died."

"We had had an argument," Spring said, "and he had moved down there—but he would have come back as soon as he sobered up."

"He told me that he was never going back to you. He said he wanted some peace." Tod went on, speaking to Butsy, "He was an old man, much older than Mom is now, and that was five years ago. I was a late child. I don't think he ever really wanted me, though he loved me well enough in his way, I guess. I don't think he wanted to have any children by Mom. I was an accident."

Spring said, "You were not! He let me have you because I wanted you. He had had me aborted twice before."

"Jesus, Mary and Joseph, don't say it!" cried Butsy.

"He didn't mean it about not coming back," Spring said.

"He said you drove him crazy," Tod said.

"Well, he drove *me* crazy," said Spring.

"But he was drunk, Mom. You were sober then. If you had only let him be, he wouldn't have gone to that firetrap to find some peace."

Butsy was lost in his own thoughts. "What if she's dead?" he said to no one. He began to cry. Jean had been sitting quietly and couldn't take all this revelatory madness. She got up and ran from the apartment. Tod started to go after her, but Spring said, "Let her go. She'll feel better if she gets it out of her system."

Butsy looked at Spring and said, "But what if Mamma is dead?"

"She isn't dead!" Spring said.

"Call her up, Butsy," said Tod.

"It's long distance—California. But I'll pay for the call, Tod. Could I?"

"Sure. Go ahead."

Butsy sat down on the couch next to a small telephone table and took out his address book. He found the number and started to put the call through.

"Your father would have come back to me, and it was cruel of you to say that he wouldn't," Spring said to Tod.

"Cruel! Don't you think the things you do—and always have done—are cruel? All you ever say is how I took thirty-eight hours to be born, and how agonizing it was for you. You could start right there."

"Well, that's the truth!" Spring said.

"But do you still have to tell me it every time we have a drink together?"

"Well, what's it got to do with you? I was the one who was in pain."

"Because I didn't want to come out and meet you!"

"That's a rotten thing to say to your mother!"

Butsy got his line and asked into the phone, "Mamma? Mamma?"

Tod and Spring were oblivious to Butsy and his call. "You're just drunk!" Spring said. "You've turned out to be a drunk like your father."

"How else could I turn out? It's all I've ever known."

Butsy jerked around on the couch and faced Spring and Tod. "She's dead! She's dead, Spring! What?" He listened again to the phone.

"You should respect your mother!" Spring shouted at Tod.

"There's nothing to respect!" he shouted back at her.

"Please, somebody—my Mamma's dead! What? What?" Butsy strained to hear someone at the end of the line.

"Oh, for God's sake! Help him, Tod. Stop *crying* Butsy! Tod, take that phone away from him!"

Tod took the phone from Butsy and said into it, "I'm a friend of—what? Oh, I see. Yes. Yes, he's had a few." Tod put his hand over the mouthpiece and said, "Butsy, your mom is in bed. She's fine. She's taking a nap. Here—" Then he handed the phone back to Butsy.

"Hello?" Butsy said, speaking again into the phone.

Spring sat down at the table and said to Tod, "I don't know why you hate me so much. I've always been a good mother."

Tod could not believe what he heard. He said, "Which is why I was dragged all over the country and never got any schooling. You should have seen to it that I was taken care of. It was your responsibility. People have no right to have a kid and then to just pretend he isn't there."

"That was your father's fault. I had to go where he went. I didn't have any money. Other women have had it easier."

"Other women have worked and worked like dogs. You could have worked. You could have made a real home for us, even if it was just a little one-room apartment.

Spring said, wearily, "What's the use of re-hashing all this now? That's all in the past."

"No, it's not, it's in the present. I'm still paying for it."

"Have you forgotten what this party is about? Your novel's going to be published. You're successful, so what difference does it make or not make what I did or didn't do?"

“It makes a difference that I’ve been a nervous wreck all my life. That I haven’t been suited for a normal life. That I’m an alcoholic. That, if this book hadn’t been accepted, eventually I would have . . . killed myself.”

“Don’t say that! You’re just being dramatic!”

“You damned old selfish insensitive bitch! All you’ve ever cared about was some paltry comfort and a good time to break the monotony!”

Butsy finished his phone call and was apparently relieved. “Mamma’s alive! I talked to her!” he said.

At that moment, the apartment door swung open and Gracie came in, carrying bundles. She was shocked, seeing the Christmas decorations and dim lights.

“Well, what’s happening here?” she said, “What is this, a party?” Then, seeing Spring, “Hello, Mom!” She saw Butsy and said, smiling, “Hello, there. Where’s Tod?”

“Gracie, this is my friend, Fred Suddeth. Fred, my daughter-in-law, Gracie.”

“Call me Butsy.” He held up his cigar, pointing to it.

“Hello, Butsy!” she said.

“Gracie, sit down! I’ve got great news!” said Tod. “The greatest!”

Spring broke in—“Tod’s novel has been accepted. Isn’t it wonderful?”

Gracie sat down and tried to take in the news. She was flustered and it dissolved into sheer joy. “Oh, Tod, it’s true, isn’t it? Honey, we did it! I can’t believe it! Tell me all about it! What’s happened?”

“Jerry called him this morning,” Spring said. “He’s got Tod a five thousand dollar advance.”

“Money! We’ve even got money! Oh, Tod, I’m so proud of you!” Gracie put her arms around Tod and kissed him.

“Would you like a drink, Gracie?” Spring offered.

"Wow! You know, Mom, I think I will have one for once—to celebrate. Tod's always complaining that I don't drink with him. Well, this is an occasion! Did you tell Sophia and Jean?" Then she said to Butsy, "They're our neighbors. And our best friends."

"They were here. Jean did the decorating," Tod said. "Like it?"

Gracie looked around the room and said, "She must have had one too many."

"And I did the cleaning," Spring said.

"Oh, thanks so much, Mom. The place really does look festive. Well, cheers!"

"Cheers!" Spring and Butsy echoed.

"To you, honey!" Tod said, "for believing in me like nobody else ever has!"

"Oh, that's meant for me," said Spring.

"You shouldn't be mean to your Mom, Tod. Look how good I feel because my mom's alive. She's nearly ninety!"

"She was probably a good mother," said Tod.

They all sat down at the table and Butsy said, "She done her best. My old man was a beast. He threw me out when I was fourteen."

"I thought it was your brother."

"That was later. I already had practice by that time. That's what I said to my brother before I broke his beak; I said I should be doin' this to the old man." Butsy laughed, and went on, "I just now asked my brother on the phone how his nose feels, does it still hurt—I hope. But what could my mother do?"

"Well, she could have stopped him from throwing you out at fourteen," said Tod.

"Naw, them were different times."

"All times should be the same when it comes to that," Tod said.

"What's going on?" Gracie said, puzzled.

"He's picking on me again," Spring explained.

"You shouldn't pick on Spring, Tod," said Butsy. "Just look at her! Ain't she cute? Ain't she something? I love that woman! She's a real individual! I love your mother, Tod. I don't think you should pick on her."

"It's between us."

"No, it isn't. Not when I'm here."

Gracie stood up. "Now wait, both of you!" she said.

"Why don't you both just get out!" Tod shouted.

"All right," Spring said, "I'll be glad to go."

"You aren't even supposed to be here, you know. You were supposed to be here yesterday!"

"I can't let you act like this, Tod. I want you to apologize to Spring," said Butsy.

"Go to hell!"

Before anyone could stop them the two men were in a drunken shoving match. Tod lost his balance and fell to the floor. His head struck with a loud crack. Gracie dropped to her knees beside him and lifted his bleeding head to her lap.

"Tod! Tod! Wake up!"

"Your dress is all blood! He's bleeding!" cried Spring.

"Christ, I'm sorry! Heads bleed something awful. But he's O.K."

"It's his ears," Gracie cried. "There's blood coming out of his ears! Oh, God! Tod? Tod? Wake up, honey!"

"Lemme see." Butsy squatted down and put his hand over Tod's heart. He looked up at the women. "I don't feel it. Christ, he's dead, I think! Christ, Spring, I didn't do nothing but push him. I didn't mean it. You know I didn't mean it. Jesus, Mary and Joseph! Oh, Christ!" Butsy jumped up and ran from the apartment.

Spring cried out hysterically, "Call the hospital! Do something! Somebody, do something!"

Grace sat on the floor rocking Tod's head in her lap.

SIGNS

What brought it all back was the double set of initials they had drawn in the soft cement after he had filled the holes left by the supporting columns of the mantelpiece. He had replaced that ancient ornate fixture with a rough wooden beam he found on a pile of jagged stars and triangles of plaster at their curb. He had forgotten the initials. After all, it had been five years since the day they drew them and three since he had walked out of that apartment for what he had thought was good.

But today he happened to be in the old neighborhood and found himself, as if by habit, turning down that narrow winding cobbled alley of a street and pausing at the wrought iron gate that opened into Savannah Mews. He glanced up at the second floor windows and felt as if beckoned, for there in a window was a *FOR RENT* sign.

The new superintendent was a laconic man who took him up, showed him the rooms he knew so well, and left him, for what he said would be just a few minutes, called away on duty. He sat down in a dusty corner on the bare wood of the floor and lit a cigarette.

How his former wife, the exacting wife of this apartment, would have objected to the last tenant not having swept up before taking leave! He looked about, wondering what he was doing there. Outside, where the sun had been so bright only a short time before, the day had darkened and a pallid opaque curtain of rain swung in a wind beyond the windows. The rain made him see again those awful fluffy curtains his wife had hung. He rose, about to shut the windows so that those ugly expensive rags should not be made wet and he get the blame. "Couldn't you have shut the windows? Couldn't you have done at least that much for me? I know you don't like the curtains, but—" He guessed it was true. He could have shut the windows. But he hated those curtains. Lord, how he hated those curtains! Still, he could have done those little things. He could have tried to respect the sanctity of her personality by giving in to the little, *petty*, traits that comprised it.

The initials *were*, however, there, at the foot of the fireplace, looking up from the small, cracked hearth, inside two hearts. They had thought that they were in this very room, and that they were in love. He had thought that he was going to the university. His wife might have thought that she was in love with his best friend, a fellow student, the man with whom she betrayed him. The rain had made the curtains wet. It was true that he had not had time to get to the windows, the storm had come up so fast, but explanations were not as good as results. He had stretched out and let the rain drift in as it would.

The curtains were wet. The storm blew up and he laughed at its fury. "It's no more real than what they think they have done to me. Am I to believe in a *Grand Guignol* storm, rain from water cans, clouds from pumps, lightning by lightswitch, brought down by some imaginatively burdened Hawthorne madly waving a scarlet letter at a crew of stagehands?" Thus, timely, an apparition appeared. She stepped in, soaked, closing her dripping umbrella. "Look! Look at those curtains!" Her ghostly voice resounded in his mind. "Couldn't you have closed the windows? Couldn't you have done at least that much for me? I know you don't like those curtains, but—"

He slammed out into the rain, and never went back—this time.

DARKLING, I LISTEN . . .

Howard recognized the moonstruck Beta at once. It was just as Porter had described it—not more than two or three feet high, built right in the earth, and about six and a half feet long. But for the small skylight on top, that looked up through the trees, and the small lifting door on the lake side, it looked like a coffin regurgitated by its grave. Porter had said that his brother, the family hermit, had built the tiny cabin for himself one summer so that he could keep his space.

"At first, there was only Alpha, the family cabin, then Matthew built Beta, so Dad decided to build the rest of the cabins for vacationers and fishermen and make some money." Howard kneeled and lit a match. Inside lay a soggy brown army blanket and a camouflaged sleeping bag. He put his can of beer on the roof and got in, stretching out on his back. Above, through the narrow window, he saw the twisted black interstices of the trees against the thick clusters of the stars, and the fancy struck him that he had fallen from above and had lodged in the narrow part of an hourglass and that he was looking down at billions of sparkling grains that rested on the bottom, below him; that he would eventually dislodge and join the others and become fixed, somehow, in the bottom of the night. Bach rolled over him, expressed in melancholy organ music, come from distant Delta, and Howard thought, "Suppose I should let time drift away without a struggle?" Then he heard the rowboat bumping against the shore, the clanking of oars and oarlocks, not twenty feet off in the gloom, and Ginger calling for Laura to be careful.

"Mommy, here's Daddy, in a little house."

As Ginger came upon him he was getting to his feet. "Just trying it out," he said.

"How is it?"

"Cozy. How did you know where I was?"

"A chain smoker like you? In this dark? Listen, Howard, you're just being dramatic. Melodramatic. It's nothing to fail. Everybody fails, but they keep trying. Besides, you haven't really failed yet."

"I've never succeeded. At anything. A failure since birth when I made my mother suffer, as she's told me often enough. A thousand hours in labor. Ten thousand! I didn't want to be born. I didn't like her milk. I don't like anything. Everything eats everything. Any God who would create such a place must be a monster. Everything reeks of pain and death."

"If you write that, nobody will read it. And think of Laura and the new baby coming now. You're drunk. You've got to wean yourself."

"It's deep pain."

"A melancholy romantic—is that it, Shelley?"

"Shelley drowned. That's not so bad. But Keats! I prefer Keats.

> I lie in the darkness and listen into silence
> sometimes, outside the stream of time
> where life hums and burns with its moths and flames,
> its mechanical tropisms of desire and death;
> I listen to the silent voice of the nightingale
> with my friend Keats, the dead boy, the poet."

"But he was tubercular, Howard, not just peculiar!"

"Ho, ho! Thank you for appreciating my poem."

"You have a child of your own to think of and another coming. Don't forget, just because I don't show yet, I'm pregnant." Her voice seemed disembodied in the darkness.

"I don't think I'm strong enough to lift all that weight," he said. Then he smiled a rueful little smile and said, "Echo to Narcissus, but your feet still crunch the leaves, my heavy-with-child." He looked for Laura, silhouetted, for an instant, in the moonlight, but flashing in and out of view. Now she was crawling out of Beta with the blanket wrapped around her, a ball of childish, female energy.

"Where's Porter and Cecily?"

"They're still at Delta. Can't you hear? Isn't it something, having an organ up here in the woods?"

"But he's stopped playing."

"Having a drink, probably. Your charade, your anatomy of melancholy, didn't work. We all just kept on having fun after you left. Porter shrugged and said, 'Well, he's a poet.' You can't bring everybody else down with you, you know."

"But you came looking."

"You're drunk. I was half afraid you'd drown, like Shelley—quite unintentionally—or not."

"Not what?"

"Not unintentionally; you've got us all worried."

"Let's go pick them up in the boat."

They rowed along the bank of the lake—easier than climbing through the dark woods.

They returned to Alpha, where Howard filled a jar with Porter's homemade wine and, at Ginger's insistence, put on a life-preserver, for he could not swim; then they groped their way through the moonlit gloom down to the dock and pushed off out on the lake. The moon broke through the glowing clouds full as the plunging back of a white elephant and shown on the lake in broken, swaying pieces. In front of the patched black and moon-drenched blue of the night sky there was a dense beribboning of frosty stars.

"It's a Van Gogh heaven," Ginger said.

Howard pulled at the oars, sending the boat rapidly out into deep water, very deep. It was the thought of freedom, of relief. But he wasn't going in the right direction. One of the oars was longer than the other and the boat kept drifting sideways, toward the middle of the lake. The deep, dark pool. At first he thought his coordination was off, having drunk so much. "Why can't I make this boat go straight?" Then he realized what was wrong and managed by compensation to get the boat back in, toward shore. Porter had begun to play again and the lake was flooded with the organ's oceanic voice. "A little night music," he said.

"Oh, Howard," Ginger said, "it's so beautiful up here. I wish we never had to go back to New York."

"So do I. Back to the bullshit world."

His hateful novel, so filled with the pain, real and imagined, of a lifetime, had been rejected, and no wonder, he thought, no wonder. Who would want to read such a shapeless agony of a thing? And yet it was the shame of failing, of failing, of coming from nothing, from less than nothing, from an ugly childhood spent with drunken and irresponsible parents, with humiliation at every turn, at school, in the streets, at home, which was no home, ever, but demon basements criss-crossed with pipes, rat-sat-upon; of coming from nothing and describing it as accurately as one could, and then going back to nothing with it, another unwanted item, another way for God to reject his life, him, thank you, thank you, your majestic cruelty, and to hell with all!

Ginger called from the dock at Delta for Porter and Cecily to come out for the ride back to Alpha.

Porter's father was an Episcopal Bishop. Cecily's father was a Port Authority lawyer. Even Ginger's father was middle-class, acceptable. But Howard remained the downstart son of a downstart father; a thief, a liar, and a drunkard, that man. Even Howard's grandfather had married a rich woman and gambled her wealth away. His mother was a moral idiot from a family of moral idiots. He felt sorry for little Laura, possessing such genes. Guilt, shame, humiliation rocked him. His drunken blood coursed through him bearing the dagger of the mind. He felt cut up and bleeding inside. But how could anyone ever know? And who should care? God didn't. God wasn't. God couldn't be—be God and be evil. For that was the world and the world said No.

Cecily came alone. "Porter wants to walk back. He's got a flashlight. But it's still too dark for me," she said. "Push off, Captain!" And back out onto the brimming lake went the boat, four aboard, the two women, the child, and Howard. "They went to sea in a sieve, they did," said Howard, cueing Laura.

"In a sieve they went to sea," she cried.

"Far and few, far and few. . ." said Howard.

"Are the lands where the Jumblies live!"

"Their heads are green," said Howard, stopping to drink wine from his jar.

"And their hands are blue. . ." Laura cried.

"And they went to sea in a sieve," Ginger finished.

"And there's the Dong with the Luminous Nose!" Cecily said, pointing toward the woods, where Porter was making his way along the dark shore, between Delta and Gamma, his flashlight bouncing before him.

"A little wobbly," said Cecily, "after an evening of beer and Bach."

"It's true, Daddy, Daddy," Laura shouted. "It's the Dong! Daddy, look! He's real!"

"The Dong with the luminous nose, the love-sick Dong," said Howard.

Next morning after breakfast they went for a walk in the woods, which rose steeply, with trees standing in uneven tiers, higher and higher, and Howard could almost see them, growing beneath the water, lower and lower, into the murkiness, the blackness, as if there were no bottom to the lake at all, the valley of drowning darkness.

Here they were in the Laurentian mountains. What were they doing up here in paradise, anyway? He should be back in New York, doing something about his failed novel, not vacationing in Canada with a couple of spoiled rich kids who had never had a problem in their lives. But that wasn't fair, either. They were friends. But what did that mean to him? Cut no ice.

And he and Ginger couldn't afford to spend money like this. Ginger had won the money on a television quiz show, of all things, and he had been able to watch the show in the market research office where he worked. She had been quite good, quite enterprising, winning while he was losing. New York, Montreal, the mountains, and the deep bottom of the lake—what did it all mean?

Now he brought up the rear, out of shape from offices and drinking, puffing and panting in an effort to keep the others in view. Some way ahead of him he could see Ginger, lifting herself by the low branches of the trees, pulling herself up the steep embankment. Ahead of Ginger was Cecily, who held Laura's hand, and Porter led the way, like an Indian scout, somehow marvelously untouched by all the drinking they had been doing.

When Howard caught up with them, the others were standing at the edge of a place where the bank dropped sharply for about a hundred feet, and where could be seen the whole lake, small now and far below. Porter jumped up and down, smashing puffball mushrooms for Laura's delight and edification, Howard supposed, for Porter taught at a private school in New York. He claimed he would be its headmaster by the time he was thirty. Howard believed him. Hell's bells, Porter could converse in Latin!

Cecily showed Laura a large, spreading shelf mushroom with an underside so smooth and velvety that a very clear drawing could be made on it with a small stick or twig.

"This is what a unicorn looks like," Cecily said, handing the mushroom to Laura. "And unicorns can only be captured by little girls like you. They'll come and put their pretty heads in your lap."

"And it has a horn like that?"

"Yes—and I think I see one now!"

"Where? Where?"

Cecily pointed through the trees. "There," she said. "But oh—he's gone now. Vanished."

They climbed on, among poplars and mossy elms, slipping and sliding on the thick matting of ancient gray leaves that lay moldering, bat-winged ashes; through nettles that brought quickly disappearing red blotches to their hands; and over slippery, green, moss-covered rocks that crouched like ancient immoveable animals, petrified life; and finally back down to Alpha, Laura crying out at the sight of numerous unicorns, scurrying among the trees like shy deer.

The others had lunch. Howard was still unable to eat, though the climb had done him some good. The beer tasted better now, and he drank some of the homemade wine, bottled by the Bishop, and soon his hangover had partially metamorphosed into the mild safety of a glow. And after lunch they took the boat and the canoe and went out into the middle of the lake to the great domed rock the Bishop had named Whalehead. There they lay on the rock, sunning, Howard sipping wine from his jar and watching Porter skim pebbles off the water.

"Tell me a story about a unicorn, Daddy."

"Well . . ."

"Yes?" Laura looked up at him, expectant.

"Once there was a unicorn," Howard improvised, "who only had an ice cream horn . . ."

"Yes? Yes?"

"It melted in the sun one day . . . and . . ."

"What, Daddy? What?"

"And the poor unicorn passed away."

"That's cute, Howard," Cecily said, laughing.

"What do you mean that he passed away, Daddy?"

"Oh, he melted away, honey, from the horn down."

"Oh," said Laura, knitting her brow, "that's sad!"

"The Bishop thinks you're a very good poet, Howard, but he disagrees with your theodicy. He says you don't look around at the joys and beauties of life enough. He respects you, though—very much."

"It's the habit of a lifetime—not looking at the good side. I'm tired of it, myself."

"Gloomy Gus," said Ginger. She was sunbathing, face up, an arm across her eyes. Howard had thought she was dozing. She was the good side of life, the beautiful side, she and Laura. They were the good side, and he was part of it, now, wasn't he? They loved him, even if his own mother and father hadn't, didn't.

Cecily shrieked, jumping up, pointing at Howard's knee, and Howard looked to see what he thought was a sparrow leave his knee and fly off in a crazy elongated spiral over the lake, into the trees.

"It was a bat, Howard!" Cecily said. "It was right on your knee."

Porter laughed. "It must have been asleep in that crack," he said. "You probably woke it when you sat there."

"Oh, I *hate* them," Cecily said.

"They're harmless," Porter said. "Some of them carry rabies, though. That's the only danger. He didn't bite you, did he?"

"No, no, he just flew off," Howard said. "No harm done." He quickly drained the remaining wine from his jar.

"Let's make artesian divers," Porter said, turning to Howard. "Like this: We put some water in those empty wine bottles on the porch and plug the tops with something and throw them up in the air and into the lake. We keep filling them a little more each time until one goes all the way to the bottom and sticks. It's a question of fine-tuning. I win, if yours stays down and mine comes up."

"Mine will be the first to drown," said Howard.

"Oh, Howard," said Ginger, "don't be so negative."

"All aboard!" Porter cried.

After depositing Ginger and Laura on shore, and picking up a case of empty wine bottles, Porter and Cecily took the canoe, Howard the rowboat, and in the middle of the lake, directly across from Alpha, they began sinking the divers. At first the bottles weren't filled enough to hold them down even for a few seconds, but soon they had reached the necessary refinement and the divers went down and remained below surface for some time, then one or the other of them would pop up, jumping out of the water.

The game was carried on by adding more water and sending them back down, whether to return or not no one could know. Howard thought it a silly, senseless game, but then what wasn't? And Cecily and Porter seemed to think it great fun.

Howard took a drink from his renewed supply of wine and pitched his diver high into the air. It smacked the water. He pulled at the oars until he came to the spot where the diver had hit, and there it was, magnified to look as if it were just below the surface. He watched the bottle, soon a mere fleck of light, scarcely distinguishable from the countless other flecks that were caught momentarily by the sun-drenched surface before they rayed down and diminished in darkness.

"He's through," Howard thought, as the boat rocked gently. "He can't take anymore."

The rowboat sank deeply on one side with his over-leaning, his peering. It floated gently sideways through water that rippled with a sound like tiny, muffled bells.

Darkling I listen; and, for many a time
I have been half in love with easeful Death,
Called him soft names in many a mused rhyme,
To take into the air my quiet breath . . .

The words ran over and over through Howard's mind, transporting him from the lake, the sky, to the beckoning darkness below. His breath came in short light whispers. Suddenly his elbow slipped off the side and the boat rocked violently, then steadied. He caught his breath. He had drifted down as far as Delta. He was nowhere near where the diver had gone down. He regained his bearing. Cecily and Porter sat off at a great, wavering distance, in the canoe. Ginger and Laura, even farther, smaller, on the shore. All of them were waving to him, smiling at him, waving to him. He belonged to these good, lost human beings. They needed him, too. There was green and gold everywhere. Even the glittering water was gold. The water was gold.

He took a cigarette from a pack, lit it, placed it between his teeth, and pulled hard at the unmatched oars. The boat angled about, spreading in its wake two curved waves in different directions. Then he saw his diver break from the water, high, shining, some distance ahead.

GHOSTS, GO HOME!

O lost and by the wind grieved,
ghost, come back again.
—Thomas Wolfe

. . . my blind left eye don't stop me I swivel quick around then get ahead back at the panorama striped down and then back up the hill to any future peak greened brown black cut through white striped like up the leg on a uniform the wind don't wall me my aerodynamics they'd lift my license for my eye full of sugar but I still drink that VA doctor's lower'n fish shit no beer no way but I drink Lite test my blood take my insulin I eat right mostly but my Drake's cakes I'm thirty-three feet back sixty-six long times to here always dreamed of motorhoming free to be you and me Maxine's you she sips at that beer stares through the wraparound like she's watching home movies and shoots bytes at me like look there did you see that she's frightened at being sixty next week I told her look at me—you plus six and I'm still steering still truckin' but I never was a trucker was a kid a soldier a vet a cop and a guard at Disney's that was my whole damned life that back there behind me on the road but it comes along with me in my sugar-eye my shotup shoulder from War Two my skin cancer from standing all those years in the sun reflecting off tarmac and parked cars at Disney World Max says look Jersey plates she says Joisey we started out in Jersey we fell in love haven't slept together in years Max thinks I'm not well interested but it's the sugar I don't tell nobody not even her not especially her suppose she knew I couldn't what kind of man would she think look she says back in back her mother sees it too I don't know what it is must be on my blind side but I don't say no way I let them know I'm blind as a blackboard over there not hurtling along at eighty they'd piss their beer you got to hold to your lane the old lady's nearly ninety but full of it not only beer either if you know look Max says shut up Max but I don't say it I don't listen about Alabama moons Georgia peaches glorious Asheville leaves I talk to myself my only friend they suck me in like black holes the old lady and Max everything goes into them nothing out toward me did I believe in love I've stopped laughing even I've been driving too long

I see us off the edge of a cliff if I don't keep him awake old man hunched up at the wheel was he my hero I think there's something wrong with his eyes now the way he jerks around to see I've noticed I ride not swiveled in a bucket by a tilted instrument pod but sometimes behind him astraddle his first Harley his long blond hair snapping in my eyes no helmets my fingers feeling in the deep holes through his shoulder and his ribs where the sniper's bullet drilled through he died he said and came alive again on a table in England I still wore his white dress shirt hanging out over my rolled-up blue jeans shiny pennies in my loafers Frank Sinatra made me scream Elvis my one daughter Buddy's blonde princess the Dead my grandson nobody sings anymore all back there somewhere with my mother boozed up at ninety a Depression-made cheapskate sipping cheap port and a hundred thousand in the bank how did we get here

where are we going why must I come Harry could save me clever with life how left-handed he mangled his right hand in the leather machine made them think he was right-handed more compensation at last a little house and money in the bank and I got us out of Jersey like war in the project then the Sixties the long hot summers bullets through the windows down to Max and Buddy in Orlando to my little house Harry why must I travel with them the youngsters even are old but Harry's gone crazy at the end fighting in the trenches again Argonne Belleau Wood gone on the road behind us dead and buried in Orlando buried and lost his grave lost we are going to sue I have no place to put flowers no place to talk to him anymore they lost my Harry tough leather guy from Brooklyn tough guy so sweet once poor old crazy man gone back to the trenches back to Pershing mustardgas and Belleau Wood another world so far away to his grave at ninety-five I don't want cable only my one soap-opera station only my wine don't even want life to come back what is the wind Star stories say some of us are aliens supermarket tabloids Maxine calls them and tries to make me think they print lies sometimes I think Buddy and maybe even Maxine too I bore her but maybe pod people have taken over her body like that old movie maybe she isn't Maxine at all she doesn't act like Maxine I could have a baby too like the hundred year old woman in Australia it would kill me at ninety they must eat something yogurt like those Russians who live forever aliens too and the little girl no older than smaller than who had quadruplets by a tom cat all of them born with whiskers the pictures were right there I saw them whiskers and pointed ears and long tails I saw them what is that going by where are they taking me

"Good Housekeeping" said the kitchen was the warm womb of the colonial home and early-American women would stand at the hearth watching the turkey turn as they pumped up the flames packing sandwiches for an airline ain't exactly the big time but we made it Buddy and I paid off the

American dream for his bedroom and my bedroom and the alligators down on the lawn to the rock seawall wanting sun what's life put the rocks back put back build up fall put back two slices Wonder Bread one slice waterpumped ham mayo mustard my long thin fingers all little silver scars I'm nobody what did I deserve not Buddy and my mother anyway sixty ain't the end yet not even with all my loose belly skin and stupid strokefoot dragging when I'm tired like Buddy on Omaha Beach but I got it right through the head like being brain-shot and nine weeks in the hospital stealing our money there she is sipping her wine at ninety defying nature and three out of five of us kids with strokes always demanding maybe she gave us the strokes but nobody's dead yet they say we are all lucky so that's what luck is not being dead a case could be made

driving into the dusk is like driving into a dream better hit the lights that big cluster of stars down there I aim my good eye on ahead now in the dusk it gets tricky but I don't let Max know extreme macular degeneration sugar-induced doc says then he says you got varicose veins in your eye laser beams he says burn 'em out so I see blue for a week from the dye and the blue fades to gray and that's it my credit's good social security veteran's pension Disney retirement I'm a triple dipper plus equity in the house poor boy makes good I'm driving fifty thousand dollars across America like I started out with anything but a piano-teaching widowed mother like I had a chance in life I play my own tapes me at the organ singing Willy Nelson songs "On the Road Again" Max hates my music she's jealous but says I could of made a living at it could of but couldn't take the joints composed some myself guitar piano organ my tape plays "King of the Road" my plates say NO MORTGAGE NO BOSS NO JOB NO WORRIES I'M RETIRED twenty years standing in the sun eating Twinkies skin cancer Harry thought Max could do better *he* never had a home like ours right on the gators' water *he'd* say he never had alligators on his lawn either only stinkbugs in his old palm tree sometimes I miss fighting with him him on the Kaiser me on Hitler who was worse all ancient history even the Commies are dead nothing left for Freedom to fight and the world moves moves into the next century away from us what we did and needed it'll all be computers and new people no more like us we're dinosaurs old people but we move and we take our houses with us like hermit crabs we circle Asheville in leaves we land at Normandy not ten minutes in and all my bones break until I wake up on the table in England purple heart silver star I remember the sea swashing puffs of smoke *our flag it still stands* yesterday's news who cares Max is sarcastic once she was proud I can't help it Max it's the sugar sugar

. . . who betrayed me so many times with his Harley with somebody else's legs around him fingers in his wounds hot stuff and joins the police to wear his beautiful blue uniform and ride his police cycle with his blond hair fluffed all around his blue visored hat and me pregnant alone with his blonde love in my belly stud making a fool of his wife making a fool of his life with nogood burgling cops only Orlando left for us thank the chief who saved us and that was when I began when I began I began began to be old

Maxine looks like me at sixty you could compare her to a picture of me then O Harry do you remember where are we North Carolina why are we here climbing this mountain full of beautiful leaves is that heaven up there what is that up there a jetstream a flying saucer why don't we just stay home where I know where things are they don't think about me how I can't see how I wish Harry were here how he was when he was young so neat courtly so kind and sweet not like at the end afraid of the Hun hiding under the table gone crazy old man with old-timers disease it was all there again for him no time had happened no me no all that life all wiped out and he was there again and it made me wonder if we aren't all just here or there or where are we

Asheville we pack it in at Nashville Max and the old lady won't go to the Grand Ole Opry so I'll leave them to themselves I'll go like I always said I would could hear it in Jersey when I was a kid could hear it all over the country Hank Williams Minnie Pearl Tex Ritter Hillbilly Heaven a southern yankee *I never get enough of that wonderful stuff* Max says we should of gone the other route to Memphis first Graceland Elvis can wait I say but it turns out to be Hank Williams Junior and Rockabilly not like I dreamed of it glitz and bang even a vet can yearn for the old sweetstuff Junior's daddy the original Hank the real thing the lyrics were in a language I could understand we fought the wars and longed for love they march for peace and seem to hate like I'm still waiting for the fat lady to sing President Truman even introduced Kate Smith to the Queen as "America" *Oh beautiful for spacious skies* but the Opry's like the rest of it now maybe we should try Dollyland at Pigeon Forge no Max wouldn't like it because

angels come to our door but Buddy won't let them in do you know these are the last days not if you have something spiritual it's on Earth he was sent by the God of Love that's why Graceland is a church even if it's like they say that his body ate twenty Big Macs a day his soul had to live on Earth didn't it had to eat so Buddy's blonde daughter tells me my daughter too but more his blonde like him now nearly bald not her him not dark like me well gray but if Elvis could bring happiness then he is a god he's one of those aliens Max he was sent here to sing and bring love they say Graceland is more beautiful than Heaven that it's all blue like the sky with no clouds no thunderbooms and tin-roof rain clatter where are we

like when Buddy grinds his choppers he is eating us up in his sleep our night war like our day war cannibal shoved our beds apart into separate rooms trumpets saxophones trombones Buddy names my snoring while he grinds on and her crazy on the convertible back there all night coughs and chatters in her sleep about chicken wing prices it's like a gone-nuts orchestra *OOMPA OOMPA OOMPA CLICKETY-CLICK BLAH BLAH* his teeth telling how much he hates his life at different times broken uppers and lowers life that never did what he wanted it to do we rocked that motorpark in Nashville hooked up Winnebago nearly laughed itself free electric lines tore out as it rolled over on its side and later shaking with screaming Mama and I had sucked the city of any last drop of Southern Comfort Buddy never came back from the Opry till it was dying out drunk himself from shit-kicking with urban cowboys I told him his sugar'll kill him he sleeps grinding his life like steak into hamburger I'm his life what's life Mama refuses to die until we do gray and stroked and sugared and beer'd under but how could we leave her at home who'd watch her nobody'll take her in if we go she has to go won't go to nursing home no way you know no how and I don't mean not to go go go before I die thank GOD for Winnebagos next stopover next postcard P.S. life's a war and you can't give up love Max at sixty

heaven is a place like Graceland they say Elvis's daughter owns it now she's the spitting image spitting image listen Max at least the foreigners don't own Graceland like they do everything else it ain't true that we don't work as hard as the Japs but the unions Max I never did trust the unions you think like a scab-cop my father was a union man Buddy her father was a union man Harry was always a good union man and a good Democrat if they're good for anything the aliens'll be UNION if I didn't belong to a union do you think they'd of paid me so much for making lousy sandwiches did you get enough sleep we should of gone to Graceland first read a "Reader's Digest" article once first it was the farmlife held us to place then industry mills and trading and later the big factories up north made cities centers now no more anyone anywhere now the computers no more fixed life no more unions no more democrats no more stay put go go go like the damned beatniks hippies used to do on the road in the sky a whole corporation inside your portable computer workforce anywhere regions don't mean nothing cities countries *my country 'tis of thee* I'm caught between the old lady back there and my grandson he'll be part of it the brave new world he said college boy and his kids won't even know what we were can't you just see it grandpa no boundaries no borders even space the moon Mars business everywhere signals flying through the air caught between times becoming part of it losing it at the same time with my sugar walking down the street I never noticed how sweet beer is injections they'll be able to fix that too grandpa and the whole world and even space will become AMERICA

you look at your mother and you think how could I have come out of that sixty years ago HAPPY BIRTHDAY Max it's a chorus of whiskey-cracked voices a duo of dead and gone ghosts calling back over their shoulders it's bye-bye Maxine you're as good as dead with your mastectomied pumped-up plastic tits what'd you need them for for *him* could of caused the stroke I'm told but then why my brother and sister stroked out too my face I had burned with acid and scraped for him forty years ago acne pits from her tea and cheap day-old cake to stuff us just before supper all of us faces like burned-red moons from her brother-can-you-spare-a-dime cheap Depression soul the old man back from Belleau Wood mustard gas and the formaldehyde stink of the tannery the whole goddamned century's been a war I could live to see the end of it no more goddamned Twentieth Century now we fight each other we can't stop fighting we're like three hairy-assed Marines landing on each other's beaches HAPPY BIRTHDAY Maxine Christ he kissed me breath like death blow out my candle if I could I'd blow them out of the Winnebago and get my wish a little time on earth alone a little life before I die

Max was always tough even as a little girl she always fought her father'd have to drag her off from a fight but he was proud my Max don't take no shit he said we had to be tough Jersey we all glow in the dark better than hard cold and cheap we had nothin' but trouble like the plague Nineteen-Nineteen she says the doughboys brought the influenza back from Europe all those displaced persons my best girlfriend died of it everybody was dying you're too young to know good to be too young for some things why do you think God does it screw that God helps them who help themselves Buddy he likes that one damned Republican but he's right it's like Elvis a success a blond guy with black hair and a cape God loves us all Max He's sending them to help us well He's got a damned funny way of showing it your granddaughter says He sent Elvis or is it Elvis sent her *I* told her he came in on a saucer they'll all be here soon Buddy singing playing the organ he installed *coming in on a wing and a prayer* his feet pumping he loves to show off he says Harry was just a leather worker says my mother taught piano class will tell your people don't have no class no way then it's a Donnybrook in the musical world

in heaven this couldn't of happened if Max would spell me I'd go back and get drunk with the old lady sit in my *Seat w/Telescoping Pedestal* and stare at her until I could see inside her BRAIN but Max won't spell me won't drive no way no how just sucks in sixpacks and farts at speed bumps I'm mustard gassed like Harry at Belleau Wood turn on the BTU's she says watch out open the vents here comes Max but she admits it was damned embarrassing we got the Arizona state troopers all over us here's the old lady telling the pump jockey at our time of life we want full service telling him I'M BEING KIDNAPPED BY ALIENS I have a lovely home in Orlando they're forcing me to go with them they want my money a hundred thousand dollars it belongs to Harry he earned it with the wrong hand call the police help help it takes some explaining but I tell them me I'm an ex-cop look I say but they got me and Max over a car hood if I had one of those BIG FOOT trucks I'd drive right over top of this traffic jam crushing cars like an angry giant that's why everybody loves Big Foot I look at the cops and twirl my finger in a circle at my temple nuts the both of them I say they feel sorry for me and because I'm an ex-cop

get real Buddy do you think God's in California or in the Painted Desert or the Petrified Forest I want to see the first Disney place is all Max is *mad* like Mel great roadman people say it's the end of America from the coast there on it's out forever and the sea climbs into the sky Buddy it's your music sometimes you sound like some godawful poet song of the open road Max there's good trucker songs Max trucker poets cowboy poets you're ignorant Max don't start Buddy don't start I tell you what Buddy Vegas is God you get a bucketful of change and pull handles until something good happens gangsters built Vegas Max gangsters built everything Buddy Bugsy Siegel is God and Vegas is heaven for shame Maxine what do you know Mama it's all a chance and to hell with your aliens can't you see saucers Maxine clouds Mama we're in the mountains Sierra Nevadas Mama

I'm not *your* mother I'm hers maybe and the white bombs of love like the Star says it's Elvis in his saucer lots of Elvises because this is the end of time they have big dark eyes and sideburns down to here real smooth cheeks and they wear wonderful jumpsuits with colors like Las Vegas that night the first or second so it was stacks of colors and everything blinking they wear clothes like that with glittery things hanging down from their sleeves I was a little girl when Dreamland burned down my mother your grand-mother Maxine said you could see Dreamland burning from Jersey I had been to Coney Island I had been to Dreamland I'm sure I saw Vesuvius erupt and a great naval battle where New York was bombarded by foreign ships and then an American admiral went out and defeated all of them you see children it is all a dream and you keep waking up to some-thing new we aren't really here at all we are here and some-where else at the same time in Dreamland *Meet me tonight in Dreamland under the silvery moon* my mother used to play that one Mama I am not your mother don't call me Mama you're alone in the world Harry never liked you motorcycle-head he called you Maxine's got me if she is Maxine of course I'm Maxine Christ of course white bombs SNOW where are we Maxine if I smashed this pedal down down hill I saw a movie once about a wagon train full of people heading west on Donner tha's it the Donner party they were going over these very mountains they were up here high like this and there was a blizzard and they got caught and they couldn't get down out of it blizzard starved and they began to eat each other don't look at me Buddy the saucers will save us they'll snatch us up into Graceland they can do anything they can make us fly can they take us back to where they came from is it a musical place of course it's a musical place Elvis is King yeah Graceland is the real true blue heaven beyond the cheap chicken wings of the world Mama beyond the world Maxine or whoever you are Buddy my ears just popped we're climbing Max it's getting dark Buddy you better stop can't stop on the highway some articulated eighteenwheeler some BIG FOOT come behind us no visibility now I nail my one good eye to the white-dark wraparound like one big cataract faint red lights turning off ahead now nothing down there's a turn somewhere down there I hit the gas down hard to the floor it's dark and white like being wrapped in ermine if we weren't doing eighty ninety a hundred it's like a toboggan like the OLYMPICS SWOOSH SWOOSH and we're out off in SPACE the cold moon and stars ahead I push my *WING-EXTENDER* BUTTON and now it's STAR TREK THE PANORAMA OF SPACE I can see through the thick clusters of stars ahead there deep GOD'S BRIGHT MUSICAL CASTLE but the saucers hold us floating in air HIGH OVER GRACELAND you can see the lights I told them I told them and THOUSANDS and THOUSANDS of GOLDEN COINS COME GLITTERING CRASHING OUT . . . *so death is luck says Maxine you can take your freaking luck and shove it Mama says it was the aliens who helped us hundreds of flying saucers piloted by Elvises in sequined pod suits they lifted us off the cliff I told you they would I told you she's nuts Buddy we're dead right now dead and floating away Max dispersing smoke and just when I thought I was going to heaven to God's bright musical castle where I could play the organ play* Meet Me Tonight in Dreamland *for all the heavenly days of my death O.K. Buddy but what in hell do you think I'm travelling for we left the other goddamned Disney place three thousand miles back I want to get away from it all that's my heaven every place is the same Max every place is Disneyland now don't you start sniveling Mama but home is where the heart is my heart is with Harry in Orlando poor old Alzheimer man I loved him so much for God's sake we got all freaking bummed out I sent a card back home to tell how you've acted you son-of-a-bitch you killed us and I think you did it on purpose you think you can drive through space now Buddy still steering Max Maxine what Mama you children are enough to drive me out of my mind but the National Star and the Pod People keep me sane look at all that space can you fly this thing Buddy an American G.I. can do anything he has to do Mama Buddy sometimes you remind me of Harry why thanks Mama doughboys is what we called G.I.s in my day like you he came back full of holes but gassed in Belleau Wood beautiful name to be so horrible I know I don't tell you very much but now that I know we are all going to heaven together or somewhere well wherever the pod people take us I love you both we love you too Mama don't we Max O.K. so all us suckers love each other just keep this smoke floating Mama I think Maxine is blubbering up crocodile tears Buddy she's hard as a rock no Mama you should see her up here shut up Buddy she's had too much beer no I think the crash is just now sinking in on me but I'm not going to stop drinking my Lite I don't care if I'm dead you are dead Max we're all dead Buddy are you sure you can fly are you does smoke rise up from a fire and finally vanish in the sky I keep on truckin' like I always done Max through war and peace Mama our flag must still wave through hell and high water Max I could go on flying this big beautiful Winnebago with the eagle wing span of an Enola Gay forever across America back and forth across this great big God bless America country* FROM SEA TO SHINING SEA

REACHING THE TOP

I hired a press agent who was said to be tops. Don't ask how much she cost me, but I had to sell everything I had. I was tired of being a nonentity. No more would people say Oh, it's just him. Instead, they would say Wow, that's him, that's him for sure! Any old how, that's the way I looked at it. So I found myself facing down a newsstand and a copy of the *Daily Do*, and there I was, in five inch headlines over an eight by ten picture. The headline read: *HE IS LOOKING AT THE PAPER.* I looked around to see if anyone nearby recognized me from the photograph. No, nobody seemed to notice. Then my eye was caught by a *People Magazine* cover. I was on it. The caption read: *HE SEES HIMSELF.* Then the newsy pointed at me and yelled, Look, there he is! Now I noticed that every magazine and newspaper on the stand had my picture on its cover or front page. The captions and headlines all read things like, *HE'S LOOKING AT HIMSELF AGAIN*, and, *WHY IS HE LOOKING AT HIMSELF?* People had gathered to see what the newsy was yelling about. I ducked out of the crowd and ran down the street, feeling a strong sense of terror. I passed a store window where I appeared on television. It looked like a talk show. Yes, it was called What About Me? I saw that I was on billboards. My name was being written across the sky. I went home and discovered myself all over the Internet. There could hardly be a soul on Earth who didn't know me. My fame brought money and soon I was one of the richest men in the world, able at last to escape my nightmare by paying my press agent to keep me out of notice so that I could achieve a life of anonymity, a shadowy figure in a penthouse looking down on the newsstand many storeys below.

HAPPINESS

Happiness is but the occasional
episode in a general drama of pain.
—Thomas Hardy

When people hear of Howard Osborne's mother being over ninety and in such rosy good health and having so much charm and spirit, they can't imagine why he should look glum. They have had to put relatives in nursing homes, and feel heavy-hearted and guilty about it. But what they don't think of is that Howard was a child when Alice Osborne was young, and was a much more powerful black hole than she was later.

Alice had wavy-bobbed chestnut hair and reminded some people of the then popular movie star, Mary Astor; but Alice was half-blind and wore harlequin-shaped glasses. She was a small, buxom woman whose sudden unreasonable fits of temper lent her a frightful dynamism. She sucked in his kindergarten class, including the pretty young teacher, on his first day at school. *Whoosh!*

Howard didn't hear about black holes until many years later; but, when he did, he recognized a figurative aptness to Alice. She forced your attention while she drained your interest, and she seemed to gain energy by sucking the life out of everyone else. For example, in the manic self-involvement and general chaos of her mind, she forgot to pick him up on that first afternoon of kindergarten, and the teachers let him slip away in the end-of-day confusion.

Lost, frightened little Howard cried his way through the long strange streets of Newark until a nice lady wrapped in furs and with a long feather in her hat like Robin Hood, appeared beside him, took his hand, and discovered where he lived through clues from well-considered questions. He told her he remembered shiny brass rails that looked to him like curled-up horns that he'd seen in movies, siding the steps of the rooming house in which he lived, and the lady knew the house he meant. They found the third floor apartment and the indignant lady questioned Alice about what had happened, how she had managed to forget that her little boy was supposed to be picked up, but Alice's bobbing head sucked the words in as they emerged from the lady's mouth, then confounded the lady with chaotic blasts, and the lady left, troubled, and with a puzzle to consider, the same puzzle that troubled Howard for the rest of his life.

It was probably then that Howard began to understand that Alice was different from other people, and he was always afraid, after that, that with her strange eyes, Alice would suck him in, too, *whoosh*, just as she had the kindergarten teacher and the concerned lady with the feathered hat who had brought him home. He guessed that she had, at least some of him, over their long, odd relationship, because now in his middle years, so many parts of him were missing—his hair, and his teeth, for instance. Especially his teeth. He was famous for grinding the teeth out of his head. When he slept, the grinding could be heard all over the house. He attributed this tooth-grinding to insecurity in the knowledge that he had nobody to depend on but himself, that knowledge dating and growing from that first dark day at kindergarten.

Howard has a lemony, humorous turn of mind, and thinks he sees a secret joke on the world. He believes that

Alice suffered brain damage in a serious automobile accident she had had when young, and that it is this damaged brain to which the world responds.

Because her two ageing sisters, with whom she did not get along because of her bossiness and interference—as they explained to Howard, apologizing—would not have her, Howard had been taking care of the aggressive, if incompetent—in material terms, to say the least—Alice, since he was thirty, when his father, Robert Osborne, went up in smoke, *whoosh*! What else could he do? When Robert died in a fire, perchance, in the very same house that the lady with the feather had guided the five-year-old Howard to, decades before—the once shiny brass bannisters were later dented and bent, finally after the fire, melted and black; it had become a flop house to where old, broke, Robert had tried to escape Alice and had failed. He left Alice with nothing but Howard, and her power to suck everything in, her tremendous gravitational pull, weakened by time, but still too strong for Robert and too strong for Howard, as well.

He was unable to escape her, to pull himself out of orbit, free of her. He has been spinning madly about her event horizon ever since, like a tiny spacecraft attempting to pull away from the event horizon of the black hole, saving himself from being totally sucked in by sheer stiff-arm will power. Isn't a black hole the very image of mad self-involvement? Isn't it true that nothing comes out of it, only goes in? Sometimes Howard wonders how he could have been born. After a few drinks, Alice was fond of telling him, in her screeching-chalk-on-the-blackboard voice, that she had spent thirty-eight agonizing hours in labor, giving him life, only to be disappointed because she had wanted a daughter, a little doll to put in pretty pink dresses and bows. Even at birth, Howard could not escape her. The thirty-eight hours were her dark refusal to give him up to the world of light. Newborn Howard arrived with golden curls. Middle-aged Howard was already balding, the hair ripped from his head in patches as by a vacuum cleaner, deracinated, Hoovered away. Now he fears for his skull, which, when he touches it, feels suspiciously pointed, as if being stretched into a cone, drawn by the self-implosive power of one of the tiniest things in the universe. He wishes someone would take a picture of him, before his image is completely distorted, to remember him by, if anyone wants to remember him. He can't help thinking, as he listens and listens to Alice's endless negative monologue, that life is already a silvery, sad, and faded—and soon forgotten—photograph. But put me in a frame while I still seem a semblance of myself, and look at me once in a while, before we are all sucked into the black hole. Thus does Howard contemplate his life. *Whoosh*!

Old Howard was exhausted. The madly spinning black hole that he had spent his life trying to avoid being sucked into, was gone. His gyroscope wobbled to a near standstill. Howard, the realtor, had planned to take the profit from the house he had recently sold and put it together with the value of a lot, which he owned, next to their apartment house, and build for his ageing wife and his blossoming children, a beautiful little new house. But there would be a necessary interim. He wanted to wait until the season when the contractors had the least work, and he could get a good contractor at a good price. And now, drained, but relieved after Alice's death, there was time, a little chunk of time available. Time to think. It seemed that he hadn't had a moment to himself in many years, a moment to explore and discover, possibly, who he was. He asked his wife to give him five weeks of peace and quiet between these strenuous, heart-stressing events—let him relax and concentrate for five weeks on art—new watercolor paintings which he loved to do. Every day his breath was coming with more difficulty. She promised. No interruptions, no disturbances. A life of peace. I'll see to it, she said.

Howard had a long-niggling idea for a series of paintings—he had had a few local shows. In fact, his art work had been favorably written up and had garnered some local critical success. This, of a man who always felt that, if he could have made Alice understand what he loved in art and what he was doing in real estate for the family; stop making nasty comments about him that sucked his heart away; and how successfully he was doing everything, he could have influenced her to being more helpful to him, less critical, more considerate of his time and his peace of mind, before her bad tempered blood pressure imploded her one day and killed his dream of making her understand. *Whoosh!*

So he began painting again, after a long stressful period, freely following his bliss, as the mythologist Joseph Campbell had put it, and one afternoon he noticed a very strange sensation. What an odd feeling! He seemed to remember it from somewhere, but couldn't place it.

It was gentle, like the rivulets of a stream, but there were little bursts of jollity in it, just gentle little bursts of jollity, nothing very big, bubbles. There was a sense of freedom, like gliding over clouds on wings, a state of well-being; that feeling of well-being one has when one is young and healthy and has all the time in the world ahead; of pleasurable satisfaction, as when one has achieved a goal which has long eluded one's achievement. Mental blue skies.

Bliss? Comfort? Felicity? Delight? What was it? He felt something he rarely experienced—that he could trust his luck. His body, held in tension for years in fear of disaster, had unclenched itself. His jaw had stopped grinding. But he couldn't place the thing, or name it.

Later, he remembered sitting down, startled, now, by it, to think, to try to understand what he was feeling, this illusive, vaguely familiar sensation. Then as he sat there, gazing over his easel at the bright white walls, with their dancing shadows and sunny drifts, he had it. It was so simple, it had eluded him.

It was happiness.

Howard realized that the last time he had felt such a sensation must have been decades before. It was shocking, to realize how rarely he had been happy, how many times in all those years, he had not been worried sick, nervous, frightened. In all these years, these decades, he had never thought about it, about simply being happy. Don't let it go away, he prayed to the glad, dancing light on the walls. Don't let it stop!

The phone rang. He could hear its threatening vibrations, like a rattlesnake's rattle, through the pillows and blankets he had buried it in. He had to answer it. It might be the police, the hospital calling to tell him that his wife had been in an accident, or his children, the I.R.S. threatening an audit, a contractor making demands, or a voice from anywhere to report some fear come true. Another black hole. *Whoosh!* It brought back a flood of interrupted moments of concentration, broken thoughts, stifled speech, a veritable tidal wave of years that threatened to engulf him with an awful drenching vividness. Paradise lost again! The sun darkened on his white walls turning them gray . . . the dancing shadows faded . . . happiness? What? He was unaware that tears formed in his eyes and ran down his cheeks. His body shook in a kind of St. Vitus dance. He couldn't control it.

Suddenly he couldn't breathe. He gasped for breath and his heart seemed to vanish from his chest. He struggled to breathe while he poured a vodka. Several shots later, he was finally able to catch his breath. But he was frightened.

What was that, hyperventilation? The breathless feeling came and went, came and went. But he mustn't let this chance to paint his beautiful roses vanish. God, he hadn't had a chance to think in years! He had failed again.

Then he had complete heart failure.

Several weeks later, on his first trip to the doctor after being released from the hospital, the doctor told him what was what.

"Stop smoking. Stop drinking. Your blood pressure was so high your heart couldn't beat. We have that under control now."

"What caused it?"

"There are other causes, but you don't have them. In my opinion, the main thing that causes primary hypertension is prolonged stress. You must learn to be happy," the doctor said, without a trace of irony.

Since then, Howard carries on, trying to live up to his responsibilities, which are fewer now, with everyone but his wife gone, and tries to paint the roses at his front door, waiting for what may come. *Whoosh!*

THE NEW GREEN CARPET

The old brown carpet and liner were ripped up and thrown out, the new green carpeting laid by an expert from the store. The man owed the store a good deal of money, but he would pay the store in time. What counted was that he had a beautiful new floor to look at. He vacuumed the new carpet every day, taking great pleasure in its neat greenness. It reminded him of a golf course lawn. Just for fun, he got out his putter and putted a few balls into a paper cup. In his house, everything was smooth.

Now one night the man vacuumed his new green carpet and went to bed feeling very good about life, feeling really quite satisfied with things. But when he woke in the morning, he discovered that his carpet had grown into tall meadow grass, and he felt water between his toes as he waded through to the bathroom. Why, the nap of the carpet must have grown at least a foot during the night. Had last night's thunderstorm sent water in under the door, water that triggered this outlandish growth? Each of his children, a boy and a girl, had a room, but they were not in their beds. The carpet-grass was growing even as he waded about the house, and now it was up to his shoulders.

"Children, children, where are you?" he called. Here and there, in the livingroom and in the dining room, he plunged his hands into the tall grass and separated it in hope of finding his children. The grass had reached the ceiling and had turned back down and become vines, so that he felt that he was in a rain forest. Then it occurred to him that there might be snakes in all of this wetland, snakes and even alligators, who could say? Had his children been eaten by them?

He groped his way back to his bedroom and found his wife. "Come with me and help me find our children," he said.

"I told you not to buy this new green carpet, didn't I?"

"Yes," he said, for he had always been a man who was willing to admit to his mistakes, "you were quite right."

"The house is filled with mosquitoes," said his wife, slapping herself in the face.

"Watch out," said the man. "That's a boa constrictor." The man reached in the giant snake's mouth and pulled forth one of his children, the little girl.

"Thank you, Daddy," she said.

"Where is your brother?" he asked her.

"He's floating in the dining room," she said. So the man and his wife and his daughter waded into the dining room, where they found the little boy floating on his back.

"It's fun," said the little boy.

"No, it isn't," said the mother.

"Don't make a big deal out of this," said the man to his wife, "it'll all be paid off in five years."

COPPERHEADS

The New York Draft Riots

Vanish these walls, vanish this wealth, with visionary eyes that see back to hot July 1863. Vanish where wealth shines shopping on Fifth Avenue, five minutes from the lion-braced library, where I turn down my book. Vanish these great, gray walls, to see when this mirage was another, of a white-winged building housing motherless humanity. Try to see out of the eyes of two hundred frightened black orphans and their saviors, or, better, the eyes of one little girl under her bed, who is to be beaten to sleep and burned alive. They come now, the first, malignant rumble of mobs is heard. A giant, bearing a huge American flag, appears. Ten thousand men and women follow. They shout: *NO DRAFT*; shout: *KILL THE NIGGERS*! One mob of ten thousand, among many mobs, one mad mob, is coming; Copperheads coming; but Mary doesn't know what they are. Snakes, she is told; and, people like snakes. Snakes? What does it mean? But behind them the sky is red, as if the sun had set in broad day, as if it had hit the earth and bounced back to the sky in cones of flame, like upward teeth, serrating the downward, hot blue. The fireworks for the Fourth, a week before, had shaken her. Looking everywhere, she saw no arms to hold her. *BOOM BOOM!* Now again—*BOOM BOOM!* But this is wilder, worse. She caps her ears, her eyes rolling for a mother, while the giant bearing Old Glory juts his lantern jaw toward the white-winged building where she hides terror in tears, holding her braided, ribboned head as, between her ten-year-old fingers, distorted clangor of malignant mob-voice penetrates with curses and screams of coves and harpies, liquored-up looters, drink-mad, blood-mouthed molls, ill-wind-shifted, now, toward Mary in the white-winged Colored Orphan Asylum on Fifth Avenue, the ghost-building, inside tall wealth, that I can reach in five minutes from this great, gray library, close my book and walk out into the Fifth Avenue festival of limousines and be inside of its smoldering, ectoplasmic doors with the orphan children, who are always poorest, with Mary, who hides under her bed, her eyes spraying terror, shutting her ears to the Fourth of July or, now, a week later, to the flag-bearing giant leading a mob through the present affluent Fifth Avenue shoppers to *BOOM BOOM KILL THE NIGGERS NO DRAFT KILL*, outside the library window on Fifth Avenue, inside of, behind, through, the tremendous modern traffic stalled at red, frustrated, Manhattan-honking. *KILL!* Mary sees feet, fast feet. She doesn't understand that the children are being herded out to safety, to Blackwell's Island on the East River. Mary sees feet scurry by her bed, sees a watery world, like one submerged, when she looks out. Then, above her bed, something huge and malignant appears, something too big. An evil thing! She will not come out from under, she will not, as the white-winged building shakes like her body with battering and the doors are pulled from their hinges. Mary tries to find her mother inside of herself, and finds an entrance and a dark hall. She goes in, finds herself upright, her legs steady under her. She pats the bodice of her pink dress, straightens her pink ribbon—for she knows her mother waits at the end of the dark hall—as the giant lifts her to the sky—knows a door will open at the end of the dark hall—and dashes her ten-year-old body down. Great doors open, her mother shimmers with beauty, with long, strong, brown open arms. In fury at his loss, the giant howls after the escaping orphans, and flames rise up around him as he moves, touching, touching the pitiful beds of orphans, touching and torching, his small mad head hissing, spitting curses upon Lincoln, the top-hatted ape, and Greeley, and niggers, niggers, for his tongue would fork with curses if it could, as the white-winged asylum crumbles in flames inside of the facades of now with its *BEEP BEEP* of prosperity. As if the great library walls had vanished, as if the market values of now, with their multi-millions of construction, were transparent, there stands the Colored Orphan Asylum, and there inside is Mary, hiding under her bed. Mary and the flag-bearing giant. Mary and the mad mob. I lean back in my library chair and push up my glasses. I am trying to see more clearly. I think I don't understand any more than Mary did, as the lion-braced library walls form around me again, shutting me off from my shopping, struggling fellow Americans on Fifth Avenue, outside, who cannot see the white-winged Colored Orphan Asylum as they pass it. But I know that all hurts must be outlived as humanity presses forward.

THE DEVIL'S TAVERN

There are three kinds of lies:
lies, damned lies, and statistics.
—attributed by Mark Twain to Benjamin Disraeli

Sam Stock is a man of his time, a hyperproductive computer programmer employed by the New York branch of the International Ministry of Wellness as a data analyst, a stat man, a Super Cruncher. He finds correlatives—hamburgers and high blood pressure, gum soles and flat feet, life and death (one-hundred percent). Everyone is at-risk. Life correlates to danger. But cyberchondria abounds. Sam thinks he might be contributing to the general unease. His work as a technocrat may have contributed to the fears of the public—their fear of walking, of breathing, of whispering (aspiration produces deadly micro-globules of sputum). This winter in New York people are lining up at the mobile Wellness Stations to get bat flu shots. Three cases had been reported in Miramar. The queues, Sam has noticed, are extraordinarily attenuated. People don't want to get near to one another. But of course, the bat flu shots are mandated. Those who do not get them are considered public enemies and are sought and found and sent on to mental health clinics. Just the other day, Sam saw that a group of senior citizens who protested the ban on donuts was rounded up and sent to the Senior Mental Health Center for examination.

Sam Stock thought that, yes, they should have their heads examined. After all, carbs can be deadly, and some of those donuts pack icing—vanilla, strawberry, and chocolate; veritable guns of destruction. But there was something troubling about declaring all those old people insane.

Sam tries to balance these thoughts as he maneuvers the lunch hour streets in search of a health food stand. It depresses him to think of the recent ban on mustard. He had to admit that mustard was the only thing that made much of the proffered food of the city palatable. But he himself was the first to find the correlation between mustard and misbehavior. It was bruited about that upscale gangs of rebellious youth in Brooklyn were now attacking public officials with gobs of grey poupon, and of course there was that incident in Atlanta where the mayor was assaulted with deep-fried hush-puppies after instituting a ban on them.

Sometimes Sam Stock thought that officialdom was going a bit too far. He understood the impulse, natural to people in power, to tell others who have no power what to do. But sometimes . . . ah, a stand full of Free-Toes—sugar-free, carb-free, fat-free, and food-free. And not even a dab of mustard to put on them! Sometimes Sam Stock thinks that life is becoming tasteless . . . munch, munch.

Twenty-twenty, the centennial of Prohibition, that was a big year for the Ministry of Wellness! The events of that year included a world-wide ban on smoking, the Bacon Act, and, perhaps the greatest coup the Ministry had ever effected, the institution of the Department of Mental Wellness, which allowed the authorities to take action against people who refused to care for themselves, people who puffed, tippled, or consumed food that was found by the experts at the Ministry of Wellness to be unhealthy. These slackers were of course costing us all money under the Universal Wellness Program. They were to be considered insane and sent to an asylum until they mended their thought-processing ways.

Sometimes Sam Stock thought the authorities took advantage of this law to declare insane anyone who in his or her life of quiet desperation heard the sound of a different and distant drummer. It was from the dark underbelly that rumblings could be heard. There was the mysterious case of the physicist who smoked, the notorious case of the tippling mayor, the amazing case of the cake-eating songstress—these stories were heard of and retold, novelized on-line by rebel writers—*Smokey, The Mad Scientist, The Red Nosed Mayor of Castorbridge,* and *God Bless America: The Dreadful Story of Cake Smith.* Sam Stock reads these cautionary tales and tries to learn from them; but sometimes he yearns for romantic adventure. The idea of sharing a chocolate-covered donut with a beauty on a tiger-skin rug set his heart racing. His Free-Toe melts like icing in his mouth at the thought.

How could Sam Stock have failed to notice Lorelei Rhinestein? She had been about the office for some time. But Sam is always intent on his production of correlatives. He sees another one—reading and suicide—and begins to run it. But he is distracted. Lorelei Rhinestein has lovely violet eyes. She reminds him of a flapper of eld. She has just come in from getting her bat flu shot and is flushed with . . . anxiety? The Ministry of Wellness does not want to tell the public about the many deaths correlating to bat flu shots. Sam Stock puts down "bat flu shots and death." He runs it—ummm! He looks at Lorelei Rhinestein. The flush is leaving her face. Not only will she live, he thinks, she will triumph. How not, with such eyes?

In the days following, he gets her name and her *modus vivendi.* She brings her own lunch. Fried chicken from home, long since banned from restaurants. She eats surreptitiously, suspicious even of associates. An atmosphere of danger clings to her drumstick. Sam Stock suspects her of transfats. He could see her in some ancient noir film, the banned-for-smoking "Casablanca" perhaps, still extant in cyberspace. Sam Stock blushes to think of it. Yes, he thought, she's like Ingrid Bergman—mysterious, beautiful, hat down over her violet eyes. But of course Ms. Rhinestein wears no hat. Though not yet banned, hats—with the one exception of cycling helmets—had been deemed bad for the circulation. The more fashionable members of the ruling class wore them; but, Sam Stock noted, Authority says yes to itself and no to everyone else. He bet that in secret they even ate cake. They did as they pleased.

Sam Stock is increasingly restive, so when Lorelei Rhinestein asks him for a date—a date with a woman of danger—he decides to give adventure a chance and finds himself saying—

"Delighted. Where shall we go?" Men do not ask women for dates, nor do they decide where their time shall be spent; men cautiously wait to be invited, and even here could be entrapment. Can mystery and candor exist simultaneously in enchanting violet eyes? Fling it, he tells himself, I'm taking a chance on love!

Lorelei Rhinestein wants to go to New Jersey. She knows a place out beyond the Pine Barrens. She drives them. It's Saturday night at the Jersey Devil's Tavern.

Where are we, he wants to know, what is this place? What does it remind him of, dark and forebody with the moon overhead? In the woods, isolated, oh, what did they call them, roadhouses, speakeasies? Something out of cyberspace on-line noir dramas.

"I don't like the looks of this," he tells Lorelei. His hackles rise, tickled, but really he does like the looks of the place. The place is like Lorelei herself, mysterious, beautiful in the moonlight, dangerous.

"I've been watching you, Sam Stock," says Lorelei. "I've been watching you and thinking maybe you need a real outing. If I'm wrong I think I can trust you to keep this to yourself, but if I'm right about you . . . well, we may be able to share something exciting. You don't look like a scaredy-cat. The last boy I brought here—a personnel director for the Nursing Corps—he ran away like a rabbit and got lost in the Pine Barrens for two days. First time he had missed a day's work in his life. He threatened to report me to the Ministry of Wellness, but I threatened to tell them that *he* was the one who brought *me* here and he kept his mouth shut."

"I'm not afraid," Sam Stock blusters. He is afraid but for some obscure reason it embarrasses him. Contradictions abound in a nature taught from childhood to be afraid of everything and at the same time to swim with Bubbles, the friendly shark. Sam Stock allows himself to be led into the Jersey Devil. People sit at candlelit tables, drinking adult beverages, smoking cigarettes and cigars, or dancing to the strains of "Smoke Gets in Your Eyes." Seated, Lorelei orders the house cocktails, two Jersey Devils, looks over the flickering candle at Sam, and, in a low voice, sings—

They asked me how I knew
My true love was true
Oh, I of course replied
Something here inside
Cannot be denied . . .

Sam tries to ignore her alluring, husky, melodious voice.

"What kind of place is this?" he asks, looking through a haze of smoke, here and there set aglow by dim lights.

Lorelei observes how wide his innocent blue eyes are in the mesmerizing undulation of the candlelight.

"Sam Stock," she says, "this is a den of iniquity, a speak-drink-and-smoke-easy, and I have lured you here in order to make a criminal of you." She is saying this in such a manner that it sends a thrill of fear up Sam's spine, but then she laughs, and says, "Don't be afraid, Sammy," and Sam is so tense that he laughs too—a nervous hack—as the aromatic Jersey Devils arrive in tall, red, steaming glasses.

Three Jersey Devils later Sam finds himself smoking. At first he coughs but then he gets the hang of it and begins to like it.

"Inhale," urges Lorelei, and sings—

Oh, so I smile and say
When a lovely flame dies
Smoke gets in your eyes . . .

Six months later, at work, Sam is dying for a cigarette. After all, smokers are people who have one friend no worse than others, the sometimes of their pleasure and the ultimate difficulties, the big troubles, the being able to be quiet in the hurried world, the holding hands without a word, the sad truth of the matter as recognized by ashes, or ashes recognized, whatever is looking up from nothing, from the smoke-filled no-bottom of everything, the oh for just a moment, the please slow it down, the oh God I'm late, the don't forget, the oh forgotten, but smokers are people who have at least one friend. The relationship between smoking and disease is merely a correlative one, he tells himself and the greatest correlation of all is life and death (100%), but right now he needs a cigarette. Everyone who has a moment of contentment, he tells himself, dies; therefore, contentment kills.

Minutes after this moment of illumination, Sam is arrested by the dreaded Green (really olive drab) Shirts of the Ministry of Wellness for smoking in the men's room and taken away to the insane asylum for mental reprogramming. His psychiatric report confirms that he may ultimately prove to be a danger to the State. He has a definite proclivity toward disrespect of authority.

Sam says, "Authority says yes to itself and no to everyone else! It says No!" Sam tells Doctor Forbrane, his counselor, to shove it.

"And all this rebellion started with a single cigarette," Doctor Forbrane tells his colleagues over cigars and port.

"Good thing we wiped out marijuana," he continues, stabbing his Montecristo into space for emphasis, "or all of the little people would have become non-productive. But have no fear. I have implanted in his brain a continuously ticking taser in order to pacify him. He will represent no more challenge to Authority than a popinjay. He will, in fact, become a useful member of society. Wellness will be his way!"

One year later, Lorelei meets Sam upon his release.

"Are you cured?" she asks as she drives him away from the asylum.

"I'm fine now, but they caught me just in time. Got a cigarette?"

"In the glove compartment," Lorelei says, hitting the gas, heading for the Jersey Devil's Tavern, which, despite all efforts of the Green Shirts of the Ministry of Wellness, exists forever just beyond the Pine Barrens.

www.ingramcontent.com/pod-product-compliance
Lightning Source LLC
Chambersburg PA
CBHW030827310726
48980CB00006B/667/J

* 9 7 8 0 5 7 8 5 0 4 7 8 0 *